Into the

Second Springtime

June Marie W. Saxton

authorHOUSE®

AuthorHouse™
1663 Liberty Drive
Bloomington, IN 47403
www.authorhouse.com
Phone: 1-800-839-8640

First published by AuthorHouse 07/21/2011

ISBN: 978-1-4520-8272-1 (ebk)
ISBN: 978-1-4520-8271-4 (sc)
ISBN: 978-1-4520-8270-7 (hc)

Library of Congress Control Number: 2010914001

Printed in the United States of America

This book is printed on acid-free paper.

For Dad, the storyteller

Thanks for always taking time to share.

Your words scattered in my heart and mind like thousands of seeds,

taking root, sprouting and growing.

Please enjoy the harvest,

I love you.

Special Acknowledgements

Hearty thanks to the fans of *Dancing with the Moon* and *Beckon*. Their willingness to read, enjoy, and pass it on is stoking the firestorm of reader interest. I appreciate Bobbi Heap, Diane Alleman, and Janalee Saxton, for their willingness to proofread manuscript pages and lend encouragement. Appreciation is once again extended to the Kevin Weston Family for their hours of reading and well-expressed interest in my stories. Thanks to my parents, Dale and Pam Weston, as well as my Grandma, Marie Weston. They told me I could so I did.

Thanks to my husband Mike, who has patiently supported my efforts to write, and bears my non-stop prattle about characters that don't exist, but who are so real to me. Thanks to my kids, Justyn and Tahnee, for saving me every time I got into computer trouble.

Special thanks to Shannyn S. Davis for her technical skills and honest opinions, and to Stacey J. Davidson for assisting my website at www.junemariesaxton.com. Carolyn W. Davidson lends inspiration to me in a myriad of ways and I am proud to partner with her artistic interpretations through the illustrations of this book, as well as the cover art. *Into the Second Springtime* provides a perfect canvas for her work and I thank her for being willing, professional, and kind.

Into the Second Springtime is a little bit different than the previous two books, but *Pirate Moon*, my fourth novel, will tie all three together, and each story is an important component of the series. *Into the Second Springtime* is meant to be enjoyed—like chocolate cake at a picnic. It's sweet and filling...and should be savored. Bon Appetite!

About the Artist, Carolyn W. Davidson

Carolyn W. Davidson spent her childhood years on a cattle ranch in the Bear Lake Valley of northern Utah. She and her husband Ted make their home in Cache Valley, Utah. They are the proud parents of five sons. Carolyn has spent her life quietly putting her family first.

Carolyn's talent in art is inspiring, and she uses her skills to lift and enlighten. She is incredibly diverse in her artistic abilities, and often uses pencil, oil, watercolor, pastel, and acrylic. Carolyn says, "To me, painting is an act of gratitude for our beautiful world."

Carolyn's background in western art qualifies her command of the canvas. She has a love for Native American people and customs, as well as for the quiet cowboy life. She captures the beauty of simple living. Her artwork is showcased on her website, www.sageweststudios.com. Carolyn is a master calligrapher and sells cards, prints, and original paintings.

Titles by June Marie W. Saxton

Dancing with the Moon

Beckon

Into the Second Springtime

Pirate Moon

To order specially autographed copies, call Bear Necessities of Montpelier at (208) 847-1176 or access email information at www.junemariesaxton.com. Fan mail is welcome!

Chapter One

The plum trees were blossoming and the fragrance turned my thoughts to Mother's home bottled plum syrup. We would enjoy the sticky good stuff throughout the fall and winter months.

Wyatt was lying on his back staring at puffy clouds. "Whatdya think about it, Wesley?" he asked, chewing on a stem of spring grass.

"Yuck, that's what." My brows furrowed and my lips pinched together, for the matter which Wyatt spoke of was not as pleasant as Mother's plum syrup. Oh no, nothing *that* good! We just spied our fifth grade teacher kissing the principal. That shouldn't have bothered us so much, I guess, but Miss Annelaise Gallagher was our aunt, and we were now afraid that trips to the principal's office would require us to stir uncomfortably before a new and unrequested uncle. It was quite a kiss if you know what I mean. Surely marriage must follow such a heartfelt puckering!

"Miss Aunt Lace is nuts if she goes for the old guy."

"Get used to the idea." Wyatt couldn't say Aunt Annelaise when he was a little boy, so he just called her *Aunt Lace* and it stuck. He couldn't break the habit when school started this year, and I'd spent the last eight months stuck in a classroom with a kid who raised his hand too often, saying, "Miss Aunt Lace." Even I had sense enough to call her Miss Gallagher in school. It didn't matter though. Wyatt was Miss Gallagher's pet, her little darling, her lamb. For some reason, I, Wesley, just couldn't measure up.

"Why do you think Mr. Mulligan was running his hands through her hair like that?"

"Shut up, Wyatt."

"You're in a bad mood."

"Do I look like an expert in French kissing or something?"

"Sick! Is that what you think was happening? They *were* acting all sweaty and breathless."

"Shut up, Wyatt."

Wyatt was quiet for a few minutes. He might have been sulking, I'm not really sure. I looked over at him. He was using his hands as a homemade telescope. I wondered what he was seeing so I fashioned my hands in the same manner and studied the sky with telescopic vision. Its kids' stuff, but technically I *am* a kid.

Wyatt grinned when he saw I was copying him. His eyes were electric blue. His skin was pale and freckled, and his hair was as red as Lady Scarlet's nightgown. Actually I have no idea what color Lady Scarlet's nightgown is—I don't even *know* Lady Scarlet—but my great grandpa uses that expression all the time and Wyatt likes to hear it.

Great Grandpa Kelly Sheehan O'Rourke is older than anybody I know. He said he is so old he was nearly young again. Great Grandpa Kelley Sheehan O'Rourke says life is like a calendar. Springtime is childhood, and during summer you're grown up. Autumn brings grandchildren thicker than apples on the tree, and then winter hits, and Jack Frost paints your hair white.

"Most people die once they turn white and brittle, but I've drug all the way through December, January, and February. I think there's indecision about my future status. God doesn't want me and the devil is afraid I'll take over, so I'm stepping along, heading for my second springtime."

I smiled, thinking about Grandpa. He said he used to be a big man but winter had shriveled him down to size. He wasn't much taller than Wyatt and me, and we enjoyed his company better than anybody's. "That's how I know I'm a going around again," he said. "I'm shortening up and my mind must be youngering, for only children seem to appreciate my company. Yes sir, it's official. I'm in my second springtime, and I plan on racing you boys into summer."

I wondered if *youngering* was a word. I couldn't find it in the dictionary and Miss Annelaise Gallagher, my French kissing, school teaching, bossy aunt said it wasn't, but Grandpa Greaty Great said something didn't have to be in the dictionary to exist. "Look up my name in the dictionary—will ye find it? Oh no," Grandpa said. "But I'm here—I exist, just as real as Santy Claus."

"Some grandpas are good, and some grandpas are great, but I'm so good I'm Greaty Great," he chanted at least once a day. Wyatt and I learned the ditty when we were very young and that's how Great Grandpa Kelly Sheehan O'Rourke became simply Grandpa Greaty Great. The phrase was shortened down over time, and so mostly he's just called Grandpa Greaty. Of course that sounds like *Grady*, and half the town now calls him Grandpa Grady O'Rourke.

That's the way things get changed. Grandpa Grady says names, words, tales, and truth gets watered down over time and with each interpretation. "Cold hard facts become liquid, boys, and as watered down as Mrs. Margaret Mahoney's pitiful oyster stew." I've never had oyster stew, but I have vowed to never eat any of Margaret's.

My thoughts were just a jumbled bunch of circles that afternoon. "Let's go fishing, Wyatt. I need to *do* something." Wyatt was game and scrambled to his feet. We dogged along the side of the highway on our way home.

Wyatt's dad is fighting in Viet Nam. It's kind of terrible when someone you love has gone to war. Wyatt cries sometimes, although he doesn't want anybody to know. Aunt Aubynn and the kids moved in with Grandpa and Grandma Gallagher. They used to live in San Diego, but Aunt Aubynn got so lonesome that Grandma told her to come home, and back to Gallagher Springs they came. We live right next door.

My Dad has three sisters, Aunt Aubynn, Aunt Aura Leigh and Aunt Annelaise. Aunt Aubynn is great—soft and kind and gentle. Aunt Aura

Leigh is indifferent, and Aunt Annelaise is basically my nemesis! She's the youngest and my mother claims she's spoiled rotten. I always agree with my mother on that subject. It's kind of interesting living next door to family, at least that's what Mother says.

We threw our books in our respective houses and grabbed our poles and tackle. Wyatt had a brand new pole he got for his birthday. I was a little bit jealous of it. It was turquoise and little metallic bits of paint glimmered in the sunshine. I had an old white pole of Dad's and tried to comfort myself by telling my friends it was good for ice fishing. "It's camouflaged to the snow so the fish don't get suspicious," I boasted one day.

The afternoon was hot for early May in northern Utah. The myriad of natural hot springs warmed the climate of our town quite substantially. Gallagher Springs was founded by my great, great grandpa, Errol Gallagher, although all of my other great, great grandparents came to America when he did. Grandpa Grady's parents were with them. According to the old men who liked to talk, the whole Irish village of Inis Pairc packed up and sailed across the sea when Grandpa Grady's father was fifteen.

We pedaled our bikes up Gallagher Canyon. We passed interesting signs as we went. The first one said, *"Welcome to Gallagher Springs, population 300."* It was a very old sign, mounted just after the settlement was built. A historical marker was near the sign to entertain bored tourists who had nothing better to do. Gallagher Springs' population was now closer to eight hundred, not counting the summer people.

The next sign said, *"Gallagher Springs boasts the largest number of red heads, per capita, than any other city in the United States."* We kept pedaling until we saw the sign, *"The end of the rainbow is officially here!"* The last sign read, *"Gallagher Springs, where shamrocks and sagebrush bring Irish luck and American pride."*

We pedaled about two miles. I was tired, and school had been long and hot. When we got to Inish Lake we baited our hooks and laid down in the shade, fishing in lazy fashion like Little Boy Blue watching sheep. The grass was cool and soothing, and I wouldn't have twitched one muscle, but I felt my pole bob and so I sat up and jerked on the rod. I whistled through my teeth while I reeled in a silvery rainbow trout.

"That's a good one Wesley," Wyatt encouraged. Just then his pole dunked down, and before I could finish pulling the hook from my catch's mouth, Wyatt was reeling in a beauty.

"Looks like trout's for supper."

I jerked my head back, so startled was I by the voice behind us. Grandpa Grady O'Rourke was nodding his head, happy to see our fortune as fishermen.

"How did you know we were here?"

"I've been waiting for you boys to get out of school. I figured you would come up here. It's too nice of a day to stay cooped up in doors. I knew spring fever would be burning your brows." Grandpa Grady helped us string our fish onto a cut willow. I baited my hook and caught another fish just as soon as my worm wiggled in the water. I whistled as I reeled in another handsome trout.

"The fish are definitely biting today," Wyatt observed.

Grady rubbed a hand along his chin. He nodded, squinting against the setting sun. "Don't catch more than your limit, or Doheny the Fish Nazi will throw you boys in jail." Wyatt and I grinned at the mention of the game warden. Grandpa Grady always went off on a tangent about the criminal behaviors of Jimmy Don Doheny. "A man tries to provide for his family, catch a few fish once in a while, and what does that Fish Nazi do? Create a stink, steal your joy, confiscate your catch, and haul you off to the big house." The exaggerations grew more and more interesting. "Why, I remember the day when a man could catch *all* of his fish on the same day if he was so inclined. I don't know what kind of an imbecile would actually do that, but this is America, and a man should have the right to be stupid if he chooses to be."

I reeled in another fish. I pulled my hook and strung it on the willow with the others, all the while listening to Grandpa's rants. "My folks came to this country because they heard that it was the end of the rainbow, and boys, it really is. Don't let old Grandpa get you riled up over nothing, but I say a good fisherman has the right to eat fish! Not four fish, or two fish, or whatever suits Jimmy Don Doheny, but just as cracking many fish as he chooses! There now, I feel a little better getting that off my chest."

I grinned at Grandpa Grady. He was baiting his hook, and his hands trembled slightly, but he was lively and spry. He always talked to us like we mattered and so his opinions sank deep. We soaked up everything he said, like young, hungry sponges. "Now what kind of grievances do you boys need to vent about today?"

Grady asked us that every day of our lives. He thought it was healthy for young people to protest about their sufferings. "Blow off steam a little at a time boys, that's healthy. Now, when you get to be pot smoking, free loving, long-haired, lazy, whining about America, war protesting couple of hippies, that's when you've gone too far! Those punks don't know squat about sacrifice or anything else for that matter. They are just squawking out loud now because nobody listened to them when they were young, and aint it grand that they live in a country where they can smoke, and dope, and whine away? We're free to march in Washington, boys, but by Jingo Jones, don't catch more than four fish a piece."

I lay back in the grass laughing silently at the wiry little man. Grandpa Grady talked with his hands. He'd been baiting his hook for the past ten minutes, but every time the worm in his right hand neared the hook in his left, his lecture would hit high point, and his hands sprang apart to illustrate the truthfulness of his statement. He'd been with us for twenty minutes and hadn't yet cast his line.

Wyatt cleared his throat. "Something's bugging me alright."

"What boy? Speak up!"

"We saw Miss Aunt Lace kissing Mr. Mulligan."

Grandpa's brows shot high. "What are you saying, Wyatt? Speak up, for bad news festers like a sliver, son, and must be drawn out to avoid the poison."

Wyatt's head bobbed in agreement with his tongue as it waggled to and fro, spilling the beans on Aunt Lace. Grandpa liked the story and seemed mighty enthralled with the telling of it.

"I don't know what they teach kids in school nowadays, but I remember when I learned how to cipher and spell. We had the three R's; reading, writing and arithmetic, which actually makes me question our skills in spelling, as technically writing begins with W and arithmetic begins with A. I don't ever recall learning *French* in school."

"I think you should tell your daughter about *her* daughter," Wyatt continued. "Grandma Gallagher wouldn't want Miss Aunt Lace smooching on the principal!"

"No—I'll not say a word to my Cora, for I'm no tattling tom! Wesley, did you also witness this grotesque display of affection?"

"Yes I did. She thought she was alone in the library after school, but we were in there getting our sling shots. We hid them in between Shakespeare's works during lunch recess. Nobody reads Shakespeare so we knew they were safe."

"Why hide the flippers?"

"They're strictly against the rules and we didn't want to get caught with them."

"That's the injustice that makes me get riled up! It's against the rules of the school for my great grandsons to carry flippers in their back pockets, but its okay for my granddaughter, their teacher, to kiss the principal! This injustice baffles reason."

"Well don't let it make your blood pressure go up."

"Annelaise Gallagher, kissing the principal!" Grady was laughing about the juicy scrap of information, and we joined in. "I'd given her up for a spinster and now she's kissing the dapper and dashing Mr. Melvin Mulligan. *How romantic!* There will be rejoicing in my Lacey Girl's heart tonight." His tongue clicked against the roof of his mouth three times.

I scowled, reeling in another catch. "This is nothing to celebrate about! It was sick!"

"I wager she'll be in a good mood tomorrow," Grandpa Grady observed, finally connecting worm and hook together. He took a wobbly step backwards and I heard the whir of his line as it sailed over the sparking water and landed with a little plop. "Don't fret about it boys."

"But it wasn't any kiss," we protested together.

"Oh?"

"It was like this," Wyatt said. He turned his back to us and wrapped his arms passionately around himself, acting out the sweaty and breathless moment. I couldn't help laughing and Grandpa Grady wiped tears from his cheeks at the charade.

"How did that go again?" Grady was baiting more than his hook this afternoon. Wyatt enacted the steamy kiss once again. "Don't mourn boys, for kisses like that bring marriage, and marriage invites the propagation of the human race."

"I have no idea what that means, Grandpa Grady, but I don't want Mr. Mulligan for my uncle."

"What makes you think Mr. Mulligan wants you two for nephews?"

I bit my lip and Wyatt sulked. "Then he should stop kissing Miss Aunt Lace!"

Grady didn't say another word about the issue, but he hummed the wedding march while we watched the sun bob over the western hills.

We pedaled home in the grey time that hovers between day and night. I was carrying the fish and the weight was dragging my handlebars off lopsided. Wyatt took them to give me a break but he managed the load even worse than I had, so before he even pedaled twenty-five yards, I inherited them back. Between Wyatt, Grandpa Grady and I, we'd caught twelve big fish, weighing a couple of pounds apiece.

"Remember Sunday School Wyatt? We learned that we are supposed to give to the poor?"

"So?"

"Let's leave some of these fish for the neighbors."

"Okay, who? The O'Reilley's?"

"No. They're not The Least of These My Brethren."

"Huh?"

"You know, The Least of These My Brethren."

"Oh." Wyatt nodded his head but I knew he didn't have a stinking clue in Heaven, or the other place, what I was talking about. He never listened very carefully in church.

"You know, Wyatt, like Gerald Flannery, for example."

"Is he one of those guys, The Least of These My Brethren?"

"Yes, remember? Grandpa Grady said he always felt sorry for Gerald because Mrs. Flannery doesn't know how to budget his money. Grandpa claims she throws more out the back door with a teaspoon than he can carry in the front door with a shovel."

"Okay," Wyatt grinned. He was game to be charitable if I was.

We pulled our bikes up to the Flannery's garage. I couldn't see piles of wasted goods thrown out the back door or anything, but still I felt nervous about going to the door and offering a fish, even if this outfit was The Least of These. "Remember how we're not supposed to let our left hand know what our right hand is doing?"

"Yes, but that doesn't make much sense to me. I always know what my right hand is doing."

"No, Wyatt—it's not like that. We're supposed to do good deeds without people knowing about it."

"Like a secret?"

"Yup, like a secret." I fiddled in my pocket until I pulled out a little notebook and a miniature pencil. The tiny set had come as a prize in my crackerjacks. I wrote in my neatest penmanship. *"To the Flannery's: if you want to fix your problem just nail the back door shut."* I opened their mailbox and stuck the beautiful trout and the note inside. I jerked up the flag. I was happy just like my Sunday school teacher told me I would be, and I had a very warm feeling in my heart.

"Let's take one to old lady McCracken. Maybe she'll feel better about life if she finds out we were willing to have charity on her poor soul."

"She's the meanest old crow! She always stares at the ground, all hunched over like she's looking for snails."

"*Ticky Tacky Wicky Wacky Mickey Mackey McCracky*, that's what Grandpa Grady calls her." Wyatt was grinning at the prospects of leaving her a fish. "I'll write the note for this one." Wyatt's head bent while he scratched out a sentiment. *'I hope you soon find a coven 'cuz no witch should fly alone.'* I nodded my approval, feeling proud to own my best cousin's occasional wit. I opened the mailbox. In went the fish and up went the flag.

We deposited fish at the Connor's house because Delma Jean was cross-eyed. *"Don't think you're seeing double,"* I wrote, *"we really did leave you two."*

The Walsh outfit merited two fish as well. They had more trouble than anyone! Most of it was due to the fact that Claude wore lipstick and Mavis didn't. *"Don't be a dipstick, let your wife wear the lipstick,"* Wyatt printed. I wondered if that comment was too mean spirited but Wyatt said, "Helping the Least of These sure is fun, Wesley."

Poor Agatha Duffy, she was out of business. Grandpa Grady often said we should pity her. "You know the economy is bad when the world's oldest profession can't make ends meet. Agatha's hen house had to shut down because the roosters were scared of the chickens."

I was always sorry to hear the poultry industry was struggling, even though I couldn't understand why she didn't just call her hen house a chicken coop like the rest of us did. I mentioned it to Wyatt.

"No, no! That's not it at all. Grandpa Grady said she ran a cat house, but the toms all ran away—whatever that means."

"No wonder she went out of business! She doesn't know cats from chickens!" I scratched my head wondering which story was correct. I simply wrote, *"Sorry business has been bad, but maybe things will improve after the war is over."* We benevolently opened the mailbox and slid the fine trout inside. I lifted the flag with a touch of reverence.

The next house belonged to Mr. Mulligan. We both laughed when we considered what kind of note we could write. We conspired together while standing in the darkening shadows of Shamrock Street's poplar trees. *"Teacher can spell and Teacher can write. Teacher can kiss but it's just not right."* We ran out of room and so the note was continued onto extra sheets. We finished by writing, *"Ooh, Mr. Mulligan, we saw you."* One by one random red flags rose all over town.

We took our last fish to Judy Brynn O'Brien's house. Judy was in our class and we couldn't stand her. She was bossy and rude—a regular know-it-all. She hovered around like an obnoxious shadow person and she smelled like dandelion fuzz. *"Mr. and Mrs. O'Brien, sorry that Judy wasn't a boy. Best of luck teaching her to be a lady for you are bound to struggle."*

"Remember Wesley; don't let our left hands know what our right hands just did." I swore an oath. At Grandma's porch Wyatt and I shook our special handshake and spat on both sides of the sidewalk to seal our secret. We then called goodnight and Wyatt disappeared into Grandma's house while I went in to dine on my mother's fried chicken for supper.

The next morning held promise of another beautifully brilliant day, and it was Saturday so that made things even better. On purpose I took off my undershirt which Mother made me wear from September to June to avoid the croup. Honestly! By the time a boy is almost done with the fifth grade surely he can go without an undershirt when the sun is shining. I was supposed to help do house chores for awhile, but I pestered my little sister Allyson so badly that Mother finally bid me to get out of her hair. Allyson's bottom lip jutted out because that meant she was stuck doing my extra chores. I sneered at her triumphantly as I walked by her to get outside.

"Mom," she whined in a savagely sing-song manner, "Wesley just smiled at me!"

Her protests fell on tired ears and Mother was sick of it. "Allyson! I don't care, now go scrub the tub."

Allyson stuck her tongue out at me when she thought I wasn't looking. I winked at her and blew her little kisses, grinning widely all the while. That really aggravated her. "Mom! Wesley winked at me!" Allyson's whining protests put Mother at the end of her tether.

"Iron the pillow cases, scrub *both* tubs, and then vacuum the floor, Allyson Jane Gallagher!" I dodged out of the back door before I could be reinstated into the middle of Mother's typical Saturday morning nervous breakdown.

Grandpa Gallagher was just climbing in his pickup truck. "Good morning Wesley."

"Hi Grandpa, where are you going?"

"To the post office and then out to the Thompson's to doctor a sick horse. Would you like to come with me?'

I nodded and jumped in the truck. I liked going with Grandpa Gallagher. He was the country vet and I was his apprentice. "Where's Wyatt this morning?"

"He was sitting in the corner helping Annelaise cut out bulletin board letters when I last took notice. Once he finished with that she was going to make him work on his science project."

"Poor Wyatt might be Aunt Lace's pet for sure, but he gets that honor on hard terms. No offense Grandpa, but I'm glad I don't live with you."

Grandpa Gallagher's lips twitched beneath a grey mustache. "You don't think you'd like living with the teacher, eh boy?"

"No sir, although Wyatt will win the science fair so I'm not too excited to try my best."

"Oh…you never know."

"Aunt Lace will see to it that Wyatt wins."

"Be respectful, Wesley."

I bit my lips together, careful not to push Grandpa too far. He wasn't as liberal as Grandpa Grady when it came to shooting our mouths off. Grandpa Gallagher loved us, but he didn't care quite so much about our sufferings, otherwise he would have flung his baby girl, and my arch nemesis, out of the house by now. I kept thinking it was high time.

I went in the post office with Grandpa because I liked to study the

Wanted posters. Several townspeople were gathered together in there and having a heated discussion.

"Hell-raising hooligans running around this town!" Judy Brynn O'Brien's father was huffing and puffing with red cheeks. I wondered why he was so upset, considering he had a beautiful trout to eat for his breakfast. Maybe he hadn't checked his mail yet...surely the surprise would brighten his spirits.

Claude Walsh nodded in agreement. I stared at his painted lips. They were a lovely shade of red raspberry but it looked sort of queer to me. Claude was very masculine in every other sense and boasted a fine set of sideburns. "Hooligans indeed," he said. "When I catch the little buggers, I'll throw them in my root cellar to rot."

Good grief! Everyone was in a bad mood this morning—especially The Least of These My Brethren. Just then the homely and unemployed, poor Agatha Duffy came blustering into the post office. "I've come to complain," she shrieked to us all. "My mailbox has been desecrated with a scaly, stinking fish!"

Of all the ungrateful, awful, old biddies! Hmph! I don't give a hoot ever again if she's out of business or not! Why I had a good mind to go get that fish and lug it off to someone who cared.

Elmer Collins, the post master looked crankily in Agatha's direction. "You're bellowing about a fish in your mailbox, too? Take a number! I've called Pistol Stewart and he'll be here just as soon as he's done coffeein' up. Nothing I can do about it so stop ragging at me. I'm not the complaint department."

Pistol Stewart, the sheriff? Um...my palms started sweating. Was I in some kind of trouble here?

"You folks okay?" Grandpa asked the milling hub-bub of naysayers.

"That's a matter of opinion," Barry O'Brien snuffed. "Our mailboxes were vandalized with *fish*." He sniffed out the last word very arrogantly—as if he was too good for a rainbow trout. I was so mad my heart was pounding and my cheeks were flaming the same color as Lady Scarlet's nightgown! I could feel it. Why, Barry O'Brien was just as no good as his uppity, snippety, bossy, know-it-all, obnoxious daughter! So much for good deeds! The whole world could just go to blank for all I cared at the moment.

"Fish you say?" Grandpa's face looked a little bit puzzled.

"Yes," Claude whiffed, feeling very justified in his annoyance.

"That's hardly anything to get worked up about."

"Ha!" Gerald Flannery cried. "Proof enough that your mailbox did not have a stinking fish shoved inside of it!"

"You're all blowing this out of proportion," Grandpa thundered. These ingrates' bad attitudes were making him mad, too. I loved my Grandpa Gallagher! He was always right and I was glad that I was his apprentice.

"It's a federal offense to mess with another person's mailbox!" Agatha cried.

It was? Well I'll be duped and doped, and hauled off in a stupor! I had no idea my best cousin and I had committed a federal crime.

"I can think of some other activities that are against the law, Agatha—maybe you'd better let this drop." The voice of Riley Gallagher had spoken again, and it was quite somber in sound.

The huddled mass turned away from Grandpa and me. I kept my eyes on the Wanted posters, sadly envisioning my school picture inside of one of them. I never meant to go to the dogs at such a young age. Grandpa bought stamps and signed for Grandma's new Montgomery Ward Catalog. The post master asked if I'd like to sign for ours and so I did, careful not to leave my fingerprints on his pen. We turned to leave but the door was blocked with the bulky figure of Pistol Stewart.

The confusion of everyone talking at once became very loud and irksome. Grandpa guided me by my shoulders past the sheriff, through the grumbling throng, and on out to the truck. "Bunch of idiotic saps," he said under his breath. He started the truck and we backed away from the post office. I was eager to put distance between Sheriff Pistol Stewart and myself.

"You think somebody might get arrested and hauled off to the big house, Grandpa?"

"Probably just a bunch of kids, and we were all kids once. I can tell you stories on every one of those angry people. Their stunts made fish in the mailbox seem Christian in comparison."

"I kind of think that someone was just trying to do a good deed when they left those presents."

"Presents?"

"Offerings."

"Offerings, Wesley?"

"Yes Sir."

"Do you want to tell me anything?"

"No sir, for my left hand isn't even allowed to speak to my right one."

Grandpa's head bobbed down and a smile teased uncontrollably beneath the mustache.

We got Thompson's horse revived. I made a poor apprentice for my mind kept traveling back to the post office and Sheriff Pistol Stewart's shiny silver handcuffs. I'd seen them before, and I envisioned them clasping around my wrists. My hands would be locked together, as if in prayer, and I wondered if they would talk to each other then.

I mourned all that morning for the loss of my best years. I believed I would face them in the big house. I would grow tall behind bars. I wouldn't get to see if at some point I actually started liking girls the way grownups always predicted I would. I wouldn't ever find out what Mr. Mulligan knew about French kissing. I would never get to shave with a straight edge razor the way Grandpa Grady did. Surely the warden would ban my razor as a weapon! I wouldn't get to be an astronaut. No moon buggy for me or a race car, either. I'd never get my driver's license. I wondered if Wyatt would be allowed to be my cell mate or if we'd be locked down in solitary confinement. Last year we visited the jail in Logan for a field trip. Our teachers took us there to scare us into being good for the rest of our lives. Tears began streaming down my cheeks and I had a stomach ache.

"Wesley?" Grandpa Gallagher's voice jerked me away from my pitiful thoughts.

"Yes sir?'

"What's the matter, Son?"

"I don't feel so good."

"Are you sick or do you just feel bad?"

"I feel *bad*."

"Well don't."

I didn't know what I should say, if I should say anything or not, so I just nodded my head.

"Heck, what's a fish in the mailbox, anyway?"

"A federal offense, apparently."

"You're just a kid. I don't want you worrying about this one more minute."

I tried to smile but more tears flooded out of my eyes and I was embarrassed. I covered my face with my arm and cried into my elbow. Grandpa stopped at Siskin's Hardware store on the way home. I stayed in the truck because I didn't want anybody to see me acting like a baby. I saw Pistol Stewart's cop car coming down the street and I hid on the floor. When I finally dared peer from the window again I saw Judy Brynn O'Brien and her terrible father walking out of the drug store. I dove for the floor the second time. I wasn't in the mood to see The Least of These ever again in my whole life.

I was still crouched low when Grandpa jerked the truck's door open. "What in the Sam Hill are you doing down there?"

"I saw a girl and—"

"Ah hell! I'm not having a grandson of mine crouching low on a sunny day. Now climb up here. What's the matter with you anyhow?

When you're a little taller you'll be hanging out the windows catcalling at all the girls, not hiding on the floor like a half-wit twit."

"Yes sir." I was mumbling and down trodden. Grandpa handed me a little paper sack. *David Siskin's & Sons Hardware* was printed across the bag, along with their company motto, '*Everything you need and only five minutes from home!'*

"See that?"

"What, Grandpa?" I peered into the little sack. There was an electrical cord, toggle switch, and two long nails inside. "What's this for?"

"It's your science fair project."

"Huh?"

"I guess if it's fair game for Annelaise to help Wyatt, Grandpa can surely help you."

I grinned, eager to see what one cord, a switch, and two long nails could become, scientifically speaking, of course. Grandpa took me out to his workshop when we got home, and it was almost enough to make me forget about my trouble.

Chapter Two

Wyatt wasn't released from house arrest until five o'clock. By that time I had my science project done and I was grinning about the prospects of the unveiling. I asked Grandpa Gallagher to keep it a secret and we shook on it and spat on both sides of the sidewalk. "I'm glad you let me come with you today."

"I'm not as great as Grandpa Greaty Great, but I'll do in a pinch." He winked a blue eye at me, and I saw his mustache twitch with a smile.

"Hey Wesley," my cousin called, jubilant to finally breathe the fresh air of a Saturday. "I finished my science project and it's a doosy!"

I nodded but didn't offer a scrap about me and my doings. "While you've been under Aunt Lace's thumb, I've dodged a bullet from Pistol Stewart."

"Huh?"

"Apparently The Least of These Thy Brethren don't like fish."

"Whatdya say?" Wyatt's eyes blinked a couple of times, as if the action would jump start his brain.

"It's a federal offense to put stuff in people's mailboxes."

"No it's not! Teddy Burke does it every day at three o'clock."

"He's the mailman, he's allowed."

Wyatt's eyebrows scrunched together into a scowl. "Who says anyway?"

"Agatha Duffy."

"Well she's not even smart enough to keep roosters so why listen to her?"

"Barry O'Brien and Claude Walsh are mad about the violation of their mailboxes too."

"Let me go get Grandpa's .22 and I'll show them violated mailboxes!" The Irish temper was coloring Wyatt's cheeks to match his hair.

"We're in enough trouble."

"Who called the Sheriff on us?"

"All of them, I think."

"Bunch of snitches! See if I ever do anything nice again!"

"The Bible says to love thy neighbor as thyself. Wyatt, you're my neighbor and I love you almost as much as me so I'm going to keep that particular commandment, and everybody else can just go to blank for all I care. I'll never help The Least of These again, and I don't care how ridiculous and pitiful they are."

"Are we really in trouble here, Wesley?"

"Grandpa said to not worry about it but Pistol Stewart's handcuffs were rattling from his belt when he came into the post office today. He looked mad because he got interrupted in the middle of his morning coffee, and I say we lay low for awhile or it's probably off to the big house."

"I'm so mad I could spit."

"Well it won't do us any good."

"Aunt Lace finally let me go tonight because she has a date."

"With Mr. Mulligan?"

"Yes and she's not even ashamed about it! She just told Mom and Grandma that they were going to a concert and then up to soak in the hot pots."

Gallagher Springs was famous for its natural hot springs. Grandpa Grady O'Rourke owned the small resort. There were eight cabins that dotted around Inish Lake, a Laundromat with vending machines and some foosball and air hockey tables, as well as billiards. A quaint boathouse sold tackle and bait, cold pop and snacks, and offered canoe and paddleboat rentals. The resort was most famous for a warm swimming pool and seven sultry soaking pools. I loved sitting in the hot pots on a cold night. Rising steam made me feel like I was all alone in an English mist or something. Occasionally I pretended I was Sherlock Holmes, solving mysteries.

The whole town clamored to Grandpa Grady's soaking pools during snowstorms for nothing was more fun than feeling snowflakes on your eyelashes while the rest of your body felt balmy and warm. Irish Hot Springs was built in the twenties and business was still good fifty years later. It wasn't a fancy place but it held memories for the whole town.

"I'm in the mood to go out to Grady's myself." I grinned at Wyatt and he smiled back at me. If being kind and neighborly didn't pay off I wondered what a little mischief could do. '*Nice guys finish last*', that's what big Bill Monroe always says. No more Mr. Nice Guy for me! "Let's go get our trunks, Wyatt."

We floated and swam until the sun went down. Grandpa Grady joined us for a soak. He blew off steam about the injustices of Communism, but we didn't spout off about anything as part of our attempt at laying low. "You boys are mighty quiet tonight, just as quiet as the Battle of Bunker Hill after the last cannon blasted and the muskets were still." He baited us but we weren't biting. We kept our thoughts to ourselves and finally Grady climbed out claiming he was nearly late for his supper. He invited us to come home with him but we declined and he didn't push the matter.

Our cousin Monty Quinn was running the joint that night. Monty was seventeen, and a real cool cat. He had Robert Redford hair and a Paul Newman smile which gave him a certain air of celebrity. He was like the *Wild Bunch* all wrapped up in one package. He was Aunt Aura Leigh's oldest boy, and he drove a Mustang. He had a girlfriend from Lakeside, ten miles south of Gallagher Springs. She was a doll, and even

I admitted the fact. Wyatt, Steve McCarthy, and I had once spied them making out in a canoe. It seemed okay for a cool guy like Monty, but totally disgusting for an old principal and my teacher. Their passionate display of affection left a sour taste in my mouth.

"Hey Monty, need us to help swab out the locker rooms?" I asked.

Monty grinned in my direction. "Sure, Kid. I've gotta scoot down to Lakeside anyway. Shay's waiting for me."

"Shaylin sure is something," Wyatt squeaked.

Monty grinned, feeling cocky and proud to have envious little cousins drooling over his girlfriend. His head bobbed agreement in a totally cool manner. "Blonde hair, blue eyes, bee-stung lips..."

"Huh?"

"Bee-stung—it means they're full and supple—delicious, you know?"

My eyebrows shot high to mirror Wyatt's. "Oh—"we stammered. I don't think I knew what *supple* meant, but if I could just dodge doing time in the big house then maybe someday I'd learn. But the term *bee-stung* was just too crazy and it sounded neat coming from a cool cat like Monty.

"I like her name," I said weakly. "It's a nice change from Cindy and Jennifer." It was a well known fact that there were nine Cindy's in Gallagher Springs, and five Jennifer's. Kathy's and Michelle's were next in number. I'd never heard of anyone being named Shaylin before, and I liked it.

"Her name?" Monty seemed incredulous. "Kid, that's not the best thing about her!" He made a curving gesture indicating the shape of a woman's body. Again my brows shot up and I didn't know what to say.

"Well...gee," Wyatt stammered. "You'd better not keep her waiting! We'll mop up and lock the doors."

"Thanks Poot—gotta scoot." Monty tossed his keys in the air and caught them, then strutted off to his car looking glorious. His life was definitely better than mine.

"I don't really like it when he calls me Poot," Wyatt said, furrowing his forehead into ripples.

"It rhymes with *scoot*, and he's cool that way. Don't take it personally or anything. I'm not sure he even knows my name. He just calls me Kid."

We filled the mop buckets with hot soapy water and went to work. The whole family helped out with Grady's place, and we all had a job if we wanted it. It was nothing new for us to help mop up. Each family also had their own key so if they felt like coming for a dip then they could let themselves in. Grady just asked us all to clean up after ourselves. Wyatt and I knew Aunt Lace would be arriving later with the dapper and dashing Mr. Melvin Mulligan for a private moonlit soak... oh, and we planned on being around.

I called Mother from the boathouse and told her I'd be home a little later. She was fine with that, imagining I was helping my aging great grandfather. I have good folks—as parents go, and I'm glad they're normal. Dad lets my mom wear the lipstick, and my mom lets Dad wear the pants. It's a nifty setup, really. We're pretty non-weird all in all. Allyson is sometimes weird, most girls are, but I wouldn't trade her for Mick O'Doul's sisters. They are ridiculous! Jilly Mae still sucks her thumb and she's in the eighth grade, which is just not right. Shellie Rae sucks on chicken feathers, and that's even worse. No matter how weird Jilly Mae is, Shellie Rae is worse, and I'm lucky to have Allyson.

"Hear that?" Wyatt whispered in the dark.

A faint motor was purring up the road. It was about ten thirty, and the sweethearts were right on time. Soon Mr. Mulligan's brand new 1972 Oldsmobile sputtered to a halt. We heard laughter and footsteps, then keys jangling at the door of the lockers. Muffled talking and more laughter followed as my scantily clad, uppity, French kissing, school teaching aunt plopped into the water with that *punk*, Mr. Mulligan. It was an intriguing show.

Miss Aunt Lace was acting coy and cute and she really made me sick! I made a gagging motion and Wyatt grinned in the black shadows of night. Using our James Bond maneuvers, we silently crept closer. It was stealthy, and there's not another word for it! We slipped around the pools and sidled up to the Oldsmobile.

We crammed a couple of Coke bottles up the exhaust pipe. Then we unscrewed Mr. Mulligan's license plates and remounted them upside down. We got the silent giggles over our shenanigans, and it was tough to conceal great bursts of laugher. Just as quietly as we could, we opened the door to the car and slid a container of night crawlers beneath the backseat. They would die and rot and stink, and that was our plan. We were going to stink up Mr. Mulligan's car the way he stunk up our lives. We snapped the radio on, turning it as loud as it would go. When the key turned in the ignition, the sound would deafen the lovebirds, wake up Grandpa Grady, and possibly blow the speakers. We turned on the windshield wipers, the blinkers, popped the hood, and set the parking break. We then dumped a container of stinking cheese bait inside Aunt Lace's purse, just beneath the lining where it had come unstitched. It would take her awhile to find the offending cause.

Wyatt crept behind me while we silently entered the locker rooms. We stole Mr. Mulligan's trousers and Aunt Lace's blouse. We stole Mr. Mulligan's shoes and Aunt Lace's undies. It was a good trick. It was naughty, but being good didn't get us anywhere but in trouble, so...we would earn our stripes.

With the stolen goods in our arms, we dashed like spies to our bicycles which were stashed in a stand of pine and aspen just down the road. We rode like there were motors on our bikes, fast and furious, for two miles down Gallagher Canyon Road. We didn't dare laugh until we neared the lights of town. We pedaled on the back street to avoid the public eye, and away from the jangling handcuffs of Pistol Stewart. The church was dark, but the sun would dawn bright and glorious tomorrow morning. Awe, the Sabbath Day, a day of rejoicing, a day of rest—we ran the stolen clothes up the church's flagpole.

"This will give our town a little religion," I said.

"Amen."

We bent low laughing, imagining out loud the looks on the faces of the sweethearts as they retired to the dressing stalls to find half of their duds missing, and then we high-tailed it for home. Wyatt spent the night with me to avoid speculation, although I knew we would eventually face plenty of that as well.

The sunny Sabbath morning didn't disappoint. I woke up to robins calling outside my window. A V of honking Canadian geese gave our house a fly-by as they returned home to nest up for the spring and summer months. They loved the grassy woodlands near Inish Lake, Eisner Lake, and Lake Washakie. Our valley was famous for the three bodies of water, and was often referred to as the Three Lakes Region. The geese came honking in each year and I wondered if they read about us in a travel brochure like the pesky tourists did.

Wyatt and I got ready for church. Mother argued with Wyatt's rooster tails, trying to slick his unruly red hair down to church standards, all the while telling him what a handsome boy he was. He yawned groggily, and Mother asked him what time we had gotten home. Wyatt fudged and I was quick to say, "Oh, about ten. Didn't you hear us come in?"

"No, did you go right to bed?"

"Yeah, we were pretty bushwhacked."

"Well, I just don't know what Grandpa Grady would do without you boys." Mother gave Wyatt's head one final sprits with a spray bottle and then hurried us out the door.

Allyson was cute with her strawberry blonde ringlets and big pink bow. She was missing her front teeth and had talked with a slight lisp for the past month. She was hoping to grow a new set before corn-on-the-cob season, but I told her not to get her hopes up. I was extra nice to her to keep myself on Mother's good side.

We headed out the door looking spit shined and polished. Wyatt and I were quiet as we walked to the church that morning. "What's the matter with you boys?" Dad asked. "Sorry so spend this pretty day in meetings?"

Yeah, that was it. I forced a great smile pretending to be as cool as my cousin, Monty Quinn. "You guessed it!" Wyatt nodded, flashing smiles all around. We weren't going to be fooling anybody in five minutes, but I kept up my good boy charade, for this was the Day of Prayer, and perhaps mine would be answered.

We turned the corner to Church Street just in time to see it...and hear it. Aunt Lace's enraged fit over the fluttering flag of mismatched trousers, blouse, lacy undies, and shoes. I tried to look confused at the goings on. A group of people approached the unfolding scene from the north side of the church as well. Aunt Lace sucked it up and stopped sputtering. Of course she didn't want to let on that the fluttering items were partly hers!

"Hey, Miss Gallagher, that's your blouse isn't it?" Judy Brynn O'Brien called, pointing upwards, drawing the attention of everyone in the gathering crowd. "But those are men's pants—" Judy pointed out, as if the milling throng couldn't see that for themselves. "Definitely a woman's underwear though!"

I believed Judy might be right. Illuminated by sunshine, the underwear seemed so flimsy, fluttering that way in the early morning breeze. I felt half dirty for touching it last night.

Aunt Lace's face turned purple and I was actually wondering if she would throw a stroke. She quickly jerked the rope down, creating a terrible squeal of the pulley's wheel. *Jerk, jerk, jerk,* down came the goods. The pulleys were rusty so it was hard work. I shared her pain for it was quite a process hoisting them up there last night.

The dapper and dashing Mr. Melvin Mulligan arrived for church. His eyeballs bulged from his face when he saw what Miss Annelaise Gallagher was fussing about. "Miss Gallagher, let me help you with that—"

"I've got it!" She snarled, acting neither cute nor coy. Mr. Mulligan caught the ferocity in her voice and quickly made haste for the church. *Run sinner run!*

Aunt Lace's hands trembled with rage as she tried to unfasten the knots. Grandma Gallagher's eyes were large and they looked our direction. Wyatt and I were still trying to look inconspicuous, but sometimes when you try to look *in*conspicuous, you actually become very conspicuous. I saw Aunt Aubynn's face pale with concern. Her eyes were all question marks as they trailed our way.

Aunt Aura Leigh's tribe came tromping through the masses. She scarcely noticed the fuss, as she was always in a hurry. "Head up and ninety miles an hour," Grady often said when he saw her. She slipped into the church without so much as "Good morning," to anyone.

Uncle Rob followed pleasantly, not seeming to care a hoot about his wife's younger sister's rage. "See you all at dinner after the meeting," he called nonchalantly.

The Quinn's kids, Dori Jo, Celia, and Monty, seemed somewhat more interested in the goings on and paused for a look. Paul Newman's smile flashed across Monty's face and his eyes locked with mine as he saw the mishmash of clothes being tugged from the pole. His eyebrows flickered upward and I caught the slightest, quickest thumbs-up signal I had ever seen. It was like a whisper of movement, an apparition of approval. I signaled back and that's when I felt a firm grip clamp down on my shoulder. I didn't need to look up to know Grandpa Gallagher was suspicious. He smelled a rat. He smelled two of them, and his other hand clamped down on Wyatt's shoulder.

"Good morning, Boys." He tightened his grip and he continued, "Make sure and enjoy the day, remember to treat your elders with respect and mind your place as children." Every sentence came out more authoritatively and was punctuated with a firmer shake to the muscles that connected our shoulders to our necks. Ouch! It was burning and sore, but I didn't try to wiggle away. We nodded. "Grandpa would surely hate to tan your hides while the sun is shining," he said sternly, and then released us. Tears stung my eyes from the residual throb of his pre-church sermon. "Be a pity to get a thrashing on a day like today."

We nodded benevolently. Monty Quinn was laughing, seeming to enjoy this display more than anything he'd seen in awhile. I was glad to oblige him, but was starting to get uncomfortable about things. The group of people wasn't disbanding very quickly. Aunt Lace was breathing very irregularly, trying to get Mr. Mulligan's shoe laces untangled from the rope, but I'd tied them on with triple quadruple granny knots. Thank Heavenly Father for Cub Scouts.

"Are those Mr. Mulligan's shoes?" Judy Brynn O'Brien's voice rasped out. My word, that nosy girl—does she notice everything? But to be fair, I did have to agree with her. They really did *look* like Mr. Mulligan's. A pious gasp sounded in the congregation.

Aunt Lace whirled around, scanning the crowd. Her eyes narrowed at the sight of me. Figures. "Wesley Gene Gallagher, you wretched little horror!" She took two steps toward me with her hand raised. I was bracing myself to get cuffed from here to Grady's house, but my mother stepped forward and grabbed Aunt Lace's arm.

"Just a minute!" Now my mother was raging, and I don't just mean a little bit, either. Her cheeks were scarlet and her eyes were on fire. She seemed to growl and snarl like any mother bear in protection of her cub. "Don't you dare lay a hand on my son!"

Miss Aunt Lace was startled by the counter attack, and the whole congregation took two steps backward, including Grandpa Gallagher. "You *know* he did it!"

"That's the wonderful thing about America, Annelaise! A person is innocent until proven guilty! Wesley did *not* do it! He was home in bed at a good hour last night. You can just take your nasty insinuations and—"

"Now, now," Dad interjected, trying to calm the firestorm of female emotions. Mother cast Dad a look that both shut him up and backed him up. Grandma Gallagher fluttered nervously, trying to smooth things over, and Grandpa Gallagher was dumbstruck at my mother's tenacity while defending her young. Usually Aunt Lace blustered and got her own way, but not today!

"He was in bed was he?" Aunt Lace's question was pointed like an arrow, and her mouth was turned upside down in the shape of a bow. Bows and arrows and mother bears were not what the congregation was bargaining for on the Sabbath Day.

"I know you never give Wesley the benefit of the doubt, on *any* subject, but you'll have to take my word for it. I checked on him myself!" Mother was lying straight through her teeth to protect my honor. I was wishing I'd have done a little better on her Mother's Day present this year.

"What's that supposed to mean—I never give Wesley the benefit of the doubt?"

"When have you EVER? Did you say one word to Wyatt just now?"

Poor Wyatt, I felt him stiffen into granite, concerned that my mother was going to toss him under the bus. Aunt Lace stopped short. She huffed and puffed at the question posed, her mouth opened and closed, but not so much as a squeak came out.

"I love Wyatt! He is like a second son to me," Mother said, collecting her emotions a little. She forced a smile in Aunt Aubynn's pale direction. "But I can't stand you needling Wesley to death every damn day while praising his cousin!"

Aunt Lace was stupefied. Mother had finally called her out, and I mean *really* called her out. Half the town was standing as witnesses, with their witnessing jaws gaping open. Half the town was also in shock, for Shannon Gallagher wasn't the blustering type. "Wesley's had a miserable year in school, and I should have requested a different teacher right from the get go." The crowd's attention flipped to Aunt Lace, eager for her reaction to that.

Judy Brynn O'Brien piped up, "It is true, Mrs. Gallagher. Miss Gallagher does like Wyatt better."

Aunt Lace glared at Judy, which delighted me, of course. I couldn't stand either one of them.

"I love Wesley, too—it's just that Wesley leads Wyatt into mischief," Aunt Lace argued.

"Bull Pucky," I thought. I was shocked to hear that Aunt Lace actually loved me, but I wouldn't count on anything changing for awhile.

Mother parroted my thoughts. "Bull pucky! If one of them did it, they both did, and you can't make my son take all the blame unless you want to start granting him half the credit for the good things these boys do. Likewise, you always dote on Dori Jo while ignoring Allyson. Why is it your sisters' kids are so much more tolerable for you than your brother's children?"

A small stretch of silence followed. I glanced at Monty Quinn. He was getting such a kick out this. I knew darn well he knew we were guilty, but cool cats are not rats. He ran a hand through his Robert Redford hair. I would have given a whole dollar to hear what he was thinking.

"Let's settle down now," Grandpa Gallagher suggested, herding people toward the church. *Onward Christian Soldiers* was pounding from an organ inside the chapel. I pictured Aunt Aura Leigh, Uncle Rob, and Mr. Mulligan singing all alone, for everyone else was outside with us. Grandpa got a hold of Celia and Dori Jo Quinn, dragging them inside with him. Aunt Aubynn jerked Wyatt by the arm, following the group into the church, all the while bending Wyatt's ear with a loudly whispered scolding. Wyatt's older brothers, Mark and John, straggled after.

Still Aunt Lace and Mother glared at each other. Grandma Gallagher wrung her hands together helplessly. "Come on girls, let's not bicker anymore."

"You!" Aunt Lace shrieked toward Monty. "You closed up last night! Did you see Wesley and Wyatt sneaking around?"

Monty looked intrigued. One brow shot up coolly. "Sure, I saw them. They helped me swab the lockers so I could scoot on down to Lakeside. We were all done by quarter to ten and I followed them down the road in my car." I smiled at Monty. Apparently he figured that since my mother could lie on Sunday, he could too. "The Kid here is pretty good help." He jutted a thumb in my direction and strutted toward the church.

Aunt Lace finally got the knots undone. With her arms full, she quickly fled down the street. She was wailing now, and no mistake. I was worried about her soul, for I truly thought she could have used the sacrament, but she was just too upset for church, apparently.

"You never give *me* the benefit of the doubt, Shannon!" She cried over her shoulder.

"Not when you act like this," Mother called coolly.

"You're just *mean*!"

We slipped into church, claiming the back bench. Allyson and Dad sat on a different bench. They deemed us a risky bet that day, and distanced themselves strategically. "It's just fine with me," Mother whispered in my ear. "I didn't want to sit by Annelaise Gallagher's brother anyway!" We got the giggles and tried to rein them in, but our shoulders shook and our faces were red as we partook of the bread and water.

In light of the situation Dad suggested that we shouldn't go to dinner with everyone else, but Mother claimed she would never wave a white flag at what she felt was a victory meal. "Let your snippety sister wave the white flag. I'll neither crawl nor hide." So we went, and Sunday dinner had never been more interesting!

Every week our families rotated houses. Today the meal was at the Quinn's. Aunt Aura Leigh was still oblivious to the blow up and trotted briskly from the kitchen to the dining room until everything was just so. Aunt Lace refused to come to dinner with Heathen Company, and Mother was still seething at the allegations against me, so everyone was really handling her with kid gloves. Grandpa Grady missed church on account of his weekly struggle with Sunday rheumatism. He always felt a little better by the time meetings were over with. He was now learning details of the Sabbath Day scandal from snatches of whispered conversations, chiefly hearing the tale from the mouths of Allyson and Dori Jo.

I felt his stare burning holes in me. I met his gaze. He knew we did it. I *knew* he knew! I shrugged quite flippantly and his bushy brows rose comically. "How are my boys today?"

Wyatt's gaze was anywhere but up. Guilt was eating him like a slow poison, but now I had Mother's honor to protect, so I must lie. She lied for me and so I would lie for myself. "We are great," I lied again. I had become a very bad person since committing the federal atrocities towards the mailboxes. It's just amazing how far a person can tumble in thirty six hours.

"Anything you boys need to spout about today? You know how I feel about blowing off a little steam. It's healthy."

Grandpa was fishing but I wasn't biting. I gave him a ready answer anyway. "Yes. I find the treatment of Chinese sweat shop workers to be very unsatisfactory."

I saw my Dad's expression morph into something quite strange, and Grandpa Gallagher's mustache twitched almost uncontrollably. Grady's face melted into a roadmap of smile lines. "By Jingo Jones, this boy is a live wire," he muttered to the men while we took our places at the table.

If my comment was funny, I felt guilty for taking the credit. Chinese sweat shop workers and their unsatisfactory treatment were featured in last week's issue of *Weekly Reader*. Contrary to popular belief, I always tried to pay attention in school.

Monty brought Shaylin to Sunday dinner. I studied her between bites of fluffy mashed potatoes. I watched her pretty bee-stung lips as they chewed and I wondered just how delicious they really were. I tried not to be obvious in my staring, but maybe I would grow up liking girls after all. I would like them now if they were more like Shaylin Parks and not so much like Judy Brynne O'Brien. Monty caught me staring and I ducked my head toward my plate and didn't dare look up again.

I forced my attentions toward Allyson and Dori Jo, who sat by each other every Sunday with their dolls in little high chairs. They got along as well as Wyatt and I, but it was true what Mother said about Aunt Lace favoring Dori Jo. That's why I had a beef with her. Aunt Lace was slighting to my little sister and it made me mad. One day I heard Aunt Lace scolding Allyson. "You'll never amount to anything, Allyson Jane Gallagher, for you are too much like your mother." Aunt Lace never knew I heard that conversation, but I never got over it, and Grandpa Greaty Great was right, festering slivers are never healthy.

Aunt Lace made a pitiful entrance sometime between my second helping of roast beef and the strawberry shortcake. I'm certain she wasn't getting enough attention at home. Her eyes looked bee-stung to me, as they were all red and puffy. She was trying hard to be the martyr, but her unconcerned sister Aura Leigh didn't realize she had been missing.

"Did you just get here, Annelaise? I'd have waited dinner had I known you couldn't get here on time."

Miss Aunt Lace sniffled sadly. Mother grinned victoriously, as she hadn't let the morning's squabble steal a bit of her fire. Grandma Gallagher quickly began talking about what she would plant in her garden just to lighten the moment, but Grandpa Grady cut in.

"Did I tell you about the doings at the place last night?" Silence as thick as frosting spread itself all over our dessert. Eyes sprang wide at his timing. Why bring this up now?

"Well, I just got my old bones to bed and my mind was starting to dilly dally all over the place, drifting into pleasant dreams, when all of a sudden the worst commotion you ever heard stirred me from my rest. Loud music, *real loud*, blared like a horn blast. That woke me, and as I was dashing to the window to see if the Russians had landed, two loud bangs thundered through the night. I thought perhaps I was back in a trench in World War I, son of a gun! I dove for the floor thinking I was getting shot at. I then heard tires squealing and gravel spraying against everything as a brand new Oldsmobile took off down the road, back firing and belching something chronic."

Aunt Lace stared disrespectfully at Grady. "It was Wesley and *Wyatt*." She heavily annunciated Wyatt's name so that Mother couldn't accuse her ever again of playing favorites.

"No, Lacey girl, your wrong," Grady said bluntly. "It was a man and a woman, and they were only half dressed, the both of them. They had been taking a romantic dip in my pools and I let them be, thinking it might have been one of you." Unbidden smiles crept up on expressions all around the table. Uncomfortable chokes and chortles muffled in napkins. "After they zoomed off in a dust I stuck my boots on and went out to inspect the cannon fire which had erupted against the night. And I'll be blasted if it wasn't cannon fire at all, but a couple of broken Coke bottles shot against my tin garbage cans! What do you suppose those lunatics wanted to shoot Coke bottles at my garbage cans for? I'd press charges if I knew who it was."

Aunt Lace was ghostly white and still as the grave after that. My dad, being the brave one, jumped to his feet and said, "That was a great dinner Aura Leigh. Thank you! I've got to run check on the cows now."

Grandpa sprang to his feet. "I'll come with you in case any of them need a sudden operation."

Grady leapt up, spry as ever after rattling everyone's rafters. "I'd like to look at your cows, Bill—I'm coming along."

Since I'm Grandpa Gallagher's vetinary apprentice I also stood up to leave. Grandpa saw me and said, "Not today Wesley. I believe it's you and Wyatt's turn to do the dishes. I want you to do all of them, and don't flood Aura Leigh's kitchen. When you're done wiping the last spoon you two may go and shovel the barn out. It needs it and can't wait until morning."

"But it is Sunday," Wyatt whined.

"The oxen's in the mire and there's no rest for the wicked," Grandpa said tersely.

"I'd rather take a thrashing, Grandpa."

"I know it. That's why it's off to the kitchen with you both." Grandpa smiled at all of his family. "Women, rest up! If there's any little thing you need, I'm sure Wyatt and Wesley would be glad to help."

That night I climbed into bed with my latest Phantom Flynn novel. Nobody wrote adventure stories like he did! Mother slipped into the room and sat on the edge of my bed. I smiled at her, for in spite of my dishpan hands, we had shared a pretty good day together. "I love you Mother."

"I love you, Wesley. I know you are as guilty as the day is long. I didn't think for a moment it could have been anyone else, but I also couldn't bear to see Aunt Lace crucify you before the town."

I smiled. She must love me an awful lot. I don't know where the tears came from, but suddenly I was fighting a whole swarm of them as they stung my eyes and trickled down my cheeks. Mother's cool hands wiped them away. "Wesley, you are the author of your own destiny. Make sure your life's book is a great read. It's up to you to determine the ending, too; happy or sad, fulfilled or unfulfilled. Be a good boy, Wesley, and you'll grow into a good man."

"I'm sorry I'm naughty sometimes, Mother!"

"I know, but I'm proud of you. Even your mischief is pretty loveable. Just bridle your energy and try hard to make good choices." She kissed my forehead and turned off the lamp before I could read any of Phantom Flynn's wily adventures.

Chapter Three

School was tense for a few days. Miss Aunt Lace wasn't speaking very much...to *any* of us, especially not to me, Wyatt, or Judy Brynn O'Brien. We were in the doghouse of the fifth grade, apparently. Instead of Miss Gallagher reading to us after lunch, which was the one thing she did really, really well, she chose different kids to read and the choppiness of their sentences nearly drove me nuts. Paul Siskin was the worst. He still sounded out little words like *the*, making it sound like *thee.* On Wednesday I just couldn't take it! I pulled my book out and started reading for myself. My favorite Phantom Flynn adventure was being desecrated by ignoramus classmates and I just couldn't handle the stammering and stuttering any more.

"Mr. Gallagher."

Paul stopped reading and the whole class turned to look at me. "Yes Mam?"

"What are you reading?"

"*The Big Irish Secret*, by Phantom Flynn—I'm just following along." I lifted my book to show her. I didn't think reading along in my own book was a federal offense—it wasn't as bad as putting fish in people's mailboxes, surely.

"Why don't you just take yourself down to the principal's office? If you're so superior as to justify rude behavior during story time, then surely you'd be happier in Mr. Mulligan's office."

I was so sick of this teacher and her load of crap! I should have been used to this by now. On and on it had gone all year. "Thank you, it would be an honor." I stood.

"Are you being smart?"

"Yes Mam. My mother sent me to school to get smart."

Aunt Lace's eyes narrowed cruelly. "Class, Wesley has just erased your afternoon recess because he is *so* smart. You may thank him later." Moans and groans bellowed around the room.

They would thank me, alright. I'd have to fist fight my way out of this one, and then I'd end up back in Mr. Mulligan's office for sure. I didn't bat an eye. I stared at the teacher for a moment. "You're full of so many sour grapes you could start a winery." That was blatantly disrespectful, but I didn't care, for it was also the truth! I slammed my desk top down and left the classroom. I guess Aunt Lace hadn't had enough of my mother yet! My darling teacher was being just as big of a jerk as ever.

I walked down the hall and right on out the end door to the parking lot. I walked down the highway until I hit Main Street, and on Gallagher Street I turned again. I maneuvered up the walk and in the back door. *Slam!* The screen door banged behind me as I stepped inside our back porch.

"Wesley?" Mother came around the corner of the kitchen. "What's wrong?"

"I'm not going back."

"What happened?"

"The same thing that happens every day and I won't go back."

"Annelaise was awful again?"

"She's just mad now."

"So am I, so why push me?'

I shrugged. "I'm supposed to be in the principal's office."

"You left?"

"I did."

"Why?"

"Aunt Lace is smooching on the principal—so what chance do I have with him? He won't listen to me. He hates me too." I kicked my shoes off and tugged at one sock.

"Put your shoes on."

"Why?"

"We are going to the principal's office."

"Together?"

"Yes."

"Um..." My mind flew for some argument to make. I didn't want to go back, not now, not ever. "It's not worth a family feud, Mother."

"We won't turn into the Hatfield's and McCoy's just yet."

I hated seeing our car turn from Gallagher Street onto Main Street, and from Main back onto the Highway. There were not enough miles between home and school! In less than three minutes we were back at Gallagher Springs Elementary, which was on the west end of the building. The junior high occupied the middle, and the high school was on the east end, far away from the little people, but sometimes not far enough. I always felt insignificant and nervous walking in the halls of the high school, but unfortunately, that's where Mr. Mulligan's office was located.

Mother and I started down the hall when the bell rang. Students poured from classrooms. Mother didn't seem tense so perhaps we were alright. My cousin, Monty Quinn, came out of Mr. Henry's science lab. He grinned at me, no doubt wondering what I'd done now. "Hey Kid," he called. "Hi, Aunt Shannon."

"Good afternoon Monty." Mother was a cool cat her own self, and I took heart. A few other high school students said hello to us, including Celia Quinn, who was a freshmen, and John Finnegan, Wyatt's older brother. Perhaps I would have been fine by myself walking down here, but it was intimidating. When we got to the office, Mother said, "You go in Wesley. See what business Mr. Mulligan may have with you. If you need me, I'll be right here, but I want you to handle it first."

I didn't like those terms and I said so. "No way—he'll be all over me."

"Then I'll be all over him. He can't eat you, Son, without becoming my supper. If you need me, I'll be right here." She smiled and I took courage in her smile. My mother was the prettiest lady in Gallagher Springs.

"Can I help you?" Mrs. Clark asked.

"I'm supposed to see Mr. Mulligan."

"Who sent you?"

"Miss Gallagher."

"Figures," Mrs. Dorinda Clark droned.

"That's what I thought."

Mrs. Clark scowled at me. Apparently only grownups have the right to an opinion. She pushed a button and talked into a box. Mr. Mulligan's voice said for me to go into his office. I looked forlornly back at Mother, but she just smiled and nodded encouragement.

I walked twelve steps, past the infirmary, and teacher supply closet to the dreaded principal's office. I'd been here plenty of times before, but it never got easier. My shoes felt heavy and full of lead. I turned the doorknob.

"Wesley," Mr. Mulligan stated glumly.

"Hello Sir."

"Why are you here?"

"Miss Gallagher sent me. I was too smart for class."

"Why is that?"

"Maybe I have a dumb teacher."

Mulligan's eyebrows shot over the top of his forehead. He coughed and blustered. "Now see here! Respect is always in order, young man!"

"Yes sir. I don't know then. You asked my opinion and I shared it. It was the wrong answer, so you tell me. Why am I here?"

Mr. Mulligan's eyes narrowed, taking stalk of me. "Are you back talking me?"

"No. You asked me a question, and I answered it incorrectly. That is all." Mr. Mulligan seemed confounded, not knowing what to do with me. *Really?* Is it that difficult to handle an eleven year old boy? He finally asked me to explain, in detail, the goings on in the classroom. I did so, but still he seemed unsure. "Am I excused?"

"No you are not excused! You impudent, impetuous little brute! We haven't settled anything yet."

I twitched in my chair, not sure of what else to say, exactly. "Listen Mr. Mulligan, my Aunt Annelaise does not like me. She cannot *stand* me to be really honest. You don't seem to like me either, and I'm at peace with that. Let's just part as enemies and call it a day."

"What?" Mr. Mulligan shrieked the word, so perhaps it was punctuated with an exclamation mark, and not a question mark. Grammar books are sometimes wrong.

"I'm certain that you'll soon be my uncle and so I don't want to start a blood feud."

"What!" That time I absolutely knew an exclamation mark was in order. "Do you want me to call your mother?"

I nodded, feeling eager for her to enter. "Yes Sir. She's here now and ready for her supper."

That set him back on his heels. He dropped the pen he was fiddling with, and his chair went careening back to the floor, resting again on all four legs. He'd been tipping on only two legs before then, which is strictly against the rules of the school. "What do you mean?"

"She's ready to come in. I can get her if you'd like."

"Of course not! Why should we bother your mother? Let's work this out ourselves."

"Okay, but I don't really know what we're supposed to be working out."

"We need to come to an understanding of what it will take to make you a better boy."

"I'm trying to be good! I was just following along with the story! Miss Gallagher has been on a mad and won't read to us after lunch! Paul Siskin is a terrible reader. I don't know why they passed him from the third grade. I just wanted to keep up with the story. Is that a federal offense?"

Purple blotches broke out on Mr. Mulligan's face and neck. "No, it's *not* a federal offense! Confound it, Wesley, why must you make things so difficult?"

"Me?" My own question was more of an exclamation, really I'd say.

"And what is that fool *uncle* talk of yours?"

"Um...don't play dumb about that. I watched you and Aunt Lace the other night. You'll be my uncle, alright."

"You impetuous little creep!" Mr. Mulligan was leaning over his desk, hissing the words at me like a mad snake. "How dare you speak of such things?"

"I saw you! I was there and you *know* I was there. And if we really get down to telling the truth, then you and I both know that's why *I'm* here! Aunt Lace is sulking about it."

"You defiled my car and I'm not going to stand for this!"

"I loaded your exhaust pipe with coke bottles, if that's what you're aiming at. Big deal—you were playing patty fingers with my aunt! I'm sure Grandpa Gallagher would be really interested to know everything I saw." I was implying pretty impertinently, and I knew it. I was taking a long shot, for it was too dark and steamy to see much of anything. I mostly only heard Miss Aunt Lace trying to act cute, and that was enough to turn my stomach for a month of Sundays.

Mr. Mulligan's face distorted into an ugly grimace. "What in the—you little extortionist! Are you trying to black mail me?"

"How would I do that?" By his reaction I was pretty sure I'd hit the nail right on the head! There *was* a lot of mischief going on! I had only been making implications, but now I took heart and blundered onward like a Christian soldier. "I don't want anything from you. I'm still explaining why I'm here, apparently."

"You just confessed to defiling my car!"

"You just confessed to defiling my teacher!"

"You had no business sneaking around!"

"Neither did you—and Grandpa Gallagher has a .22, a Long Tom rifle, and a Remington 30.6, so you might want to be more careful from now on."

"Is that a threat?"

"No sir, just a fact."

Blotchy spots stretched across his knuckles where his hands were angrily clasping and unclasping. His whole body seemed bee-stung and it was not attractive. "You have not seen the last of me, young man. I'm considering expelling you from the school."

"My mother better hear it then—and better from you than anyone."

His lips pinched together forming a white line. Perspiration dotted along his brow and I could now see why Aunt Lace closed her eyes when he kissed her. He wasn't much to look at. "Perhaps we should just let this all go."

"We could, but then you'll have to explain it all to your sweetheart. She wants me hung and won't settle for anything less. Maybe you should call for Pistol Stewart to come haul me off to the big house. There would be a trial and I could tell everything I know! Then we'd both be happy. Aunt Lace would be rid of me, and I'd be rid of both of you."

"I'm giving you ten seconds to get out of my sight!"

"Should I go back to class now?"

"No, you should not! You should go home for the day and see if you can find some manners and respect."

"Alright, that's just what I'll do. I'll be back tomorrow, sadly."

"Perhaps you'll get the flu." He sounded hopeful about that.

"I doubt it. I'm *very* healthy. Besides, tomorrow is the science fair and my project is a doosy."

Eyes rolled in Mr. Mulligan's head. "I'm sure it is."

"I think I will win unless you and your library lover are the judges."

"Library lover?"

"I saw you."

He wiped a tired hand across his eyes. "Did you also defile my mailbox?"

"Not intentionally—I was leaving a present for The Least of These My Brethren."

"That's ridiculous! Why on earth did you lump *me* into that category?"

"I felt sorry for you."

"Why is that?'

"I knew you'd be out of a job once the town found out about your stunts with the fifth grade teacher."

"I am free to date whomever I choose!"

"But not during school…I'll just bet."

"Get out of my sight, NOW!"

"I win." I opened the door and removed myself from his sight.

"How did it go?" Mother asked.

"He says I can go home for the afternoon."

"What else?"

"Um…I'm not really sure. He blustered about stuff, but I'm still not clear about it all. I offered to get you so he could explain it better but he didn't think it was necessary."

"Isn't that a pity?" Mother clicked her tongue impatiently and we strolled from the school. I noticed Monty Quinn staring from a window. I grinned at him and he grinned back.

Mother drove me up Gallagher Canyon. "You need to spend some time with Grady," she said. "He's a great champion of children's sufferings, and surely you can vent."

"Where are you going?"

"Back to the school."

"Why?"

"Tomorrow you'll be in Mrs. Leison's fifth grade class."

"But there's only two weeks left of school!"

"Yes, I know, and won't you enjoy them, Son?"

"Wyatt needs me."

"Surely he'll be fine for two more weeks."

"Stan Tomkins is always looking for a fight."

"And?"

"I usually give him one."

Mother smiled, and then pursed her lips together contemplatively. "Wyatt doesn't?"

"Wyatt's too gentle and Stan's too mean."

"I will take Aubynn with me to the school. It sounds like Wyatt needs a new location as well."

"Aunt Lace will *die* before she gives up student custody of the lamb, that *darling* boy."

"Well either way..."

I laughed and climbed out of the car. Grady was waiting for me in the doorway, and his eyes were shining.

Chapter Four

The afternoon was pleasant at Grady's. Maxine Flanders tended the resort and so Grady and I launched out on Inish Lake in his motorized fishing boat. We didn't even grab our poles. "It's just a pleasure trip," Grady said. "It's necessary to take a jaunt just for the simple enjoyment of it every now and then. Grandpa let me drive and we motored over to a little island. We pulled the boat onto the grassy slope and then settled ourselves beneath the shade of some black willow trees. We talked about my trouble and Grady listened well. Grady was right of course, it was healthy to blow off steam. I felt refreshed after the first hour had passed.

"I'm sorry to hear that my Lacey Girl didn't have the sense to read to your class. It's a let-down to have a good book blundered through that way. It's like giving a bucket of fresh oysters to Mrs. Margaret Mahoney, expecting a delicious stew. Her pitiful, watered down version is such a disappointment. Great books are like that too—they're meant to be feasted upon and nobody wants the watered down version!"

"You always understand me Grady."

"Some grandpas are good, and some grandpas are great, but I'm so good I'm Greaty Great." I smiled. My great grandpa was steady, like the sun or the polar star. "Tell me about this Phantom Flynn writer—what makes his books so enjoyable?"

I grabbed my novel from my jacket pocket and tossed it towards Grady. He studied the cover, asking me questions about the plot and characters. He listened while I brought him up to speed, and then he flipped the book open to the right place and started reading. Grady was even better at reading than Aunt Lace, and my mind was soon swept up in the story. Several times Grady paused to laugh at the boys' antics saying, "Son of a gun! These little characters remind me of you and Wyatt!" It was a perfect ending to a lousy day.

Mother came and picked me up at six. I had a couple of bum calves to feed and chores to do. Allyson helped me feed the baby Herefords, Fudge and Freckles, and we got done in record time. "Are you sad, Wesley?"

"No, I'm alright."

"Mom's got you in a different class. Aunt Lace is wailing something fierce at Grandma's house. She called Mom and Aunt Aubynn dirty rotten traitors, but I think it will be okay. Aunt Aubynn said it would be better for her not have so much trouble in her classroom so she's settling down a little bit." I nodded. Allyson looked sideways at me. "Sorry she's so mean, Wes."

"It's okay Sis. She doesn't matter anyway."

We shoveled out the chicken coop and scattered fresh straw in the nests. We gathered the eggs and filled the troughs with wheat and water. The chickens clucked idiotically even though they could see we were being kind to them. "Shut up, old biddies," I scolded, and then I laughed, for the whole town sometimes felt like a bunch of awking, squawking chickens to me. "Oh, go lay an egg," I hollered, "lay dozens of them!"

Dad came whistling from the barn. He was a pleasant man and seldom ever cross. I'm glad I don't have a mean dad like Stan Tomkin's father. He beats Stan's stepmother. I think he whips his kids too, and that's why Stan thinks he has to prove how tough he is all the time. He couldn't best me though. I've already pushed his face in the dirt on several occasions, each time making him cry *Uncle.* For some reason Stan has a beef with Wyatt, and just waits to pounce on my best cousin. That's why I have to trim him down to size every chance I get.

"Hello kids," Dad called. "Got your homework done?" I didn't think I would bother finishing my math assignment since I would have a new teacher in the morning, and I said so. Dad laughed and his head bobbed jovially. "I thought we'd drive down to Eisner and see a movie tonight, how does that sound?"

"What is the movie?"

"Jeremiah Johnson."

I was delighted, but Allyson stomped her foot, bemoaning the fact that she wanted to see something from Disney. Still, a trip to the movies was a treat and no mistake. We picked up Grandpa Grady and motored twenty miles north to the quaint town.

Eisner Lake was the largest body of water, stretching from the town of Eisner, located on the north end of the Three Lakes Valley, to Lakeside on the south end. Gallagher Springs was built smack in the middle of those two communities, and was sprawled between Eisner Lake and Inish Lake to the west, while Lake Washakie crowned the northwest border of Lakeside. It was the prettiest country in the entire world, and I watched the waves of Eisner Lake lick against white-washed rocks near the shoreline as we traveled.

Skip Doheny, the Fish Nazi's kid, Macie Marie Owens, his redheaded girlfriend, Monty Quinn and Shaylin Parks were at the show house when we got there. I spotted Monty's Mustang first thing. Grandpa Grady headed straight for the teenagers, offering a large sack of popcorn and a jumbo package of Milk Duds to the double-dating teenagers. I wondered if Monty would be annoyed at the old man, but he ran a hand through his hair and smiled coolly. I felt myself mirror his action, trying to do it like he did. He was all ease and smiles with Grady, and the other teenagers seemed to like Grady's attentions as well. I grinned, for perhaps Grady was a cool cat, too. Who would have thought? I snapped my fingers, thrilled to have such a neat family.

Just as I was settling in my seat for the cartoon preceding the movie, I noticed my two enemies snuggled together about six rows ahead of us. Grady was delighted. "I am now eagerly watching a show of a different specter," he whispered loudly in my ear. I looked across the aisle to Monty Quinn. I caught his eye and motioned toward Aunt Lace and her beau. Monty's mouth dropped open and he smacked his forehead. I was pleased to have shown him such a funny thing.

The movie was good, although it could have used a bit more action and a few less dire circumstances. The life of a mountain man is apparently very grim! Very grim, I say, and I have already scratched it off of my list of things to be when I grow up. However, my favorite part of the movie showed a man buried up to his chin in the sand. He looked so peculiar with his bald head sticking out of the ground like a saltbush. I wanted to say something to Monty Quinn about it, but they were long gone when the lights came back on. I figured Shaylin must have had a curfew and Monty still had to take her clear down the valley to Lakeside.

We funneled out of the theatre to our car. We were just climbing into the Buick when a heck of a commotion stirred from several cars away. We craned our necks to inspect the situation, only to find Mr. Mulligan's shiny new Oldsmobile in a bad way, for someone had chained the back bumper to a telephone pole. He obviously hadn't seen the shenanigan and pulled away from the curb, leaving his bumper behind. I was dumbstruck at the sight. Of course we laughed at the spectacle. Other vehicles full of movie goers joined in. Aunt Lace's eyes were wild and Mr. Mulligan looked completely stupefied.

Silas Rex, a well-known man from Eisner, walked over to inspect the goings on. "Phew, Melvin! What have you got—a dead body in the trunk?"

"I'm not sure what smells—I've looked everywhere, and promise I haven't spilled any milk on the seats."

I thought of the worms and ducked my head for another chuckle, although they shouldn't have been so putrid already. That's when I saw it—Aunt Lace's purse slung over one shoulder. The stinking cheese bait must be positively reeking by now, and if she wasn't careful, she'd entice rabid mice and lousy varmints to her person. I noticed her sniffing about, looking mystified at the horrific odor. "Really Melvin, the stench is getting worse and worse," she complained. "You'd better take your car in for a thorough cleaning."

Mr. Mulligan seemed out of sorts at the moment. He had worse problems on his hands, by the looks of his bumper. Someone had done a first rate job of removing it for him, and I had a good idea who it was. I had a hunch that loud laughter was probably rocking Monty Quinn's Mustang as it bucked down the road with four gleeful teenagers inside.

Silas, Dad and Grady inspected the damage. Aunt Lace refused to look at Mother, Allyson, or me, which was fine with the three of us. Mr. Mulligan was red faced again, and buzzing like a hornet. "I've had it with hooligans!" His yelling attracted another crowd of people from the theatre. Ace Rushling was among them, and he happened to be the owner of the Three Lakes Insurance Company. He inspected the damage on the spot and approved it for repairs, assigning the work to be done at Silas Rex's garage.

"See, that's snappy service," Grady cackled to Mr. Mulligan. "That's why I live in a valley where things are simple. No red tape, no fuss, just get 'er done, and that's the best way!"

"Follow me to my repair shop and leave your car tonight. I'll get on it first thing in the morning," Silas said, eager for the job.

"Then how would I get home?" You know, for a principal, Mr. Mulligan sure wasn't very bright.

"You can squeeze in with Bill and Shannon, of course!" Silas didn't know that Mr. Mulligan and his poisonous little date was in a tiff with Bill and Shannon Gallagher at the moment. He didn't know beans about fish in mailboxes, stolen clothing fluttering from the flagpole, or the drama in the principal's office that very afternoon. He didn't know that my mother had just requested a new fifth grade teacher for me. He didn't know that none of us wanted to ride together.

A horrified expression crossed Aunt Lace's face at the suggestion. That was so hysterically funny that I burst out laughing. Grady noticed it too, and jumped all over the suggestion. "Capital idea, Silas! Melvin, Annelaise, jump in with us!"

All eyes focused on Mr. Mulligan then. Grady and Silas just jammed him in between a rock and a hard place! He had an executive decision to make, and judging by his work as our principal, I knew he wasn't very good at them. "Sure, if you don't mind, Bill."

"Not at all, hop in." Dad was grinning from ear to ear. He loaded Allyson and me in the front seat with Mother, and opened the back door for his snippety, foot stomping sister. Aunt Lace was seething at the humbling situation she now found herself in. Groveling for a ride with her much despised family members was not what she wanted to be doing! Grandpa Grady scooted into the middle, leaving the only available space for Mr. Mulligan on the other side of him. That was the funniest thing of all! Grandpa Grady separated the lovebirds!

Mother's head ducked into peels of silent laughter. Allyson kept quiet, only meekly saying, "Yuck, something really stinks in here! Do the rest of you smell that?" It did! Aunt Lace's purse was terrible, and I noticed she kept fumbling through it, looking for the offending problem but never seemed to come up with anything. I kept peering at the goings on from the side mirror through the window. I enjoyed gazing at Grady's smile and Aunt Lace's angry frown. Dad kept patting Mother's back affectionately, thinking the whole scenario was too crazy. Mr. Mulligan grumbled and snuffed about the ills of modern society.

"For the record," I said about six miles from home, "I didn't do it."

Dad and Mother lost it then, laughing raucously at my comment. "Of course not, Wesley," Grady called heartily. "This was another hoodlum attack—probably committed by those same punks that vandalized my garbage cans the other night. Don't you worry Melvin; I'll sure be on the lookout from now on!"

Mr. Mulligan mumbled a quiet thanks and I turned over my shoulder to smile jubilantly at him. He shut his eyes trying to make me disappear.

"What are your thoughts on things, Lacey Girl?" Grady asked.

Her nose shot in the air and her eyes rolled while she returned his gaze. Her whole manner seemed disrespectful. "Hmph! That no matter how bad things get, they can always get worse!"

"You're right Lacey Girl. Things *can* always get worse, and I don't mind saying it." He shook his white-topped head against the basic discouragements of life. "And what about you, my lovely Shannon? What do you think this fine night?"

"That no matter *what* things can always get better. Tomorrow will be better than today." Mother patted my knee.

Grady smacked his lips together. "That's another thing I like to say! Things can always get better, and they might just as well get better as *worse*."

Dad kept slowing down, driving slower and slower to further aggravate the situation. He winked at me when he saw me checking out the speedometer. Finally we were puttering along at only twenty five miles per hour. That's the thing about brothers—they never outgrow the need to torture their sisters.

"What's wrong with this idiot car?" Aunt Lace snarled. "Is the gas pedal broken?"

"I don't think so, Sis."

"Then step on it!"

"Yes Daddy, please," Allyson whispered, "Because it really stinks in here."

I was too tired to fight sleep that night. I dreamed I was buried up to my chin in desert sand. A jackrabbit hopped by and blinked at me. His whiskers tickled my nose lightly. A slow tortoise crawled past. My eye balls had seen him coming for hours before he finally crept past my face. A coyote came sniffing by and lifted his leg and saturated me. I hollered at the mangy beast and he nipped at me, drawing blood from my ear. I wanted to touch my ear, but my hands were buried at my side and it was impossible. A bobcat purred through the scraggly, sparse grass. Its eyes narrowed down and it suddenly leapt at my face, claws out and sharp teeth grinning maniacally. Suddenly the feline's face distorted into the features of Aunt Lace. She lunged and scratched and howled again and again, toying with me like a mouse. I jerked awake and my pajamas were drenched in sweat.

I dreaded going to school the next day. I felt like the new kid and I'd lived in Gallagher Springs my whole life. Mrs. Leison just lived on the end of Main Street and had once babysat me when Mother and Dad went on a vacation with Grandpa and Grandma Gallagher. She was very nice so I didn't know why I was so petrified to walk into *5th Grade A* instead of *5th Grade B.*

Wyatt was nervous too and his teeth chattered like he was freezing to death. "Whatdya think Wesley?"

"I dunno. It'll be alright, I guess." I turned the door knob and we walked in. Mrs. Leison looked up and smiled.

"Hello boys. Class, we are lucky enough to get two of our friends to join us for the remainder of the school year. Won't that be nice?"

Margo Walsh raised her hand. Teacher called on her and she said, "What's wrong with Wyatt and Wesley? Did they get kicked out of Miss Gallagher's class?"

I scowled at Margo. *At least my dad doesn't wear lipstick, you little fleabag!* I was ready to say it out loud when Mrs. Leison interjected. "That's none of your concern, Margo!" Her words were sharp and Margo cowered down and shut up. "We are just very lucky to welcome two boys to our classroom who are our good friends already! Wesley and Wyatt's great-great grandfather settled our town." Mrs. Leison invited the kids to welcome us in.

Wyatt relaxed a little bit while he saddled up at his seat. Our desks had just been drug across the hall with all of our stuff still in them. I noticed Margo cranking her neck backwards like a hooty owl to stare at me. Was there a Judy Brynn O'Brien type in every class? I stuck my tongue out at her and she turned around. I glared at the back of her head. I heard a little snicker to the side of me. I glanced sideways. Avery Anne Applewhite was grinning at me. Avery had been in my grade forever, but we'd never ended up in the same classroom yet. I didn't know her too well, but suddenly took a small interest. Her hair was strawberry blonde, like Allyson's, and very shiny. It wasn't full of snarls and static like some of the girls'. She had a sprinkling of strawberry blond freckles to match and I found myself thinking it was very clever to coordinate so well. I smiled back then ducked my head. Perhaps when I grow up and learn to like girls I would like this one.

Math was first in Mrs. Leison's class. I was embarrassed to get called up to the chalkboard the very first thing to show how to multiply fractions. Of course I worked the problem out alright, but it put me on the spot. I poked my tongue out at Margo as I walked back to my desk because she was making googly eyes at me.

Spelling came next and Mrs. Leison clapped her hands together three times. "Spelling Bee!" The classroom clamored into two lines. Wyatt and I stumbled along like dumb sheep in a corral, being driven with the herd, trying to learn our duties in the new class. Apparently every Thursday was spelling day. Mrs. Leison said it was boys' turn first. The word was *Translate.* Miles O'Reilly spelled it correctly and earned us a point. Then it was the girls' turn, and on and on. If you misspelled a word you had to sit back in your desk. I thought this was a great idea, as competition was healthy. It made learning feel like a sport and I was always game for a game. Miss Gallagher should have done something creative like this in her classroom. She only believed in having us write each word into sentences until it blazed itself into our minds.

"Turquoise," Mrs. Leison's voice said. I felt Wyatt go stiff and could practically hear him sweat. He wasn't a grand speller, but I hoped he could work it out.

"Turquoise," Wyatt repeated. "T-U-R-K-O-Y-Z-E, er, um… something like that," He hesitated for a moment and then said, "Turquoise."

"Incorrect, take your seat Mr. Finnegan." Now it was the girls' turn to spell, and the well-coordinated Avery Anne Applewhite was next in line. She rattled off *turquoise* very smoothly, and I was impressed.

Around and around we spelled, sending students to their desks one by one. I was sad to see that the girls were better spellers than the boys. By the time twenty minutes had passed I was the lone boy standing for my team. I faced Avery, Margo, and one of the nine Cindy's. "Albuquerque." Mrs. Leison challenged. Sweat broke out between my shoulder blades. Did it have a K in the middle somewhere, or was it a Q? I couldn't quite remember.

Margo tilted her head off smartly and spelled, "Capital A-L-B-

U-R…K-," she stammered midway through the word so I knew she wondered the same thing I did, "U-E-R-Q-U-E, Albuquerque."

"Take your seat." Margo's shoulders slumped and I wasn't sorry to see her go, and I knew I would spell the word correctly for I'd learned from Margo's error.

One of the nine Cindy's messed up on *arthritis,* assigning an E-S at the end of the word instead of I-S. Now it was down to Avery and me. We squared off and it gave me a good excuse to really look her over. Her mouth was prettily shaped and her lips weren't chappy at all, so it sort of looked neat when letters came out of her mouth as she spelled, "H-I-P-P-O-P-O-T-A-M-U-S," correctly.

"Wesley, can you spell *spaghetti*?"

"No, but he sure can eat it," Steve McCarthy quipped.

I spelled the word, silently thinking Steve McCarthy could eat it, and now the pressure was back on my worthy opponent. Mrs. Leison gave her the word *illustrious* and she nailed it.

The ball came whizzing back into my court. I looked expectantly at my new teacher. Mrs. Leison smiled and her twinkly brown eyes were hopeful. *"Voluptuous."*

What kind of a word is *that*? Boys don't go around spelling things like that! Avery grinned at me and her nose wrinkled up, seeing I was in a tight spot. "I pass," I said, admitting defeat. "I wouldn't spell that word if I could."

The whole class burst into laughter, Mrs. Leison included. Then Avery Anne did something really nifty. She said, "I pass too, Teacher."

"Oh dear, there are no takers for such a delightful word? How about *rheumatism*?"

I cleared my throat, figuring my options. "Voluptuous," I said, "V-O-L—"

Mrs. Leison doubled over, leading the class into a hearty roar. I was surprised that my humor could be so appreciated. Had this all taken place in Miss Gallagher's class I would have already been to Mr.

Mulligan's office twice. "Oh Wesley, you are a hoot! I'm so happy you are with us now," Mrs. Leison said. "Now, try again with *rheumatism*."

I blundered and failed. Avery spelled the word correctly, beaming triumphantly at me the whole time she was spelling. Defeat had never felt so good and I didn't mind losing to her a bit.

At recess Stan Tomkins started riding Wyatt pretty heavy about being a classroom fink. I wrestled him down, and after a tough scuffle, made him cry, "Uncle!"

I didn't let up right away. "Not yet Stan. You leave Wyatt Finnegan alone from now on! Do you understand? I'm sick of you heckling him!"

"Get off me, you butthole!"

"Jerk!" I slammed his face into the dirt some more, willing to hold him down for as long as it took even though my muscles were shaking from fatigue. Stan was bigger than I was and hard to handle. "What?"

"Uncle!"

"That's not the magic word today."

"I'll leave Wyatt alone!"

I thrust his face downward again, feeding him a little dirt before I released my hold. "Keep your word," I warned. When I straightened up I was surprised to see Miss Aunt Lace looming over me.

Stan's nose was bloody and he tried to use the situation to his advantage. "Miss Gallagher," he moaned pitifully, "Wesley's roughed me up."

I looked Aunt Lace right in the eye, waiting for her tirade to start, but she simply said, "Hush up Stan. I didn't see anything," and walked away. My mouth gaped open… for wonders never cease.

The science fair was that afternoon. It involved each student from third grade through the eighth grades. The whole town was invited, and so was the student body, including the big high schoolers. Grandpa Gallagher came at two o'clock, bringing me and Wyatt's projects. We lugged our stuff secretly into the gymnasium, not wanting others to see the goods before the unveiling.

I carried our large picnic cooler and that drew a lot of stares. I grinned at Judy Brynn O'Brien. Her project about taste buds looks tasteless compared to mine. I smiled at Stan Tomkins, who hadn't put much effort into a dinosaur panorama made out of modeling clay. I beamed at Avery Anne Applewhite just because she was smiling at me—I have no idea what her project was. Mrs. Leison and Miss Gallagher were buzzing around trying to help each fifth grader, but Grandpa and I had my project well in hand.

When I could stall no longer, I dramatically lifted my project onto the table. Confounded stares peered my way. I knew they would remain befuddled until I really got down to business. I plugged my invention in. I unloaded ketchup, mustard, and Mother's pickled relish. I set a stack of napkins on the table, several bags of buns, and then mounted a poster. "HOME MADE HOTDOG COOKER by Wesley Gallagher HOTDOGS FOR SALE .50 a PIECE." I was in business.

It worked like this: the two nails were driven through a block of wood. I engraved my trademark initials into the wood with Dad's wood burner. It looked professional. I had wrapped electrical coils around each nail head, turning the nails into electrical conductors when the cord was plugged in and the toggle switch was on. The nails were spaced three and a half inches apart, with the dangerous looking things jutting out of the wood base like cooking prongs. I mounted wooden spools on the bottom of the cooker to conceal the nail heads.

I thread the first hotdog onto the prongs, flipped the switch, and let the electricity cook the wiener. It was genius, really I'd say, and it made the gym smell good. Grandpa Gallagher was as excited as I was! We hung a big poster that explained electricity and how my project worked. I drew a big CAUTION sign that warned curious idiots against touching my apparatus while it was turned on. It cooked hotdogs very quickly, and I could cook six of them each minute.

Wyatt's light-up solar system paled in comparison although it looked quite interesting to me. He had a network of gears that made the planets rotate around the sun. Aunt Lace would be furious with me for unseating the little scientist, but I knew I'd win—heck, I'd known all week, and I couldn't even be humble about it. Interested students streamed to my station from all over the gym. The public wasn't here yet, for we were supposed to be looking at each other's exhibits for the first thirty minutes. I was swamped with customers from the junior high. They all had coins jingling in their pockets and they thought my homemade concession stand was brilliant. Grandpa kept me in hotdogs and supervised the safety of the whole thing.

The smaller kids looked enviously at my electrocuted hotdogs, licking their lips, but claiming poverty. "Maybe your parents will buy you one when they come," I said hopefully, but I handed Allyson and Dori Jo one for free, making them the envy of the third grade. I felt really pleased when the town started trickling in. Many of the mothers and dads were quite generous.

"Hey Kid." I was counting my money, but I jerked my head up to see Monty, Skip, and some other big seniors. I grinned. "This is pretty cool stuff, Kid." Monty flipped a fifty cent piece in my direction, and Skip unloaded a whole dollar, buying one for himself and Macie Marie. "Good show last night," I said, flashing a phantom thumbs up at Monty just as he had done to me. They broke out in raucous laughter, and Grandpa Gallagher seemed puzzled by the inside joke.

"This hotdog cooker is too cool! You should have brought some Cokes, and Crush, and chips to sell, too."

"Yeah, but Mr. Mulligan would have made me buy a business license so I didn't want to push my luck."

The big kids laughed irreverently again. Monty squeezed a line of mustard onto his bun. "See what I mean? The Kid's got class. He's sharp."

I grew about nine inches just then, and my confidence took a healthy enough jolt to launch me into adolescence. "Thanks Monty."

The jostling crew moved on to Wyatt's set up. Monty cranked the handle and watched the planets go spinning into orbit. "Good job, little Poot," he encouraged. I saw Wyatt scowl sideways at me.

Business was so brisk Grandpa had to run down to McCarthy's Market for some more hot dogs and buns. I explained my project to all interested persons while demonstrating the marvels of cooking with electricity. Everyone seemed pleased to have a bite to eat while they studied science. I saw Avery Anne slip into line. I fidgeted nervously. I felt all flushed as she dropped five dimes into my hand, and yet my confidence was riding high. "Hey," I said.

"Hi Wesley."

"You are a good speller, Avery."

"You too."

"What's your science project? I've been too busy to come and see."

"It's about nutrition. I have some celery stalks in mason jars of colored water. The stems are drinking the water, and you can see red and blue streaking up the veins of the celery."

"Like blood poisoning?"

"Sort of, I guess. Anyway, it proves that plants really do drink in water and nutrients."

"I've never cared about celery very much, but I'd like to see it. I'll walk over there when I can."

Avery smiled and her nose wrinkled up just right. "Well, it probably won't slow down for you." She dotted little spots of mustard along her hotdog and then squiggled a line of ketchup in between. I'd never seen such artistry! I'll bet she could make celery do whatever she wanted it to!

"Hey Kid, I'll man your booth so you can scoot around for a minute." Monty had doubled back.

"Okay...be careful to shut the switch off before you load or unload a hot dog."

"Kid, electricity doesn't shock me—I shock it."

Wow...it just doesn't get any cooler than that, does it? I didn't know what to say so I just shuffled along, following Avery to her station. I liked her celery a lot and said so. She smiled and crinkled her nose, and

I ducked my face because I was embarrassed and out of anything else to say.

"I know who the judges are."

I jerked my head back up. "You do?"

"Dr. McGee, Mr. Henry, and Mrs. Clark, and they just came in, but I overheard Miss Gallagher talking to Mrs. Leison."

"Yeah?"

"She said you would win."

"Was she mad about it?"

"I don't think so."

I was dumbstruck, but high tailed it back to my station before the judges milled near. I took a crank on Wyatt's gears as I passed. "Monty calls me Poot even when it doesn't rhyme with *scoot*," he grumbled.

"Oh well. He doesn't know my name but he likes my style," I boasted.

"You're dumb."

I didn't blame Wyatt for sulking at me. He hates braggarts and so do I—usually. "Thanks Monty," I said, sliding back behind my table.

"No prob. That girl was cute."

"You think so?"

"Yep, she's the kind that grows up to look like *this*," and his hands made that curvy motion again. Now I really blushed and the heat in my cheeks could have roasted a hotdog, too.

Monty laughed and went in search of his buddies. School was out and the high schoolers were free to leave, but the students in the science fair had to stay until five o'clock. I was happy when Mother and Dad came in with Grady, Grandma Gallagher, and Aunt Aubynn. They bought hot dogs, and took pictures of Wyatt and me in front of our stations. I imagined they snapped photos of Allyson and Dori Jo, as well. Aunt Aura Leigh and Uncle Rob came later, Aura Leigh streaked through the gym, head up and ninety miles an hour, pausing only to examine Dori Jo and Allyson's exhibits, Wyatt's, and mine. Uncle Rob bought several hotdogs claiming nothing was more American.

Grandpa Grady was slow. I watched him hover over each child, making a fuss, building character and confidence. He seemed to have scoped out each kid without folks attending, too, and magically slipped them all quarters for a hotdog. Stan Tomkins loomed before me. "I want a hotdog, you butthole."

"Haven't I trimmed you down to size enough for one day?"

"I said I'd be nice to Wyatt. That means I'm gunning for you now."

"No you won't. I'll fight back and cowards hate fair fights." He made a mean face and called me something I'm not allowed to repeat. I rolled my eyes. "You do it," I said, handing the hotdog to him.

He triumphed, cramming the weenie down carelessly. A little devil whispered in my ear that I should hit the toggle switch and I listened. Stan jerked his hand back, wincing from the jolt. I saw a blister pop out immediately for it both shocked and burned him.

"I don't care to be called a butthole," I said. "And the next time you want to say that word, just softly croon it to yourself as you look in the mirror." He glared at me, but that was the end of it that night. He loaded up his bun with about a half a jar of relish and snarfed the hotdog down. I wondered how long it had been since he'd eaten something besides dirt. I couldn't stand the big bully but I felt really sorry for him at the same time.

The judges had split up and gone off in all different directions of the gym, obviously running a divide and conquer strategy. I smiled at Mr. Henry and launched into an explanation of my project.

Mr. Henry listened soberly. "Electricity is dangerous."

"Yes sir, and should be respected, hence my CAUTION sign." I like the word *hence* and use it whenever possible.

Mr. Henry's mouth twitched a little, like Grandpa Gallagher's often did. He asked me questions about my project and I answered them rapid fire, eager to show him what I had learned while building my cooker. "It's obvious you have done this for yourself," he finally said.

"Yes, my Grandpa Gallagher helped me though."

"Certainly, certainly. And how old are you?"

"Eleven since February."

"In whose classroom?"

"Miss Gal—I mean Mrs. Leison's, sir."

"It looks as if she's done a top notch job with you." I thought the timing of such a statement was funny, and if I won, Mrs. Leison would get all the credit, and Aunt Lace would be duped again, just as I was making progress with her.

The hours passed quickly. It felt like I had fed the town that night while Wyatt lit up the sky with his cranking gears and spinning planets. Grandpa Gallagher bragged about us both, and Grady worked the crowd, making special efforts to show an interest in the students. Finally Mr. Mulligan stepped to a microphone. He awarded a third place certificate and twenty-five dollars to a girl from the eighth grade, Karen Tripp. Her project was a dissected crayfish demonstration. Fifty dollars and second place was awarded to a seventh grader, Bradley Benson, with a homemade erupting volcano. Suddenly Wyatt and I looked concerned, for we thought we were both in the running for first and second.

"And the first place honor and hundred dollar grand prize will be split this year, as we have a tie between Wyatt Finnegan and Wesley Gallagher. They are both students in *Mrs. Leison's* fifth grade class."

I didn't mind sharing the accolade with Wyatt one little bit, for aside from fifty dollars, I had a lot of money rattling around in my can from hotdog sales. We stepped up to the podium and shook Mr. Mulligan's hand. He looked pained by the responsibility of having to announce our successes, and I ginned and said, "I win again."

The phone rang at nine o'clock that night. Mother took the call. Her brows shot up and she passed the phone to me. I gulped once, "Hullo?"

"Wesley, this is Aunt Lace."

Oh dear, I wondered what I'd done wrong now! Little beads of sweat surfaced beneath my pajamas. "Uh huh?"

"Congratulations on the science fair. Your superiority was obvious."

"Um...who did you say this was again?"

"Aunt Lace."

"Oh," I nearly fell down on the floor and kicked my feet like a squashed rabbit alongside the road. "You liked my project?"

"Very much, and the two most capable students won. I'm so glad!" She almost sounded pleasant and the weirdness of it was uncomfortable.

"Well—you'd better tell Grandpa. He helped me."

"Good night, Wesley."

"Um, okay, well…goodbye."

My family stared at me as I hung up the phone, expecting a report on the phone call. "Yes?" Mother baited.

"Um…I think it was a wrong number," I mumbled and headed off to bed with my Phantom Flynn novel in hand.

Chapter Five

A week sped by. Wyatt and I settled into our routine in Mrs. Leison's class. At lunchtime Miss Gallagher looked longingly toward the lamb, her darling boy. Wyatt pretended not to see but every once in a while I noticed him smile in her direction.

"Wyatt, are you sorry you got moved with me?"

"No."

"Sure?"

"Yep."

"Promise?"

Wyatt crossed his heart and gave me half of his pears as a solemn oath of truth, and I figured he couldn't be more sincere than that, that's what I figured.

Avery Anne Applewhite sent one of the nine Cindy's over to our table with a cookie. "Special delivery for Wesley, from a secret admirer," she said, handing it to me. I feigned shock at getting a cookie although I'd seen Avery place it in Cindy's hand just seconds earlier. The boys all made googly "Awe," sounds.

"Wesley's got a sweetheart," Steve McCarthy drawled.

"A sweetheart? Is that what this is?" I asked, eyeing my cookie suspiciously. "I thought it was just a cookie!" I pointed down the table at the line up of trays. "Look guys, you've all got sweethearts!" It was a good move as the boys let it drop, and starting oohing and awing at their own ginger snaps. Miles O'Reilly even kissed his, saying he had a smack for his snap. Of course, Miles O'Reilly was quite a chubby boy and I figured he kissed most of his food.

The fire alarm sounded then, screaming and angry, and we all filed out of the school in an orderly way just as we'd drilled a dozen times. We grabbed our cookies and munched on them on our way outside. The classes were organized into groups so that our teachers could get a headcount. Mr. Mulligan supervised the evacuation with meticulous skill. High school and junior high students poured from the east doors and milled around until they were near us.

The clamoring bells of the town's fire truck came clanking up the road. The fire department was the only ones authorized to shut the school's fire alarm off once it sounded. Many of us covered our ears to avoid the jarring clamor. The truck pulled dramatically up to the school and volunteer firemen went running inside. Soon the alarm shut off and Captain Drake Murphy strolled from the school shaking his head.

"Is everything okay?" Mr. Mulligan asked.

"Wull..." Mr. Murphy said in a funny way. "That's probably a matter of opinion."

"What do you mean?"

"Wull..." Murphy said again, grinning over a mouthful of horse teeth, "There's a car in the cafeteria."

"There is not!" Mr. Mulligan protested. "We were just in there, and—"

Murphy grinned again, this time the teeth exploded from every direction in a cheesy smile. "Better see fer yerself," he said, swinging the lunch room door wide open.

I blinked several times at the spectacle. Mr. Mulligan's shiny, newly repaired 1972 Oldsmobile was sitting smack dab in the middle of the room! Lunch tables were scooted against the cafeteria walls with our trays still setting on them. I couldn't believe it!

Wyatt sputtered, "That's Mr. Mulligan's car, and I can *smell* it from here!"

Teachers' jaws gaped and children blinked stupidly. Mr. Mulligan's hands doubled into fists and he hopped around like a mad troll beneath a bridge. "Who has done this? Who?" His face was mottled purple, looking like it was plastered with huckleberry jam. "Who, I say, who? Who? Who?" He sounded like a hooty owl *who-ing* away like that, and a few chuckles stirred around the crowd.

"Not only who, but how?" Mr. Voss asked comically.

"How? Yes, how? How! And why? *Why* would someone do this?" Mr. Mulligan wrung his hands, walking around and around his car.

More students filtered into the lunchroom, looking dumbfounded. Margo Walsh grimaced and pulled her shirt up over her nose. "Sick, that car really stinks!"

Wyatt looked at me. "Hasn't he found the worms yet?"

"I guess not," I whispered.

High school kids were now bending with laughter as Mr. Mulligan hopped up and down, shaking his pudgy fists. "I'd just drive it out of here if I knew *how*," he sputtered angrily. That did it. Fifteen or twenty students and teachers bellowed with merriment.

I was plum amazed at the intricacy of this covert operation. Someone had to have had this planned out well in advance, and been driving or pushing the car into the school before the fire alarm even sounded to have mastered the stunt. They moved swiftly and with precision. Someone had to have had connections to pull it off.

Just then I saw it, alright. Ever so slightly John Finnegan slipped a bill into Monty Quinn's hand. Monty's lips pinched together coolly. Then Celia Quinn slid a greenback into his hand, followed by Tom McFarland, big Bill Monroe, and Cindy Somebody. Jentz Cooper and others huddled near, doing the same thing. So sly, *ever so sly*, bet money piled up in Monty's hand. Skip Doheny smiled smugly, so I knew he was in on it and Macie Marie Owens as well. I smelled a whole town full of rats and one rancid can full of rotten worms under a seat.

"How? How?" Mr. Mulligan fumed toward Mr. Henry and Mr. Voss. "How can I get it out of here?"

Mr. Henry's head bobbed in thought. "The only doors that open wide enough are in the gym and the auto shop. You'll have to maneuver the automobile out of one of those places."

"You think they brought it in that way?"

Mr. Henry shook his head, "Well, it got here somehow."

Mr. Mulligan stared at the high school students, scanning the faces for an honest looking one. "John Finnegan!" he cried.

Wyatt's older brother's head snapped up. "Sir?"

"How do you suppose this car ended up in here?"

"I don't know, Sir. I was outside."

Laughter rolled like lunchroom seconds. Even the cooks were getting a hoot out of this. "Well, I *know*," Mr. Mulligan persisted, "but what's the best way to get it out of here?"

John was a bookworm and very smart. He had a dull personality but kept his nose clean most of the time. I was happy to see he could let his hair down enough to slip a little bet money in Monty Quinn's direction. He didn't like being singled out now, and his cheeks flamed as red as Lady Scarlett's nightgown. "Sir, would you like my friends and I to remove the car for you?"

"Do you think you know how?"

I was laughing on the inside at this little turn of events. *Do you think you know how?* How did Mr. Mulligan think it got in the cafeteria in the first place? I shook my head, trying to keep the laughter contained, but I locked eyes with Monty Quinn and flashed a faint thumbs up, so fast and so faint it's like it never happened.

"I'll bet we could figure it out," John said respectfully, trying hard to hold a straight face.

"How many friends do you need to help you?"

"Oh, probably two or three," John answered confidently.

Mr. Mulligan considered John's petition and granted him permission to choose a couple of helpers to remove the car. John looked like the cat that was in the cream to me. His eyes glistened while he gazed at his fellow students and comrades. "Oh I dunno," he said lowly. "Maybe I'll take my cousin, Monty Quinn, 'cuz he's a sensible guy, and perhaps... Skip Doheny."

Wise choices indeed! The wolves stepped forward, modeling the innocent fleece of sheep's clothing. This was just too much! Monty looked studiously at the problem at hand, trying to work a suitable conclusion. Mr. Mulligan warmed right up to his ploy and cozied closer to work up a joint vehicle removal strategy.

"Whoever did it," Monty offered, "must have come in the gym doors, then down the south hall, through the junior high commons, and in here. That's the best way I can figure it."

"How did they get it around the corners?"

"Very carefully," Skip noted stoically. "They probably had to ease it around the center fountain."

"Can you boys *ease* it back out of here so I can get the kids back to class?"

"You want me to drive your car?" Monty seemed shocked, as if he hadn't just done that.

"Well, you are a well respected young man in this school. Go very carefully, and I'll oversee the finishing of the lunches so that the elementary can get back to class and the older grades can come and eat.

"I'm afraid to drive your car, Mr. Mulligan."

"Why? Why are you afraid?"

"I think there's a dead body in the trunk. It really stinks."

"Yes," hissed around the crowded room. It was true—all of the windows were rolled down on the Oldsmobile and the stench was unmistakable.

"There's no dead body!" Mr. Mulligan was blustering and purple faced again.

John Finnegan raised his hand and Mr. Mulligan recognized him. "Our car smelled like that once. We finally found an old carton of night crawlers under the back seat, but not before Wyatt puked all over the side of the station wagon."

"But I haven't been fishing!" Mr. Mulligan jerked the back door open, practically standing on his head to dig beneath the seat. Much to his consternation he pulled out an offending container of dried worms. "How did these get in here? How? And why? Why!"

Everyone laughed again, and Monty Quinn's blue eyes locked with mine and we smiled.

Mrs. Harris, the head cook, ran into the kitchen and came back with a can of Lysol. She misted the car like a fumigator. Students coughed and chortled in the fog of aerosol, wheezing and hacking until we all agreed we preferred the stink.

"What if the guys who did this beat us up?" Monty asked, feigning concern.

"Anyone who lays a finger on you boys will answer to me," Mr. Mulligan assured, very authoritatively. He surveyed the student body. "These are good boys and not low life hoodlums! This is a warning!"

I was giggling inside at the prospects of Monty Quinn punching himself in the nose. Miss Aunt Lace's eyes narrowed in my direction. "I didn't do it," I said defensively.

"But I think you know who did."

"Scouts honor, I didn't have anything to do with this!"

"Innocent? Surely not." Her words were sharp and curt.

I was wrong. She wasn't getting nicer! Somebody drives a car into the school and I'm immediately a suspect? Give me a break! "I think *you* know who did it!" I countered. "I think this all came from the faculty, and I'm suspecting you and Mr. Voss are involved."

"Wesley, don't be *ludicrous*." Miss Gallagher's tone was icy.

"Then don't you be *presumptuous*."

"Presumptuous?" The word was spoken quite shrilly.

"P-R-E-S-U-M-P-T-U-O-U-S. Mrs. Leison is one heck of a good spelling teacher." My sass was uncontrollable.

"Honest Miss Aunt Lace, we don't know anything." Wyatt protested meekly.

Aunt Lace studied the earnest face of her little lamb then turned with a huff and walked back outside muttering, "If you say so, Wyatt."

Twenty minutes later Monty Quinn and Skip Doheny motored past the fifth grade classrooms. We ran to the hall door. John Finnegan was motioning them back with his hands. "This way now," he encouraged. The car went into reverse, and John kept baiting them back farther. Apparently they had now driven up and down every hallway in the school in their efforts to gingerly make the corners and get it on outside. We hooted at the sight.

"Oh dear," Mrs. Leison said. "I fear you boys are milking this a little."

Monty grinned at his old fifth grade teacher. "Us?" he asked innocently.

The car reversed until it finally looped around the junior high fountain and disappeared into the gym. It circled the school yard several times before parking. It was a crazy case and Monty was getting away with it all—and with Mr. Mulligan's protective blessing, too!

Mid May breeze ruffled whitecaps on Eisner Lake. I studied them while the bus chugged to my drop off. Wyatt and I skedaddled up Gallagher Canyon to Grady's on our bikes so we could relay the events of the day. Grady laughed and laughed. "We once hoisted the bishop's wagon on top of the church," he gasped. Wyatt and I were impressed.

"Tell us about it," Wyatt urged while we motored toward the island in Inish Lake. I had my Phantom Flynn novel in my pocket and figured we could talk Grady into reading some more. He did. I laid under the Black willows, tracing the branches against the sky while my mind ran wild, painting illustrations to the words of the story. Grady was the greatest reader ever and I was sad to see the sun sink down.

Chapter Six

School was out and Grady planned a Grandpa Greaty-Great Holiday. He invited his great grandsons to join him on a camping trip. Monty pulled to a halt in front of Grandma's house. He drove Grady's old Studebaker truck. We threw all of our stuff in the back, then Mark and John Finnegan jumped in the cab with Monty while Wyatt and I climbed in the back. We rested against our sleeping bags and steadied our fishing poles and tackle boxes with our boots. When we got to Grady's place Mark hopped into the back with us and Grady climbed in the front. We chug-a-lugged up to the very top of Gallagher Canyon then drove on top of the ridge for a ways. Grandpa Grady made Monty stop for a minute so we could survey the view. All three lakes glistened like deep blue jewels and it was no wonder our ancestors thought they'd come to the end of the rainbow! We continued on until we hit a little road that carved off of the backside of the mountain and wound down Washakie Fork.

The glacial waters of Washakie Creek cut through the narrow valley with a mighty rushing sound. Aspen and pine grew heavy along the banks. The valley was green and fragrant and was Grady's favorite fishing place in the whole world. We set up camp, pitching two good sized tents. The three older boys got one, while Grady, Wyatt and I would sleep in the other. I grinned the whole time we were working just because I knew how lucky we were. Not every kid had a chance to live like we did. I loved the mountains and nature. My eyes worked the canyon while I dug a fire pit. This was our place—being owned by

Grady, and ranched by my Dad, Uncle Rob, and Grandpa Gallagher. Surely most people never had the opportunity to have the Garden of Eden planted in their own back yards. I felt so happy to be a country boy just then that I had to whistle.

Once we got everything set up to Grady's standards, he wrangled a cooler open and passed out sandwiches. They were Grady Specials, sliced ham and cheese with tomato, lettuce, cucumbers, and bleu cheese dressing. The bread was homemade and full of walnuts and sunflower seeds. That's the way Grady liked it, nutty and chewy. He sold these sandwiches on occasion at the resort and city folks just clamored for them. "Good food," Grady said.

"Good view," I added.

"Good company," Mark offered.

"Good day," John declared.

"Good for us," Wyatt agreed.

"Good grief!" Monty said, chugging a swallow from a bottle of orange Crush. "Let's not use all of our conversation up during lunch!"

We laughed noisily, and then Grady said cleverly, "Good one."

After lunch Grady wanted to take us hiking. I wondered about the wisdom of it since he was slightly wobbly in the legs, but he grabbed a big stick to steady his steps, and invited us to keep up. We walked south, toward the Lakeside end of things.

"Right up here boys, is what I want to show you."

We trailed through a dense thicket of chokecherry bushes and into a clearing. "When I was a boy the Shoshones camped here all of the time." We were definitely interested, every one of us, and listened close to every word.

"They set up their tipis all around this flat right here. See where the soil is black? That's where their campfires were. They came through here every fall, and they could fish and hunt a plenty. Sometimes they slipped over the ridge in the evenings and soaked in the hot springs where my place is. Of course it wasn't developed and fancy like it is now, but the spring water was warm and they loved it. I once saw them carry an old

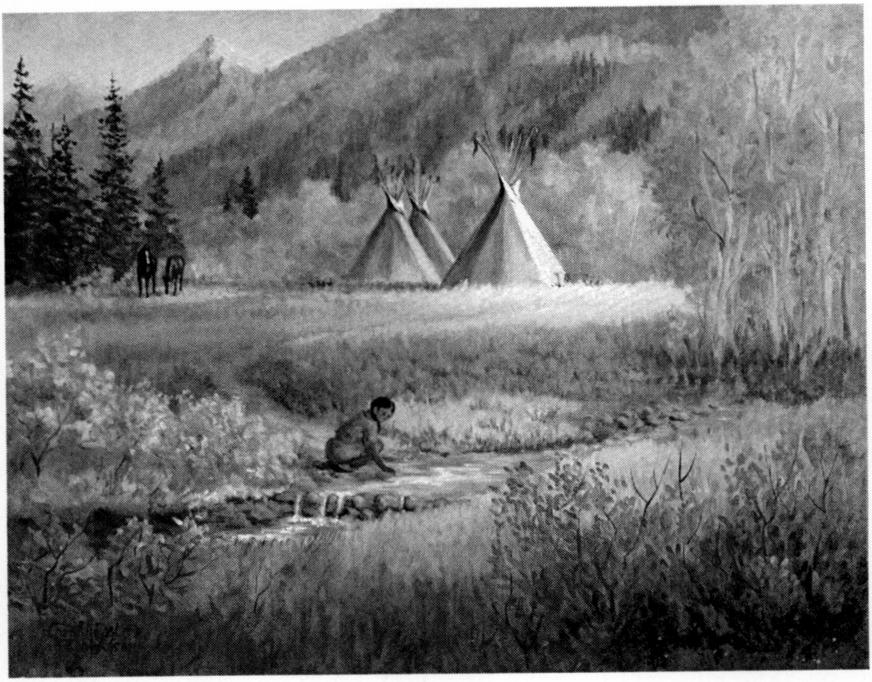

man into the water. His legs were bent with age and he was crippled. He soaked in the water all night, and when morning came he climbed out of the water on his own power and mounted a horse, smiling. He claimed the water was poured to earth from The Great Spirit to heal the suffering."

My mind whirled with the thoughts of seeing Indians camped like olden days. It was weird to me how times had changed in Grady's lifetime. No one said a word while he continued talking. "Sometimes the town got a little nervous when the Indians came to camp but I loved it. The native people mesmerized me. I came near at nights, sitting in the trees. I huddled in the shadows and watched them dance by the fire."

"Weren't you afraid?" Mark asked, hating to interrupt the stories, but yearning to know.

"Yes, I was always afraid, but so terribly fascinated! Adrenaline sped through my vessels the way Pistol Stewart speeds through town to catch a jaywalker." Chuckles rumbled among us. Grady was a one of a kind grandpa, and no mistake. "But I got so I'd bring some kind of an offering with me just in case I was captured somehow, in violation of a treaty or something."

"What treaty?"

"Brigham Young had agents working with Chief Washakie to keep peace for the settlers. Washakie promised to clear out of the Three Lakes Valley if the agents could secure his people the Wind Rivers, over in Wyoming. Brigham's agents worked with the government to form a decent treaty, but Chief Washakie set a condition of being able to come back and hunt and fish without trouble, and they smoked the peace pipe over it."

"They did?"

"I'm certain of it, boys, although I wasn't there, but that was the condition of our valley at that time. When the Shoshones came to stay, we were to clear out and not make any trouble for them, and they mostly left us alone."

"What kind of offering, Grady?" I needed to know.

"Well, at first I shot a couple of rabbits and had them with me, just in case. No trouble came, but after they all bedded down for the night I stepped closer and laid them near the glowing embers of their fire. The old man saw me and smiled. I made it back home with my scalp *and* my horse, so the next time I took a couple of turkeys. My dad found out I wasn't afraid to get near the Indians and he sent me up with some coffee, sugar, and cornmeal. On another occasion he sent me here with a couple of ewes. Father liked to keep on the right side of them."

"That was nice."

Grady grinned at our rapt attention. He bent low, raking the fire blackened soil with his hands. He clicked his tongue to the roof of his mouth as he picked up an arrowhead. We went gaga at the discovery and soon we were all carefully sifting through the dark soil with our fingers, looking for any sign of native artifact. Grady showed us how to identify little chips of flint. "These are the pieces that were chipped off the rock while forming an arrowhead. See? Anywhere you see these chips you know Indians once made an arrowhead there." I was amazed and began picking up the delicate slivers of flint and obsidian.

"Is this something?" Monty handed a find to Grady.

"Look, it's a part of a scraper, see?"

We gathered around. Monty had found a tool with a sharpened round end. Grady showed us how a squaw would have used the tool to scrape the hair from a hide. I thought it was too bad that it was broken. A breeze rattled through the trees around us. "Hear that?" Grady asked.

Our heads jerked up, wondering what he was hearing besides the wind. "What Grady?" Wyatt asked.

"That rustling sound is a composition of whispers echoing from long ago."

I scowled, considering Grady's words, and for some reason, a batch of goose bumps tumbled down my neck and arms. The other boys peered at Grady, eager for more. "What do the whispers say?" John encouraged some detail.

"The whispers just ask you to reflect, respect, and remember." Another round of goose bumps shivered. Grady was being more serious and contemplative than I'd ever seen him, and his stories were holding us spellbound.

"Did the Shoshones like your offerings—the rabbits and turkey?" Mark dragged an old stump over for Grady to sit on while he answered his question. We sat around the old man, listening, with our hands loosely combing through the dirt for relics.

"I guess they did. They left that year and I didn't see them for another one."

"How old were you then?"

"Fifteen—just your age, Mark." Mark nodded. "The next year they came back. I'd ridden my horse after some cattle on our summer range southwest of Lakeside. I was eating a chunk of cheese for my lunch beneath a stand of willow trees on Elmer's Point. I saw the Indians coming, but I made it back here before they did. I rode up here with two fifty pound sacks of sugar on my father's orders, and had it waiting in the clearing when they arrived. Dad always liked to keep peace with the Indians but was fearful of them himself. Well, it caused a great stir among the people, and although I was hiding, that old Shoshone man spied me and smiled."

"Was he crippled again?"

"Not as much as the year before, but during the next couple of days the people again journeyed to the hot springs and soaked. The old guy drew strength from the mineral waters and offered some kind of prayer over the springs."

"I had no idea your resort had an Indian blessing," I said.

Grady smiled at me. "Maybe that's why I'm still here," he mused. "That wise old sage was older than Santy Claus, but now I'll bet that I'm older than he was then, and look at me! Hiking and camping with a bunch of young sprouts, and nary a hair missing from my head! The water does me good too, and so does the fresh air and the mountains and streams. The lakes are crystal clear, and I'm a talking about the end of the rainbow, boys, I really am. Never forget about home! Always remember—that is what the rustling voices are whispering today." He looked specifically at Monty Quinn, and I wondered if this trip was for him, especially. Grady wanted him to have a life lesson before he strutted off to college in the fall.

Grady leaned back on his stump, stretching his left leg out. His eyes looked distant and he continued, "Some of us town boys hovered near the perimeter of the hot springs that night. A Shoshone girl named Awinita stole my heart away."

"How Grady?"

Grady smiled at the inquisitive eleven year old redhead. "She unfastened her long braids and shook her hair loose. It tumbled down past her waist. She was the most beautiful girl I had ever laid eyes on in my life." We sat in silence, only the whispers of the past rustled around us. Grady clicked his tongue to the roof of his mouth and stretched his right leg out. "Awinita and I locked eyes and you boys can believe whatever you want to about love at first sight, but I'm here to tell you, that's sure enough what it was, alright. I talked my buddies into heading back to town and I rode with them, but doubled back with some canned peaches and a hairbrush."

"What?" John leaned closer, straining for more.

"I swiped a hairbrush from my sister Mary's dressing table, and I've never been sorry. I took the gifts back up to the hot springs. I didn't stand in the shadows that night, but walked closer to the band of Shoshones than I ever had before. Of course it was steamy and so everyone looked dreamlike anyway. I just stood in the water with them very quietly."

My heart pounded in my ears at the strange tales. Grady had never said anything about this before and I was amazed. "Grady! Is this the truth?"

"Yes it is, and I've held this in too long! Time has woven around my memories, spinning like gossamer threads, forming cocoons, and now they have wings and must be set free before I die." The statements made us stare, and it was more reverent in that grassy clearing of Washakie Fork than any grand cathedral. None of us wanted Grady to mention death, and we hoped this wasn't his way of setting us up for such a grim occasion.

Monty combed a hand through his bangs. "Go on," he said, completely intrigued with the story.

"I noticed the old man smile at me again and I smiled back. I refused to gaze at anyone but him until he looked away. I noticed several Shoshones looking me over rather suspiciously, but the old man said something to them, and a few nods turned my way. They let me be and I stood in the water, surrounded by the mist in the darkness. A small ripple behind me got my attention. Awinita was looking at me. She motioned me back a few steps, where warm water spilled over a tumbling cascade of rocks. We were alone in the night, I tell you."

"Where did everybody else go?" Wyatt asked daftly.

"Hush Poot! They were there—they just didn't matter, that's what Grady's saying."

"Oh." Wow, Monty was really good at figuring out these romantic mysteries, if that's what Grady was telling us.

"Well yes," Grady nodded, "but also they disappeared from view by a rising curtain of steam."

"What happened then Grady?"

"She talked to me in English—and I was surprised. She didn't know a lot, but she thanked me for the rabbits, turkeys, sheep, and sugar."

"How did she know it was you?"

Monty let out a huffy breath. "Go wait in the tent Poot, and we'll fill you in later when we can draw pictures for you to look at."

Wyatt's brow furrowed and he bit down on his lower lip and I knew he wouldn't ask another question—even if curiosity killed him.

Grady smiled at us, making eye contact with each one. "That girl was perfect! I don't know how she knew a lot of things, but I'm telling you," and then he let out a low whistle. "I handed her the brush and told her I wanted her to have it. She didn't understand so I reached out and ran it through her dark hair. She watched me for a few minutes while I brushed and then she closed her eyes and smiled softly while I finished. That was it! My heart hung on her belt like a scalp. Later I opened some peaches for her and you've never seen such surprise in your life, as what registered on her face as she tasted the fruit. I gifted the other cans to her and then I rode home, but boys I didn't sleep. I couldn't even breathe properly."

"I'll bet Mary killed you when she found out her brush was missing," Wyatt said, forgetting his vow not to speak. John hurled a pinecone in his direction.

Grady smiled at the interruption but continued undeterred. "I went back the next night. They were gone from the hot pots, and so I came here. Right here," he said, pointing to the very spot. "I stood closer to them than ever before. I felt several eyes study me. The old man smiled, and then the others went back to their places, letting me be. I felt a tug on my shirt. I turned around and Awinita was behind me. My heart leapt in my chest and I couldn't conceal my joy at seeing her.

She tugged my hand and we walked through the trees. We talked to each other and then she took the brush out of her pouch and brushed *my* hair with it. It did weird things to me and I wanted to marry her right then and there."

"Grady this is too much," Monty said coolly. Wyatt grumbled at him, wondering why it was okay for him to speak. Monty ignored him and said, "So…then what, I mean—did you kiss her, or what was the custom exactly?"

Grady looked solemn and his eyes were lost in yesterday, yet his mind was keen and he said, "I don't know Monty—what the customs were. I only know the way we fell in love and it was a beautiful thing. We went riding together the next day and I gave her a poetry book. It was my mother's."

"Did you swipe it?" This time I was the one who interrupted, but nobody yelled at me.

"Yes, I swiped it and never told my mother where it went. Awinita cried when she looked at it. She touched the delicate golden embossing on the pages and wept. I was amazed at her gentle spirit, grace, and beauty. I read the old Gaelic poems to her and I translated them into English the best I could and told her that the love sonnets were meant from me to her. We placed our hands on each other's hearts and yes, I kissed her."

I was getting embarrassed by Grady's sappy behavior and I said so. He nodded agreement, "But Wesley, that's what love does to a man. It softens him down and humbles him up; otherwise we would be too rough and crude to be any good to a woman. You remember that! Always be tender with women. They are sacred and not to be toyed with! They are not possessions. They are not to be treated lightly, nor bragged about with buddies in locker rooms. You boys learn this well, I want you to always honor women. God made them special for a reason!"

Even Judy Brynn O'Brien? Impossible! I had a lot of thoughts racing through my mind but I kept silent and Grady continued, "I taught Awinita how to dance the way we did in town. She taught me the dances of her people. We rode together every day and lied down together beneath the stars and wondered about Heaven. I pledged my love to her and we made some plans."

"What happened?" Mark asked frantically.

"Nothing." Grady's eyes watered and I wondered if he might cry. I wanted to help the story along, but it wasn't mine to tell, and so I was helpless.

"What do you mean *nothing*?" Monty was going as crazy as I was.

"I rode back the next day and they were gone. Awinita tied a couple of feathers in a tree, they fluttered for me, but I knew she was gone for that year. My heart ached and I started to bawl. I rode home, making plans to trail them to the Wind Rivers, making plans to leave."

"What happened?" Mark was still frantic.

"Nothing."

All five of us slapped our foreheads at the same time. *"Nothing?"*

"Father stopped me. With his thick Irish brogue he asked me where I thought I was going. I told him and he whipped me. *'That will teach you for running after what you can't have, lad,'* he said to me."

I hated my great-great grandfather right then and I said so. Grady shook his head. "No Wesley, he was right. Where could we have fit in? In her world I was tolerated, but ignored, and in my world she was feared and despised. Where in the entire world were we to go?"

"When *was* this?"

"1899." It seemed so long ago and yet not so long on the other hand. "The next year they returned and I tried to stay away."

"What happened?" Mark again.

"I woke up with a start, for one thing. Awinita was looming above me in the darkness of my room, brushing my hair." I thought that was bold, and tingles again worked my spine as Grady spoke. "I stared at her in the moonlight, then took the brush and pulled it through her long, heavy hair until it glistened. I pulled a piece of her hair to my lips and kissed it. She slipped away from our place before sunup, and I snuck back out here before sundown. I was seventeen and didn't need to listen to my father."

I felt uncomfortable, knowing there was a sad ending in here somewhere, for the lessons in life always ended in "I should have listened to my father."

"Then what?" This time the plea came from John.

Grady smiled, and stood up, stretching his back. "Well boys, I believe you've had enough for one day. Too much isn't healthy either. Let's get a fishing now." That's it. That's how he left it, and I wanted to holler. The others felt the same, for moans and protests rolled around the group of us. "Go ahead boys, and blow off steam." He hummed back up the trail, listening to our protests but ignoring our pleas.

We fished the afternoon away, listening as Grady rumbled about the crimes of the Fish Nazi, Jimmy Don Doheny. The rants were familiar, yet each of us was strangely subdued. Grady was a more complex person than we had ever considered, and learning of Indians and forbidden love trysts set us into sober moods, and we wandered down the stream, seeking solitude as well as fish.

I cleaned my fish near the creek and headed back to camp when I heard Monty whistle. The others came straggling in toting their suppers, with the exception of John, who never seemed to really catch anything. I don't know if he was unlucky or a bad fisherman, but he was welcome to one of my nice catches. Grady rolled the trout in flour and set them to crackle in a hot cast iron skillet. "Oh my, my, my," he smacked, "our supper is much exalted above Mrs. Margaret Mahoney's pitiful oyster stew." We didn't laugh the way he expected us to. "Why so glum, chum?" He asked Wyatt.

"I've been worrying about you and that Indian girl all day. Please tell us more."

Grandpa looked at the boy for a moment, a shadow of sadness crossing his face before launching off a song about an old Ford machine. He didn't sing it as funny as Grandpa Gallagher did—because Grandpa Gallagher swore in the song and Grady didn't.

Old Ford Machine

I bought myself a Ford machine, filled it full of gasoline.
I cranked it up but the darn thing got away!
It didn't wait for me to get in; now all I've got's a pile of tin—
All I've gotta do it walk right up and pay!

So that was it—he wasn't talking any more about it that night.

Before we parted company at the campfire, Grandpa warned Monty, John, and Mark not to scuffle too loudly, claiming it would disrupt his beauty sleep. They grinned at the old man, promising to hold it down a bit. "Hey Grady," Monty said. "You're a cool cat, you know that?"

Grady laughed, raising his right hand in oath position. "I hereby certify that I, Kelly Sheehan O'Rourke, am not a scruff." Monty gave him a respectful little salute. I practiced that same salute from where I was standing because it was downright nifty.

In our tent Wyatt again pleaded to Grady for more. "Not tonight, boy. Now you rest up, eh? Old Grandpa loves you boys."

Sleep wouldn't come for me, or Wyatt, and I could hear his thoughts drumming around, unsettled like my own. About one o' clock I heard Grady unzip the tent flap and he stepped outside. I waited a minute or two and stealthily crept after. I was worried about him stumbling around in the darkness. It took me a minute to get my bearings in the night, but then I saw Grady kneeling by the creek. The moonlight silhouetted his form against the shimmering water. He held his face in his hands. A few steps further and I could hear him sobbing quietly. I froze, every fiber of my body burning at the sight. How could I help my poor old great grandfather? What on earth did the trees whisper to him that weighed him down with such sorrow? I didn't know what to do as Grady's bony shoulders shook beneath the heartache of remembering.

I knew I must not trespass any further, so I turned back to camp. I was startled to see Monty, Mark, John, and Wyatt, standing behind me, witnessing the same haunting site, but feeling just as helpless. They walked with me. Monty was the only one who spoke. "Kelly Sheehan O'Rourke is definitely *not* a scruff, and we will never forget today."

I must have slept sometime that night, but my dreams were strange and spooky. I was standing in the hot pools surrounded by mist. An Indian girl stood before me, putting her fingers to her lips, shushing me. I waded toward her. I wanted to make sure she was real, but as I put my hand out she faded into a vapor of rising steam. She was only a ghost and not solid at all. This thing happened again and again until a woodpecker pounded a tall cottonwood tree like a jackhammer, jarring the images from my subconscious mind. I stirred from my sleeping bag, seeing sunlight through the tent's vinyl.

I pulled my boots on and threw a sweat shirt over the top of my head. I slipped from the tent, knowing the others were awake, but trying to ignore the annoyances of the woodpecker to catch a few more early morning zzz's. I built a fire and chopped some wood. I filled Grady's coffeepot with water so we could enjoy some hot chocolate with our breakfast. I rummaged through a cooler and found some eggs and started cracking them in a dish. Monty stepped out of his tent and joined me.

"Mornin' Kid."

"Good morning."

"I'll help you with breakfast."

"Thanks."

Monty whisked pancake batter in a bowl and soon we were in the business of cooking breakfast. I liked having some time with Monty and I felt fairly grown up as he talked to me about stuff. I said something and he laughed, which sort of startled me. "Kid, you are so full of firecrackers. I get a kick out of you."

I felt proud about that. "I get a kick out of you, too! I liked what you did to Mr. Mulligan's car."

"Oh Kid, that was too crazy! I was hoping you'd get a bang out of that."

"I did, and was jealous not to be in on it!"

"I thought about getting you out of class..."

I jerked my head toward Monty, feeling ten feet tall to think he'd thought about me at all while planning such shenanigans. My eyes must have been full of question marks because he bobbed his head, saying, "It's true Wes, but I knew too many red flags would fly in the air if I did."

"Who pulled the fire alarm?"

"Celia."

"Celia?" I was astonished as ever, for Celia Quinn was good and proper, and did crocheting and needle point while watching television at night. "I was thinking it was Macie Marie, perhaps."

"Well she was in on it, but we had her distracting Mrs. Clark at the office. She pretended to be in a fainting way, and so Mrs. Clark was fluttering over her in the infirmary when the fire alarm blasted. She escorted Macie out of Mulligan's private office door just as Mulligan's car went by her station."

"Who moved the lunch room tables?"

"John and Mark."

I thought about those quiet Finnegan cousins, feeling proud to own them at that moment. "So they worked pretty fast—"

"Yeah, we all did. Me and Skip hopped out of the car and beat it down to the south east exit just as the firemen ran into the school. We milled around until we were mixed up with the other students in Mr. Voss' fourth period class, crying 'Here' when Mr. Voss took a headcount. John and Mark bailed out of Mr. Henry's lab door mixing in very inconspicuously. It all went down like butter on bread, smooth and creamy."

"Well, it was crazy and I liked it." I stirred the eggs and sprinkled them with salt and pepper.

"You were still in on it."

"How's that?"

"The incredible stench emanating from under the seat."

"Oh yeah, that."

"That was too funny when Mulligan pulled that old can of worms out. Too funny, I'm telling you. He's such a geek, that Mulligan."

"Aunt Lace is swooning for him."

"Well just between you, me, and Woody the Woodpecker up there, she's kind of geeky too, so they look pretty good together."

I laughed and laughed. "You really think so?" Gee, for a cool cat and a graduated senior, Monty sure was nice.

"Um...*yeah!* I mean, I think Aunt Lace is really pretty, but she's just so snippy! She drives my dad nuts, too." I couldn't imagine anything in the world driving Uncle Rob nuts—he was so pleasant all of the time. "He says he can never divorce Mom just because he'd miss out on all of the good entertainment that's provided by being part of her family." That little scrap of information tickled my funny bone like a feather. "Dad says the best way to annoy Aunt Lace is by ignoring her, and it's true. She gets fuming mad when she's not spinning in the center of everyone's attention."

"She makes my blood boil because she treats Allyson rough."

Monty looked sideways at me for a second or two. "Is that what the problem is?"

So he had been wondering what ruffled my feathers against her. I told him what I'd overheard Aunt Lace telling Allyson. Monty's eyes narrowed and he chewed against the inside of one cheek, listening and flipping pancakes.

"Well Kid, I've got an inside track on this."

"What?"

"Mom told me that your mother and Aunt Lace were in the same class in school, vying for valedictorian. Your mother edged her out, which caused a rift, and Aunt Lace vowed to hate her forever. Your mother also beat her out of a very prestigious scholarship which re-ruffled the peacock's strutting feathers. Then she beat Aunt Lace out for the title of Miss Three Lakes Valley that summer. To add insult to injury, your dad fell in love with her and married her the next spring. Aunt Lace erupted over it all, declaring Shannon never made use of her academic honor, scholarship, or title, just because she didn't finish college. Aunt Lace fussed and fumed, claiming such accolades were wasted on a stupid girl who gave it all up to marry an ordinary cowboy."

"That cowboy happened to be her own brother! Wasn't he good enough?" I was annoyed at her snippety, uppity attitude all over again.

"Well, you know Aunt Lace. She's got a healthy opinion of herself and likes to look down on what she should be looking up to. My mom claims Allyson is a miniature Shannon, and so that's probably why Aunt Lace blusters like she does."

"We're enemies." I said it so matter-of-factly that Monty choked for a second.

"Yes Kid—and the town knows that! You're a pistol you are, fully loaded and just as apt to pop off as not." We were still smiling over our conversation when the others stumbled from their tents for breakfast.

Grady took us hiking the other direction that morning. Monty, Mark, and John had their .22 pistols strapped around their waists in holsters. I felt like part of the wild bunch and couldn't wait until I was twelve because Grandpa Gallagher gave his grandsons guns at that magical age.

We lined up some tin cans on rocks and had target practice. "Nice shooting," Grady encouraged every time a can would fly in the air. "You're better with that pistol than a fishing pole," he said to John.

Once Mark missed his target completely. "Now you're taking aim like Ticky Tacky, Wicky Wacky Mickey Mackey McCracky," Grady chided.

Wyatt and I chuckled at that. "That old witch can't shoot," Wyatt cried.

"I know, that's what I'm talking about," Grady chuckled.

Mark looked disgusted, drew bead on the can and blasted it sideways, vowing to never miss again if that's who he'd be compared to.

After we shattered the peace and did a proper job of killing the cans, we gathered them up and hiked back to camp. My ears were still ringing with the residual effects of our sport. Grandpa started telling funny stories as we went. "Old McCracky wasn't always wicky wacky," he said. "She earned her nickname from me after one very memorable St. Patrick's Day celebration in '28. It was prohibition times and our town was proper and law abiding except for a few cheats once in a while. St. Patrick's Day was one such festive occasion. McCracken's had a distillery set up, and the McCracken boys got rich bootlegging. It was a lot more profitable than keeping sheep apparently. They set up a lemonade stand on Main Street, only there wasn't any lemonade in their barrels, if you boys catch my meaning. Dark Irish Ale flowed and the festivities got happier and happier, with many folks stomping jigs right in the middle of the road. The town lined up for a parade. We had a brass band and everything. *The Society to Stop Demon Liquor* had an entry in the parade. Pious Peter Pellingham from Eisner was leading the little group of do-gooders. He sat on a strapping black stallion, carrying a banner. He looked stuffy and disgusted at our little celebration. Violet McCracken was drunk as anything, because for every glass of lemonade she poured for her customers, she'd throw down one for herself. She asked several of us how much we'd give her if she shot the hell right out of the *Demon* on the flag. She took one pickle-eyed aim and squeezed off a shot. *Bang!* Down went Peter's fine prancing stallion. Pellingham's horse was dead but his banner remained unruffled."

Gee, I hated stories where good horses and dogs got shot. It was a darn shame, and now I knew why old lady McCracken couldn't stand up straight and look people in the eye. She was bent with remorse, no doubt, and possibly not a snail-spying witch at all.

That afternoon we got in the truck and drove south again as Grady's hips were bothering him. Monty just rolled along making a road where there wasn't one. We meandered through the grassy clearing where Grady had found the arrowhead. The afternoon wind rattled through the leaves and Grady became more and more subdued as he strained to listen to those whispers. We felt a sense of melancholy and I wondered if Grady would speak of Awinita some more. We traveled about three miles southwest from the grassy clearing, crossing the creek twice. A maple grove covered the base of a ragged mountain. We chugged over to it and Monty cut the engine.

A small cabin nestled in the grove. It was snug and tight and undisturbed. "Are we going in that ranger station?" Wyatt wanted to know.

"This isn't a ranger station." We were surprised by that but let it pass.

A padlock wrapped around a small gated yard. Grady produced a key and to our dismay we walked up on the steps of a little porch. Another key unlocked the door and we stepped inside the small cabin. My eyes worked the shadows, adjusting to the inside dimness after the brightness of outdoors. An old bed was in the corner. A small table and two chairs rested against the south wall, and I spied a little cradle in the corner. Grady reached above an old cook stove, striking a match on the chimney rock. He lit a little coal oil lamp and the objects in the cabin danced with new light. Dusty hides covered the backs of the chairs, and the cradle was lined with soft rabbit fur. I had a feeling this tour was leading us to the rest of Grady's story.

I looked over at the old man. His eyes were tearing and his chin trembled at the view. I felt so guilty of trespassing then, and we were all uncomfortable, not sure of how to proceed. None of us knew what to say so I just looked around, hurting from shared pain and old memories. Monty pulled a rocking chair into the center of the room and helped Grady sit down. "Welcome to our house."

"Whose house?" Wyatt didn't mean to be daft; he was just trying to get things processed like the rest of us.

"Awinita, my beautiful bride's and mine."

"So you *did* marry her?"

"After a fashion, I guess." I wondered what that meant, but just kept listening, hoping to fish out some answers. Grady drew in a deep breath. He started right off where he'd finished up the night before. "That fall when the people left for their homes in the Wind Rivers, Awinita stayed with me. We built this cabin together with the help of my father and brothers."

"But I thought your dad whipped you for—" Wyatt began.

Grady winked in his direction, lifting a bony hand to still the question. "But the old elder from the tribe married us in Shoshone custom and it was all over but the crying then. We couldn't live in town and be accepted. Father knew we'd have to have some place to live, and I was willing to walk away from the society of town. We built this cabin in a few days and my mother sent up some furniture and quilts, bottled fruit and soap cakes—things like that."

"That's great," Monty said. "You were *my* age and a real man."

"In many respects Awinita and I were just kids, growing up together in our own world, removed from both of our previous ones. A little like Adam and Eve, I suppose, but of course we had good sense and didn't talk to serpents or eat nonsensical fruit." We blinked and coughed at such a statement, but Grady went on. "I loved her!" Tears came and he made no effort to wipe them away. "Lord I loved that woman!"

"We hunted together, fished together, and rode together. I taught her to read, getting several books from my Mother's library. We herded sheep for my Dad through the summer months, and visited my family occasionally, careful not to make other acquaintances in town. We were outcasts of course, and would have been snubbed anyway. In the autumn her people came and Awinita camped with them, talking with her mother and sisters in the old way, and dancing at night by the campfires. I was chiefly ignored by her family, but it didn't matter so much to me as they'd been kind enough to agree to our marriage. We were married for a couple of years and a little son came to live with us. Awinita insisted on calling him Kell, which is what she called me. I shot rabbits from time to time and Awinita skinned them, tanned their hides, and sewed soft blankets for our little son." Grady leaned toward the cradle, grabbing one of them. He shook dust from it then buried his face in the softness and cried.

Monty, Wyatt, John, Mark, and I looked at each other suspiciously, wondering somehow if we were going to learn that we were one-eighth Shoshone. Wyatt's red hair and freckles pretty much removed any doubt from my mind that we *could* be, but all of these tales were news to us anyhow.

"When little Kell was about two we went to the hot springs—we went there every week to bathe. It was a perfect night, as no one was around. Little Kell loved the water and we bathed, and soaked, and swam. I was playing with my little boy, lifting him on the same rocks where I'd first brushed his mother's hair. He was a fearless little brave and would jump into the water where I would catch him. Things were going along just fine, but all of a sudden Kell jumped awkwardly, catching his foot against another rock. He smacked down, head first along the cascading rocks. He bled to death before we could get help."

Eerie and sad, that's the mood that fell upon us inside the cabin. Grady cried some more, telling us how his heart broke when he buried his beautiful little brave, all wrapped in rabbit skin blankets. "Awinita and I wept together over our loss many nights. She conceived again and we hoped for happiness, but both she and our daughter died of the fever a couple of years later. I buried my little Fawn in her mother's arms."

Tears rolled from Monty's eyes, and he didn't care. "Where?"

"I'll show you boys." We walked out of the cabin and around to the back. There were two grave markers made from flat stones. The first one read, *"Here lies our little brave, Kelly Sheehan O'Rourke Jr. June 1, 1902-August 4, 1904"* The other one said, *"My beloved Awinita and our golden Fawn."*

"I didn't feel like carving a date on that one, but they died on November 2', 1907."

We filed back inside the cabin. Grady knelt at an old cedar box. He lifted the lid and pulled items out. I'm just a rowdy boy, but even my heart panged at the contents. Out came the hairbrush once owned by my great-great Aunt Mary, and given to Awinita.

"Awinita's hair always smelled like mint and clover. I heard old timers talk when I was just a boy. Some claimed that Indians stunk—but it's a lie. Boys, if you like the smell of campfire smoke, and leather—if you like the way meat cooks as it roasts on a spit, and the smell of horses, and fresh air, then you've got to know it was a lie. Awinita was clean and beautiful in every way! She collected mint every time she found it growing somewhere, and often wove the leaves right into her braids."

We held an old poetry book, owned by Grady's mother before she came to America. It was written in the ancient Gaelic language, but the pages were delicate with gold embossing and flowery designs. Grady removed a leather pouch, the one carried by Awinita. Interesting bits were inside—scrapers, a needle, thin strips of burlap, thread, and matches. The contents were a mix of native and white items, just like their marriage had been. We saw a baby rattle made from a dried gourde, little moccasins, and a beautifully beaded shawl. Grady held each item to him, hurting, reminiscing until he almost bled.

"How many years were you together then?" Monty asked quietly.

"Seven. Seven beautiful years, but seven hundred would not have been sufficient for me."

"Then what?"

Grady moved a quilt, hand-stitched by his mother. I was finding all of it to be neat; all of this old stuff was full of memories and stories. "You boys will like this," he said, lifting a burlap bag. "This is a cache of tools Awinita's mother left with her when we were married. He was right, we floundered over the tools. Grinders, knives, bone needles, awls, arrowheads, and all kinds of interesting relics were in the burlap pouch. It lightened the mood a little bit, our fussing about the curious workmanship of the artifacts.

"This is the best show-and-tell I've ever seen," Wyatt claimed.

Mark rummaged through the cedar box until he found a Celtic whistle. Grady laughed to see it. "This was mine as a boy," he said. It's really similar to a Native American flute. Awinita's flute is in there someplace." Grady lifted the slim little instrument to his lips and suddenly Irish music filled the room. Mark then pulled out a wooden flute. Grady also played it for us, and they were oddly similar, yet the Native flute seemed to call out the whispering winds again, and Grady sank into a deeper melancholy than before.

"What are you going to do with this stuff?" Monty asked pensively.

"I don't know what to do. I guess I'll make a list, and when I'm dead you boys will take care of it for me."

"Does Grandma Gallagher know you were married to Awinita?"

"Yes, but it's only vaguely been discussed. Cora never seemed very interested in it—never wanted to know any details."

That was odd, but female jealousies are something that Dad says are not to be messed with. Perhaps Grandma was just jealous for her mother's sake, in some silly way.

"I'm certain that none of your parents even know."

"When and how did you ever move on, Grady?" John's question was searching. We wanted to understand.

Grandpa placed all of the items back into the cedar box, opting not to answer right away. He dragged the cradle back into its place and smoothed the hides on the bed where we had rumpled them. "Boys, would you mind waiting in the truck for a few minutes?"

We slid out silently, staring at each other, wrapping our minds around Grady's disclosures. "I had no idea his life was so much like Jeremiah Johnson's," I said to Monty.

Monty nodded, recalling the Indian wife Robert Redford acquired in the movie, but he said, "Grady's life was better. It was a beautiful thing. That's why it hurts so badly to remember, Kid." I leaned my head against the seat and closed my eyes against the sun. I wondered what Grady was doing in the cabin but I knew he must be saying goodbye to it one final time. "Kid, Grady had to come back here. You know that's why he brought us, don't you?"

"Yes. He's too old to come alone."

"I'm never gonna forget this, Wes."

"Me neither."

"See that you don't."

The Finnegan brothers were talking together in the back of the truck, too, but I couldn't hear what they were saying. I figured their conversation was probably a lot like Monty's and mine. We were subdued and felt kind of drained. Grandpa Greaty-Great's Holiday was a little more than we were expecting.

That night we ate cheese sandwiches around the campfire. Grandpa Grady sensed the levity of our camp trip and tried to lighten it up with more funny tales about the townspeople and brighter days gone by. It seemed to me that at one time the snow was deeper, horses were better, the coffee stronger, the girls prettier, and boys had more sense. Grady never told us what we really wanted to hear. I guess he was too tired to tell us more, and so he stayed in a safe zone as far as stories go.

Chapter Seven

We fished again the next morning, lighting out bright and early. By lunchtime we'd caught our limit and fried trout in the cast iron skillet. Grady tended a Dutch oven full of potatoes and onions, too. We ate our fill then cleaned up camp. Grady lay down in his hammock and took an afternoon snooze. John went into the tent with his book, and Monty whittled on a stick. Wyatt and I started building roads in the dirt, using sticks for bulldozers. Mark fell asleep in the shade of the aspen tree, using his sweat shirt as a pillow.

Wyatt and I had a swanky set up going. We buried some pop cans to make overpasses and bridges, and constructed fence lines with little pine twigs. We also built tiny cabins from sticks, stacking them like Lincoln Logs. We played the afternoon away, me and my best cousin, and then Grandpa Grady woke up and asked us if we were up for another ride. We hopped into the truck, only Monty requested that I ride up front with him and Grady. I felt a little cocky as I scooted into the cab. Wyatt scowled slightly, but if he could be Aunt Lace's pet lamb, surely I could be Monty's junior sidekick. There seemed to be a little justice in it, and I grinned like a boaster.

We drove through a winding canyon, from Washakie Fork into Inish Flat. The combination of Indian and Irish names and locations was all so symbolic of the history of this place, and especially Grady's life. At Inish Flat Grady showed us some old grizzly bear markings in a tall tree. He told us stories of herding sheep in the area, of once shooting some wolves that had gotten into the sheep.

We must have driven ten or fifteen miles. Grady directed Monty to a steamy spring. "Here's another hot pot, boys. Want to swim?"

Of course we were game, and soon we were splashing and frolicking in the naturally warm water. Monty Quinn fastened a rope on an overhanging cottonwood limb and we swung like Tarzan, dropping into the welcoming depths. Even Grady took a wild run at it. His spindly legs wrapped around the rope in a comical manner and he thumped on his hollowed chest like a wild jungle man.

John and Mark squared off against Monty and me in a chicken fight while Grady and Wyatt judged the winners. I rode on Monty's shoulders and my job was to wrestle John off of Mark's shoulders. John had three years on me, and long lanky arms, but I was sturdier and faster. In the end, Monty and I won, and we pranced around like Mohamed Ali in the boxing ring.

"Rematch!" John was huffy about the outcome. "This time I ride Monty. Mark's a bad horse."Mark slapped water at his brother's comment. So I climbed on Mark, and personally, I thought he rode okay. Grady was laughing to beat the band as we started again. After several tries, I bested John again, knocking him into the water. Mark and I took a victory lap around the natural pool.

"See, it wasn't the horse, it's the rider," Mark said to John. So they traded places and I saddled up on Monty again. I threw Mark even quicker than I had John, and Grady and Wyatt cheered and clapped.

"I'll face you Kid." Monty grinned and picked Mark to be his horse.

I climbed on John's shoulders afraid I had met my match…and then some. "This isn't really fair," I said. "You are seventeen and going to college soon. I'm only headed off to the sixth grade."

"Which makes it all the worse if I lose to you," Monty said, taking a swipe at my arm.

"Of course Napoleon was short and look what *he* did," I bluffed.

Monty's head tipped sideways at my crowing confidence. "Well to every Napoleon comes a Waterloo, and you are about to meet yours!"

He reached out for me, grabbing for my upper arms. I quickly wrapped my arms around his and jerked upward at his elbows, hooking them in the wrong direction, hyper extending the joints. I didn't truly hurt him, but my action startled him off center—and that was the secret, really. I wasn't tougher, I was just good at leveraging these cousins of mine off balance. He toppled too far for Mark to keep supporting him and they both went under.

Monty was red faced when he bobbed back up and I was afraid he was going to whip me, but he shook his head and laughed, threatening us all with our lives if we told. He extended a hand. I shook it and he said, "Good job, Champ."

Wyatt was proud of me, and had rooted for me all along. "I love the underdog to win!"

"Then you should have been cheering for the rest of them," Grady answered.

"I want a turn," Wyatt said.

Grady thumped on his chest again, offering to give him one. So that's how the funniest thing I've ever seen in all my life happened. Wyatt climbed on Mark and Grady climbed on Monty. There wasn't ten pounds difference in either one. Wyatt's muscles weren't developed yet and Grady's were past their prime by a few years. They grappled and sparred while their horses laughed so hard they could scarcely stand. John and I wiped tears from our cheeks at the drunken spectacle! Grady doubled up his fists, challenging "Come and get me, Boy!"

Wyatt kept baiting him forward, toughly saying, "Bring it! Bring it right here."

They finally locked arms with each other and it was quite a match. They shoved, pushed, and pulled, but neither one went anywhere. Finally the bellowing horses collapsed for lack of oxygen, and the chicken fight was over as Grady and Wyatt plunged into the water in a stand still.

We dried off as best as we could, and pulled our boots and shirts back on. The ride back to camp was merry and full of laughter. Everyone called me Champ and I couldn't wait to tell Dad about it. Half way back to camp, Monty stopped the truck. "I say the Champ should drive," he said. Grady agreed, and I was ten feet tall as I walked around to the driver's side and climbed in. I've been driving since I was seven on our ranch while Dad pitched hay to the stock in winter, but this was lots more fun.

The campfire blazed hot that night. There was a sense of brotherhood between us all that hadn't existed before Grady's Great Holiday. I felt sorry for every other kid in the world who didn't have what I had. How many kids got to carry pistols and fish in their own streams? How many boys my age got to drive a pickup truck through the hills? How many could say they knew their great grandfathers? And how many could boast that their old Grandpa had lived among Indians, marrying and living in a fearless and free way? Someday I hoped to love a woman as much as Grady loved Awinita, but I figured I'd have to head off to the Wind Rivers of Wyoming to find such a girl, for the Shoshones had stopped visiting our valley many decades ago.

"Grady, what happened to you after Awinita died?" John asked.

"Are you boys still nagging me for more?" Grady was surprised. We nodded and so he started talking, seeming pleased that we cared so much. "I was nearly twenty-four years old, and I'd already buried my wife and two children. I rode into town and told my folks goodbye. Mother wanted me to stay, but she hadn't been able to boss me around for years, and nothing had changed. I lit out of Utah altogether and went to California. I worked at building roads and bridges there—even tried my hand on some fishing boats. I finally had enough and came back home."

"I'll bet they were glad to see you."

"Yep, I'd been away five years. I was now twenty-eight and a threat to society, apparently." Smiles lit our faces at the stray comment. Grady sure was funny sometimes. "Mary and Mother fretted and fussed about me living and dying as a lonely old man. Mother blustered until I started courting again. Of course I was rusty with women. There had been but one fire in my life, and with Awinita, rules of courtship didn't apply. I knew I couldn't find anything to match our passion, and so I didn't even try. Society is very limiting where love is concerned."

Monty grinned, running a hand through his hair, nodding. "And?"

"I started looking around, at least. A fiery redhead from Kilkenny Point caught my eye." Kilkenny Point was located between Gallagher Springs and Lakeside. "Her name was Adelaide Danaher, and my mother approved of her because she was *'in all ways Irish.'* I courted Addie a few times with mixed feelings. I felt a little guilty, like I was cheating on Awinita's memory, and I also felt guilty for trying to compare Addie to Awinita. That wasn't fair, for Irish American girls couldn't behave as a wild, impulsive Shoshone could—and so I struggled with mixed emotions."

"I'll bet you never woke up with Addie brushing your hair," Mark said.

Grady's face lit up at the very suggestion of it. "That would have been scandalous to say the least, but see; you boys understand my difficulty in finding a suitable mate. Going to church socials didn't really do anything for me."

"What did?"

"Well...do you boys happen to know the dashing and dapper Mr. Melvin Mulligan?"

We choked at the question, wondering when *he* entered the picture. "Yes," we answered.

"Well his grandfather was dapper and dashing, also. His name was Finn Mulligan, and he fancied himself to be a quite a catch. He started courting Addie as well and it got my ire up."

"Yeah?" Monty asked, grinning widely.

"Yeah! I started to get more earnest about seeing her just because the competition stirred my blood."

"Just like a spelling bee," I muttered. "Competition is healthy."

"Finn took Addie to the Harvest Social, but I outbid him on her box lunch."

"By how much?" Mark and John asked together.

"By fifty dollars, that's how much."

"What? Wasn't that a lot of money then?"

"It's a lot of money now! But I was prepared to bid double that amount if it meant Addie ate with me and not with that dopey milk dud that brought her. He was purple faced when I slid my arm around her waist and led her to a quiet spot in the park to eat our meal."

We grinned at the very thoughts of Grady besting Mr. Mulligan's grandfather. "I asked if I could see her home after the social just because Finn was still fuming, pacing back and forth against the pavilion. She consented even though the action was considered brazen, for a girl always left with the guy who brought her, you know. On the way to her house we visited about things. I don't remember what I said, but she laughed, and the sound was joyous— like the peeling of silvery bells. I looked over at her then, really studied her for the first time. Her eyes were shamrock green, and her hair was deep auburn. Her complexion was milky and smooth, and I saw genuine beauty there. I went back to see her the next evening and we took a stroll along the shore of Eisner Lake near her home."

"Did you tell her about Awinita?"

"Well, I kind of had to ease her into that. It was difficult for her, really. Women have a hard time with things like that, and Addie vacillated back and forth with her feelings on the subject, but she accepted a proposal of marriage anyway. After we had been married for a year, she was quite convinced that she wanted to come out here and see the cabin where Awinita and I had lived. I didn't think it was a good idea, but she fixed bouquets for the gravesites and everything, wanting to prove to me how large-hearted and good she could be. We came."

"What happened?"

"She became agitated the second we stepped into the cabin and flew into a jealous rage. She ranted about burning the cabin down just to destroy the bed in the corner, and all kinds of nonsensical things! She sulked for a week afterwards, refusing to speak to me. In fact she went home to her mother's in a petty huff to sulk, and I came back here, doubly disgusted. We had a few turbulent times, boys, and I won't lie to you about that. She was very young...only twenty."

We considered that for a few minutes. Women *could* be difficult, and not one of us needed convincing on that subject.

"But I *did* love Addie. It was a gentle love which swelled over the years. She was truly refined and beautiful, and sometimes very proud. She had a hard time not being a little bit haughty. Annelaise reminds me of her quite often, and yet Addie had tremendous strengths as well, and we carved out a good life together."

"When did you get married?"

"1914. We had your Grandma in 1915 and lost an infant son to the great flu epidemic in 1919. We named him Danaher James O'Rourke, and we mourned our little Danny boy, I tell you."

I winced at more bad news...but something wasn't computing. "When did you serve in World War I?"

"My life *felt* like World War I, but I confess, I wasn't ever there." We blinked with amazement for Grandpa always talked about fighting in the trenches and old army wounds.

"What a fibber!" Wyatt cried.

"Everything I've told you this week has been certifiably true," Grady argued. "We built the resort in 1920, and I've been fishing, and swimming, and soaking, and boating, and loafing every day since then. Father died in 1930, and left his whole place to me. I kept a few sheep and cows, but not more than I could handle. When Cora married your Grandpa Gallagher, I turned the ranching side of things over to them. I had more than I could handle just wrangling dudes." We laughed. Grandpa Grady was no loafer. He was constantly building things and making improvements.

He got a far-away look in his eye. "One of the first things I did while building the resort was tear the waterfall down where little Kell slipped and died. I didn't want something like that to happen to another child, *ever*, especially not my darling little Cora."

Grandpa checked his watch and jumped at the time. "By Jingo

Jones it's past our bedtime, boys. Better shut my mouth so we can all shut our eyes."

We stood up, stretching. "Hey Kid, you game to sleep out under the stars with me tonight?"I looked at Monty, surprised. "I mean, you are the champ and everything."

"Sure, I'm game."

"Poot, John, Mark—you guys wanna come?"

Wyatt's eyes were big as saucers. He didn't like the dark very much and shook his head. "No, I'll take my beauty rest with Grady." John and Mark also declined, and I think Monty knew they would.

I grabbed my sleeping bag and flashlight out of the tent and followed him up to the ridge. "We gotta be up here, out of the trees," Monty said, "so we can see the stars and stuff."

To be honest I was a little edgy, being exposed like this, to who knows what. I thought about those bear marks in the tree, and Grady's tales of wolf packs and such. I felt a trifle spooked and no mistake, but I spread my bedding down, talking tough. I kicked my boots off and climbed inside my Coleman bag.

"I like you Kid," Monty said. "You don't act like an eleven year old—more like fifteen, at least."

I stretched a little taller in my sleeping bag, feeling confident and happy. "Thanks. What about Grady's stories, huh? Can you believe he was married to an Indian girl? Do you imagine she had bee-stung lips?"

Monty started giggling. People don't think teenage boys giggle, but I can argue that fact, for Monty was giggling. "You crack me up, Champ!" He rolled over on one side. I could see his teeth in the moonlight. "Yes, I picture her with bee-stung lips, alright, and I gotta tell you, Indian girls are sexy!"

"Huh?" This time I giggled 'cuz that was a pretty bold statement.

"Very sexy," Monty reiterated, "they come with pre-packaged suntans, you know? *Me-ow*!"

I thought about Allyson's Malibu Barbie. It had quite a suntan. "I guess that *is* sexy," I said, feeling brazen for even saying the word.

"Just picture that yummy tan skin in a buckskin dress, standing in the steamy hot pots, with hair down to *there*! Oh Kid, that's too much! I get sweaty just thinking about it."

"Well I blush just hearing that you get sweaty." We burst into another ripple of man-giggles. It was fun, this bonding with my older cousin, talking about what was *sexy*.

"Grady's a cat, a cool cat, and I dig that old man. I hope he doesn't ever die...except he wants to, you know, to see Awinita again."

"I know, but what about Addie? She'll pitch a fit in Heaven if he pays attention to Awinita, and you know he will. I'm worried about that, kind of."

"That's a weird thing to think about Wes."

"I know, but how do you think that will all go down? I mean, I don't want Grady to be in Grandma Addie's doghouse. I think that's why he's going around again. He's *afraid* to die. Once he does, he's going to be smack dab in the middle of a very tricky, sticky, situation."

"An eternal love triangle?"

"Maybe."

"Hmm...interesting. Don't worry about it, Wes. There are probably rules about stuff like that on the other side. I think he'll be able to spend time loving both of them for the rest of forever if he wants to."

"I think Grandma Addie will stomp off mad the first thing, and then it won't matter what Grady does."

Monty laughed again. "Well...maybe so."

We were quiet for a minute, listening to the sounds of frogs from down below, near the creek. A rustling sound rattled through the trees, whispering, whispering, until I felt a sudden chill. I closed my eyes against the eerie strains and dosed off. My mind was just starting to shilly shally into sleep when Monty started talking again and I jerked awake.

"I won't be scared to go off to college, now. I just have to remember Grady dared stand in a pool with a whole band of Shoshones, staring the old elder right in the eye. I'll remember he dared defy his father and ask for Awinita's hand in marriage. He built a house when he was my age for crying out loud! Surely I can handle English 101 at the U."

"Yeah," I said, sliding beneath the veil of sleep. I was fishing near Inish Lake, just cranking on the reel, then I was playing construction with Wyatt in the school yard. I was riding with Grandpa Gallagher in his truck, turning the radio knob. I heard drums and native flutes, and rattling whispers of yesterday.

I jerked awake. My eyes were wide open to the brisk night air. I would have given anything to not really be seeing what I saw—for leaning over me, studying me, was an ancient old Native American man. His eyes were black and searching. He smiled at me and I wondered if he fancied my scalp, or just thought I was a handsome boy…I couldn't breathe under his penetrating gaze and I was more scared than I'd ever been in my life. I was petrified, like a piece of four thousand year old wood, or a fossil, perhaps. The old man whispered something to me, but I couldn't understand it. The hair on the back of my neck stood up, as well as the fair fuzz on my arms. Tingles tangled and my heart sped violently. This was not a dream, and I wished it was! I reached sideways to get Monty's attention but he was already sitting up, staring at the apparition as well. We heard the faint beating of a drum again, and then the spirit faded into the night.

I bolted out of my bag, stuffing my feet in my boots! I didn't even wait until my heels were inside them all of the way before I took off. Monty passed me like I was standing still, and I followed him pell mell down the hill toward our camp. We jumped into the Studebaker and locked the doors. "Holy crap!" Monty cried. "We've seen a ghost, alright."

"Who *was* that creepy old guy?"

"Could have been Chief Washakie for all I know."

"Hoo-wee! That was scary—I was hoping for a nightmare, but I'm afraid I was wide awake."

"Oh Kid! Awake is right, and my flesh is crawling!" Monty's eyes were the size of dinner plates, and his face was ghastly white. We slept in the cab the rest of the night, and I was careful to keep one eye open. I didn't want anything or anybody sneaking up on me again.

When Grady came out of his tent the next morning, Monty and I had breakfast ready again. "How was your night beneath the stars?"

"Um..."

"What?"

"I sure enough believe in life after death, Grady," Monty said.

Grady's eyes twinkled and a smile cut into the lines of his face. "Why's that?"

"An old Indian leaned over me last night. Honest, Grandpa—we saw him!" I was talking fast.

Grady rubbed a hand along his chin, grinning. "Is that a fact?"

"Yes sir!"

"Well boys—the veil that separates this world from the next one is very thin sometimes."

"I guess so," I agreed. "Sometimes it's so thin it's not even there."

Grady nodded. "Old man you say?"

"Yes, and he was smiling at me."

"Probably that same old tribal elder who married Awinita and I—he's Awinita's grandfather. I've seen him a few times over the last fifty years myself." Our heads jerked up. "He loved Washakie Fork, and who's to say they're not *all* back here again?"

Shivers crept along my hairline, and I had been so spooked in the night that it didn't take much. "Well why did he single me out?"

"Probably thought he was looking at me again. You are the spitting image of your great old great-granddad."

I cocked my head sideways, looking Grady up and down. Is that what I'd look like in another seventy-five years or so? "Well you are quite handsome, Grady." Wyatt and his brothers rousted around and they milled closer wanting in on our conversation. They laughed at my comment.

Monty told our cousins about our night and Wyatt's face paled. I kept nodding to verify Monty's stories. Not one of the Finnegan boys doubted our tale, and not one was sorry to have missed out on our adventure. Not one.

We fished and shot the morning away. We fried more trout for lunch, and then Grady decided he wanted to visit the cabin again. We were hesitant to go, but Grady wanted to take wildflowers to the graves while he was so nearby. We hiked along the stream, gathering large bunches of wild geraniums, dock flowers, Indian paintbrush, and wild bluebells. We drove through the clearing where Awinita's people once camped. We stopped for a while and hunted through the blackened soil for more arrowheads. We didn't find any, but I had an old tuna fish can full of chips and a few beads, and it was all proof enough that they had once been here.

We got to the cabin and Grady unlocked the gate. We patiently tromped behind our aged grandpa as he walked around the back of the cabin. We froze into place as we neared the gravestones. A tribute of eagle feathers fluttered off of each one. The offerings hadn't been there a couple of days earlier—the stones were undecorated and barren then. Chills worked curiously down our arms, and across our necks. None of us spoke. We just watched Grady as he stared at the mystical offerings. His jaws worked together as he gazed on the sight. Finally he said, "Mark, put the flowers down."

Mark stepped forward and placed the bouquets on the graves, looking pensive all the while. I saw him reach out a rigid finger and stroke a few of the feathers just to make sure they were real. "Who left them Grady? Nobody's been up here but us."

Grady nodded but said nothing. Finally after several long minutes he asked us to take off our hats because he wanted to pray. We complied with his request. Grady started off, "Heavenly Father, we're thankful for this hallowed piece of ground. We're thankful for the heritage and history of this place, and so fully recognize the cycle of life and the beauty of living—and dying. We're thankful to have spent this time together. It's been fun, it's been powerful, and it's been sacred. Let this experience burn and blaze in these boys' hearts throughout the rest of their days, and throughout eternity…" He asked the Lord's blessing to be with Monty as he headed off to college. He asked for protection to be on Uncle Aiden Finnegan, who was fighting in Viet Nam. He asked for blessings to be with all of us—every single family member. It was a long prayer, and goose bumps kept working mysteriously against my flesh. My heart burned with many different emotions and my mind kept shouting questions at the Universe about the meaning of it all.

Just as Grady's prayer was winding down, he paused for a long time and said, "And Lord, we ask a special blessing for Bill and Shannon's family, that they can get one last child here to live with them." I was extra stumped about that! Wasn't Allyson and I enough? I wasn't aware of any special attempts, *or failures*, at making more babies at our house. Curious, that's what it was—but I chalked it up to the meanderings of an old man's extra long prayer.

After amen was said, Grady asked us to wait in the truck, and he went again into the cabin. He was in there for a long time. When he came out his eyes were red and puffy and he was carrying Awinita's hairbrush. He held the brush to his nose, hoping to smell the minty fragrance of her hair, but I'm certain all he caught was the odor of cedar. He said, "Boys, when I die, you are to bury me here, and not in the town cemetery. You'll have to fight your Grandma and your parents about that, but this is what I want! I won't brook one argument, and if you don't comply with my request, I'll send every Shoshone in Heaven or Hell to haunt you."

"I promise, Grady!" Wyatt was earnest and tearful as he said it. We nodded.

"But I hope it's not for awhile," John said, and we nodded again.

The truck lurched forward, and Grady's head craned backward, watching the cabin disappear into the distance. We crossed the creek twice and then caught our breath as we hit the clearing. There, where Grady had picked up the arrowhead, was a burning fire right in the middle of the blackened soil! Smoke curled and wafted to the Heavens. Monty hit the brakes and we stared again, dumbfounded.

I reached over and locked the doors—although I don't know what good that would have done.

"What do you want me to do Grandpa?" Monty asked.

"Drive closer."

We inched toward the phantom campfire and Grady unlocked the door and climbed out. He walked near, sitting himself down on the stump. He put his hands out, feeling the warmth of the flames. We stared from the truck, crying. This was bewildering, life changing, and definitely not normal. This was exactly what Grady told the Lord it was—powerful. A powerful, mind blazing, scene played before our view while Grady warmed himself near the campfire of yesterday, lit by nobody quite knew who—and it was all too much, and that's why we cried.

Chapter Eight

How was I supposed to be able to tell my folks about our camp trip when I got home? I didn't have the words to describe it! Where to start? I had to factor in the believability of some of my stories, and I just couldn't make myself talk about a lot of it.

"Well?" Mother asked. "How was it?"

"Perfect. We fished a lot and shot some tin cans until they were dead. We had chicken fights in a hot pool, and I was the grand champ. Grady found an arrowhead, and...it was all really great!"

"Are you glad to be home?"

"Not really."

Mother's lips pinched together—I think I disappointed her. We'd been gone seven days and she was homesick for me. I thought about Monty and the Finnegan boys. They were probably being interrogated by their mothers as well, and just as helpless to answer appropriately. Nobody could possibly understand the kind of week we'd had.

By late afternoon I was already homesick for Grady. I asked Mother if I could go check on him. She sighed heavily and said, "Go ahead."

I rode my bike ninety miles an hour, surprised to see the Finnegan's bikes already parked at Grady's place and Monty's red mustang in the driveway. So...we hadn't had enough, not one of us.

We soaked in the pools together that night after the tourists left, recapping our week. Grady beamed at us, surprised I think, by the power of Grandpa Greaty Great's Holiday.

"I thought you'd be down to Lakeside tonight seeing that lovely Shaylin," Grady said to Monty.

Monty hedged. "She's working—and I've got all summer to be with her." So that was it—Monty and the rest of us had been left to wonder about how much time we had left to spend with Grady. He'd been getting things in order pretty good the last week.

"You have all summer with me, too."

"I hope so."

"Boys, I've got it on good authority that I won't die until I'm ready to."

"You're not ready?" John asked.

"Not quite. It's true that I miss my kids, Awinita, and Addie, but… if I die then I'll be missing all of you." That did it—we all teared up again, although it was easy to cry in the misty pool of steam without detection. "In fact, I'm in my second springtime boys, and I plan on racing you into summer."

The season hustled by in a blur, and we helped in the hayfields, helped at the resort, and most evenings found us all back at Grady's, requesting stories, wanting more.

It was tough the day that Monty left for Salt Lake City. We didn't want him to go, not one of us boys. Only Celia seemed excited about it since she was getting his bedroom. We had a cookout at the resort, a big family party. Shaylin came, crying through most of the festivities because she said she would be so miserable without *her guy*. She would just be a senior in Lakeside and feared he would gallop off to college and forget about her.

The sun sank low and we all knew Monty must go. "See you Champ," he said to me. He shook my hand then gave up the macho stuff and hugged me to him roughly. "Never forget those spooks, huh Kid?"

"Try to toughen up in a chicken fight."

"Don't get sent to the principal's office."

"Try not to remove too many bumpers."

Monty grinned. "Stay solid, Wes."

We watched the sporty car disappear around the bend, and my unemotional Aunt Aura Leigh got very emotional and so Uncle Rob took her home with Celia and Dori Jo.

Aunt Annelaise had invited Mr. Mulligan to our family party, and I ignored both of them, in fact, I'd ignored them both all summer. They were beneath my notice and out of my book as far as I was concerned.

Dad motioned for us to get into our Buick. I said goodbye to Grady, and just as I was climbing into the backseat of our car, we heard it—a terrible commotion. We bailed out to see what the trouble was, only to find Mr. Mulligan's bumper had been chained to a telephone pole and was now lying on Grady's driveway. I laughed until I was sick! We drove home before we got stuck giving Mr. Mulligan a ride anywhere, leaving before the blustering and insinuations could start.

School began and I had Mr. Despain for a teacher. We got along good and I was happy that he was also a Phantom Flynn fan, making story time interesting. Avery Anne Applewhite was in my class again, although she had eyes for Steve McCarthy this year. It's just as well. I smelled her hair in the lunch line, and although it *was* very shiny, it didn't smell like mint. Or clover.

Margo Walsh and Judy Brynn O'Brien were not in my class this year, which was a definite plus, and proof that good things come to those who wait, for I'd waited and waited to be rid of them both.

With Monty and Skip graduated and gone, Mark and John Finnegan became the cool cats of the high school, which was sort of weird, but Grady's holiday had changed them. They were less quiet and bookwormy, and a lot more confidant. I boasted to my friends that I could best them both in a chicken fight, but they didn't believe me, and Wyatt told me to stop being a boaster.

I only had to grind Stan Tomkin's face into the ground twice that fall. He was starting to get tired of a butt whipping ever other day, apparently. Some folks are slow learners, but better late than never Grady and I always say. Recesses were spent playing soccer, kickball, and Smear the Queer, which was a lot like football, minus the padding and most of the rules.

In November I got a letter from Monty. I was excited and went into my room to read it. He told me about school and college girls. Then he got down to business and started talking to me about our camp trip with Grady. "After lots of thought over the matter," he wrote, "I think I know who lit the campfire in the clearing. It was Awinita. It was her way of telling Grady that the flame of love is still burning for both of them." I considered the words, reading them again and again, then carefully folded the letter into the envelope and put it in the top drawer of my dresser.

I got a lead part in the Christmas play. My character was Mr. Grumpy, and I owned Mr. Grumpy's Toy Shop. The younger kids in the school were dolls, teddy bears, and tin soldiers, and everyone tried to convince me to like Christmas, which was comical to me since in real life I just adored the holiday. Some little second grade girls got crushes on me from rehearsal, and they tagged me around the playground at recess, throwing snowballs. I threw snowballs back at them and they chanted, "*Missed me, missed me, now ya gotta kiss me!*" I couldn't wait for Christmas break so they would go home and hopefully forget.

Monty spent a lot of time in Lakeside during the holidays, so I guess those college girls didn't hold a candle to what he had here—which speaks volumes about country girls and country living in general. I hope to never live in a city, even a small one. Gallagher Springs and its eight hundred people sometimes felt too crowded for me.

1973 rang in with a blizzard, closing the roads and schools, businesses, stores, and everything. Three Lakes Valley ground to a stand still for three whole days—no power, no phones, no anything. Aside from Grandpa Gallagher and Dad's worries over the stock, it was pretty neat I'd say. On Sunday night Grandpa hitched up his team of Clydesdales to the big sleigh. The horses clopped on top of the drifts, and we picked up the Quinn's, and we all headed up to Grady's place to soak in the hot pools. Grady lit lots of lanterns and the place looked like a fairy land. Dori Jo and Allyson bathed their new Christmas baby dolls. Wyatt, John, Mark, and I had contests to see who could do the craziest stunts in the water. It was fun! We had Dutch oven potatoes and chicken, and then Grady fried hot scones and served them with fluffy golden honey butter.

"A little blow and snow can't get my family down," Grady crowed, serving up seconds on the scones. "Eat up, kids, for there's plenty! While the whole world wallows in inflation, corruption, and gasoline that sells at forty cents a gallon, we'll live like kings we will!" And then he started off about OPEC, railing against the dirty rascals who oversaw all of the mischief in the world. "You're all apt to see gas hit two dollars a gallon, but I hope I never live to see the day that happens! This ole' world spins in a drunken stupor, it does, and half reminds of Ticky Tacky Wicky Whacky Mickey Mackey McCracky on a certain St. Patrick's Day afternoon."

Grandma Gallagher rolled her eyes at the repetitive stirrings of her father, and I winced, wondering if Grandma Addie would have done the same thing, being a little haughty and all. I liked Awinita better myself, and half wished she was my great grandmother instead of someone who reminded Grady of Aunt Lace.

Oh, speaking of Aunt Lace, she was busy fluttering from lantern to lantern, gazing at her new diamond ring. Yep, I was right. The dapper and dashing Mr. Melvin Mulligan *would* my uncle. Whoopity-doo! Mr. Mulligan came smirking into the pool with us boys. "I guess I'll be your uncle now," he said rather stupidly.

"I guess it's a free country," Mark observed. "Our silly aunt is free to choose for herself."

Mr. Mulligan laughed, trying to make a great lot of fun out of the statement but none of us even smiled. "And what if this was a society of arranged marriages?"

"We would have arranged it differently," Mark stated bluntly.

At that we did smile, in fact we laughed. I threw my hand out, bidding the principal to shake it. "Let's be friends," I invited, "and congratulations for succeeding where your most dapper and dashing grandfather failed!" We laughed some more. Mr. Mulligan blinked dumbly and fled to a different pool, not understanding my comment at all.

My birthday was February fifth, and we had another celebration. Roe v. Wade was splashing the headlines as abortion had just been granted as a constitutional right and Grady was scorching mad over the depravity of it. "I buried three children of my own—and grieved over each one. How can people do this? It's madness! It is genocide, and now it's *legal*? I'm worried about us, for I fear that the greatest nation on earth will rot from within—forget the Commies! We are our own worst enemies now." We all listened, wondering about it, helpless to change a thing.

My father looked puzzled. "Three children, Grandpa? You've only buried one."

"No, I've buried three, and I'll tell you about it if you'd like."

"Let's have cake!" Grandma Gallagher interrupted her father, hoping to shanghai the conversation.

Grady let it pass but said to my Dad, "Talk to Wesley, for he knows about my life better than you do."

We ate cake and I opened my presents. Grandpa Gallagher gave me a .22. I knew he would and I was thrilled. I got new Levis and shoes from my folks, and some fishing tackle from Uncle Rob and Aunt Aura Leigh. Grady gave me a little card. I opened it, feeling dimes taped inside. Instead of coins, a little arrowhead fell out. It was the one Grandpa found while we were camping, and the card said, "Always remember."

In March I got the mumps. It was going around our town like a juicy secret. Mother made me a breakfast tray, but my jaws were tender and my neck hurt badly. I had a fever and thought perhaps I'd have to die to feel better. Television was swirling with news reports about the Watergate investigation, but all of the political stuff was boring without Grady's take on it. I watched *The Price is Right* and then fell asleep. I was dreaming that I was bidding on fabulous prizes in the game show. I won a bunch of cash in Plinko and then a new car, a boat, and vacations to both Brazil and Switzerland in the showcase showdown. The audience was clapping for me and Bob Barker took my arm and led me toward my prizes. The Price is Right models, Janice Pennington and Dian Parkinson, were sexy and I thought I would tell Monty about them. If anyone had bee-stung lips, surely it was them! I climbed into my new car but I heard the faint pounding of drums. An old Indian smiled at me from the backseat. Feathers fluttered from his hair and I woke up in a sweat.

"Are you okay?" Mother asked. She touched my forehead. "Oh, Wesley you are burning up!" She guided me into the bathroom and made me take a bath, then kept pushing a thermometer in my mouth the rest of the day.

The next morning Allyson woke up with a swollen neck, too. She was a whiney, fevered, miserable little thing, and I did feel sorry for her. It didn't stop me from arguing with her about which one of us was sicker, though. I also stuck my tongue out at her once or twice just to see her lip quiver. It quivered alright, and she started bawling and snitched on me.

"Happiness is!" Mother complained, dragging Allyson into her bedroom and away from me. "Honestly, there are many days when I'm glad there's just two of you."

Suddenly I remembered Grady's prayer in Washakie Fork, near the cabin. He prayed for my parents to get another kid, and now I just found out that Mother didn't want one. I was a little bit worried about it. "Don't you want another baby?"

"Not today, no I don't."

"Ever?"

Mother looked at me strangely. "Why?"

"Um...well...I just wondered if we were trying to have some other kids around here, that's all."

Mother felt my forehead again and dragged me back into the bathroom, making me climb in the tub. "Stay in there for an hour," she said, "until your fever breaks or you stop talking nonsense, whichever one comes first."

That afternoon at five o'clock the phone rang. It was Aunt Lace and she asked if she could come and see me. I wondered if she too was getting ill, and expected to see her neck and jaws puffy and swollen when she bolted through the back door.

"Wesley!" she shrieked. Her eyes were red. "Wesley!"

"I didn't do it," I said, not knowing what crimes had been committed, nor where.

She shook her head in a flustered motion, tossing her long dark hair. "Stan Tomkin's beat up Wyatt today! Dad's just taken Wyatt to the hospital in Eisner. He beat him badly, Wesley."

I felt sick inside as I considered the state of my best cousin. I couldn't help crying. "Will he be okay?"

"I hope so, but his face is black and he's acting slow and stupid. Dad thinks he has a concussion, but it's possible his eye sockets are shattered, as well as his nose."

I wanted to vomit; in fact I did start heaving, for I'd done that all day. "Oh no! Aunt Aubynn should have kept Wyatt home since I wasn't there to protect him."

Suddenly Aunt Lace was sobbing and wailing uncontrollably. She threw her arms around my sore neck and squashed my head to her bosom. My space was definitely being invaded and I couldn't breathe, but I heard Aunt Lace shriek apologies to me. "I blamed you for starting trouble all last year, and here you were, just defending my guileless little lamb! I'm sorry I was hard on you Wesley! I do love you, I do! Please get better. Pray for Wyatt. Pray for Aubynn—she's had a bad day. No mother wants to go find her son in that condition."

I pried my face away from the headlock. "Where was he?"

"He was lying in a pool of blood in the bushes on the west end of the playground. He didn't come home on the bus, and Aubynn called up to Grady's after awhile, but he wasn't there, and that's when she went looking for him." I was sick *and* mad now, and Stan Tomkins had no idea what was coming for him. *None!*

We called down to the hospital about an hour later to check on Wyatt. Grandpa came to the phone, explaining that Wyatt was in getting X-rays. "He looks rough to me," he said. "I've put animals down that looked this bad." That wasn't comforting at all! Of course I wanted to go see Wyatt, but I couldn't because I was too contagious. Dad promised he'd drive down to the hospital and call me personally. Mother stayed with Allyson and me and we fretted the evening away.

When Dad finally called the news was grim. Wyatt had a shattered eye socket on the left side, a busted jaw, again on the left, a broken nose, and three teeth had been knocked out. "The kid's got a broken collarbone. He has a concussion and two cracked ribs. "Aubynn found a crowbar in the bushes. That's what Stan clubbed Wyatt with, apparently. My, my, isn't that Stan Tomkins a big, brave boy?"

My fists clenched and I shouted into the receiver, "I'm going to kick the shi—"

"Wesley!" Mother jerked the phone away from me before she had to wash my mouth out with soap. I knew she couldn't have born doing it—not with me in a mumpish way, of course.

Around and around I paced in my room. I was shook up and inconsolable. The phone rang again. It was Mr. Mulligan. So far this had been a weird night. "Hullo?"

"Wesley—I'm sorry about Wyatt. I should have listened to you last year when you told me about Stan bullying him."

"Yes you should have, but you're not too bright so I can't hold it against you."My sentence came out like a mouthful of water cress. It definitely had a bite to it.

It was quiet on the other end, as Mr. Mulligan tried to answer that. I didn't know how he was supposed to, exactly. "Well…I hope Wyatt's well soon. Please accept my heartfelt apology." I mumbled something, then hung up and called Grady. I needed to blow off steam before I erupted, grabbed my new pistol, and went outlaw, vigilante style.

"Hold on Boy, I'm coming to see you!"

Five minutes later the Studebaker rolled to a stop in front of the house. Grady was sitting on a stack of pillows to see out. He seldom ever drove anymore so he must have deemed this to be an emergency. He stayed with me that night, claiming he'd already had the mumps and wasn't afraid to get them again. He truly was fearful that I'd go shoot somebody, I think. He talked to me for a long time in bed that night. We blew off steam together, actually, and I did feel better. We each prayed for Wyatt. Grandpa's prayer was a long one, and should have been sufficient to heal the dead, let alone the half dead, so I took hope on my best cousin's behalf.

It took three or four days, but I was finally proclaimed well enough to go to Eisner. Wyatt was still in the hospital. He had an IV in his arm for his jaw was wired shut and he couldn't eat. His eyes were completely black, with a thick gauze pad covering his left one, and his lips were cut and swollen. A metal brace was taped onto his broken nose, and little tubes were shoved up his nostrils to hold them open. His jaw looked ten times worse than mine or Allyson's put together. His shoulders looked small and puny beneath a collarbone brace. His ribs were wrapped with medical tape to help support the injuries, and his skin was red and irritated around the adhesive strips.

"Hey Wyatt…it's gonna hurt when they pull that tape off." He couldn't smile at me although he probably wouldn't have anyway. "I'm really sorry I wasn't with you, Wyatt."

His fingers moved, letting me know he understood, but he looked so pitiful laying there that I had to bawl, and I didn't want to. I was twelve and it was time I stopped getting so emotional. I only felt better when tears trickled from his eyes, too. "If it makes you feel any better, I'm planning on killing Stan," I said. Wyatt's fingers wagged horizontally, as if to tell me no. *I didn't know why not!* "I will, and then you won't ever have to go through this again!" Again his fingers moved and his head turned, ever so slightly. "You can't stop me," I cried.

"Don't." The word was muddled and thick, and spoken between wired jaws.

I stopped short, reexamining the situation. "Why?"

He didn't answer and I didn't push it. I tried to tell him some funny stories to help cheer him up, but without his ability to respond I didn't know if I was cheering him up or bringing him down. "Do you want me to shut up?"

This time the fingers worked vertically, like a yes nod, and so I did. I shut up and stared at him for a while. My thoughts were loud though, and I think my visit was more irksome than pleasant to the sacrificial lamb. Mother took me home after twenty-five minutes and I bawled the whole way.

Chapter Nine

In any other school district in America, Aunt Lace would have to step down, being engaged to the principal and all, but after being put to a vote at a school board meeting, it was concluded that she would stay on staff. It was also decided that Stan Tomkin's would be indefinitely expelled. He had been lugged off for a five month stay in juvenile hall, where no doubt he could learn to be a real delinquent.

Quality people, the Tomkins' outfit; Aldean was never sober, and Suzy was usually gone, cleaning rooms at the Fat Shamrock, a local hotel. The Best Western it wasn't, but it provided steady income with lake-loving tourists always coming to town. She was only Stan's stepmother, as his own mom hung herself in a bedroom closet when Stan was three. There was a passel full of little mouths to feed at the house, because Suzy gave Aldean four more kids. It was a sad affair. Suzy often wore sunglasses to hide bruises leveled by her drunken husband. Was Stan expected to be more than just a chip off the old block?

Wyatt didn't return to school that year. His jaw was still wired shut, and he sipped broth and Jell-O water through a straw. Aunt Lace tutored him in the evenings so he could keep up with his class and be advanced to the seventh grade. He turned twelve on May fifteenth, and got a .22 pistol just like mine, but he didn't take any pleasure in it. His life was grim and I wasn't sure if he'd ever be well enough to hunt and fish, and play again.

On the last day of school Avery Anne Applewhite trailed me off of the bus. She had a little pan full of strawberry tarts for Wyatt. Apparently her affections had transferred to him, and she was bearing gifts of glad tidings and cheer. I led her through Grandma's kitchen and into Wyatt's post on the couch. His cheeks flushed beneath the mottled purple and yellow bruising on his face. He sort of rolled his good eye at me, letting me know he didn't appreciate the intrusion into his misery. I shrugged my shoulders, letting Avery speak for herself.

"We all miss you Wyatt. My mother and I made these strawberry tarts for you. I see now that maybe you can't eat them, but you could always offer them to your company and well wishers." Avery was very articulate and polished. Aunt Aubynn gushed about her thoughtful ways and beautiful, shiny hair.

"Avery, would you like me to drive you home?" Aunt Aubynn asked.

"Yes, please, Mrs. Finnegan. I sort of twisted my ankle playing hopscotch today and it hurts. Get better Wyatt."

She primly followed Aunt Aubynn out to the garage. I watched her leave, marveling at her composure. Perhaps she would vie for the title of Little Miss Utah at some point, even if her hair didn't smell of mint. Or clover.

I turned back toward Wyatt. He scowled at me. I was surprised since he hadn't yet been able to show us many facial expressions—usually we saw only two: pained and blah. "Why are you frowning at me?" I asked incredulously. "She asked me to bring her, what was I supposed to say?"

Then I saw it—the hand motion again, only this time his middle finger stood straight up with the others held down. My best cousin was flipping me off and I almost couldn't believe it. "Rest up, little lamb," I cooed. "Get that jaw better quick...so I can re-break it!" I slammed out the back door, nearly knocking Grandma Gallagher off the steps.

"Wesley?"

"Hi Grandma, you'd better get in the house. The bum lamb needs a bottle." I stomped across the yard and into my own. The situation didn't get funny to me until I was in bed that night. Wyatt had never flipped the bird in all his life—I didn't even think he knew what it meant. I giggled to myself in the darkness. The doldrums of being banged up and shut in must have been getting to him, but I didn't figure it was all bad. It was time he got a little bit of fire burning inside. The next time somebody swung a crowbar in his direction maybe he'd do something about it!

I got out of bed and called Grady. I told him about the events of the afternoon and he laughed and laughed. "By Jingo Jones, I believe that boy's a getting better," Grady said. "He'll be okay now."

The end of May brought a lot of work. We branded calves and fixed fences. I guzzled lots of Orange Crush while we worked the days away. Grandpa Gallagher believed in having a daily treat, and we drove to Milner's Station for a soda every afternoon. John and Mark always took one back to Wyatt who was still pretty laid up. I wasn't speaking to him just yet.

The first of June came and with it swarms of people. Monty called from Grady's, asking if I could help out with boat rentals and stuff. The resort was hopping and more than they could see to. Dad told me to just take the car and I felt a little bit cocky as I pulled the Buick to a halt in Grady's driveway.

"Hey Kid," Monty grinned when he saw me. "I see you've got your license."

I laughed and nodded, "Yep. They've lowered the legal age, you know." A fat man in skimpy plaid shorts bumped into us, nearly knocking Monty into the pool.

Monty glared at the dude, muttering, "Idiot."

"City people," I said. "I'll bet you're glad college is done for the year so you can get away from them."

The man bumped into us again walking the other direction. "What do you mean?" Monty asked. "They all followed me here!"

The big pool was packed. Heads dotted along the seven soaking pools, and beyond that, boats bobbed colorfully on Inish Lake. I saw people, people, everywhere, and understood Monty's request for help! I stepped into the boathouse and started selling bait, answering questions, pedaling sodas and Grady's special sandwiches. He'd made up about fifty of them that morning, and they were selling fast.

"We need your hotdog cooker, eh?"I grinned at Grady's suggestion. I would get richer than old Sam Locks selling hotdogs around this place! "Bring it tomorrow, and I'll have my Cora girl order up some hot dogs and buns."

So I was in business for earnest the next day. I made two hundred and fifty-one dollars on hotdog sales, minus the cost of the goods. Grady was grinning at the profits and claimed his outfit was just like Sutter's Mill.

Two or three days later I followed Grandpa Gallagher into his workshop. We constructed a super-duty hot-dog cooker that zapped ten weenies at a time. "Now you've gotta be careful with this contraption, Wesley," he said.

"Roger that."

I put the invention into the car and drove right back up Gallagher Canyon. I passed Sheriff Pistol Stewart on the way. I nearly wet my pants, but I stretched up, sitting tall and straight, and I saluted respectfully as he went by. I kept checking the rearview mirror for red and blue lights to come on, but didn't see any and decided the good Lord really does answer prayers.

"The Fuzz didn't get you huh?" Monty asked as I parked again that day.

"No. When I *wuzz* with the *fuzz*, this is what I *duzz*," I said moronically, saluting, and craning my neck to look very tall. Monty burst into a belly laugh and slapped me on the back, calling me cool.

Hot dog sales were brisk and Grandpa Gallagher's invention worked like a little wonder. The fat man with skimpy plaid shorts appeared at the window ordering several. He flipped a five dollar bill at me like money grew on trees.

"I don't wonder that guy doesn't turn into a big wiener," Grady said.

I answered, "Well…you *are* what you eat."

We laughed at that and later Grady filled Monty in on our conversation. "The kid's a pistol, Grady."

Grady nodded, "I fear he reminds me of me."

Amusement, that's what we had all day long, every day. Tourists weren't always brilliant, but usually amusing, and to quote my snowy-topped great grandfather, "They pay the bills and then some."

July was hot and the hills looked sunburned. Grandpa Gallagher took me with him to doctor a sick cow at Kilkenny Point. John and Celia were working at the resort with Monty. Mark and Uncle Rob were helping my dad haul hay. Grandpa and I came upon a broken down Volkswagen bus. It had peace signs and rainbows, sunshine, and flowers painted all over it. *"Clack with Butterflies"* was printed on the side. One bumper sticker said, *"Make love not war."* I read a second one, *"Heaven waves a white flag and Hell runs a victory lap."* A third bumper sticker didn't say anything, but a picture of Uncle Sam hung upside down in a bull's-eye like a target. Dirty drapes clung from windows and smoke poured from the cab.

"Is it on fire?" Grandpa asked. He climbed out of the truck and strolled warily up to the vehicle. I got out and walked with him, interested.

Two or three people were crammed into the front seat smoking kooky smelling cigarettes. So there was no fire, and I suddenly knew what dope smelled like. Grandpa jerked the door open, looking disgusted. "What's wrong here?"

A long haired, unshaven, unkempt, and all around dirty guy was slumped behind the wheel. "Peace," he said, laughing in the dignified face of my Grandpa.

Just then the back doors of the bus swung open and three other people staggered out, looking around, dazed and dumb. One of the dirty things was a lady—a real hippie chick with matted hair and a tatty collection of necklaces. She wore a long tie-dyed skirt and a little tank top with no bra. Her feet were bare and dirty, and I wondered how old she was. "Hey Mister," she said. "We're all broke down."

"Hell yes," Grandpa agreed. His mouth was tight and grim, and his jaws clenched and unclenched. He didn't mind helping people in need, but this sight was appalling to him.

The back door opened wider. A tiny little girl peered out at me. The stench from inside the bus was atrocious—worse than any can of rotting worms. It smelled of dirty, filthy, unwashed bodies, bad smoke, and I didn't know what else. I stared at the intolerable conditions of the hippie wagon. It was the filthiest thing I'd ever laid eyes on, with clothes, food containers, garbage, beer cans, and stained blankets scattered everywhere. I cast my eyes around, counting one more chick and four grown men. Were they living in this caravan? A five gallon bucket of human sewage in the corner told me they were, and my stomach turned.

I looked at the little girl again. She couldn't have been more than three or four. I felt sorry for her. Black hair, oily and matted, clung against her head. She wore an oversized T shirt and didn't have on shoes. Her little hands were black with grime, and her face hadn't been washed since Roe v. Wade sold America down the clapper.

"Mister, that kid's hungry," the first chick said, jutting a thumb towards the child.

The tiny black eyes peered up at Grandpa. He groaned at the sight of the child. "Wesley, meet The Least of These," he said.

Of course! Gospel lessons bigger than Sunday school slapped me right in the face. The poor, filthy little girl was but innocence in peril. "Bring me my tool box, Wes."

I did as Grandpa said, and he talked to the woman, "Pop the hood on this traveling junkyard and let me see what's wrong." The woman responded, reaching past the stoners in the front seat. She seemed to be the only capable one in the bunch, and her judgment was questionable.

"What's your name?" Grandpa asked.

"Joni."

"Well Joni…do your folks know where you are?"

"No."

"That's a damn shame, don't you think?"

"My folks are squares, and I am free from the bondage of society."

"Pfft." Air hissed between Grandpa's cheeks in a disgusted manner.

Grandpa turned to me. "Take that little girl down to Maggie's at the Point. Get her something to eat." He handed me five dollars and I took it, feeling awkward and kind of ashamed to be seen with the bedraggled thing.

"Want something to eat?" I asked her. She nodded and climbed outside, squinting in the sun. "Does she have shoes?" I asked Joni.

"She did, but I haven't seen them for awhile."

"Pfft." This time the sound came from me, and I locked eyes with Grandpa and he just shrugged his shoulders at me, bidding me to use my head. "Come on little one," I said. I picked up the dirty little thing, hoping I wouldn't catch head lice. The smell of her sickened me, the barnyard odor of the sick cow had been more to my liking, but I bucked up and trudged toward the quaint café on the corner with the love child in my arms.

"What's your name?"

"Yarrow."

Yarrow? That's a terrible name! Surely yarrow wasn't even a *real* flower—just a plant, and not beautiful sounding at all. "Yarrow?"

"Uh huh."

"Not Heather?"

"Nope."

"Not Cindy, Jennifer, Kathy, or Michelle?"

"Nuh uh."

I switched to the plant names again, hoping the little girl would find one she liked better, "Fern? Ivy? Rose? Are you *sure* your name's not Heather?"

A small breath blew against my neck. "You are funny."

"How about Lilly? That's sort of beautiful."

"My name is Yarrow."

"Yarrow who?"

"Just Yarrow."

"How about Sparrow? That rhymes—or maybe Birdie? Robin?"

"Don't you have ears? Myself is named Yarrow!"

"Okay," I said, letting the subject drop.

We walked into the front door of the café. Archie Gallagher, Grandpa's cousin, was saddled up at the counter sipping on a cup of coffee, and a pair of tourists in golf clothes canoodled in a booth, but other than that the place was empty. I pulled Yarrow into the bathroom and locked the door.

"What are we doing?"

"Washing your hands." I started the water and pumped the soap dispenser. I began scrubbing those little dimpled hands, and blessedly the drain carried the sludgy water away. Yarrow giggled at the experience. "You like washing?" I asked.

She bobbed her head, "Yes."

"When was the last time you were clean?"

She just stared at me, and so my suspicions were correct—it had been ages since her last bath. With moist paper towels I scrubbed right on up both arms. Drips of water left clean marks everywhere they ran. Soon I pushed her sleeves up past her shoulders and scrubbed. Her arms looked good, and Yarrow examined them excitedly. "My face?" I nodded. Of course, I must wash her face. We lathered soap on our hands, both of us, and started scrubbing. I wiped her face dry with a paper towel, and then lifted the little girl up to see in the mirror. She stared at herself, blinking. "That's Yarrow?"

"Sure, it's you." I was befuddled by the question. "See how pretty you are?"

Yarrow smiled at me. I smiled back at her in the mirror, and then I spied her poor, greasy, horrible hair, and I disapproved. I hoisted her up, making her tip her head over the sink. With another wad of soap in my hand I started washing the tangled mess of hair. I scrubbed her head like grimy sox to a washboard. The little girl smelled better and better. I patted her dry with more paper towels, longing to scrub her filthy T-shirt as well, but I was helpless on that account, as I didn't know what to put her in while I did it. I tried to smooth her hair with my fingers, but the child needed a good brushing.

"Myself is clean?"

"Kind of." The top half looked a lot better than the bottom half. Her legs and feet were still polluted looking.

"You'll let me eat?"

I nodded and we left the bathroom. I parked Yarrow in a back booth and walked up to the counter. Maggie noticed me. "Hi, Wesley. What can I do for you?"

"I need a couple of cheeseburgers, an orange soda and a glass of milk. Just holler at me when it's ready and I'll come up and get it and save you the trip."

"Well, alrighty then," Maggie said pleasantly, throwing a couple of patties on a hot grill. I was afraid if Maggie saw the hippie child, she would refuse service, for she wasn't wearing any shoes, and a sign on the door said, *"No shoes, No shirt, No service, No exceptions."*

"Where's the foods?" Yarrow seemed angry with me when I sat down empty-handed.

"It's cooking."

"What's that?"

"It means it's getting ready." And I felt sick to think the girl didn't know what cooked food was. "What do you usually eat?"

"Crackers."

"Potatoes and gravy?" She shrugged, not knowing what I was talking about. "Pudding?" Again she shrugged and by now I wanted to bawl. "What's your favorite food?"

"Little meats in a can." She motioned with her fingers and I thought she might have meant Vienna sausages. I was glad she'd experienced such cuisine. At least it was something.

"Order out, Wesley!" Maggie's voice made me jump and I made haste to the counter, grabbing Yarrow's plate and mine. I doubled back for the drinks. I opened a straw and stuck it in the glass of milk for the girl. She stared at it, full of wonder.

"Here," I said, sucking out of my straw. "Like this."

Her eyes danced as she tasted the cold milk. She stared at me while I took a bite of my burger. She bit into hers hungrily, chewing only a few times before gulping the food down. Truly she had been starving and tears burned against my eyes at the thoughts. I'd never gone hungry a day in my life.

"What is this?" she asked around a whole wad of burger.

"It's a cheeseburger. It's good huh?"

"Uh-huh!" She guzzled some more milk and then tried some fries. She smiled from ear to ear at the golden delights. "What's this?"

"French fries."

"I'll take some for my Joni."

"Is Joni your mom?"

"She's just my Joni," Yarrow said, "but my Joni loves French fries."

This was the saddest thing I'd ever seen or heard. "I'll bet," I choked. "Listen Yarrow, you eat all of your fries, and we'll take mine back for your Joni, okay?" I didn't want the child to go without one thing.

"You're nice."

"Thanks."

I handed the money to Maggie at the register, and then pocketed Grandpa's change, careful to leave a quarter on the table for a tip. I didn't know if that was enough, but technically I'd waited on our table, myself. I walked out of Maggie's at the Point, surprised to see Grandpa's truck parked in front.

He was just climbing out when he saw me coming. "Put the kid in the truck, Wes."

I did and then joined him in front of the truck to see what he wanted. "I got the van started. They took off. They took off without the kid and without looking back! I had a mind to chase the dirty, rotten sons-of-bitches down, but I'm not sure that would have been fair to the kid." His hands were trembling and his jawbones worked overtime, clenching with tension.

"What will we do?"

"Hell if I know." Grandpa was really rattled because he was cussing up a streak, saying words he generally saved for working with sheep. "Take the kid home, I guess, and then call the Sheriff and I don't know what..."

I nodded, feeling the weight of lots of problems pressing down on us, but also a sense of relief. I didn't have to put that little girl back into the dirty bus! We rode into Gallagher Springs.

"Mister, I'm taking these foods to my Joni," Yarrow said to Grandpa.

"Pfft. You've got to come with us first," Grandpa explained as kindly as he could for as rattled as he was. The pickup pulled into the driveway.

"I'll take her with me," I said. Grandpa's brows shot high, but he didn't argue.

"Yes, maybe your mom can put her in some of Allyson's hand-me-down clothes, and..."

I didn't wait for any more suggestions. I had Yarrow in hand, and I hit the back door, ready to show Mother what I'd found and ask if I could keep her.

Chapter Ten

If I live to be as old as Grady I'll never forget the look on Mother's face as I presented the small black eyed girl to her. Utter mystification—shock, and I'm not sure what else, played across her face. "Start the tub, Wesley."

I did as she instructed. I filled the tub and retrieved a fluffy blue towel from the linen closet, and then I hurried into Allyson's room and snatched a couple of tub toys.

Allyson stared wide eyed at the creature in the hallway. "What's your name?"

"It isn't Heather," Yarrow said.

"I didn't ask what it wasn't, I asked what it *was*."

"But that boy," Yarrow said, pointing to me, "kept asking what it wasn't."

"Her name is Yarrow," I informed them.

A sour look crossed Allyson's face, "Yarrow?"

Mother's lips pinched together and she gave Allyson a stern look. "I think Yarrow is a *beautiful* name!" Yarrow smiled from ear to ear at the woman. "Now Yarrow, let's get you into the tub."

"What's that?"

Mother's eyes were wild at the inquiry. Unspoken questions flew my direction. I planned on answering them just as soon as I could. "Come here and I'll show you." Mother led the girl by her recently scrubbed hand. "See, you are going to take your shirt off and climb in here and swim and scrub. Doesn't that look fun?"

"Oh, scrubbing some more? Can that boy help me?"

"No. Boys don't wash girls."

"But he washed me at the food place."

Mother's head tilted as she spied me strangely. "But not a whole bath, dear."

"Oh."

"I will help you."

They went into the bathroom and the door shut. Allyson and I stood in the hallway, curious about the little stranger. Soon Mother appeared in the doorway. "Allyson and Wesley please run downstairs and bring up the gray chest. Allyson's old clothes and shoes are folded inside." We did as we were told. We took the chest into Allyson's room. Mother came in and sorted through items, finding a little pair of pink panties, a yellow sundress, and small pair of white patent leather sandals. Allyson had fun spying all of her old clothes from days gone by.

"Do we get to keep her, Mother?"

"I doubt it Wesley. The sheriff will come when he can. I'm certain that it will all have to go through the state. She will probably be awarded to a grandparent or some other relative, if possible. But we can clean her, feed her, and love her while she's here."

"Just don't let her go back with those hippies. It was awful Mother—you should have seen inside that van."

Mother nodded and stepped back inside the bathroom. Allyson and I laughed because we could hear Yarrow singing, "This is the best day of my life, and this is the best day of my *li-i-iffffe*." She dragged the word out, climbing the scale higher and higher with it as she went. "My food was good, and my food was *go-oo-ood*! I like to scrub, and scrub, and scru-uu-uu-b!"

"How are you doing in here, little one?" Mother asked.

"Fine! I like the tub! Myself never swimmed in one before."

"Never?"

"My Joni took me to a ditch once."

"Is Joni your mommy?"

"She's just my Joni."

"I see...do you have a Grandma or a Grandpa."

"Nope."

"Are you sure, Yarrow?"

"My Joni has a ma."

"She does?"

"Yip. Ma Bell. My Joni sometimes stops at stations to call Ma Bell."

Allyson and I had our ears to the door, hearing every cute word, but my eyes teared at the mention of Ma Bell. Obviously Yarrow's Joni had been talking about the phone company, and little Yarrow thought it was a relative.

"Who's Joni?" Allyson asked.

"Her stinking lousy mother, I think."

"Why doesn't she call her *mother*, then?"

"Her mom is a wasted member of the counter-culture—a hippie chick. I'm sure she's *too free from the bondage of society* to raise her kid with the security of having a mother. I'm certain that she is raising her as a little friend, instead. *Some friend!*" Allyson's eyes were wide and she nodded, although I'm not sure what she really understood.

An hour later Mother finally pried Yarrow from the tub. "What's wrong with my fingers and my toes?"

"They got shriveled from that nice long bath, little one, but they will un-wrinkle in a few minutes."

Mother and Yarrow emerged from the bathroom. I couldn't believe the transformation of the bedraggled little love child! She was absolutely sugar and spice with her hair all clean and brushed. Allyson's sundress was darling on her, and she smelled sweet—just the way a little girl should smell.

"Hi my Boy," she said to me. "Look at myself!"

"I see."

"Do you live here, my Boy?"

"Yes and my name is Wesley."

"I will call you Heather," she said, and tiny sparks of mischief were in her eyes. We laughed at that, and Yarrow clapped her hands and spun around and around, so tickled by the attention. "Myself is funny?" We nodded. "Do you live in this house?" We nodded again.

The phone rang and Mother went to answer it. Allyson took Yarrow to her bedroom to play with toys. Yarrow squealed with excitement, and I do mean squealed! She asked what the bed was; being in complete dismay that Allyson had one all to herself.

I walked into the kitchen. Mother was staring at the wall, deep in thought. "Who was on the phone?"

"The sheriff."

"And?"

"He said he is in a bit of a commotion right now and asked if the child was okay for at least tonight."

"And?"

"I said yes, of course."

Then we heard it—sirens and horns blasting through town. The emergency vehicles seemed to come into town from Eisner, and left Gallagher Springs, screaming south toward Lakeside. I always felt sick at the sound of sirens. Somebody somewhere was in trouble.

At suppertime, Dad came in, looking bewildered to see such a tiny guest, although I knew he had been talking to Grandpa. "Hello," he said. "Whose little girl are you?"

"I belong to that boy right there," she stated emphatically, pointing in my direction.

Mother filled Dad in on the strange events of the day. Dad just nodded. We prayed over the meal and then Mother dished up some mashed potatoes and gravy for Yarrow. She cut a pork chop into tiny bites. Yarrow floundered on the food! "I love this stuff!"

"That's what mashed potatoes and gravy taste like," I said.

"Yeah," Yarrow agreed, "and it was cooked, too. I never ate so much foods before this day."

"God bless *this* day, then," Dad remarked.

After supper we went into the front room. *Gunsmoke* was on television, followed by *McMillan and Wife.* Yarrow scooted close to me on the couch. She was mesmerized by the program, but soon fell fast asleep against my shoulder. Dad lifted her into his arms to carry her to Allyson's bed. Yarrow startled awake. "Where are you taking me, Mister?"

"Into Allyson's room for night time. You can sleep with her."

"I want to sleep with my boy."

"No, for little girls don't sleep with boys."

"My Joni does."

Dad's expression was quite humorous, but he didn't say what he was thinking. "Yarrow, at our house you may sleep with Allyson."

"Alright. If my Joni comes while I am asleep, just tell her to come back again in the morning, but myself is not leaving without him." She pointed at me.

"I'll be sure to tell her that."

Yarrow was sound asleep before Allyson could even get her teeth brushed. We peeked in at her, not caring if we were missing our favorite programs on TV. "Don't get attached to her!" Dad warned but I knew it was already too late.

At ten o'clock a knock pounded against the door. Pistol Stewart stepped inside. "Hello folks," he said. Mother asked him to sit down and we faced each other tensely. "Thanks for taking the kid. Is she alright?"

"She seems well enough. She's very bright, and has an incredible appetite."

"Did you catch her mother?" I asked anxiously.

"Well…there's been a heck of a commotion in Three Lakes Valley today."

"We heard the sirens, is everything okay?"

"That dang idiot-wagon drove off a pier into Lake Washakie, right off the east side where it's deep. Some fishermen saw it speed ahead and then plunge right into water. As near as I can tell, it was a group suicide attempt, and a successful one at that. Dive teams from Eisner have recovered all but one of the bodies." Sickening shivers tied my stomach into a frozen knot. "Apparently Doc Riley Gallagher repaired the hippie bus just so it could drive them all to hell. It seems that the girl's mother saved her kid's life by sending her with Wesley for something to eat. Thank you, Wesley. I guess I'll have to look the other direction *every* time I pass you driving up to Grady's place. Just so you know—I've been looking the other direction all summer."

I twisted in my chair, unaware of his keen eye and knowing ways. It's amazing I'd avoided doing time in the big house this long. "Thanks."

"My deputies have been trying to identify bodies and contact the next of kin. Joni was presumably the girl's mother, and we know her last name was Whitecliff. That's about it."

"I'm so thankful the girl's mother sent her to eat!"

"I would imagine she did it out of love—no matter how strangely lousy her choices were."

"Yes, of course. Well—now what?"

"We'll let you know. I have the authority to take the child and put her in state custody, but I can't think of a better place for her temporarily than staying right here, if you are agreeable to this."

"Sheriff, if you find out nobody wants the kid then I'd like to adopt her," I said. I meant it and I flushed instantly because my Dad chuckled at me. "I'm dead serious!" I scowled at him.

"Yes, of course, we'd take the little one," Mother said briskly. "But... I'm sure she'll have tons of relatives clamoring for her."

"There'd be no better home on earth to take her in, the poor little bum—but it'll just depend. Well, thanks much and I'll be in touch." He shook my parents' hands and left.

I prayed that night, long and hard. I wanted to keep the girl. I didn't know why—'cuz at first she really stunk, but she was so tiny and cute, and she called me her boy. I had only known the kid for eight hours, but I loved her. "Finders keepers," I said to the Lord. "I found her. Please let me keep her because no matter what my dad says, I am already attached."

I couldn't sleep and climbed out of bed at eleven thirty. I knew it was late, but I phoned Grady. He answered on the second ring and didn't mind at all that I had interrupted his beauty sleep. "She's the one you prayed for, Grady!"

"Boy, I think you might be right."

"Make it be so."

"I haven't the power."

"Don't let them take her."

"I am not the boss, but I'll see what I can do."

"I think she might be an Indian."

"Why?"

"She has pretty skin, black eyes, and her last name is Whitecliff."

"That's no sign of a duck's nest."

"Can't you make that old Indian spirit pull some strings or something?"

"Well…I can't say that I *can*, but who's to say that he hasn't helped out already?"

"I dunno."

"Go get some sleep, Wesley. Que Sara-Sara, whatever will be, will be, and we will just do as the whitecaps do, and go with the flow."

"Pray!"

"Okay—but when we pray, we pray to God and not to men. You remember that."

"I know that!" I felt exasperated. I didn't intend for him to *pray* to the spirits, for heck's sakes! "But I know you say really long and good prayers. Please help us keep that little girl."

"I said, OKAY!" Grady's voice sounded shrill in my ear. "Laws almighty, Kid, you're as monotonous as Claude Walsh's raspberry red lips—the least he could do is try a different shade."

I smiled. "Good night, Grady. Thanks again."

Sleep did not come. I don't know why I had to do it, I just don't, but I snuck out of the house and up behind Grandpa Gallagher's workshop. I started his pickup truck and drove up Gallagher Canyon, then onto the high ridge. I drove to the exact spot where the old spirit had leaned over me and Monty Quinn as we slept beneath the stars. I turned off the truck and got out, willing any Shoshone still camping in Washakie Fork to come find me.

"I'm here!" I called into the darkness. Rattling and rustling whispered up the hill from the grove near the creek. I listened, but couldn't understand. "Have you been watching over Yarrow? Did you choose me to find her?" I waited. Crickets stirred and frogs called, but the air was still and eerie. "I am not afraid anymore!" Even as I said it I knew that was a lie, but I continued, "My great-grandfather walked among you when you were alive, and so I can be brave among the memories of the dead." I listened in the darkness for over an hour.

Nothing, just the night, but I don't know what I expected.

"Well anyway, if you somehow led Yarrow Whitecliff to me or me to her, then thank you." I let my gaze sweep the valley on both sides of the ridge. To the south I saw it. Past the distant bramble of chokecherries trees a solitary campfire burned in the clearing. I thought I heard the faint pounding of drums and flute music, but then again, my imagination was soaring and adrenaline surged through my veins the way Pistol Stewart sped through town to catch a jaywalker.

I stood absolutely still, watching the distant flicker of flame, smelling smoke as it curled in the night. "Thank you," I whispered. The aspen whispered back. I got into the truck and went home feeling like I had trespassed against the sacred wonders of hallowed ground long enough.

The sun rose before I wanted to wake up. A small voice asked, "My boy?"

I cracked an eye open. Yarrow peered at me, just inches from my face. "Good morning, Yarrow."

"My Joni let me stay all night."

I wondered how we could ever tell Yarrow about her mother. She didn't even know what a bed was—how on earth could we explain death? "She's decided to let you stay for awhile."

Yarrow climbed onto the bed and laid her head on my arm. "Do you have books?"

"Yes."

"Allyson can do a book."

"You mean read? Yes, and I can too."

"You will do a book for me?"

"I will *read* a book to you. Say it."

"Read."

"Go pick one out."

She came back into my room with *Bambi*. I was wondering if she couldn't have found one where the mother *didn't* die, but I didn't end up reading to her anyway because she talked too much, asking questions about the animals. There was a picture of a butterfly. "That's a butterfly."

"Yes it is."

"That's where my Joni is going—to clack with butterflies."

I wondered if there were butterflies clacking in hell. Who knows, exactly? I only know the stoners took a trip and then drove off the deep end…or maybe it was the other way around.

I hated to go to work that day. I gave Mother strict orders not to let the state take Yarrow away while I was gone. I thought I had it on good authority that she *would* be staying, but I could have literally been *up in the night.* Perhaps the campfire burned every night in Washakie Fork, and the old Indian was playing me for a dude.

I rented out paddle boats, canoes, fishing boats, sold bait and tackle, and zapped hotdogs all day long. My mind was preoccupied, and at quitting time I beat it home without sweeping up. Grady grumbled after me.

"Sorry Grady, but I am out of here."

"Out of here? I don't think you ever showed up today."

I let the comment pass and hopped into the Buick and drove home. I passed Pistol Stewart and waved without even trying to look tall in the saddle, and he was careful to look the other direction. Nobody was at home when I got there. I panicked before seeing a note on the table. "We are at Grandma's."

I washed up and went next door. Yarrow was curled up next to Grandpa Gallagher on the sofa. She was watching *The Wizard of Oz* on TV and the flying monkeys were tripping her out. "Hi my boy," Yarrow called. "There are bad monkeys flying away with the kids, but this nice man is keeping *me* safe."

I looked at Wyatt. He stared back. John came up behind me, whispering, "Do you think this the kid that Grady was praying about last year?"

"I hope so."

"Weird."

"I know."

I stared at Wyatt again. "Can you talk yet—or are you still performing sign language?" Shoulders shrugged and so I let it drop. What a big jerk! It had been six weeks since he flipped me off and I was the one who should have been mad! "You're acting like a sulky hen."

"We can't all be strutting roosters," he countered.

My brows shot high and my head angled sideways. "What's that supposed to mean?"

Shoulders shrugged again and I stormed out of Grandma's back door and went home. I didn't know what to do about Wyatt, and I didn't know what to do about Stan when he came back to town. Perhaps I'd send them both to clack with butterflies!

An hour later I stormed back over to Grandma's. Wyatt had gone to his room, for he hated *The Wizard of Oz*. He had nightmares for two weeks after watching it the last time it came on TV. I pushed the door open, seeing Wyatt was alone in the room. Mark was on a date with Michelle Voss, and John was out in the front room. Wyatt looked up from a Phantom Flynn book and scowled at my intrusion.

"What's your beef with me?"

His one good eye looked hollow as it stared. He didn't say anything! He shrugged and looked back at his book. That infuriated me! I grabbed his novel and threw it against the wall.

"Get out of here! You have your own house."

"Not until we talk! Why are you so hissy pissy?"

"I'm sick of you! I get my bell rung—right? And what do I hear? Fluttering! Fluttering in all directions about why Mom should have kept me home because *you* had the mumps! That's a load of bull pucky!"

"What?" I was trying to understand Wyatt's fury now that he was venting.

"I don't need you to fight my battles."

I blinked twice, wondering what to say to that. The kid had been down and out for three months and I didn't savvy. "Um…"

"Shut up. You are such a little hero, Wesley! I'm sick of you thinking you're my big protector."

"Of all the dirty, rotten—" my mind deserted me for more fitting adjectives, "low-down, snake-in-the-grass attitudes! I've gotten fat lips and bloody knuckles for you, and this is how you *thank* me?"

"You didn't do it for *me*! You did it for *you*! There's nothing you like better than mixing it up. You crave a good scrape at least once a week. You're a selfish little braggart."

"I am not!" I yelled, although it *was* true that I was somewhat of a pistol—anyway Monty thought so, and Grady agreed. "I've been watching your back."

"From now on, I've got it. I'd rather be a steady target than an easy one."

"I don't get you."

"I didn't ask you to!"

"Some wise butt rang your bell with a crowbar—actually intended to *kill* you, I think, but I'm the problem?"

"Where's your man?" Wyatt mimicked. *"Not here to save you? You're worthless Finnegan...Wesley's the Lone Ranger but you're only Tonto! Wesley's Bat Man and you are Robin. Wesley's Marshal Dillon but you're nobody but Festus. He's Sherlock, you're Watson. Wesley's Tony Orlando and you're Dawn! You're a sidekick, you butthole! This aint Mayberry, but you sure as hell are just like Barney Fife."*

Actually that was pretty good. "That was a great impersonation, Wyatt."

He rolled his one good eye and winced as the action must have strained his bad one right along with it. "You're puffed up."

I considered his opinion of me. "Kind of," I admitted. "But I'm no different than I was before you took a crowbar to the head."

He glowered at me, considering my words. "I'm sick and tired of being compared to you! Monty Quinn calls you Kid, and Champ, and Pistol! He calls me only Poot. Grady let you drive his truck! Where was I? Riding in the back—never once in the front."

"That wasn't my doing—"

"You threw all of the big boys in the chicken fights. Who fought me? A ninety year old man—and I couldn't best him."

"Grady's tough—there's no shame in that! You didn't *lose* to him either, I'll remind you."

"I ask one question and I'm told to go wait in the tent! You ask a question and the whole world scrambles to answer it for you."

Gee, when Wyatt decides to vent, he really goes at it. He wasn't even giving me time to respond now.

"I spend three weeks slaving over a science project and you stroll into the school after one Saturday afternoon and rob half of my prize money."

I was getting riled again...I hadn't minded sharing the first-place title with him! "Well—"

Wyatt cut me off. "I'm just sick of the whole world catering to you. I'm certain you can't *possibly* understand."

My fists clenched and unclenched. I stared at the kid who had once been my best cousin. "Welcome to my fifth grade *hell*," I said. "I know a little bit of something about playing second string." I stared, intending to blind Wyatt with super-hero lasers blasting from my eyeballs. "Just ask Aunt Lace which one of us is A-Number One!" He looked a little stunned by that. *Good!* "I was willing to bear her ridicule and harsh disciplines all year just to feed Stan Tomkins a little dirt in your behalf. Why? Because I thought it *mattered*!"

Wyatt's head swung back while little shards of illumination burst upon him. At least I hoped he was seeing the light. I turned to leave.

"Where are you going?"

"Monty and I are going fishing. I'm headed up to Grady's right now to spend some quality time with my...*best* cousin." I swaggered from the room in a braggedy manner, *on purpose*, letting the words knock him from side to side like the cruel blows of a crowbar.

I climbed into the Buick and drove up to Grady's. Monty was mushing it up with Shaylin in the hottest pool. Definitely steamy. I lied about us fishing together because I was sore at Wyatt for being so petty. Grandma Addie's blood flowed healthy and strong in his veins, I guess. The thing that riled me the most was the fact that he was right about most of it—but then again so was I. Nobody's perfect! I'd been willing to look past his faults, but apparently mine had been piling up around him. I knocked on Grady's door but went in before he could answer it.

He seemed delighted to see me. "Wesley, what's bothering you this evening?"

"Wyatt."

"Better let it out boy, for bad news keeps like sour milk."

I blew off steam, alright. I told Grady everything, hoping to get a reassuring pat on my back.

"I'm sorry you boys are having grief," he said.

"And?"

"And what? Either you'll patch it up or you won't."

"But he's been my best cousin!"

"Good friendships are hard to part with and are usually worth mending."

I gulped. Grady wasn't helping me at all! "He's acting haughty, like Aunt Lace, or Grandma Addie."

"Don't be disrespectful!" The hazel eyes narrowed in my direction. Grady suddenly sounded like Grandpa Gallagher and I choked. My head snapped sideways to study him.

"I didn't mean to be."

"First of all, the aunt that you don't like just happens to be a granddaughter that I love! Secondly, you've taken up the notion that your great grandma wasn't a good woman, and it's an infernal lie! I lived with her for over forty years and I'm certain she'll rise to the very top of the Celestial Kingdom, with or without the rest of us."

I scowled. "But she blustered and fussed about Awinita and your cabin—she was so jealous."

"So what? I blustered and fussed over her attentions to Finn Mulligan!"

"But you said—you had stormy times, and..."

"I know, and everybody does! But none of it meant I wasn't happy with her! I'm sorry if I said anything about her that you misunderstood. I didn't talk about Addie so much while we camped because I thought you already knew about her. I love my Adelaide Danaher O'Rourke! I know my tales of Awinita are exotic, strange, and wild. I know they are appealing to you—more to you than the other boys, I think, and that's fine, but don't you start judging about who's *petty* and who's on the level."

"You said I was like you, and—"

"My hell, you are! It's no wonder I get pained with you on occasion."

"You want to be buried by Awinita!"

Grady rubbed his tired eyes. "Yes, I do. Those lonesome graves make me feel awful—my Addie is buried in the cemetery, surrounded by our kinfolk. I just can't bear for Awinita and those two little babes to lie in such a lonely place."

My brows furrowed and I was confused as ever I'd been in my life. Blustering to Grady had done no good tonight, for he was blustering back and I didn't care to hear it. "Sorry I bothered you," I grumbled.

"Adelaide Danaher O'Rourke was a fine, spirited, beautiful woman! She could sew and quilt—crochet, knit, everything! Her handy-work was unmatched. She was the best cook in the county! You never tasted caramel until you tasted some of hers! She kept a big garden—had a green thumb, but she was refined, too. She often gave readings at community events, and her voice was soft as velvet, lilting lines for the entertainment and cultural edification of others. Addie liked to dance. We often danced beneath the stars, waltzing to the melodies of the old Victrola. Every so often we'd paddle out on the lake, pretending we could sail to the moon by following its golden path on the water." Grady paused, swaying slightly. "Adelaide was proud—but then again, she had a right to be!" Grady smiled, sighing. "Oh my Addie…what a gal!" Grady's eyes were teary and his expression wafted to some distant place.

"I'm sorry if I misunderstood."

Grady's wise eyes trailed back to me. "Wesley, fix things up with Wyatt or move on. That's the best advice I can give you."

I brooded at the kitchen table. Grady's clock ticked against the wall and a chime sounded ten o'clock. "Guess I'd better go."

"Guess you'd better. Take tomorrow off! You look like you could use a day."

I scowled again. I didn't want a day off! Dad would just shoo me out to the hayfield, anyway. "I want to work."

"No. You can come back day after tomorrow. Stay home and play with that little stray girl."

"Whatever," I said, pounding down Grady's walk.

"Wesley!"

I turned back. Grady was standing on the back steps. "I'm sorry I wasn't in good humor tonight. It's Addie's birthday today, and my thoughts have been hovering around her all day."

I felt small and stupid, and worst of all, humbled. "I'm sorry I'm a jerk!"

Grady smiled. "Now you've learned to say it, go repeat it to your cousin. He's a jerk too, but one of you has got to say it first. By Jingo Jones, one of you must break!"

My thoughts were heavy as I raked a plume of dust behind me. The Buick ate up the two miles in no time. My folks were just finishing the ten o'clock news when I pulled to a stop. I ran in the house, making sure Yarrow was still there. She was curled up in Mother's arms wearing a ruffled white nightgown.

"She waited up for her boy to come, but finally nodded off."

"Grady doesn't need me tomorrow. I will play all day with her unless you can use me, Dad."

"Oh...I don't need you tomorrow either. The hay's not ready to rake so enjoy the day. Help your mother." That sounded like an oxymoron to me, *enjoying* my day while *helping* mother, but I let it pass.

I went down the hall to my room. I grabbed a piece of notebook paper and printed, *"Wyatt, I'm sorry I'm a jerk."* I signed my name and then added, *"P.S.—I did not go fishing with Monty. You are still my best cousin if you wanna be."*

I looked around my bedroom spying a racecar model I'd gotten for

Christmas. Wyatt had really envied it. I grabbed it and snuck across the road and in through Wyatt's window, a thing I had done many times before. He wasn't in his bed. John stared at me from the top bunk. *"Tie a Yellow Ribbon 'Round the Old Oak Tree,"* was crooning from a radio on the dresser.

"Where's Wyatt?"

"Search me. He was here awhile ago. Maybe he's in the bathroom." He went back to his book.

I sat the model and note down on Wyatt's pillow where he was sure to find it. "See ya, John."

"Bye. Come back sometime and try the front door. We have a doorbell and everything."

I chuckled and John winked at me. "See ya, Kid."

I snuck back around the bushes against the side of the house, making a beeline for my backdoor.

I stealthily crept back into my room. I shut the door and turned on my light. Wyatt's metallic blue fishing pole was lying on my bed with a note that said, *"I'm sorry I'm a sulky, hissy pissy, little idiot. Guess I'm only sidekick material after all. Enjoy the pole. You're new best cousin would not be impressed with your old white one."* He signed his name with a flourish. *"P.S. Don't tell Grandma or Mom that I said pissy. You know how they feel about that word."*

Tears stung like darts and I started wiping them away, even though I was twelve and a half and should have been past such nonsense. I sprang out of my room noisily, dashing back across the drive way to Grandma's house. I met Wyatt, who was scurrying over to ours. We grinned at each other.

"Hey Wesley, I'll trade a nifty racecar model for your fishing pole," he said.

"It's a deal." We smiled and sealed the truce with our secret handshake, then spat on both sides of the sidewalk.

Chapter Eleven

The whole family pitched in and helped Grandma Gallagher get the yard ready for Aunt Lace's wedding, even Monty and Uncle Rob were there. So that's why Grady told me not to go to work. Maxine Flanders and Big Bill Monroe had matters in hand at the resort. Dad lent me to Mother because our yard needed to be spruced up as well. Wedding attendees would have a wide view into our yard as well.

Yarrow followed me around like a shadow talking a mile a minute and asking questions. Dad mowed and I was raking grass and hauling if off in the wheelbarrow. Yarrow wore an old pair of Allyson's jeans and claimed she was a farmer because of it. She demanded to ride on top of each grass load claiming they were haystacks. She prattled and I grinned at her nonstop comments. I don't know if other four years olds could possibly be as bright as she was.

"My boy and myself are doing haystacks," she called to Dad. "My boy and myself are working hard," she said when Mother was near.

At lunchtime Grady's Studebaker bounced into the driveway. He was sitting on the pile of pillows again. He smiled at all of the activity, unloading a cooler. He'd made a whole bunch of Grady Specials and brought them down for our lunch. "I've seen less industry in a beehive," he said jovially as we all gathered around.

"Who is that?" Yarrow asked.

"Grandpa Grady."

"*Another* Grandpa?"

"Yes." I pulled the plastic wrap from Yarrow's sandwich and held it for her while she took a bite. Her eyes sparkled while she chewed. "Do you like it, Yarrow?"

"Uh-huh!" She said in her usual way, dragging the *uh* up an octave and a half then quickly slamming it down with *huh*.

Grady studied her thoughtfully, tears brimming against his hazel eyes. He had not yet seen the child. "Hello my fair and lovely," he said, bowing before our little guest.

"Thanks for coming," Yarrow said, wiping a bit of bleu cheese dressing from her lips.

Everybody laughed. Grandma shook her head at her father. "She's the brightest little thing I've ever seen."

"She's just what we ordered," Grady commented. The grownups looked stumped by that. Monty Quinn flashed me a thumbs up and I crossed my fingers back at him.

"Yarrow, would you like a soda?"

"Myself might want a sody if it's good."

Grady chuckled again. "I think it is. You may have grape, orange, root beer, or 7-up."

Yarrow looked into the cooler, utterly dismayed. "Myself will take the one my boy wants me to have."

Grady grinned, liking the girl's pet name for me. "I like this kind the best," I said to Yarrow, grabbing a bottle of Orange Crush.

"Me too!" We pried the lid off with the pop opener and Yarrow laughed at the small hissing sound. "Do it again."

"I can't, silly. I can only open a bottle of pop once."

"Make the other kids open some, then."

Grady passed out sodas to all of us, and Yarrow clapped her hands every time the lids came off.

"Haven't you had an orange soda before?" Allyson asked.

"No, but myself's had a Budweiser. That's Moon and Bong's best sody, I guess. I don't think it's orange."

We were mystified, mortified, and disgusted, the whole group of us. "Who are they?" I asked.

"Bong and Moon are the drivers. My Joni sleeps with them at night."

Mother wanted to faint away, I just know it. This little kid had seen things that would curl our hair, I'm afraid. "Budweiser is *not* a soda," Mother corrected, "and should *not* be given to children!"

"Well," Yarrow shrugged. "Myself doesn't like it."

"Well I should think not!"

Yarrow stuffed another bite of sandwich into her mouth, chewing thoughtfully. "I wonder where my Joni is this day. She would like to eat."

"Oh really?" Grady asked.

"Yip. Joni sometimes talks about food to help her tummy feel full." None of us quite knew what to say to that. "My Joni is very good to me. She doesn't let Bong and Moon, Skitch or Roscoe hurt me."

"Have they tried to hurt you?" Mother baited, fearing the answer.

Yarrow didn't answer the question directly. "One time my Joni took me and we sneaked away when it was dark."

"And?"

"Bong found us. He said we couldn't leave because my Joni was too sick. He put a shot in her arm and dragged us back to The Clacker."

"The Clacker?" Grady looked puzzled.

"Yip. We live in The Clacker. When my Joni comes back myself will show it to you."

Uncomfortable silence followed, and I soon took Yarrow by the hand and we loaded more hay. By three o'clock our yard was as good as it could possibly get. There wasn't a wayward blade of grass anywhere! Dad was sprucing up the house's trim with a fresh gallon of exterior paint, and Mother, Allyson, Aunt Aura Leigh, Dori Jo, and Celia drove down to Siskin's Hardware for some more summer bloomers and planting pots while Grandma and Aunt Aubynn painted Grandma's porch railing.

Wyatt shuffled restlessly from Grandma's front porch. I was glad our friendship was patched up. I went in search of Dad. "Can I take Wyatt and Yarrow up to Grady's place? I want to take Yarrow swimming, and it would be good for Wyatt to do a little something—besides nothing."

"That kid has been all summer healing," Dad agreed. "Go see if Allyson has an old swimming suit that's the right size. If not, a little sun suit should work."

I found a small blue swimming suit with a little ruffled skirt. I told Yarrow to go into the bedroom and put it on, and she came back out with it stretched over the top of her farmer clothes, and on backwards, to boot. "This isn't *conshtrable*," she complained.

I grinned at her mispronunciation of *comfortable*, but I had to agree. It did look a might awkward! I told her to go back into the room, take all of her clothes off and try again, turning the suit around the other way. She did, and mostly got it, only having one arm jutting out of the neck hole. I helped her readjust and we went out to the car. She was excited that her boy could drive.

"It's clean in here," she observed, eying the interior of the Buick suspiciously. We drove up the road and unloaded in Grady's driveway. He made a beeline for us, grinning to see Wyatt and I together, and also to dote on the black-eyed girl.

"Hi Old Mister, myself came to see you already! Did you been missin' me?" Grady took her hand and led her into the smallest soaking pool. It didn't take Yarrow long before she splashed and kicked and blew bubbles out of her mouth and nose into the water. Grady had her well in hand so Wyatt and I set out for the island in Grady's boat. It was good, and although we were hesitant at first, we were soon talking and goofing in the old way.

"Avery Anne Applewhite has been to see me three more times

this summer," he confessed. "Geez, it's embarrassing when she comes, but she's sort of...cute, too." He gulped and his Adam's apple worked against his throat.

I nodded, understanding Wyatt's predicament, feeling a wee bit envious of Avery's attentions. "She's not annoying like Margo and some of the other girls."

"I'm embarrassed to tell you this, but...I like her."

"I liked her in fifth grade. She's cool." Wyatt grinned, grateful that I understood and didn't pounce all over him for liking a girl. "But she's a little bit fickle, so don't feel bad if she likes some other guy by September."

"Oh, I won't. We're just friends, anyway."

Right. Friends. That's why he was going into a holy confessional with me. "When do you get the bandage off of your eye?"

"Next week, if the doctor thinks it has healed well enough."

"I'll bet you are excited. It's been a long time since you've been able to look out of both peepers."

"Wesley, are you going to get to keep Yarrow?"

"I hope so, but Dad says not to get my hopes up."

"No?"

I shook my head and we sat in silence for awhile. "I wonder why Grady prayed for her to come to my house."

"Mark, John, and I talked about that the other night."

"Yeah?"

"Grady's the man, that's all. We don't know why he would have prayed like that otherwise."

"He *is* the man...he's the man that called me a jerk last night."

"Oh yeah?" Wyatt laughed.

"He called you one, too."

"I know. I talked to him on the phone. He hung up because he said somebody was knocking at the door. I suppose it was you."

"That's kind of funny, Wyatt."

"So, if you get to keep Yarrow that means God really listens."

"I guess it does."

"So maybe Grady's prayers about my dad will be answered too; you know—that he'll soon be able to come home to us." Wyatt started wiping tears. "I hate the war!"

"Me too."

"I just wish I knew how to be a better boy so God would want to answer my prayers."

"Is that why you're so mild—most of the time anyway? You weren't too mild with me last spring—but usually you're the perfect lamb."

"I guess it is."

"That's as good a reason as any."

"He's been gone longer than his tour of duty already."

"So let's go on a Spirit Quest like the Indians used to do! We'll hike into Washakie Fork, fast and pray, and see what happens."

"Just the two of us?"

"Yeah."

"Can't we just do that *here*?"

I couldn't help laughing at his hesitation. "I guess we can, but that's more like just being angelic at home, not really a *Spirit Quest*, I'd say."

"You're whacked if you think I'm going camping in Washakie Fork, *alone* with you. Monty Quinn spent one night on the ridge with you, and got scared out of twenty years of his life! No way."

My head bobbed with the humor of the whole situation. "Well, I went back up there by myself night before last."

"You did not!"

I nodded, making the motions of our secret handshake. "I did."

"Why in the name of Pete would you do that?"

"I needed to—I was wondering about Yarrow."

"What does she have to do with Washakie Fork?"

I told Wyatt how it all went down. He was flabbergasted that I stole Grandpa's truck and dared drive on top of Gallagher Ridge in the middle of the night! "Did you keep the truck doors locked?"

"No. I climbed right out and invited every ghost in the place to come do business with me."

"Jump back," Wyatt said, disbelieving.

"Scout's honor."

"What happened?"

"Nothing, for a long time. Just the rattling whispers of the wind. And then I saw a fire burning in the clearing."

Wyatt clamped his hands over his ears begging me to tell no more tales. "You're giving me the creeps! You really are the hero type, and I'm okay with being a sidekick, Wes. I'm the kind of sidekick that doesn't do Spirit Quests. If you go back you'll have to go alone."

"Sometimes the Lone Ranger rides alone," I goofed.

"Shut up, Kemo Sabe."

We motored back to the dock. Grady and Yarrow were fishing by the side of the lake. Yarrow was wrapped up in one of Grandma Addie's crocheted afghans, looking content in the peaceful surroundings. "Hello, my boy! There's a fish down there and we're gonna catch it."

I nodded, hoping the line would bob. It did, and Grady helped Yarrow reel in a nice trout. She squealed and squealed. "This is for my Joni! She likes fish, I bet."

Grady helped get the hook from the fish's mouth. "Good job, Golden Fawn." Wyatt and I were surprised. Grady faced our silent inquiries. "She reminds me of my little girl—the one I didn't get to know for long enough. I'm glad I'm still here and getting acquainted with this one."

Chapter Twelve

Yarrow twirled around and around, squealing in front of the mirror. Mother drove us to Logan for some city shopping, claiming we needed new duds for Aunt Lace's wedding. Yarrow was wearing a spring green dress with tiny yellow rose buds and a frilly white pinafore. She was so cute—I shuddered to remember the awful T-shirt she was wearing when she came to us. I didn't know how Mother would ever bear giving her up now…after four days.

Allyson donned a dress in matching fabric, but more grown up of course, and minus the pinafore, for she was nearly ten. Her eyes were shining as well so I assumed that shopping for clothes was a lot more fun for girls. Personally, I hated it.

"It's my wedding dress," Yarrow cried to the sales associate at ZCMI. The woman smiled and brought several boxes of shoes for Yarrow and Allyson to try on. Yarrow danced with every pair that slipped on and off her tiny feet. "Oh, these make my toes happy!" She spun and twirled, and the sales lady was getting a real kick out of her enthusiasm.

"My goodness, haven't you ever tried on shoes before?"

"No, she hasn't," Mother replied.

"Myself doesn't remember any shoes before my boy took me for foods," Yarrow rattled.

The sales associate let it drop.

Allyson fell in love with a pair of white sandals with a one inch cork heel. I knew she thought she was getting away with high heels in them, for most of her shoes were flat. She kept turning one direction and another, checking out the shoe from every angle. Her eyes were shining and her heart was set.

"I would rather you chose a flat heel, dear. You are apt to turn an ankle."

Allyson smiled, "Please."

"But," Mother sighed, "Since your *favorite* aunt only gets married once, I suppose we could make an exception."

Yarrow pranced around and around in the new white patent shoes. "Myself can dance with these on!"

"We'll take the Mary Jane's," Mother said to the clerk, pointing to the shoes on Yarrow's little feet.

Disappointment clouded Yarrow's face. "Myself doesn't want Mary Jane to have *these* shoes!"

The sales lady clucked, "Well for pity's sake…I've never heard anything so darling in all my life!"

Mother scooped Yarrow up, explaining that the shoes were called Mary Jane's, but they would belong to her. A big smile covered Yarrow's face as the realization donned on her.

"The shoes are Mary Janes?"

"Yes Yarrow."

"Look My Boy," Yarrow called, pointing to one foot and then the other, "this one's Mary and this one's Jane!"

"Why are you spending money on her if we don't know if we get to keep her?" I asked Mother, near her ear while Allyson and Yarrow chose hair ribbons and sox.

"Because she is mine for today, Wesley."

We ate lunch at Dee's drive in and Yarrow was delighted to have another cheeseburger and some French fries. She wrapped most of her fries up in a napkin. Mother asked her what she was doing.

"Myself is taking these fries for my Joni. She is going to have so much foods when she comes to get me!"

Mother's lips pinched into a tight line. Until she knew the fate of the little girl, she didn't dare say anything, but she sighed beneath the weight of needing to.

I wasn't picky. At JCPenney I opted for the first pants, shirt, and tie that Mother made me try on.

"Wesley, are you sure? There are some nice blue pants over there."

"Nope. These are fine."

"Because we could do the light green shirt with the blue pants as easily as those tan ones."

"Are you crazy? I *love* this outfit," I said sarcastically, parroting Allyson's typical girly comment.

Mother's eyes rolled but she went along with it. "Yarrow, don't you think Wesley looks handsome?"

"Not as handsome as Allyson and myself."

I got a kick out of that and had to agree. Personally, I don't know why everyone has to dress in matching colors at weddings! I imagined the whole bunch of us walking around like a goofy rendition of *The Partridge Family*, minus the stage.

When we were all done shopping, Mother drove us out to Willow Park to look at the animals and play on the slides. Yarrow scampered along, chattering, brimming over with the wonders of life beyond The Clacker. She fed the fish in the lake, saying, "They aren't as good as Old Mister's fish. See? They look sick."

I got a bang out of that. "Why Yarrow?"

"They got spots in the wrong spots."

"They're German browns."

"Myself likes rainbow fish better."

"Rainbow trout?"

"Yip. That's it."

The festivities of the next day were tiresome. Several times I snuck away from the reception and mish mash and went home. I didn't dare stay away for long as my aunts kept making a headcount every so often. There was dancing after sundown. I spied Wyatt dancing with Avery Anne Applewhite and I nearly fell down at the sight. Mark and Michelle Voss were dancing a little too closely, and I saw Aunt Aubynn looking a bit concerned a few times. Monty and Shaylin were still wrapped up in each other and I was left to wander over to John's side.

"Is it bedtime yet?" He asked.

"I'm afraid not."

"I don't go for this type of thing."

"I don't blame Grandpa for celebrating though. It's high time Aunt Lace moved out."

John grinned, "By the way, you look smashing in your pale green shirt."

"Thanks, I like yours as well—it's perfect pastel!" We had been complimenting each other all day, using phony British accents. "I also find your tan trousers to be quite dashing!"

"By Joe! You, Wyatt, and I look like a set of mismatched triplets, I must say old chap! One is pale, one quite tall, and the other most scrappy!" Then John shed the accent, asking, "Wanna hit the hot pots?"

"You think we can slip away?"

"Mom's got other things to worry about," John said, throwing his head in Mark's direction.

We walked out of the yard without drawing notice from any one. We took Aunt Aubynn's car and drove away. Suddenly John got the giggles.

"What?"

"We'd better go decorate Mulligan's car. I don't think anyone has."

"They were leaving it at Mulligan's house so it didn't get toyed with," I said.

"Exactly."

The Ford looped around in the road and drove back toward Shamrock Lane. Sure enough the 1972 Oldsmobile was parked in his driveway. We sped on by, stopping in at McCarthy's Market for some stuff. John had fifteen dollars in his wallet and we blew most of it on string, Kool-aid, Oreos, whipped cream, balloons, and a twenty-five pound bag of rice.

I separated the Oreos, sticking them all over the windshield while John frosted the car with whipping cream. It looked quite delicious. We dumped twenty five pounds of rice inside the front and back seats, and then finished stuffing the car with blown up balloons. I found some pop bottles in Aunt Aubynn's trunk, and shoved them up the tailpipe so Mr. Mulligan's neighbors would know when they left for their honeymoon, no matter how late it was. I unscrewed the license plates and remounted them upside down, chuckling over the pleasures of such a sport. We tied some old tin cans to the back of the fender, wishing we had the heart to just chain it to the garage door or something, but we didn't.

John dumped the packets of Kool-aid into the wiper fluid tank. I thought that was especially creative, and could only be owned to the fact that he was well-read. "That a good one," I commented and John giggled. Yes, we both were, for boys definitely knew how. Then we hightailed back to the dance, milling around, purposely bumping into people so that we had an alibi.

I wanted to tell Monty what we'd done, but he and Shaylin were gone so I drank some more punch, had one more piece of cake, and then took a seat next to Grady on the patio.

"Hi Grady."

"Where have you been?"

"Oh just around."

"Uh-huh," he said, sounding unconvinced. "I hope nobody did anything to Melvin's car—because he and Annelaise are taking

Riley and Cora's to the airport instead, and Riley will be driving the Oldsmobile while they are gone."

Whoops.

Grady studied me. I was trying to seem unconcerned. "Riley will tan somebody's hide if he has a mess to clean up."

Um...

I twisted uncomfortably in my chair. "Well, it was nice talking to you, Grady. I guess I'd better go see what John's doing over there."

I made it to him just in time to see Aunt Lace toss her expensive bouquet of roses. Celia clamored to catch it, but Michelle Voss beat her to it, and Aunt Aubynn paled significantly. Then the newly wedded couple drove off in Grandpa's Plymouth looking blissful and starry-eyed.

"Whoops," John said.

"Um..."

"Well, now what?"

"I dunno but I'm glad we didn't chain the bumper to the garage door."

"Me too."

Aunt Aura Leigh began bossing us all to fold up chairs. The guests filtered away before they had to help with the clean up, and the night was shot before we could go back to Shamrock Lane and undo our deeds.

I slept well in spite of my shenanigans, and by morning light, mostly managed to forget about it all. The phone rang at seven thirty and I answered.

Grandpa Gallagher's voice said, "Wesley, come with me this morning. I've got to do a health check today with the brand inspector. We won't need to take the truck. I'll have you drive me over to Annelaise's new place and I'll pick up their car. We'll take it."

Whoops.

I dressed in feelings of dread that morning. It was *unconshtrable*, like a backwards swimming suit stretched over farm clothes, really I'd say! With my neck and head feeling like they were sticking out of an arm hole, we drove over to Mulligan's. Grandpa saw the car and groaned. "What in the Sam Hill! I expressly told Melvin to leave his car home so this *didn't* happen!" He heaved an exasperated breath.

"Perhaps too many people know where he lives, though," I suggested hopefully.

Grandpa was muttering. He found a stick and wiped off the windshield on the driver's side. "I'll just clean this up good enough to see out of, he said." He opened the door to climb in, but couldn't. The interior was smooshed to overflowing with balloons. "Oh for Hell's sakes," he stirred, getting angrier by the minute. He started pulling them out and throwing them on the cement. A few popped in his haste, and I saw cross-eyed Delma Jean Connor peer out of her living room window to watch, being neighbors and all. I secretly wondered if she saw *two* Oldsmobile's and *four* guys in the driveway next door.

After Grandpa got the balloons pulled out of the driver's seat, he swore again. "Rice? Who in the *blankety blank* thought of this? There's gotta be fifty pounds of food storage all gone to waste in here."

Wrong. Only twenty-five, but I didn't say anything. Grandpa climbed in. "Wesley! Follow me back home. I'll have the Finnegan boys wash this car. We'll have to take the truck anyway."

I was climbing in when I heard the commotion. And saw it. Oh my! Someone had chained the bumper to the garage door, and Grandpa pulled away, not noticing. The bumper stayed on, but the garage door was now lying on the driveway and Delma Jean was fluttering with excitement from a nearby window. I suddenly knew why Monty Quinn wasn't still at the dance when we got back last night. I'll bet he never bargained for this!

Grandpa Gallagher climbed out of the Oldsmobile, red faced and mad as I'd ever seen him. Interesting language, both colorful and diverse, flowed into the bright sunshiny morning. I'd never heard such a unique array of adjectives, adverbs, pronouns, and dangling participles. The fact is, his sentences would have been impossible to diagram. Grandpa was livid! Delma Jean must have heard the cussing, for her mouth dropped into a large, gaping O.

"We'll have to fix this later. Come on Wesley; follow me back to the house. We're late!"

I did as he bid, wanting to shriek with laughter at the sight in my rearview mirror, the garage door was bent and crumpled, lying in a heap behind me.

That's when I saw what was in front of me. Grandpa hit the switch to the wiper fluid, wanting to clear his view a little better. Cherry colored liquid sprayed against the glass, smearing with Oreo remnants, making a thick pasty substance. The wipers worked the muck like a mason spreads mortar. Grandpa nearly ran off the road before he could stop the car. He climbed out, kicked a tire, huffed and puffed, while I watched from a safe distance. He wiped off the windshield the best he could while yelling, "What in the hell is that?" He smelled his sleeve. "Cherry? Cherry! I'm gonna kick some butts until heads roll," he proclaimed, and I believed him. Just then a bottle belched out of Mulligan's tailpipe. It shot like a missile, straight back at me, knocking a headlight out of Dad's Buick.

Whoops.

Chapter Thirteen

The next day was Sunday. Allyson and Yarrow wore their new dresses to church. Yarrow was excited to see what church was all about, and I have to admit, it was more fun than usual. The song leader mesmerized her, and Yarrow's little arm fluttered in time with the chorister's. *"Then wake up and do something more,"* we sang, *"than dream of your mansion above! Doing good is a pleasure, a joy beyond measure, a blessing of duty and love."*

"We never sang that one it The Clacker," Yarrow whispered to me.

"What did you sing?"

"I know *Puff the Magic Dragon* and *The Yellow Submarine*," she said.

I'll just bet.

Yarrow sang the tune around the house all day. "Then wake up and do something more!" She piped loudly, and would then forget the lyrics and just make stuff up until she hit the chorus again.

Dinner was at our house that afternoon, and Monty and I grinned when Grandpa Gallagher rehearsed his anger over Mr. Mulligan's car for the nineteenth time. John nudged my foot beneath the table and I felt so welded to him now. Getting into mischief together is the stuff good friendship is made of, apparently.

Everyone left at four, and at four-thirty Pistol Stewart knocked on our door. I felt sick inside, and Mother asked Allyson to take Yarrow over to Grandma's for a visit. "Well folks, how are things going?"

"Fine, come in." Mother was tense and she was pinching her lips together until they were nearly white. She was going to fly all to pieces if he took that kid away.

"I appreciate you keeping Yarrow," he said. "As far as we've been able to tell, she's got a grandfather still living.

Mother's eyes closed and her chin trembled. Dad put a soothing hand on her shoulder. "Go on."

"But he's ninety-eight years old."

Mother's eyes sprang back open and she took a breath, feeling suddenly hopeful. "Yes."

"He's a great grandfather, really, and probably too old to care for the child."

"Probably?" I asked incredulously. "There's no *probably* to it."

"But he wants to come meet you folks before he decides anything."

"Of course! When?"

"*Sometime.* That's all he told me," Pistol said.

"But he can't *possibly* see to the child," Mother said.

The sheriff nodded, "He has never laid eyes on her either, but he wants to see for himself where she has landed."

"But you did put in a good word for us?" Mother asked again. "I mean, you did tell him that we would love to keep her?"

"Shannon, I did. I said all of that."

"And?" She persisted.

"He said he would come, *sometime.*"

I wondered if a ninety-eight year old man could live until *sometime* came. "But I don't understand. Joni Whitecliff told Grandpa Gallagher that she had parents."

"The old man claimed they were killed last summer in a car accident in Wyoming. I'm sure the girl never knew they were dead."

Pistol shook my parents' hands and left. I wanted to jump for joy at the news. I would worry about Yarrow's old grandfather sometime, *another* time, and I ran over to Grandma's to share the good news.

"Can she be ours?" Allyson asked when she saw me burst through the door. Yarrow was busy playing with modeling clay in the kitchen.

"At least for now," I said. "She can stay until her old great grandfather comes to meet us."

August crowded into July and the hills were the color of faded straw. Yarrow's clothes now hung in the closet like a permanent resident of our household. One day I went to call her in for lunch. She was standing on top of a big rock in our yard.

"Yarrow? What are you doing?"

"I'm just watching down the road for my Joni. I thought she would be back."

I closed my eyes, wondering what to say to that. "Well, maybe she's decided to let you stay with us. We love you so much."

"I love you, my boy. But my Joni would like it here, too. She could stay here with myself and Allyson and you."

I nodded, lifting her down from her perch. "Guess what Yarrow?"

"What?"

"I think your name is beautiful."

She laughed. "You want myself to be called Heather."

"Not anymore. Yarrow is lovely. It's my favorite girl name in the whole world!"

"Myself likes it very goodly, too!" And she skipped ahead into the house.

Yarrow had been with us for a month. I was starting to feel confident that she would always be with us, ever hopeful at least. I was at Grady's zapping hotdogs when a man stepped to the counter and ordered one.

I turned around, spying him suspiciously. He was ancient, with long white braids that hung past his belt. He wore a snazzy Johnny Cash style black western shirt; open at the throat, and a buckskin vest with intricate beaded detail along the pockets. A large belt buckle held his Levis up, and he sported snake skin boots. He wore copper bands around each wrist, and several chains hung around his neck, including a bear claw necklace. I spied two or three rings on his leathered bronze hands. He smelled of tobacco and sen-sens.

"It's fifty cents for the hot dog, a buck if you want a soda and chips."

He tossed a crisp bill in my direction, eyeing me closely. "That's highway robbery, aint it boy?"

Considering the century he must have been born in, I had to agree. "Welcome to 1973."

"Inflation is a damn nuisance," he said.

I nodded again, shuffling uncomfortably before his searing, black-eyed gaze.

"Boy, you remind me of a little white fart I used to know."

My eyes sprang open, but my mouth stayed shut.

"You don't happen to be related to Kell O'Rourke, do you?"

"I do. He's my great grandfather, and this is his place."

The ancient smiled. "Ha!" He blasted. "This used to be *my* place! I used to swim here all the time."

I didn't know how to answer that. Grady built this place from scratch, but this was one old guy, so...

"You're a likeness of Kell, right down to your plucky manner."

Plucky manner? "Well, thank you. Yeah," I went on, "this is his place. I'll get him for you, if you want."

"Kell's alive?"

"I couldn't go get him if he wasn't."

"You're Kell's, alright—just as plucky, just as strutting, and cocky as a rooster." He paused, silently gauging me. "I like you, boy. I will call you *Little Irish*."

"Why?"

"Because we called Kell the *Big Irish*." I laughed at that, never having heard that nickname before. "I take it you're Shoshone?"

"I'm Kell's brother-in-law."

Awinita's brother! Suddenly the swirling stories came into focus. This old relic was a piece of Grady's past. This man had once worn buckskin leggings and feathers in his hair. He had hunted, fished, and camped in Washakie Fork. Perhaps he had once made arrowheads by the fire. He'd slept in tipis and lived the tribal customs of old. He had been born in a time of great change, and he had seen it. From the nomadic traditions of his forefathers, to the era of space travel and moon buggies, he had seen it all. I wondered at his thoughts as he witnessed the demise of yesterday. Of all the changes that had rolled across our nation, possibly none were as great as those born by the Native Americans.

"I'm Wesley Gallagher." I put out a hand.

He took it, laughing at me. "Gallagher? So the Irish are all still bottled up, I see. I repeat: I will call you Little Irish."

"Then what may I call you?"

"Howahkan."

"If you'd like to sit down I'll go get my Grandpa." I pulled a chair out for the man and went in search of a less ancient old guy.

Grady was mopping around the pools, keeping the boardwalk swabbed up and safe for walking. He smiled when he saw me coming. "Awinita's brother is here," I cried, not waiting to make small talk.

"Surely not Howahkan?"

"Yes, he's here!"

"I thought he was dead twenty years ago."

"He was surprised to hear you were among the living as well."

"Well I'll be jumped by a pack of bunny rabbits! Call Celia and see if she can come help out."

"Are you going to take Howahkan to your house?"

"Yes."

"I'd like to come."

"Then tell Celia to send Monty up, too."

"When was the last time you saw this guy?"

"1929, and it was such a disappointment. The Shoshones came that year in cars, and stayed in my cabins. No more horses or tipis, or doing things the old way. I was busy keeping things in order and didn't have time for social calls."

I jogged back to the boathouse. Howahkan was bent over some new fishing reels, whistling *"Bye Bye Miss American Pie."* That wasn't exactly the tune I was expecting.

"You know that song?"

"Listen Little Irish, I've got a radio."

"We can go see Grady—I mean Kell, just as soon as my cousin gets here."

"Who invited you to this pow-wow?"

"The Big Irish."

"Typical—so bossy."

"You don't mind do you?"

"Not really." A hint of amusement played against his wide-set mouth. I thought he might be the handsomest ancient I'd ever laid eyes on. His looks were typical of most natives. His forehead was high and I could envision a headband encircling it very well. His cheekbones were also high and well pronounced. His nose was one to be proud of, too, and a hollow beneath his bottom lip gave his chin character. In his day he must have really turned heads, for I noticed him turning many now. His features seemed chiseled, like a fine carving.

"It's rude to stare." His words startled me and I flinched, searching his expression to see if he was angry or not. He was smiling.

"I like to look at you."

"Am I an enigma, a haunt, or just a pleasant threat?"

I didn't know what enigma meant, and I'd seen better haunts, alright. He was too old to scare me much, so I answered, "A remnant of the past," I suppose.

"You make me sound as if I am the lone buffalo."

Celia docked the boat. She'd been across the lake cleaning cabins. "I'm here," she called. "Monty's coming. I'll keep an eye on the boathouse and the lockers until he comes."

Her eyes noticed the man standing next to me and she stared. She had lots of questions, but choked them all down and went to work. I led Howahkan past the locker rooms, hot pools, and over to Grady's house.

Grady opened the door and I stepped past him into the house. The men stared at each other for several minutes. "You are shrunk, Kell! You are not Big Irish, for Little Irish is bigger than you!"

"Winter shriveled me down to size, but I am still strong, and if you slap me about, I will not cry."

Howahkan laughed, and it was deep and gravelly. "Are you still sulking about that?"

"No, but neither have I forgotten."

"I had to make sure you were man enough for my sister."

"And so I endured it without kicking the living daylights out of you."

Howahkan laughed again. "Kell," he said, opening his arms. My great grandfather stepped forward, and the men embraced each other roughly, pounding each other on their backs. Then Howahkan sat down in Grady's recliner and kicked his feet up for a visit.

Grady went into the kitchen and brought back a cola and a platter of cookies, offering them to his guest. Howahkan grunted. "No beer?"

"Not here."

"Not yet?"

"Not ever."

"You don't have much longer to find out what you've been missing out on," Howahkan said, smiling. He eyed a cookie suspiciously. "What is this?"

"It's a Snickerdoodle."

"Real men don't eat *Snickerdoodles*." He heavily emphasized the word, finding it funny.

"It's really sweet," I interjected, reaching for one myself.

Howahkan jerked the plate away from me. "Perhaps in this case I will make an exception," he said, grabbing several.

Grady sat next to me on the couch. "What business brings back to Three Lakes Valley?"

"Must I have business?"

"Not necessarily."

"Then do not be so nosy, Big Irish."

"But if you have no business, then was it business that has kept you away for so long?"

Howahkan looked up from his cookies, and his eyes narrowed at Grady's question, careful not to step in a verbal trap. "My business is to mind my business, and business is brisk!" He smiled, seeming pleased with himself.

"How have you been? It's been many decades."

"I dare say it has, and life is hard, but as you can see, I am still here, so it can't all have been bad." Howahkan smiled impishly, adding, "And I see you are still here as well, so it can't all have been good, either." Grady didn't laugh. He wasn't feeling jovial, merely reflective. Howahkan seemed interested in the response. "Do not start crying or I shall slap you."

"Awinita was always worth having to put up with you."

Howahkan tilted his aged head back against the chair, laughing heartily. "Little Irish, this is a good man," he said to me.

"Are you two friends?" I asked.

"I respect the Big Irish. I do not love him."

Grady blustered back, "It is better to be respected than it is to be loved."

"But we both loved the same woman, and that is enough perhaps," Howahkan persisted. "You just wait, Little Irish—when some dude comes stepping around, making his play for your little sister. You have one, I presume?"

"Yes—Allyson." I truly considered his words, and my ire rose just thinking about it. It was true, I felt protective of her, and would gladly feed some guy a little dirt to protect her. I said so and Howahkan and Grady got a kick out that. Then I considered my little Yarrow. I'm certain that there couldn't be a fellow anywhere who would dare come around if I was home. "So, fill me in here…you slapped Grady?"

"Who is Grady?"

I pointed at the man next to me, and Howahkan seemed perplexed, so Grady sang out, "Some grandpas are good, and some grandpas are great, but I'm so good I'm *greaty* great. Hence the shortened version: Grady."

Howahkan's eyes rolled. "You are a braggedy, braggedy man, Big Irish."

"And you are arrogant and proud and have always gone stomping around doing just as you pleased."

"Back to the subject," I invited.

"Yes. Big Irish came and waded in the water with us. I saw Awinita making eyes at him and knew she was interested. *Hmph!* The next night Big Irish came walking into camp, just as brazen as you please, as if he was invited." He gazed at me for a second, adding, "Kind of reminds me of you."

"So then what?"

"Awinita grabbed him and they disappeared into the night. I wanted to follow with my tomahawk, but Grandfather wouldn't let me. But after Awinita slipped back by the fire, I dodged away, following the Big Irish to his barn. He pulled the saddle off of his horse and I cuffed him once."

"Once?" Grady's brows were high.

"I slapped him once to get his attention and then a few more times so he knew I was serious."

"About what?"

"My sister, you little green horn!"

"Oh."

"He slapped me forty times; I swear to you, I was nothing but handprints for a week."

"Kell never cried out, and didn't fight back either, although his cheeks were red. He was mad! Ooh, was he mad! He bore it though."

"Then what?"

"He came back the next night, letting me know he was serious about my sister, too. You've got to respect a guy who staggers back, knowing what the odds are. I don't know why Awinita looked twice at him though. His lips were cut and swollen, and one eye wouldn't open."

"I came back to prove I was bigger than you were."

"Yeah, Kell's the Big Irish, after all!" Howahkan taunted his brother-in-law with a cruel and haughty laugh, but then he sobered. "You impressed Grandfather, and that's all that mattered. The Big Irish was nothing if not brave."

And so conversation played back and forth like that for a couple of hours. Finally Grandpa asked, "Why are you here, Howahkan?"

I knew why. He was here to take my little Yarrow away, and I would not let him. I said as much and both men studied me.

"You know about the girl?"

"Yarrow has been staying with us."

"And?"

"Finders keepers."

The silence was heavy. Grady wasn't breathing, fearing I'd really gone too far, piping off to one as proud as Awinita's brother. He was also astonished at the connection of Yarrow to his beautiful bride of long ago. I felt like the silence might deafen me, and so I broke it, saying, "Howahkan, you can slap me, beat me, cuff me, kick me, and leave me for dead, but please don't take the girl." The silence returned, settling like a blanket on the room.

"I don't take orders from a sprout."

"If you have to take her then also take me. I can tend her and then she won't be a problem for you."

Howahkan sneered at my words, wincing backwards, as if he could never saddle himself with the burden I would bring. A leathered hand wiped across his eyes, and he suddenly seemed sullen and tired.

Grady's tone was quiet, but he said, "Be still, Wesley."

I bit my lips together, but I could feel blood throbbing in the vessels of my neck and face. Perhaps I would have a stroke. Wyatt would always wonder what happened to his best cousin.

"You are a damn Indian," Howahkan finally said to me, shaking his head. "I don't usually see such tough stock among the whites."

Then Grady let out a shaky breath, and I myself took a gulp of air, feeling hopeful again of making it home with my scalp, among other things.

"Let's make medicine by the fire in Washakie Fork," Howahkan suggested.

"Don't be a fool. We are old men." Grady said.

"You couldn't make medicine when you were a *young* man," Howahkan laughed. "You nearly choked to death, unable to speak, and unable to walk properly! Haw, haw," the ancient teased. "One puff, that's all it took."

"I don't smoke," Grady said defensively.

Howahkan laughed again. "How about you, Little Irish?"

"Are you talking about smoking peyote?"

The old man scowled, and lines rippled across his high forehead. "Hmph! *Hollywood,*" he scoffed. "Take me to the Fork," he asked Grady again.

"I don't drive well anymore."

"Then lend me a horse. I still ride every day."

"Wesley will take us. We'll leave in the morning."

"We're going camping?"

"I need to go back," Howahkan said. "We'll see if we can make medicine."

I didn't know exactly what that entailed, being so polluted by Hollywood and all, but it sounded like a great adventure to me. I didn't know many white kids that took a real Shoshone with them to a place called Washakie Fork, but I was feeling hopeful about peace talks around the fire. I would try my hardest to be brave for my Yarrow.

It was an interesting conversation with my parents that night. Mother didn't understand why Yarrow's grandfather didn't just come to the house for dinner. "It's kind of a native thing, I think." I didn't explain Grady's connection to Howahkan, other than they'd known each other in days gone by.

"How long will you be gone?"

"I'm not sure."

"School starts in September."

I laughed at Mother and gave her a quick hug. "I will convince him to leave her here, Mother, and it shouldn't take me four weeks to do it."

I packed some clothes into a duffle bag and rolled my sleeping bag into a tight bundle.

"My boy is leaving?"

"Hi Yarrow. I'm going camping with Grandpa Grady and his friend."

"If you see my Joni, bring her home with you."

I closed my eyes for a moment, wondering what to say, and knowing this must soon be resolved so we could all move forward. Yarrow needed to know that her Joni wouldn't be coming to live with us. "Yarrow? Do you want me to read to you?"

She grinned and dashed to the bookcase in the hallway. She came back with *The Poky Little Puppy.* She leaned her head against my arm as I read, pointing at the pictures. Her hair smelled of apples, and I couldn't help noticing how clean her tiny hands were. I was thankful that she was here, nestled next to me, instead of rattling around in the back of some crowded, filthy clacker.

"I love you, Yarrow."

"Myself knows that."

Chapter Fourteen

We were set to leave Grady's at ten the next morning. Mother scowled as I climbed out of our car, not trusting this whole operation. "Don't worry," I soothed.

"You're not supposed to be driving yet—not here, let alone all over in the hills!"

"I'll be careful."

"Be sure and invite Yarrow's grandfather home for dinner. I just don't understand the need to romp around like ruffians from a century ago…and remember who you are!" I smiled at that, grabbed my gear, and shut the door.

I drove up Gallagher Canyon with my two doddery charges. One was ninety-eight, and the other ninety-two, respectively. I was only eighty-six years younger than Howahkan, so I figured we shouldn't have any problem with a generation gap. I had to chuckle at my thoughts.

I rolled onto the top of Gallagher Ridge. Grady told me to stop and he and Howahkan climbed out. They cast their eyes in every direction, soaking in the view, remembering the vistas from days gone by.

"What do you think, Little Irish?"

"I think this is the end of the rainbow."

Grady chirruped at my answer, saying, "I should say it is! And I say so myself!"

"My people loved this country," Howahkan agreed. He chanted something in the Shoshone tongue, but it was foreign to me. *"Tsaangu beaichehku, Tsaan dai neesungaahka."*

"What did that mean?"

"Good morning, all is well," he translated.

When the old men were ready, we got back into the truck and meandered off the ridge. I got the shivers when I passed the hallowed place of the spirit's visit to me. Down we went into the grove of trees where Grady camped with us last summer.

"This is where I first proclaimed my love for Awinita," Grady explained.

"Spare us the details, old man," Howahkan grumbled, but his smile told me he was only kidding.

"Oh my Awinita," Grady said again, clouding up. "I thought I told her goodbye last year. I did not expect to come back."

"Do not cry, Big Irish, for soon you will tell her hello. Stop the truck," Howahkan barked to me. I did, and again he climbed out. He walked over to a stump and listened as the August breeze danced through the aspen. The rattling whispers swirled about and Howahkan was lost in the listening.

I walked down to the creek and fished while the men talked of olden times, golden times, and what was wrong with the world today. We were going to hell in a hand basket. Traditional values from every culture were being eroded like friction to sandstone. In our quest for equality we were losing our identity. "The evil one hangs a shroud over Mother Earth, blinding the people to the goodness of the sun," Howahkan said prophetically.

"The kids today," Grady began. I listened to the banter, sometimes hearing, sometimes losing the murmurs to the loudness of my own thoughts. "…but I told my grandsons last summer that the whispers of the past are urging them to reflect, respect, and remember."

"That is right," Howahkan agreed.

I reeled in a couple of nice fish, baited my hook and let my line whiz again. A horsefly bumbled against my shoulder and I squashed him. "I hope my kids just hold on," Grady was saying. "I love my family so much, and hope they all make it through the sludge. Life's not simple—the waters are polluted and not easily chartered."

"Bring back the buffalo, and with them the traditions of my people! Bring back the campfires and the ceremonies. Bring back the freedoms of this land. Bring back common sense!"

"Amen to that, brother."

Another fish bent my pole and I reeled in again. I thought about casting my line for another one, but didn't want to face Howahkan's heat for wasting anything. Mr. Despain had schooled us well on native culture and beliefs, and I knew that I must not shame Grady by being greedy with my fishing. I cleaned them and walked back up to the grove. Our fire ring was still undisturbed from the summer before. I piled wood and struck a match while the men talked. I got a cast iron skillet from the back of the truck and found the container of flour. I rolled the trout and started them crackling in the pan.

The aroma was tantalizing and soon Howahkan came over to the pan to inspect his lunch. He smiled. "I see the creek is still full of Tsaa-Baingwee."

"Tsaa-Baingwee?"

"Trout, you little green horn."

"Lots of trout."

"Do you like fishing, Little Irish?"

I nodded. "Of course. I like doing lots of things. I never want to live in a city. I belong here."

"Where?"

"Right here in Washakie Fork."

"Why?" Howahkan persisted.

"Because of the meaning of my name—Wesley means *west meadow.* This is the west meadow from Gallagher Springs, is it not?"

Grady laughed, surprised by my knowledge and willingness to

impress Howahkan, but Mr. Despain said Natives appreciated the meanings of names, and every name had a meaning.

"Little Irish, you have big ideas," Howahkan said pleasantly.

We enjoyed our Tsaa-Baingwee and Grady and Howahkan stretched out for a nap after lunch. I cleaned up and went to inspect me and Wyatt's construction site from the summer before. A few bits were left. I restacked the twig houses, and rebuilt the fences. I found a stick and pushed dirt back into place, recreating roads and bridges. A breeze stirred the leaves and shivers spread down my arms. I remembered my solo jaunt to the top of Gallagher Ridge last month; of seeing the fire burning again in the clearing. I thought of the smiling old Indian spirit, and of Grady's prayer for another child to come to my family. I wondered about all of it—and I couldn't believe Yarrow's coming was a mere coincidence.

I felt eyes on me, and I looked up from my play. The handsome figure of Howahkan was looming over me, smiling. "What are you doing Little Irish?"

"Nothing," I said, feeling ashamed almost, for playing.

"You drive like a man, and speak like a brave. You cook like a squaw, but you play like a boy."

"I am a boy."

Howahkan smiled gently. "Yes, Little Irish, you are for a fact, but I think your spirit is older than others your age."

I wondered about that statement for the rest of the afternoon and asked Howahkan about it later. "Your heart is mature," he said. "Who knows for sure, but your spirit could be older than mine."

We drove to the clearing. Howahkan's eyes surveyed every fire blackened circle. He walked the length of the clearing and back. His feelings were harrowed up, just as Grady's had been. He grasped a handful of soil, lifted it above his head, and chanted, *"Damme sogopeha ne masunga'a, Sogobia, gwiizo 'naipeha nemmi sundehai. Tsaan dai neesungaahka."*

"What's he saying Grady?"

"I touch the earth, Mother Earth, bring life to us. All is well."

"You understand?"

"Just a little."

"I recognized the *all is well* part. He said that on top of the ridge when he said good morning."

"We will camp here," Howahkan said.

"But..." I started to say, remembering the blazing phantom campfire that I had seen burning on two occasions. I felt a little nervous about it, but let it pass.

"But what, Little Irish? Speak up!"

"This ground is hallowed."

His brows rose expectantly. "Yes."

"A campfire sometimes burns here."

"What do you mean? Stop talking in ridiculous riddles, you little white fart."

"A campfire burned here last month. Yarrow had just come to us, and I wanted her to stay. I could tell she was native so I borrowed Grandpa Gallagher's truck, and drove to the top of ridge and asked the spirits to let me keep her."

The black eyes narrowed down, and Howahkan's neck was ramrod straight, as proud he stood, not wanting to be trifled with. "What do you know of spirits?"

"When we camped here last summer, I awoke to an old Indian kneeling over me. He chanted something strange. I was frightened and ran away."

"So why did you come back?"

"I just wondered if he could pull some strings somewhere." As I stammered out an explanation, I noticed Grady's eyes bulge from his head. He was not privy to my midnight adventures of a month ago. "Howahkan, when I pray, I pray to God, and not to men or spirits, but I just needed them to know I believed Yarrow was a gift, a blessing.

I requested to the night and everything that had ears to listen, that I wanted to keep her."

"Sounds like you came to make some medicine of your own. What kind of a Little Irish are you, anyway?"

"I dunno, sir."

"Don't call me sir. It makes me sound pompous and white." We laughed together and the trees whispered harmoniously. "And what was your answer?"

"I heard the trees rustle, but I did not know the answer—and then I saw the fire."

Howahkan nodded. "My name means *mysterious voice*. I belong here too Wesley, and perhaps I can understand what the whispers say."

I set up camp to the men's orders. Howahkan did not take to so much fuss. He didn't think we needed the comforts of home. I didn't cotton to the idea of sleeping under the stars again, and I think Grady understood. "Set a tent up for me, Wesley. My bones would shrivel in the open air."

"It already looks like you were born in a whirlwind," Howahkan said smugly.

I set up the tent and unrolled our bags. I brought a foam pad for Grady's bed and snuck it beneath his blankets without Howahkan's notice.

I was starving by the time night fell. It seemed that Howahkan didn't merit much supper, but Grady told me where to find some bread. I made a sandwich for us and my stomach was grateful.

"Any more Snickerdoodles?" Howahkan asked.

Grady grinned at me, telling me where to find them. That's what the ancient had for supper—six Snickerdoodles and some sage tea.

The campfire popped and smoke curled toward the stars. The sky was brilliant that night. We heard a coyote mourn from a neighboring ridge. I wondered if he was truly howling at the moon. Howahkan fixed a pipe with tobacco, and a pinch of sage and cedar. He began chanting, wafting the pipe smoke upward. Howahkan was sending a prayer upon the smoke. I was fascinated and kept quiet, not asking for translations. I didn't want to disturb anything. Howahkan's voice sang out in a clear and haunting tenor, calling the words of an ancient language. It seemed mystical and magical, almost, and I couldn't stop goose bumps from rising against my flesh.

He passed the pipe to me. I didn't know what to do. Mother wouldn't have wanted me smoking, but I was here to make medicine. I looked at Grady while Howahkan continued to cry the words of the prayer. Grady nodded acquiescence to me and so I puffed on the pipe and handed it back to the man with the long braids and beautiful features. Nothing happened—I didn't have a vision, nor even feel dizzy. I said a prayer to God that if smoking the pipe was wrong, would He please forgive me. And if He smiled upon the ancient custom, wouldn't He please answer my prayers. I closed my eyes and began praying for our family to keep Yarrow. I prayed for everyone I could think of, including Aunt Lace and Uncle Melvin! I especially prayed for my best cousin Wyatt. I prayed for his eye, his jaw, and his ribs. I prayed for his father most of all. I prayed that he could come home from Viet Nam. I prayed for Stan Tomkins and what I should do about him. I prayed for Yarrow's Joni, wherever she had gone. I prayed for Grandpa Kelly Sheehan O'Rourke to not be in trouble with Addie when he got to Heaven. I prayed that he could love two women and all of his kids without going to anyone's doghouse. I prayed until the sounds of Howahkan's voice faded into the crackling of the fire. I was falling into deep communion with a higher power, and the experience drowned out the other sounds of the night.

I felt myself stretching into a sacred band, or frequency of speech. My mental tongue was loosened and I prayed about many things at once, thrilling my own heart and stirring my soul with a burning fire. I loved my life, and gratitude burst like a breaking dam, flooding every subconscious level of my being. My spirit seemed to be rising with the smoke, curling higher and higher. My energy finally spent itself out, and the pleadings of my spirit hushed, and then I strained to listen for answers. I heard a faint beating of drums and opened my eyes to a glorious spectacle. Campfires dotted all throughout the clearing. Smoke rose, mixing, and wafting ever upward. The smell was ridiculously good, and with imagination's eyes, I saw the dancing and life from a hundred years ago.

I spoke and the sound of my voice was strange. "Yarrow has been sent to me, protected and cared for all along by unseen power. Awinita has been called to act as a guide for the child, and favors me because of my likeness to Kell. I am the Little Irish. I have been taught to respect God, and to me it is a privilege to reflect, respect, and remember. I have a great love for the Shoshone people, as well as my own."

The night was bigger than I was. It was sacred! I was only a boy, and tomorrow I would play and talk, and act like one. I would do foolish things, and fall into scrapes and mischief, but tonight I was making medicine and it was a powerful thing.

I watched the fires burn all around me until they were only glowing embers, and then I fell asleep by the side of our own campfire. I dreamed of nothing and in the morning Howahkan looked at me strangely. "Boy, when you make medicine, you really make medicine."

I grinned at him. "Really?"

"I only wished I had another little sister, for I would marry the two of you myself."

"I'm not ready for that!"

Howahkan nodded reflectively and Grady said, "Forget what I said about kids today. Judging by this one maybe our nation will stand a little longer."

"I will not call you Little Irish again. To me you are Little Shoshone now."

"Why?"

"I have never heard such words come from one so young."

I bit my lip. I thought I had been praying silently, in my mind. I felt a little bit embarrassed and I said so.

Grady said, "Wesley, last night you uttered phrases in English, Gaelic, Shoshone, and I don't know what else."

"And I thought *I* was Howahkan, the mysterious voice. I had but to interpret yours."

I didn't understand! The frequency was gone, but I felt a huge amount of respect emanating my direction from both men. I would try hard to be good all day and not ruin it. We drove to the cabin, and Howahkan looked upon his sister's old home, as well as her final burial site. "You named your daughter the English interpretation for her mother's name?" Howahkan asked Grady.

Grady nodded. "Yes, we called her Fawn."

So that's what *Awinita* meant. I smiled and looked wondrously at the tribute of feathers fluttering from the headstones.

To my mother's dismay we were not gone for a month, only one night. Howahkan said he didn't need to make more medicine, for anything less than last night's dose would seem like a sugar pill. "No need to make placebo. I got plenty of medicine already."

"Mother wants you to come home for dinner."

"She does not need to bribe me. Although I thought I would take Yarrow and place her with another granddaughter, Gloria, I believe she is better off with you, the Little Shoshone. I cannot argue with Awinita's will—and I never could, otherwise she would not have married *him*." He jutted a thumb towards Grady.

Tears coursed down my cheeks, and my legs felt weak. I sat down suddenly, feeling no support in them. I buried my face in my elbow, crying shamelessly. "Thank you! Thank you!" I sobbed with relief, with gratitude, and I could not hold it back. "I love you Howahkan!"

I expected him to take a swipe at me, to sober me and wise me up, but instead he reached down and jerked me to my feet. One arm reached around my shoulders, and he hugged me saying, *"Tsaan dai neesungaahka."* All is well.

I couldn't quit tearing up, not all of the way home. Grady made small talk to ease my emotional come-apart. Once in a while he patted my knee, saying, "The Lord hears and answers our prayers."

We got to Grady's and I skinned into the house not wanting anyone to see my bee-stung eyes, for they were *not* sexy. Howahkan eased himself back into the recliner. "I'll take a beer now, Kell."

"Not here."

"Not yet?"

"Not ever."

"You are stingy, Big Irish! I've just given you my great granddaughter."

Grady laughed and Howahkan joined in. Grady retrieved a Pepsi Cola from the fridge and a Hershey bar from a drawer. "Will this do?"

"You can always bribe me with shoog," Howahkan said, using the broken English word from days gone by. "You brought us a hundred pounds of sugar once. Old Grandfather kept saying, "Shoog. Shoog! The Big Irish is always good for shoog." Howahkan's head bobbed pleasantly at the recollection. "But…the Big Irish never brought us any beer."

"Washakie didn't want his people to drink—he claimed that was the behavior of the Arapaho, not Shoshone."

Howahkan nodded his head. "And Brigham did not want *your* people to drink—he claimed that was the behavior of the gentiles, but come now Brother—surely you must admit to cheating a few times over the years."

"I haven't, personally. It has always been a goal of mine not to break promises to myself like a common hypocrite."

"But many Mormons have celebrated well; honoring the grain that good beer is made of."

"So?"

Howahkan grinned mischievously. "I long to be like *those* people."

I was getting a kick out of their banter. "I'll give you a beer, Howahkan."

I thought Grady would pass out at my bold declaration. "Wesley! You certainly will not!"

"I will too! Howahkan has given little Yarrow to me, and he can have whatever he wants!"

Howahkan whistled between his teeth, interested as all get out. "Little Shoshone, where will you get your beer?"

"I can't tell you."

"Why not?"

"Just because—but if Grady will let me take the Studebaker, I'll be back in just a minute."

Howahkan grabbed twenty dollars from his wallet and threw it down on the coffee table. "I'm betting against you, Little Shoshone! I don't think you have a clue in hello mighty where to get one."

Grady was stupefied and didn't know what to say. I jumped in the truck and drove down Gallagher Canyon, turning on Gallagher Street. I slipped into the back door without anyone even knowing I was home. I grabbed some money out of my bank, from my summer hot dog sales, and then I went to the Fat Shamrock. Suzy Tomkins was pushing a maid's cart down the hall. I grinned at her. "Hello Suzy." She had always been friendly to me in the olden days when Stan and I were friends. Of course those days were gone now, but she still looked genuinely glad to see me.

"Wesley, what are you doing?"

I pressed a fifty dollar bill into her hand. "Will that help out with things?"

Her chin trembled, seeming surprised. "The children are hungry—how did you know? And why?"

"I've really been given a precious gift today and I needed to share. The only problem is I need to get my hands on a beer."

"Oh Wesley, don't start that! It's a terrible habit and leads to drunken behavior and trouble."

"It's not for me, Suzy."

"Who then? Mrs. McCracken?"

"It's for an old Indian man. I just want to be hospitable."

"Aldean is passed out in the front room. Just go in the kitchen door and take what you need."

"Thanks Suzy."

I drove to the Tomkin's place. I felt nervous, but did just as Suzy told me to do. I opened the kitchen door. Jamey was playing with a toy car on the floor, staring wide-eyed. I winked at Stan's little brother. I put all of our left-over food into their fridge—what we hadn't eaten on the camp trip; cheese, bread, Snickerdoodles, sodas, eggs, syrup, and grapes, for Grady had supplied us for three or four days, at least. Then I swiped a six pack feeling well justified. Aldean couldn't go ape over finding it gone, for surely he'd think he drank it already. I handed Jamey a cookie. "You didn't see me," I said.

He smiled delightedly at the treat and said, "No I didn't."

I was back at Grady's place twelve minutes later. I handed Howahkan the brews and he bellowed with laughter to see what I had produced in so short a time.

"I shudder to ask where you got that," Grady said dryly.

"I thought this stuff was illegal in Utah," Howahkan teased, slapping his leg with pleasure. He cracked a can open, making a great sport of drinking a beer in Kell's house. "To the Big Irish!" Howahkan toasted. He took a few swallows. He lifted the can again. "To the Little Shoshone," he said again. "To making medicine!" He lifted the can one final time before draining it. "To the damnedest kid I ever saw!"

"To the damnedest kid with the biggest heart, the stiffest lip, and the strongest backbone," Grady agreed. "Of course, of course, he *is* a perfect likeness of me."

I picked up the twenty dollar bill eager to recoup part of my losses. "Come to dinner with me Howahkan."

"I will and I'll bring the Big Irish with me. For many decades we have been brothers."

Chapter Fifteen

Grady sent me home in his truck. I walked in the back door. Yarrow saw me this time and came running. "My boy!"

I picked her up and kissed her head. She was clean and precious, and worth the world to our family. She was a gift—and I'd earned her!

Mother looked concerned when she saw me. "Wesley! You've been gone only a day and a half!"

"I promised I'd be home in time for school," and I laughed because it was only the seventh of August.

"Well?"

Tears streamed down my cheeks again, for I was about to deliver the best news of my life and I couldn't contain my feelings. Mother saw my emotion as a bad thing and nearly flew all to pieces before I could settle her. I reached out and steadied her by the shoulders, giving her a little shake. She was stunned by that, and with her eyes wide open and looking at me, I said, "She is ours."

Well, I've never said a better thing! Mother did the same thing I had done earlier in the day, and sat right down on the floor, weeping and laughing. Allyson and Yarrow ran into the kitchen to see what terrible thing happened to Mother. Mother grabbed both girls, pulling them down to the floor with her, hugging and kissing them both. "Yarrow," Mother said, "You get to be our very own girl now. You must call me

Mother, and Mister is now your Dad. Wesley and Allyson are your brother and sister. You are part of our family."

Allyson cried too, so happy was she, and she twirled all over the kitchen doing a dizzy dance. "Wesley, you're my hero!"

"My Joni is part of our family too."

"Yarrow, I need to tell you about Joni."

"Myself is listening."

Mother grabbed her hand and led her toward the picture of Jesus in the front room. "Do you remember me telling you about Him?"

"Yes. He's Jesus. He's nice."

"That's right. He is taking care of Joni now."

"Because my Joni is sick?"

Mother nodded. "Yes."

"Will Jesus ever bring my Joni back?"

"Yes, when He comes again, He will, but that might be a long, long, long time."

"Myself will be old then?"

"Perhaps."

"Oh. Will Jesus give my Joni foods?"

"Yes."

Yarrow smiled. "And a bath? And can Joni have a bed?"

"Yes."

"Awe," Yarrow sang happily, "Jesus is *so* nice! And Jesus is so ni-i-ice." Yarrow spun around with Allyson. "I get to be here always! This place is as good as Jesus' house, Allyson! Myself has a bed, and a bath, and foods, too!"

Mother nodded again, and that was it. Yarrow was fine with her Joni's new address.

I drove to Grady's place at six to pick up Howahkan and Grady for supper. They climbed back into the truck with me. "We are like the Three Musketeers," Grady said.

"You're white," Howahkan grumbled pleasantly. "The Little Shoshone and I are musketeers, and you alone are one of the Three Stooges. Haw! How does that suit the Big Irish?"

Grady didn't answer.

"Howahkan, how did you get to Gallagher Springs, anyway?"

"A granddaughter brought me. I made her drop me off at the resort. She will pick me up in a few days."

"Joni's sister?"

"Yes."

"Is she a hippie?"

"No, she is a nurse."

I thought about the difference in the girls. "I'll bet you are proud of her then."

"I am. Gloria is a fine woman. She's the oldest girl of my youngest daughter, and Joni was the baby of the bunch. She was always a good girl, but she got running around with a damned idiot from Jackson Hole. He was a one-man walking catastrophe! He was on drugs, and in to the new scene; a real side show. Joni ran away with him and his flea bag friends. That was a dark day in our lives. We haven't heard from her in four years."

"How old is Yarrow?"

"Gloria traced a birth certificate to a clinic in Casper. She'll be four on September fourth."

"Will Gloria be sad that you've given Yarrow to us?"

"Probably, because she is a woman, and they are strange where children are involved, but she will respect my decision."

"Tell Gloria that she is welcome to come and visit anytime."

I pulled into the driveway. Howahkan's eyes looked around the yard. "Nice," he said. Of course it was still spruced up from Aunt Lace's wedding, and Howahkan was impressed.

I led him into the house. Yarrow came running to give Grady a hug. "Old Mister, myself will call you Grady now." She stopped short, eying the ancient Indian suspiciously. "Who are you?"

"Howahkan. I am your grandfather."

"*Another* grandpa?"

"I've come to see if you are happy."

Yarrow's eyes glistened and she pranced happily. "Myself gots a bed and I scrub and scrub and scru-u-bb in the bathtub every day! Myself thinks that is so happy! And myself gots a boy and an Allyson!"

Howahkan reached out a hand and shook Mother's and Dad's. Grady made the introductions and then we took our places at the table. Mother had outdone herself. The table was set with a juicy beef roast, mashed potatoes and gravy, Yarrow's personal favorite, along with sliced tomatoes, fresh cucumbers, corn on the cob, and baking powder biscuits.

"Our family knows how to eat well," Grady said after the blessing on the food.

Allyson stared at Howahkan the way I must have at first. Her eyes were large and she was mesmerized by his features, braids, and mannerisms. He stared back at her, trying to shame the girl into looking away. "It's rude to stare," he finally said.

Mother fluttered about, trying to make excuses to lighten the situation. Howahkan raised a leathered hand to shush her, and she stopped short, choking off a word in progress.

"But I like to look at you," Allyson said. "I wish I could take you to Show-and-Tell."

Howahkan's smile spread. "And why is that? Am I an enigma, a haunt, or just a pleasant threat?"

Allyson's eyes blinked, trying to process the meaning of her choices. "You're just really *old*," she said to Mother's dismay. "And really beautiful."

"I do turn a few heads," Howahkan boasted. "I am not shriveled and white like some old farts I know." He threw a playful elbow into Grady's side.

"Did you two play together when you were younger?" Dad asked, being woefully ignorant of so many important things.

Howahkan's brows rose. "Boy, you are not made out of the same metal as your son."

Dad paled and Mother's cheeks flushed. They didn't know what to think about Howahkan. They did not know how I had wooed him out of Yarrow. They did not know what to say.

"I'll bet you couldn't make medicine by the fire if you tried," Howahkan went on. "You'd better spend some time with the Big Irish, here, and learn some things," he said. "Either that, or ask the Little Shoshone. He can fill you in on a lot of good tales."

Dad took a bite of potato, not sure how to answer. "Of course," he said simply.

"But I like you, Bill."

Dad looked up from his plate expectantly. "Yes?"

"Because you've taken good care of the Big Irish's land and stock, and you've provided well for your family. You've married a beautiful woman with good sense, who can cook, and more importantly, she has taught the Little Shoshone how to pray and *be* somebody. The Little Shoshone has represented you well, and his light illuminates you as a good father, a good man."

Wow. The only thing Dad could do with all of that was chew on it. Mother smiled at me.

"And if you slapped my dad forty times, he still would not cry out," I boasted.

"Why would he slap me forty times?" Dad was incredulous to most of the conversation.

"He slapped Grady forty times," I said, giving only enough information to make Allyson's chin drop, Grady chuckle, and Howahkan smile.

"Shannon," Howahkan continued, "you must be a hell of a woman. You've got the best kid, here. He's been taught a thing or two, and no doubt that's your fault. He has respect and good sense. He knows what he believes in, but he's not close-minded either. He made medicine with me by the fire last night. I know you people don't use tobacco, but the Little Shoshone was courageous enough to honor my custom of prayer. He opened visions for us last night." Now Mother chewed on that! I was afraid Howahkan was working on getting me grounded for life, but he said, "Because of this kid right here, and *no* other merit, Yarrow will stay."

"I am so thankful to hear those words," Mother said. Her eyes were teary and her voice sincere.

"I ask only one thing in return."

"Anything!"

"Do not be so quick to answer that," Howahkan warned sternly.

"Anything, Howahkan, I mean it!"

"Give the boy to me."

And then we all saw that Mother meant *anything* but that. Her chin trembled. "What?"

"Where sacrifice is requested, sacrifice must be made. The boy offered himself to me."

Howahkan wasn't playing fair. I simply asked that if he took Yarrow, would he also take me, so that I could watch after *her*. He was mixing it up and pushing Mother's buttons in a serious way. I heard Grady click his tongue to the roof of his mouth. He was as entertained as ever he'd been a day in his life.

"I cannot give you my son!"

"That's selfish, Shannon. I just gave you my girl."

Silence. Nobody even chewed for several long minutes. Howahkan waited.

"But—" Mother's tears were spilling down her cheeks now, for Howahkan required too much of her.

"And my stubborn mysterious ways are proof enough that you should always admire the Little Shoshone's ability to make medicine with me."

"Yes, but—"

"Yes but nothing! Appreciate this boy, damn it! His spirit is old, like the great ones. I will not take him from you, although it would have been fair. And now you will always know how difficult a thing you have asked of me, to give up the girl."

Mother was sobbing softly, relief washing over her like the tidal wave on *Hawaii Five-0.* "Thank you Howahkan!"

"But, whenever I request it, the Little Shoshone must be sent to me for a visit."

"Yes!"

"And if I come back here he must be given permission to drive me all over hello mighty, and wherever else I might want to go."

"Yes."

"And he will be allowed to bring me beer and shoog, and make me comfortable."

"Wesley does not have access to beer."

"The Little Shoshone is craftier than you give him credit for."

That's it. I'm grounded until I'm fifty...

"Yes," Dad said, answering in Mother's behalf.

"Good. It's finished, pass the gravy."

That was the meal to end all meals. After dinner we walked into the living room. Gabe Fleischer, a lawyer from Eisner, came and adoption papers were drafted. The legal fees were going to be staggering. I went into my room and grabbed my hot dog money. I returned to the living room with the full sum of it. I handed it to Dad.

"Wesley, what is all of this?"

"Four thousand sixty-one dollars, minus my tithing money."

"Where did you get this?"

"Wages from Grady's, Grandpa Gallagher, and hot dog sales. Business has been brisk."

"You've sold four thousand hotdogs this summer?"

"No, more than that," Grady offered. "That's just his profits."

"What in the Sam Hill?" Dad sounded like Grandpa Gallagher just then. "Why am I breaking my back raising cattle and hay when there's money in hotdogs?"

Howahkan tipped his head back and laughed, it was loud and gravelly. "You don't know what kind of a Little Shoshone you're doing business with," he cried.

"Wesley, I'm not going to take your money," Dad said.

"I want you to."

"It's the sacrifice, don't you see?" Howahkan explained. "What don't you people understand? There's no such thing as something for nothing in this world. The Little Shoshone petitioned the Heavens and was granted the blessing. Now he will sacrifice the fruits of his labors to pay for it all."

"Of course," Dad whispered hoarsely.

"The median wage in America is only twelve thousand per year. The Little Shoshone has made a killing in two months. How much have you made Bill?" Howahkan asked tauntingly.

"My dad is a good worker," I boasted, defending him against Howahkan's verbal cuffing.

"Be still, Little Shoshone," Howahkan reprimanded. "I'm making sport."

Papers were signed and Fleischer left. Yarrow sidled up to Howahkan with a story book. He lifted her onto his lap. Several times he kissed the top of her head while he read to her, and the sight was poignant. He would have been a very good grandfather to her, and we felt his sacrifice keenly. Yarrow pointed to different pictures, asking cute questions and making precocious comments. She held one of Howahkan's braids in her dimpled hands, mindlessly tickling her own cheek with it like a feather.

She fell asleep in the ancient's arms. He studied her face and kissed her softly on the forehead. He handed her to me, saying *"Tsaan dai neesungaahka."* All is well!

Chapter Fifteen

Aunt Aubynn was pale and wiping tears with the backs of her hands as Grandpa read the telegram. Uncle Aiden had been rescued from a war prison near Hanoi, and would be returning stateside after spending eighteen months in captivity. The house was deafeningly still with gratitude for several seconds and then it exploded into hearty cheers of thanksgiving. Mark and John leapt around, shrieking hallelujah while Wyatt burst into tears. He hadn't been able to do much since the beating. His eye patch was now off, but movement jarred his head with splintering pain and so he was very careful to walk and move cautiously.

"Tsaan dai neesungaahka," I said to myself. I was relieved for the Finnegan's.

Amid the jubilation of hearing good news, I noticed Wyatt's body shaking uncontrollably. "What's the matter?"

"My dad," he chattered. I called for Aunt Aubynn to come.

"Wyatt! What's wrong with you?"

His skin was ice cold and clammy. "My dad," Wyatt said again. He shivered and shook and couldn't seem to stop. His lips were turning an odd black color.

"Is he in shock?" Grandpa Gallagher was concerned. He knelt down by Wyatt's side. The bunch of us was still again, being upset by Wyatt's spell. "Get me some salt water, now!"

I scrambled to the sink, being Grandpa's vetinary apprentice and all. We must save the lamb! I dumped a tablespoon of salt into a cup of warm water and stirred it up. Grandpa propped Wyatt's head up, gently supporting him while the boy sipped the salt water, but the shaking was intense. Suddenly Grandpa scooped the boy into his arms and ran for the door, saying, "I'm taking him to the hospital!"

Aunt Aubynn and Grandma Gallagher followed them to the car. Aunt Aubynn sat in the backseat, cradling Wyatt's head and he was tucked in with several heavy quilts. Grandpa backed out of the driveway looking tense and driving fast.

That put a damper on the celebration, and we all paced, concerned over the frail boy. Grady kept clicking his tongue, saying, "Poor Wyatt's had one shock too many this year."

At ten o'clock Grandpa finally called. He said Doc Hooper thought the boy had suffered a serious nervous breakdown. His nerves hadn't yet recuperated fully from his brush with Stan Tompkins, and his body went into a meltdown, with his adrenals pumping out more adrenaline than he could handle. Doc Hooper sedated Wyatt with heavy tranquilizers and he was sleeping, but Doc wanted him to go to Primary Children's Hospital in Salt Lake City for an evaluation.

"Poor Mom," Mark said to John. The three of us walked into their bedroom. "I don't suppose this would be a good time to tell her Michelle is pregnant."

John slapped his forehead, "Mark! You idiot! What were you *thinking*? Don't answer that—because you weren't thinking."

I was thunder struck, unable to say anything of value. Mark was seventeen, and just beginning his senior year. Mr. Voss taught math to the junior high and high school students, and I was afraid to face him now—after Mark had knocked his daughter up and everything. I knew he liked her a lot, but I didn't know he liked her *that* much!

"What are you going to do?"

"Marry her."

John hissed out a disgusted breath. "What?"

"I *will* marry her."

"You're a kid, you dough head!"

"I'm as old as Grady was when he married Awinita."

"Yeah, but life was different then! You can't just move to the hills and live off the land anymore. It's against the law."

I scowled, wondering if it really was against the law, for I'd considered it myself.

"I've talked to Grady. He's going to give me lots of hours at the place and he found an old Dodge Dart for six hundred dollars at the dealership in Eisner so I'll have wheels."

"You're a lame-O!" John cried. "You're a doofus and scruff! I can't believe you are bailing on me this way!"

"But if I don't I'm bailing on Michelle, and I won't do that to her."

"She could put the kid up for adoption."

"She doesn't want to! Seriously, I'll work this out. We're getting married."

"Dad's going to tan your hide when he gets home!"

"He's been gone—and it's been a while since I've answered to him anyway."

"You're killing me here!"

"Sorry John."

"It's embarrassing!"

"I'm not the first one to put the cart before the horse. That's what Grady says."

No wonder Grandpa Grady's hair was white and he was shrunk and puny. He was the one to bear everyone's problems, it seemed. I wondered when he'd been hit with this news and asked.

Mark looked at me for a moment and said, "The night before that old Indian showed up."

I wondered if Grady had prayed at the campfire too. Surely it was a mixture of all our prayers that made the best medicine. "It will be okay."

"Thanks Wes." Mark smiled at me although he looked defeated. He was scared and he had every right to be.

"You won't live to see Dad again," John continued. "Once Mr. Voss finds out, you are a dead man."

Mark nodded, looking grim. "I know that."

Wow…so many problems…I thought of Howahkan's words. Happiness and good news was granted on one front, but the reward carried the penalty of Wyatt's breakdown, apparently. And I didn't know what to think about Mark. His life had suddenly become very complicated.

"Where will you guys live?"

"Mrs. McCracken has an apartment for rent above her garage."

"You would live *there*?" John was crazy eyed.

"She only wants fifty dollars a month rent."

"On hard terms! She's a whack-O."

"It's not too bad. Of course, the couch converts to a bed. There's mostly just the one room."

"One room?"

"And the bathroom."

"Outside?"

Mark laughed wearily. "No dumb-dumb, it's inside."

"Sounds great," I smiled weakly. To quote Howahkan, there's no way in hello mighty that I'd ever live there!

"I'll graduate next spring, and then we'll go off to college or something."

"Will you enroll the baby as well?" John asked sarcastically.

"Um…I'm not sure."

"This is ridiculous!"

Mark sighed and leaned against the wall. "I'm sorry nothing will ever be the same again, John."

"I wish they would." John didn't look up. He rested his face in his hands as the Carpenter's crooned, "*Yesterday Once More"* on the radio.

September rolled around and we said goodbye to summer with a birthday party for Yarrow. She had never known what a birthday was before and danced and pranced excitedly with each present. The Quinn's and Mulligan's came, as well as Grady, Grandma and Grandpa Gallagher, and John. Aunt Aubynn was still in Salt Lake with Wyatt, and Uncle Aiden was not home yet. As best as we knew, he was recovering in the 95th Evacuation Hospital near DaNang, close to the South China Sea.

Monty went back to the U for another year of higher education. Mark stepped in, filling his place at Grady's, as business was still busy. Mark was working every spare minute, and I knew why, but the heavy secret still rested with John, Grady, and I, because Mark hadn't been able to come forward yet, not wanting to trouble his mom.

Wyatt wouldn't start school with us again. He was having a real challenge. He was receiving some kind of treatments in Salt Lake City, but the doctors didn't think he was ready for school. The neurological damage was worse than originally thought. I would start junior high alone, without my best cousin. My heart was heavy and often my guts tied into knots fearing for Wyatt in the long run.

Allyson was worried about fifth grade, but she would be in Mrs. Leison's class, and I assured her it would go well. She had grown two inches over the summer, and she was getting pretty. One day I would hear about some boy trailing her home from school, and I would secretly threaten him, and possibly sneak into his barn and slap him forty times.

"Happy Birthday to myself," Yarrow squealed. She opened a present. "Another wedding dress! Look my Boy!"

"That may soon come in handy," John whispered.

Yarrow started to pull her clothes off in order to put the dress on, but Mother stopped her. "No, we'll try it on later," she explained. "You must keep your clothes on in front of the guests, and finish opening your presents."

"Myself loves birthday parties," Yarrow said. "Let's do another party yesterday."

"Tomorrow," Allyson corrected.

"Yesterday and tomorrow," Yarrow squealed.

That night I dreamed I was in Washakie Fork. I was riding horses with John. We were dressed like Daniel Boon, with coon skin caps and buckskin jackets. We were hunting bears and trapping beavers. We came upon a man, buried up to his chin in the dirt. It was an odd sight, seeing his head blooming out of the ground like a salt bush. We dismounted our ponies to help him, only to find it was Mark.

"You're nearly in over your head," John said.

"Nearly, but not quite."

"That's quite a hole you dug for yourself."

"I didn't bury myself!" He argued. "Mr. Voss did it."

"No," John challenged. "You dug the pit and Voss shoved you in."

My alarm sounded. I grimaced to face the seventh grade and I dreaded the beginning of another year. Yarrow wailed from the house as Allyson and I left that morning. "Please don't go," she sobbed. "Myself wants my boy at home!"

Myself wanted to be home, but I sucked it up and walked to the bus stop on the corner of Gallagher and Main. I saw Stan Tomkins coming my way and my fists clenched before I knew what was happening. I charged him and we rolled head over heels down the street, scuffing our new clothes.

"You dirty rotten, mean, low-down, son-of-a—" *Pow!* He cuffed me in the lip. *Bam!* I punched him in the jaw, wishing to break it. Language was flying, and we were a mass of arms and legs as we rolled and scuffled, wrestling each other on the pavement. Allyson was shrieking, and all of the little Tomkins' brood was bellowing as well, with the exception of Jamey, who seemed to be rooting for me. "You nearly killed Wyatt, you son-of-a—"

I finally got a headlock on Stan, and I was twisting his head down to a more manageable position, bracing my feet against the curb. I wanted to kill him and was wondering just what the best possible method would be. Just then a hot swipe seared against the side of my head, then a strong arm dragged me upward, pulling me to stand. I refused to turn Stan loose, so he rose off the ground with me, and whoever had a hold of me was getting a workout!

"Wesley, turn him loose!"

"He nearly killed Wyatt!"

"Turn him loose!"

"I won't!" I didn't know who had me, but I wasn't giving up.

"Wesley Gallagher, damn you, listen to me!"

I didn't listen and the man's grip slipped from my arm. Stan and I fell back to the ground with a loud thud. The man, *whoever he was*, landed on top of us. My neck was kinked beneath the bulky figure, and the wind was knocked out of me. I had no choice but to finally let go. It was a spaghetti bowl of stray arms and legs and grunting for a minute, until we all got untangled and untied. Stan was wheezing and purple faced. I was gasping for air, myself, unable to suck wind. And some big fella was cussing to beat the band. I saw his shiny tin star as he finally got off of me, shoving his self from the ground in push-up manner.

"Damn you Wesley Gallagher," Sheriff Pistol Stewart spat. "You are coming with me. You too, Stan! You've been back in town for two days and already causing a ruckus!"

Stan wanted to cry foul, but he still couldn't talk and neither could I. We panted like dying dogs on the cement. The school bus pulled to a stop and Allyson and the others boarded the bus, wide eyed, and silent. I saw Allyson's face press against the glass and the bus pulled away, leaving me and Stan to go to the big house together. Pistol's knuckles were bleeding where they scuffed the asphalt as he fell. Blood was coming from my lip and Stan's nose. We sat in silence, drawing wind for a few minutes. Curious onlookers drove by slowly, wondering about the fuss.

"Are you boys breathing good enough to get into my car?" I nodded, ready to get out of the public view. Stan struggled to his feet as well. His windpipe was still a little bit smooshed, I think, because he whistled with every breath he took. "Now have I got to handcuff you two together?"

"No, not unless you want me to finish what I started," I wheezed.

"Stan?"

"No."

"Then get in and try not to bleed all over my seats!" We rode clear to Lakeside, because that's where the Sheriff's office was. I tried not to think about anything, for I refused to cry in front of Stan Tomkins. He glared at me when I looked his way.

It was a long ride, but not long enough. We were soon being herded into the Sheriff's office and my shoes grew heavier with every step.

Deputy Parnell looked curiously at us when we entered but didn't say anything. Pistol took us into a holding cell. It possibly was only a room, but it felt like a holding cell. He stared at us, long and hard. Neither one of us said a word. "Stay here," he said. "And if you move one inch from your chairs, I'll throw you in the slammer."

Stan held a Kleenex against his nose, sopping up blood. I just let my lip bleed, hoping it looked gruesome for my mug shot. If I was going down, I'd go in style, just like one of the bloody Clanton brothers at the O.K. Corral.

Twenty minutes later Pistol came back into the room leading Suzy Tomkins and Shannon Gallagher. Why did he have to drag our mothers into it? I groaned beneath Mother's gaze. Anybody but Mother, and I could have born it—but it would be hard going down in style in front of her.

Mother shook her head, being so disappointed in me and everything. I knew she was sorry that she hadn't traded me for Yarrow when she had the chance. She was sorry that I wasn't living on the reservation with

Howahkan. Making good medicine didn't count for anything here in the sheriff's office.

Suzy was nervously fidgeting for a cigarette, but Pistol told her she couldn't smoke inside the building and she put her lighter away, looking ill at ease. She picked up a pen then, clicking it to distraction. Click on, click off. Click on, click off. Click on, click off. Click on, click off. Click on, click off.

"For hell's sakes, Suzy! Please have a smoke," Pistol grumbled, confiscating the pen.

"Sorry," she whispered, but dug into her purse, frantically producing a cigarette in no time. She lit it and a ring of blue smoke encircled her head. It looked like a sorry excuse for a halo, but then again, this wasn't Heaven.

"What is going on?" Pistol finally asked.

"He charged me," Stan said.

Attention turned in my direction. "Yes, I did. He nearly killed my cousin last spring. I'm not going to invite him over to watch *American Bandstand* with me. Yes, I rolled him."

Mother's eyes closed. Perhaps she would do well to start smoking herself…

"This is the first time you've seen each other since the incident last spring?" Pistol pressed.

"Yes."

"I see," Sheriff Stewart said, clicking the pen of his own accord. "So this has been festering, Wesley?"

"Like a sliver."

"I see."

"I didn't know he was back in town. I can't believe they decided to let him go back to school!" My voice raised an octave and I sounded like Allyson.

"It was the recommendation of the Juvenile Court," Suzy explained, blowing smoke from her nostrils like a dragon lady.

"Yes," Pistol agreed. "They felt that it was important to get Stan back into a structured schedule rather than let him roam wild all over town."

"I *have* to work," Suzy stated, feeling defensive.

"Yes," Mother said, breaking her silence. "Of course, Suzy."

"Well folks, how are we going to resolve this? Because I've recovered my share of corpses this summer, and I really hate doing that." I thought of the hippies floating and dead in Washakie Lake. Poor Sheriff Stewart! "I like both of you boys, and shouldn't like to scrape you up after you murder each other."

"I wasn't *really* going to kill him," I said, disgusted.

"Then why charge him?"

"I told you! I'm sore. I've got to avenge my cousin. Wyatt's wrecked all to hello mighty and not able to come to school or anything!"

Mother's brows shot high. I'd gone off and parroted Howahkan Greathawk right in front of her. Oh well, I was already going to jail, how much worse could it get?

"You didn't need to avenge Wyatt. The juvenile court already did that."

"Well...he needed to know I wasn't gonna stand for his sh—shenanigans, either."

"Stan? What do you have to say for yourself?"

"I'm really sorry."

Likely story! Everyone looked expectantly at me. What? What was I supposed to say to that? I shrugged belligerently.

"I don't understand why you two aren't still friends in the first place," Suzy droned, taking a deep puff on her cigarette. The butt glowed red with the activity.

"We used to be friends," Stan sulked.

"*Used* to be," I emphasized.

"And then Wyatt Finnegan moved into town. No more Wesley! He disappeared to Wyatt's side, leaving me high and dry. No more fishing. No more swimming or boating at Grady's place. No more football. No more nothing! I hate Wyatt because he robbed me of my best friend."

I couldn't believe any of this! "You were still invited! You just treated Wyatt bad and I got sick of your comments and crap!"

"Well, still…you shouldn't have dumped me like that, Wes."

"You should have been a nice guy and you'd have been with us."

Stan wasn't done milking sympathy. "No more going to your house for sleepovers. I like your family a lot. Your dad's nice! Remember that time he took us down to Eisner to see *True Grit*? He bought us ice cream and everything." Stan started blubbering, and bloody snot blew all over the front of him as he cried.

"Yeah, so?"

"I liked your Mom, too! She's the best cook around and she never yells."

"I don't have time to cook much," Suzy said defensively. "And I *have* to yell to hear myself think!"

"Yes," Mother said softly, "of course, Suzy."

"Your Mom used to read to us, remember Wesley? She read *Where the Red Fern Grows* to us underneath the trees in your backyard. Remember?"

"Yes."

Suzy sucked on the cigarette again. "I've never been much of a reader. I aint got time for fantasy or fuss."

Stan ignored her comment. We all did. "Well…Wyatt ruined all of it. No more forts, no more trading stuff at lunch time."

Stan was trying to pack my bags for a guilt trip, but I refused to travel! "If you wouldn't have been mean to Wyatt you could still have hung around with us," I argued instead. Was no one hearing me? Was I talking to the wall?

Stan started sobbing. "I'm really sorry about Wyatt! I'm sorry! My dad was so drunk and mean the night before! He used the crowbar on me and Suzy, and then something snapped, and I just hauled off and used it on him. I don't know why I did it! Just to get Wesley's attention, I guess."

All eyes reverted back to me. "You're dad is not worth much," I said, and Mother kicked me under the table. "I'm sorry he's so mean, Stan. You have it on hard terms at your house."

Suzy's head sank, feeling embarrassed. "Well, he's not *always* mean—I mean, sometimes Aldean's in real good humor." She sucked at the cigarette until I was afraid the whole thing would disappear into her mouth.

"He is not," Pistol argued. "He's a miserable cur, and you really lowered your standards when you fell for him." That did it! Suzy frantically began searching for another cigarette, and the room was blue with pollution already. Even the flies in the window sills buzzed their last.

"I'm sorry," Stan repeated forlornly.

I was sick of everybody and the whole deal. I wished I was living in the Wind Rivers beating up Shoshone boys just then! I wished I was *anywhere* but where I was. Mother kicked me again.

"I'm sorry I started it this morning," I conceded. *Boy was I sorry!*

"And?" Pistol nudged.

"What? I'm sorry we didn't get along after Wyatt moved to town, but he's my best cousin, and I won't apologize for that."

"So now what? Can you two leave each other alone? Can you just make yourselves be invisible to each other? Can I trust you to ride the same bus, and attend the same school without launching into a war?"

"I don't know," I said.

"I'll try," Stan conceded.

I wanted to knock his block off just then, but I let it pass. "I'll try too."

"Suzy, Shannon, get them out of my sight!"

Our mothers whisked us away. Stan whimpered because a beating was waiting at home for him. I was whimpering because I didn't know *what* was coming. We walked toward the car.

"I'll drive if you'd like me to," I offered politely.

Mother's lips pinched together and her nostrils flared. I climbed into the passenger's side of the Buick, realizing my offer had been rejected. Mother was quiet for three miles and then she said, "I'm so disappointed in you, Wesley." That's the worst sentence a boy can hear his mother say.

News travels faster than lightning in a thunderstorm in our town. Everyone knew about our tussle, and when I walked into school the next morning, I was greeted by strange looks and handled with kid gloves. Margo Walsh, Judy Brynn O'Brien, and two of the nine Cindy's stared at me and tittered nervously.

"It's rude to stare," I said, sounding eerily familiar to a ninety-eight year old full-blooded Shoshone by the name of Howahkan Greathawk.

"Um…" They stammered, feeling awkward. More kids gathered around, including some high school students. I detected Celia Quinn in the group.

"What am I, an enigma, a haunt, or just a pleasant threat?" Junior high kids stared blankly, but a few of the older ones snickered. Celia winked at me, chewing on the inside of one cheek, looking amused.

"Good job, Wes!" Miles and Steve, Mick, Paul, and Ross thumped me on the shoulder, and suddenly I felt claustrophobic beneath the weight of so much admiration. "Way to avenge Finnegan," one of the boys said. "How is he anyway? I heard he was nearly dead."

"He's in Primary Children's Hospital, right?" Another voice asked.

Avery Anne Applewhite appeared from nowhere proclaiming her concern. "I'll just *die* if Wyatt's not okay."

"He'll be home sometime this week, but he can't come back to school for awhile."

"That's too bad," a few kids said. Others remarked, "It's good he'll soon be home."

Stan Tomkin's walked into the school. The huddle of students parted, staring him down. Nobody said hi to him. Nobody slapped his back with admiration or congratulations. Nobody said anything. Stan looked bad. Both eyes were black, and I hadn't done the damage. While I admit to possibly dislocating his jaw, bloodying his nose, and squeezing him down in a choke hold, I never touched his eyes.

"You sure gave it to him!" Steve quipped. Kids laughed and jeered raucously, giving me more credit than I deserved.

Stan's eyes were wild beneath the bruises. I realized how hard it was for him to show his face in Gallagher Springs after maiming a mild boy as well liked as Wyatt Finnegan. I knew his heart was hammering in his chest right now, wanting the kids to stop staring. He didn't have anything to say that was clever or coy. He didn't have an old Indian friend, or anybody else in his corner. At best he had a drunken father and an unconcerned, overwhelmed, stepmother. He'd taken a butt whipping from me and had gone home for a worse beating by the looks of him. I found myself doing the unthinkable.

"Stan," I said, surprising everyone, including me and him. "Put 'er there!" I extended my hand. He looked warily at me, expecting a trick. "Let's let sleeping dogs lie," I said, thrusting my hand forward again.

He reached out slowly. Our hands connected and we shook a truce. I didn't want to but I did. His face lit up the wild gleam in his eye was replaced by a jubilant one. "I'm sorry, Wes. I'm sorry everybody."

"Stan and I nearly took a ride to the big house together!" I said. He nodded, smiling oddly.

Silence alarmed teachers for the halls were never quiet before school, and soon several joined the scene, peering curiously over the heads of students. For Stan's benefit, and definitely not my own, I continued, "Stan's well paid for his crimes against my cousin, and maybe we should all just let this drop."

Kids sighed and curious brows rose, not quite expecting what they got. Disappointment was the general feeling, but they couldn't argue.

Stan got his, and they figured I'd given it to him, so there was no use pursuing the matter. The throng disbanded. Still Stan gazed at me and I stared back. Through clenched teeth I whispered, "If you *ever* attack another kid again, so help me Stan, I'll finish our fight."

"I know."

I released his hand and turned away, pitying him, and despising the situation. Mr. Voss was standing right behind me. He reached out a hand, grabbing me by my shoulder. "Come with me, Mr. Gallagher," he said.

I did as I was told, but wondered what on earth my crimes could have been to merit a private conference with the math teacher. We went into his classroom. "Have a seat," he said, motioning toward a chair near his desk. I sat down and waited. I was used to being in trouble as it naturally followed me like a shadow. "Wesley that was an incredibly big thing you just did a few moments ago."

Relief. This conference was a good thing, apparently. "Thank you, sir."

"We just convened a faculty meeting, wherein concerns were expressed over the feared treatment of Stan, after returning to school. We have all been gravely concerned about how to accomplish what you just accomplished."

"What's that?"

"With astonishing ease, you extended a hand of friendship to Stan. It needed to come from you, as the town is well aware of your close friendship with Wyatt. Now the other students may follow your lead and not feel compelled to crucify him themselves. In short, they must forgive him since you have."

"I see."

"I am impressed."

"Thank you."

"I am surprised, also."

"Why?"

"Because of your influence over the temper and attitude of the students. You possess uncanny leadership ability. I've scarcely ever seen it in one so young. I am amazed at your tenacity and spunk."

"Thanks."

"I just want to say, be careful, Wesley. Leadership skills like that can be a blessing or a cursing, depending on which way you go. If you jumped off a cliff the others would follow, and you don't want to be responsible for that."

"Yes sir—no sir." I wasn't sure which answer was correct. "Yes sir, I'll be careful, and no sir, I won't lead anybody off a cliff."

"I'm serious. You must discipline it."

"I'll try."

"It bodes well for Mark to have you as a cousin. I'll see you in fourth hour."

I skedaddled out of the room hoping it still boded well for Mark when Mr. Voss found out what he'd done to his darling little girl. Actually, I still hoped it boded well for *me* when he found out.

Just before lunchtime, half way through English class with Miss Pell, we heard Mrs. Clark's voice over the intercom. "Wesley Gallagher, please report to Mr. Mulligan's office, *immediately*, if not sooner!"

Students looked sideways at me and color crept into my cheeks. Miss Pell seemed intrigued saying, "Wesley, you may go. It's difficult to report sooner than *immediately*, however. Mrs. Clark is silly." I couldn't argue with that. I gathered my books and left the classroom, feeling gawked after.

My folks were seated in Mr. Mulligan's office when I entered. I didn't know what to expect, for good news and bad news slapped me this direction and that lately. I usually had a hard time preparing myself to receive the next pending situation, never knowing what it might be. Yesterday Mother was so disappointed, this morning Mr. Voss had been so impressed, etc. It was hard to know what I was in for this time.

"Have a seat, Wesley," Mr. Mulligan said. I only call him Uncle Melvin in my own mind while making sport.

I pulled a chair out. I looked down at my hands not daring to pre-investigate the predicament by studying my parents' faces. Just then the door opened again and three members of the school board stepped into the room along with the superintendent. Oh no—this *was* bad—much worse than I thought.

"I guess you know why we're all here," Mr. Mulligan began.

"No, I *don't* know, but I feel like the lone buffalo," I said. Everyone laughed at the comment, and so I straightened up a little, not wanting to look like a scruff.

"Boy you do beat all," said Howard Smith of the school board.

Superintendent Cantwell spoke up, "We are here to recognize you for good deeds."

I was shocked and so were my parents! Obviously Mother suspected more trouble, and her face melted into pleasantries then.

Mr. Voss entered the room and explained the situation of the morning. "I was so impressed to see Wesley extend a hand of fellowship to that boy, Stan Tomkins," he said. "He turned the very temper of the student body as easily as one flips a pancake. It was astonishing, and a little heroic, for I know it couldn't have been easy for him to do. Wesley acted more mature than his years and now I don't think there will be any more trouble."

Mr. Mulligan clucked approval, as did the others. Superintendent Cantwell presented me with a certificate. I shook hands around the table. Mother pulled me from my chair with a hug and the men chuckled.

"Oh I'm so proud of you, Wesley!"

I smiled…because that's the best sentence a boy can hear his mother say.

Chapter Sixteen

Howahkan sent for me during UEA, which was our fall break. I was nervous to go, but excited too. Mother was hesitant to let me leave, but she's the one who agreed to Howahkan's request. "Remember who you are," Mother said as I climbed out of the car.

Yarrow was sniffling from the backseat. "Be careful my boy! Myself is missing you so much."

I acted brave and boarded the Greyhound, set for destinations beyond my wildest imagination. The trip to Lander, Wyoming felt long and the bus was hot even though I had my own seat. I closed my eyes for a ways, reflecting on the events of the past month.

Wyatt finally came home from Salt Lake City. He had hypo-functioning adrenals and that meant he had to take hydrocortisone shots and some other medicine to keep his body functioning properly. He was always in risk of having his blood pressure drop too low, and had to take it easy. His headaches were still bad, yet less severe than they had been. He was skinny and pale, and very sober. Instead of scuffling and swimming, hiking and running, we mostly just played checkers and board games. Occasionally we fished, and he always seemed to enjoy the sunshine. He was being tutored at home by Aunt Lace in the evenings. Avery Anne Applewhite visited him regularly, and sometimes she cramped my style, for I now played second fiddle to her in Wyatt's eyes. I rued the day I'd ever led her to him.

Mark went to visit Mr. and Mrs. Voss on the ninth of September. I remember that night very well, as he'd posted John and me out in the yard to make sure he made it out of the house alive. We listened for the violence to begin, but it never did. About two hours after Mark entered the house, he came back out. His eyes were red, so he'd been crying, but he was more relieved than anything.

"Well?" John asked.

"I'm still alive."

"Oh…how did it go?"

"It was the hardest thing I've ever done in my life."

"Why didn't Mr. Voss cream you?"

"Because Michelle kept begging him not to."

"Otherwise?"

"I'm sure he wanted to pound me into oblivion."

"Yeah. I'll bet," John said. "So now what?"

"We're getting married on Friday."

"So soon?" I was surprised.

"Not soon enough." Mark's mouth set in a grim line.

"Yeah."

"I've really disappointed everybody."

"But…you're doing the honorable thing," I persisted.

"I really do love Michelle. I just promised my left kidney to Mr. Voss if I don't honor her forever."

John and I laughed. "Your left kidney?"

"Yes, among other things," Mark chuckled, shaking his head. He heaved a sigh of relief. "Well…that's over. Now I just have to face Mother then clear out Mrs. McCracken's spare apartment."

I'll never forget how pale Aunt Aubynn looked when Mark told her the news, nor how red faced Grandpa Gallaher became. "You dumb-bum!" he hollered. "Your mother has been sick with worry over your dad and Wyatt, and now *this*? Of all the idiot tricks! What in the Sam

Hill were you thinking?" He railed on and on for twenty minutes. "I ought to kick your butt up around your ears so far you'll have to part your hair to use the bathroom!"

Mark bore it. He had no choice, and in the end, he *did* marry the girl. It was a very private ceremony with just close family attending. Grady gave Mark an undisclosed sum of money after the wedding, and my cousin looked relieved. He was lucky to have such a man in his corner. We all were.

We ate cake in the shade of a weeping willow tree in the Voss's backyard. Aunt Aubynn wiped tears, and so did Mrs. Voss. It's a mother thing, I suppose. Our families were cordial and the men visited pleasantly, and I could see that life would go on even though I knew Mark had wondered a few times during the past few weeks.

No matter how mad Grandpa Gallagher was at his second oldest grandson, he handed Mark the keys to his car, explaining that a nice hotel in Salt Lake City was waiting for them for a couple of nights, all paid for. Michelle squealed and the newly-weds left in style with well-wishes from us all. Nobody messed with the car...our backsides were still smarting from the last wedding.

"I guess he'll be grinning in school on Monday morning," Monty quipped. I was too embarrassed to give it much thought.

"What I wonder," Wyatt said, "Is where they'll eat lunch?"

That was a good question, for the boys sat on one side of the cafeteria and the girls on the other. Where *do* the married people go? "I'll let you know," I offered.

"Kid, I'm kind of curious about that too," Monty said, laughing again. "Write me with the details, will you?"

I gazed out the window for a stretch. Wyoming was big country, and it seemed like a long way to where I was going. I couldn't believe Awinita and Howahkan had trailed back and forth between the Three Lakes Valley and the Wind Rivers when they were young. They must have had mighty adventures! I felt like a spoiled white punk for taking the bus.

My stomach tied in knots as the bus chugged into Lander. I grabbed my duffle bag and climbed off the bus at my stop, dreading the uncertainty of what came next. I looked about the milling crowd, trying to find a familiar face. I didn't come up with one and my heart sank. I looked up and down the street, and then settled myself on a bench to wait. I closed my eyes to utter a silent prayer.

"The Little Shoshone looks like Custer as he made his last stand," I heard a pleasant voice call out. My eyes sprang open and Howahkan stood tall and handsome before me. He was smiling. Another native man was just behind him.

I reached out and shook their hands. "I'm glad to see you Howahkan," I cried.

"This is Amos. He's my grandson."

Amos seemed cheerful enough, but didn't say a word. We walked toward a brand new 1973 Dodge pickup truck. It was nicer than anything I'd seen in Gallagher Springs, although I'm not sure what I expected. We climbed into the truck and headed down the Wind River Highway toward Fort Washakie. John Denver's *Rocky Mountain High* wailed from the radio. I saw lots of small, run-down reservation homes, but there were nicer vehicles parked near each one than we had back home.

"There are lots of nice trucks out this way," I commented.

"We've got our level," Howahkan said. "I wouldn't be caught dead in the Big Irish's old Studebaker. Not here. We're proud!"

"I see that," I said, driving past a splintery hut. I did a double take, making sure it was livable.

"That was my place," Amos boasted proudly.

"Oh…"

"I've got two TVs!"

I craned my neck around, trying to get a better look at the ramshackle place. It didn't look big enough for *one*. "Is one of them outside?"

Howahkan laughed at my question, but Amos scowled. "You're dumb."

I was delighted to see a few actual Tipis. One Tipi had a television antennae poking out of the top with the lodge poles. I assumed that meant it was lived in. Interesting. We passed a handful of Indian kids riding bikes. Another boy carried a lamb in his arms. He waved as we went by, and I waved back, wishing I could tell him I was a vetinary apprentice.

We turned onto Deadhorse Road and drove a short distance. We pulled up in front of a little house. It was smaller than Grandpa Gallagher's workshop, but it was clean and well-kept. Feathers fluttered from a gate in front of the house. "Thanks Amos," Howahkan said. We climbed out and Amos chugged away in a plume of dust.

Howahkan kicked a couple of cats off his doorstep and we went in. My eyes worked the room, as I was keenly drinking in every detail of the ancient's dwelling. A cook stove sat against the north wall. A coffee pot was sitting on it. A shelf ran the length of the wall holding a set of canisters. They were just like the ones we had at home, and I was surprised by that. Salt and pepper shakers and a can of Crisco clustered on the shelf as well. I had to smile.

Howahkan watched me. "What are your thoughts, Little Shoshone?"

"Nothing—I was expecting dried strips of pemmican and venison to be curing by the fire, I suppose."

"Amos is right, you are dumb."

I nodded, laughing. My eyes swept to a table and chairs. A plant was in the center of the table, just like home. Little violets crowded the window sills and a John Deere calendar hung above an old fridge. Magnets were stuck all over it, holding newspaper clippings, photographs, and things that were important to the living relic. I was tickled to see my school picture hanging up there next to a Peanuts cartoon.

A rocking chair was angled next to the woodstove, and several hides draped over the back of it. An Indian blanket was crumpled in the seat, and I could imagine Howahkan drinking his tea near the fire, all cuddled up and warm. A stack of Louis L'Amour novels rested on a small stand. He was currently reading *Bendigo Shafter* and I could tell because a feather was stuck between the pages as a bookmark.

"You like westerns?"

"Why not? I'm western. *Bendigo Shafter* takes place near here, in the rugged mountains of Wyoming. He boxes, and I've always admired a man who was good with his fists."

I nodded. "Have you ever read any of Phantom Flynn's novels?"

"Haw!" Howahkan snorted. "Sounds Irish."

"Well L'Amour sounds French!" I retorted hotly.

Howahkan rubbed his chin. "Tell me about him then."

"He writes good stuff, too. I love his books!"

"What are they about? Leprechauns and lucky clovers?"

I scowled at the old man. "No! They're westerns, most of them. A lot of them are about Indians, too. Some of them are tales about fisherman on the open seas, but they're all really good."Howahkan's lips strained into a smile, but he agreed to try one. He was in luck, for I had several packed in my bag.

Howahkan sat me at the table and rummaged in the fridge. "Suppertime," he said. "Would you like pemmican or venison to eat?" He taunted me wickedly while placing raspberry jam and peanut butter sandwiches on the table. They were made of soft, delightful Wonder bread.

"Grady makes his own bread," I said, biting hungrily into the sandwich.

"I'm not a squaw," Howahkan grumbled.

We ate in silence for a few minutes then Howahkan reached over and turned the radio on. "I told you I had one." Cher was singing *Half-Breed*. I'd never listened to the lyrics before.

"My father married a pure Cherokee
My mother's people were ashamed of me
The Indians said I was white by law
The White Man always called me Indian Squaw
Half-breed, that's all I ever heard
Half-breed, how I learned to hate the word
Half-breed, she's no good they warned
Both sides were against me since the day I was born..."

I was thinking about Grady and Awinita's tough struggle, marrying at a time when it was so unpopular, when Howahkan said, "Sounds like your new little sister to me."

"Yarrow?"

"Yes, she's just a half-breed."

"Yarrow is perfect and I don't care."

"What used to be unheard of is popular now anyway. In fact," Howahkan persisted, "The most unheard of things seem to be clamored after."

"Grady and Awinita could be married *and* live in town now."

"Yes, or even here with us."

"They were brave, Howahkan. You know that."

He nodded, reaching for another sandwich. "You know why this jam is so good?"

"Yes I do—because raspberries are delicious!"

Howahkan's shook his head in disagreement. "No. Lots of shoog."

We stepped into a small adjoining room. A couch hugged a wall. It faced a television set. There were interesting things hanging on the walls: Indian rugs, trophy antlers, old muskets, Shoshone spears, a Catlinite pipe, and some photographs. I saw Howahkan's wife and children. He was proud to show me, even eager. An old fashioned photograph in an oval frame sat next to the TV. I picked it up, studying it thoughtfully. A young Shoshone girl peered behind the glass. She was the most exquisite thing I'd ever seen—Monty would have even said she was sexy. Even though the photo was very old, antique in fact, with the image in tones of sepia, I could see the sheen of her hair; appreciate the glow of her pretty bronze skin. Her cheekbones were very high, and her eyebrows were delicately shaped over piercing, dark eyes. Her mouth was pretty and the chin was perfect. She couldn't have been more than sixteen. "Who is this?"

Howahkan didn't answer straightly. Instead the response took a detour of annoying lengths. "One summer we were going about our business. Some green horn from Saint Louis came driving up in a peddler's wagon. I thought he was brazen as all get out, but he claimed to be a photographer. He wanted to take pictures of *"the American Savage,"* as he put it. He showed us samples of his work. He had photographs of Sitting Bull, Chief Joseph, and Geronimo, among others. Many of us were ready to throw him into the Little Wind River, but Grandfather was interested in the camera contraption, asking how it worked. The man showed him, arranging Grandfather on a rock. The man disappeared under a black cloth for several minutes. Finally a loud *poof!* And grandfather was free to wiggle again." Howahkan reached for another photograph on a high shelf. "Here is that photograph."

Goosebumps raced against my flesh! The man behind the glass was the one who knelt over me as I slept beneath the stars on the ridge above Washakie Fork. I said as much, and Howahkan was intrigued, prodding for more information, needling me for details.

I motioned toward the girl in my hands, "But who is this?" I finally asked again.

"That green horn photographer was crazy about the looks of her; he took many pictures of her, and told us they would be printed up in the white man papers and books of Saint Louis, New York City, and other areas. He said she would be the face of the Shoshone. Years afterward, these photos came back to us, mailed from far away. That is my sister, Awinita. She had been dead many years when the photographs came."

Awinita! I stared at her again, nearly croaking that Grady had loved and won such a prize. I gulped heavily and Howahkan laughed. "You look just like the Big Irish used to when she was around!"

"Howahkan, I have never seen anybody more beautiful, and I mean it."

"I agree. That's why I slapped the Big Irish around so hard, for *that* is what he intended on trifling with!"

I nodded, conceding reason behind his actions. "She's the most amazing girl—really!"

"Beauty like hers is rare, but your little Yarrow will look similar."

"Yarrow is cute, but this is something else again!"

"Awinita was *cute* once too. Give Yarrow a little time, and then see what happens, for I'll be damned if the cutest buds don't bloom into the finest flowers."

"Grady doesn't have a picture of her, Howahkan."

"I know."

I hesitated, wondering how rude it was to ask for this one, knowing nothing could mean more to the Big Irish. Howahkan read my thoughts, pushing the frame closer to me. "Take it to him. Kell must have it now, and I've been selfish long enough." Tears bit against my eyelids, for this would be the finest thing he could ever receive.

"They were a handsome match," Howahkan went on. "The Big Irish and Awinita."

"Grady just looks like me...but *me-ow*, look at her! That is a poor match."

Howahkan bent his head laughing heartily. "Do not underestimate your good looks, Little Shoshone. One day you'll cut a handsome figure and then watch out."

Someday. That would be a long ways off.

Howahkan led me into a tiny room, and I mean tiny. It was big enough for a cot and my duffle bag. I'm not so sure it wasn't a closet at one time, but it suited me fine. There was a small bathroom, and

Howahkan's room, and four days to spend together. I stayed up reading one of my Phantom Flynn novels, pushing to finish it so I could begin his newest one, but fatigue crept in and sleep silently stole my sight until morning.

I took a jar of Mother's home bottled plum syrup since Howahkan loved shoog so much. I made pancakes for breakfast and the old man nearly floundered on them. "Your mother will send more if I make medicine right."

"She would send you more even if you didn't."

Howahkan sent me out to bring his horses. I was truly tickled to see they were Paints, as that's what Hollywood told me to expect. I've ridden horses all my life, but we didn't have Paint ponies on our place. It was an impressive thing to see the ninety-eight year old man climb in the saddle. He was half cocky about it and strutted tall and straight in the saddle.

"I didn't ever ride with a saddle until I was eighty. I always rode as I did as a boy, no saddle. I could run by the side of horse and then swing myself onto its back, but I stopped doing that at eighty because my daughters whined about it. I'll bet the Big Irish couldn't ride even with a saddle."

"Grady could."

"He's too short. He'd have to mount by standing on a stump."

"I wonder why you haven't shrunk much."

Howahkan thumped on his chest. "Shoshone stock."

"The Irish stock isn't too shabby either," I protested. "Grady is amazing! He still drags boats back and forth, keeps his whole resort in tip-top condition, fishes, shoots, and encourages young people to express themselves. Last summer he swung on a rope like Tarzan and dropped into the hot pool at Inish Flat."

"At his age? He should be embarrassed!" Howahkan laughed for he was a verbal bully and difficult to handle in an argument.

We rode along. Howahkan sat ramrod straight, with his chin pulled down to show his stature in the saddle. He looked proud and beautiful clopping along the fields of Fort Washakie. I could tell he was Awinita's brother, for their looks were just something special—a cut above. I never knew someone could look so fine at such an age, but I was proud for people to pass by and see me riding with him.

Howahkan took me to the Sacajawea Cemetery. I was surprised to learn that she was buried there. Wyoming is fairly close to home—but I thought she had died back east for some reason. It was neat to see. I also walked among the other graves, thrilling inside, at the feathered offerings hanging from the headstones. I thought of the eagle feathers that fluttered behind Grady and Awinita's cabin, paying tribute to Grady's bride and children.

We rode to another cemetery, Washakie cemetery, and paid our respects to the great chief. I felt tremendous reverence there. "Did you know him Howahkan?"

"Yes. I knew him. I revered him! He lived to be older than I am now. I was twenty-five when he died, and there was great mourning among our people. I have had the privilege of making medicine with the great chief."

"Really? How was that?"

"It was something to always remember, but Little Shoshone, the greatest experience I have ever had near a campfire came last summer as I prayed with a twelve year old boy."

That put a lump in my throat and I was quiet for a while, considering his words. Howahkan took a tribute to his wife Anna. He showed me the burial sites of his children, for he'd outlived them all. "I called this son after my grandfather—the same grandfather that you claim you saw. *Bodaway Greathawk*. "Bodaway means fire maker." I was goose bumping—for what could I say to that? Bodaway was still good at making phantom campfires burn in the green valley of Washakie Fork.

"Here is another son." Howahkan said.

I read the name of the stone, "Kell O'Rourke Greathawk." My mouth dropped open and my head snapped up to study the tall Indian next to me. "You named him after Grady?"

"No. I named him after the Big Irish. There's no *Grady* to it."

"That's great! Does he know?"

"I'll wager he'll soon find out."

"Why did you name a son after the man who you slapped forty times?"

"Because he bore it. I respected Kell, and Awinita loved him."

"This makes me like you even more, Howahkan."

"You know what the great Washakie called my little son?"

"No, what?"

"He lifted the infant toward the sun, saying 'Kell O'Rourke, our little shoog.' My people called that boy Little Shoog for many years."

"Well…what could be sweeter?"

"Indeed," Howahkan said. "Washakie also respected the Big Irish. Washakie also liked shoog."

"I can't believe Grady *knew* Washakie."

"He didn't actually—but Washakie knew him."

That gave me something to think about for the rest of the morning. We rode through the streets of Fort Washakie, seeing some old stone buildings, and Roberts Mission. Howahkan introduced me to many people, all curious about the white kid riding with the eldest elder of the reservation.

We went into a store and I nearly floundered! There was lots of neat stuff in there. Rabbit pelts, like the ones Awinita sewed together to make blankets for little Kell and Fawn. There were pipes and arrows, vests, gloves, and finely beaded ceremonial clothing. There were drums, moccasins, and Indian jewelry. Howahkan bought a little pair of white beaded moccasins for Yarrow. "Will these fit the child?"

I nodded, feeling confident about it. I had some money in my wallet so I also bought a pair for Allyson so she wouldn't feel bad. Having Indian moccasins *actually made by Indians* was the grooviest thing imaginable. I couldn't carry a lot on the horse, so I asked Howahkan if I could come back for more souvenirs before I left to go home.

He smiled, seeming pleased that I was so crazy over the culture, but shook his head, saying, "You're such a tourist."

For lunch Howahkan asked me to make more pancakes. He smacked his lips, pointing to the bottle of plum syrup. Mother would be happy to know his appreciation was keen. I cooked while Howahkan read his book. After lunch I washed dishes and cleaned up. Howahkan taunted me, by calling me squaw and housewife, but the comments didn't bother me much.

Howahkan wanted to read some more after lunch. "Let's trade books," I challenged.

Howahkan scowled, but accepted a Phantom Flynn novel. "This any good?"

"I haven't read that one yet. It's the newest one. It just came yesterday morning before I left. I belong to the Phantom Flynn Book Club, so they come automatically."

"What are you, a travelling library?"

"I suppose."

I settled down with a Louis L'Amour to satisfy the literary-loving Ancient. He flipped the Phantom Flynn novel open and his face froze—his neck raring back in shock.

"Howahkan? What's the matter?"

"What in hello mighty is the meaning of this?"

I shrugged, motioning with my hands that I didn't know what was wrong.

Howahkan cleared his voice and read, *"The brave was handsome in the lantern light of the barn. I stared at him, both curious and alarmed. He had followed me without my knowledge and I didn't like that. I studied him, trying to decipher his intentions while shadows leapt."*

"That's cool—see? Completely identifiable for you. Read on." I didn't know what the big deal was.

Howahkan cleared his voice and continued. *"Suddenly his hand slapped against my face. A hot flame ignited beneath my cheek, and I wanted to yowl, but bit my tongue, and looked again at him. He smiled, curious I think, by me as well. Then a sharp blow cracked against my other cheek and I staggered back a step, but I refused to cry out. The horses skittered in their stalls, whinnying for me."*

Howahkan was a better reader than Mrs. Leison and Mr. Despain, and I begged him to keep going. "Damn you, Little Shoshone! Don't you see? The Big Irish wrote this! Kell is Phantom Flynn!"

The statements were absurd! I was at Grady's nearly every day, and surely I'd know if he was a writer. He never let on to anyone…although there *was* a typewriter in his bedroom…and some of the stories *did* remind me a lot of Gallagher Springs…and Wyatt and I. My heart raced at the idea that Grady actually *could* be Phantom Flynn. My imagination was prone to going wild, and so I said, "No, Grady is too busy to write books."

"Listen to this," he challenged. *"The blows came with a fury then, marking my body, drawing painful welts. One eye began swelling before the assault could finish, and my lips were torn and bleeding. I bore it, for the brave's sister was Awinita, and I could endure anything for her; otherwise my fists would have exploded with fire because my blood was prone to running hot."*

"Oh my heck! Howahkan! My great grandfather wrote that? Grady *is* Phantom Flynn!" I was impressed, ecstatic, overwhelmed, and suddenly star-struck. Who knew? Did any one of us? "I've got to use the phone!"

"I don't have one."

"I've gotta call Grady *now*!"

"Take the horse back to the store. There's a phone there."

"Aren't you coming with me?"

"No! Hello mighty, no, for I've got to read and make sure Kell got it right." His ancient nose buried back behind the book. He chuckled.

"Kell described me as being a *perfect specimen of manhood.* He sure as hell got that right."

I raced out of the house, clicking to the pony again. I climbed on bareback, without the saddle. I didn't have time to mess with it. I loosened the bridle reigns and we took off. I had to squeeze my knees into the horse's side to keep from coming off, but I made it.

A payphone was mounted on the wall in front of the store. I hit the operator and requested a collect call. Grady answered on the second ring. "Hello?"

A nasal sounding operator droned, "Collect call from Wesley Gallagher. Will you accept the charges?"

"Certainly I will!"

"Grady!"

"Wesley? How are you my boy? Is everything okay?"

"Grady!" I gulped, finding it difficult to talk to my favorite author. "I know about you!"

"I should hope to shout."

"No, I mean—you are Phantom Flynn!"

He chuckled into the phone. "Oh...you've got it figured out, I see. I expected I'd start getting phone calls."

"It's true then?"

"Yes."

"I can't believe it! Howahkan is going crazy reading it, and I can't wait to get my hands on it! What on earth made you write about Awinita?"

"It's the only way I can get Cora to really know her old dad, I guess."

"It's a great way!"

His laughter was merry and pleasant. "I'm glad you approve of my methods."

"Grady, you're my hero! I wish I was home right now so I could monopolize your time, and motor to the island and make you read this book to me."

"No, you enjoy your visit with Howahkan. You are Grandpa Greaty Great's good boy, and I love you. There will be plenty of time for us to get together after your holiday."

"Grady, please don't hang up! I just want you to know that I love your stories. I just never dreamed in a million years that it was *you* writing them. You are the most popular author in our whole valley—every school teacher reads your books and quotes you, too."

"That's because the stories are about all of them, really—or their grandparents. I only changed the names. They love the stories because they are reading about themselves."

"You amaze me. I love you Grady!"

"I'm not different than I was yesterday and you mustn't get too excited."

"But I *am* excited! But you didn't change the names in this story, did you?"

"No. The book that Howahkan's reading is my own personal tale, and too sacred to my heart to mettle with. Enjoy it, Wesley."

"I will. The beginning is a doosy already! Howahkan was reading it, completely stunned to discover this side of you. He likes you. He named his son Kell O'Rourke Greathawk."

Grady's tongue clicked, but then he said, "Wesley, I've got to go, for Monty just screeched to a halt in the driveway, and he's running to the door with his book in his hands. I'm afraid my secretive days are over." I heard Grady's door bang open and knew Monty was already inside. "Oh—and now here comes John running up the walk."

"Tell them hi for me. Tell them I beat them to it."

"Good bye, Wesley."

I hung up. My hand was trembling and my mind whirled with the knowledge of who Kelly Sheehan O'Rourke was, and of all the tales that he'd ever spun. I wished I was at his house at that very moment, experiencing the shared shellshock of John and Monty. What would Mark say? And Wyatt? I smiled, turning for the horse. A large Shoshone boy was sitting on it, staring at me. I startled at the sight, and my blood began pumping for a different reason.

"Hey Whitey. Looks like you stole my horse."

"That's my horse and you'd better climb off."

"Says who?"

"Says I."

"I don't take orders from the *mighty whitey*." His manner was surly and taunting.

My ire was rising, and I could taste blood which was never a good sign. "Who *do* you take orders from?"

"Nobody."

"That's too bad. I was taught to have respect. What have you been taught?"

"Nothing."

"Again, that doesn't speak well for you or the traditions of your people."

And then he swore kind of nasty and started riding away with Howahkan's horse. I leapt ahead, grabbing the bridle near the bit. The horse faunched sideways but I held on. The kid kicked at me with his boot. I grabbed his boot, cranking his foot at a bad angle. He tried to kick loose but lost his balance as the horse shied, and fell with a thud in the road. Several people were coming out of the store, watching the goings on. I hoped I made it through this scrape with my scalp.

He began swearing and talking rough, threatening to kill me. What could I do but scrap back? He crouched low ready to spring at me. I was ready and thrust my arm out, stopping him mid-lunge, clothes-lining him beneath the chin. He went down and I followed, leveraging my arm around his neck until I had him in a chokehold. He flailed, punching me several times in the leg. My knee banged at the shock, and the only way I could get him to quit was by increasing the pressure around his neck. My arms were searing with muscle fatigue and I was seeing double from the exchange.

"Maybe this will teach you a lesson in respect," I huffed between clenched teeth.

Being a scrapper he got one leg under his butt and was able to launch himself into a better position. I had to release the chokehold to get better footing. He took a hot swipe at my ear, making contact. That rang my bell with reverberating clamor. I shook my head to clear my vision. I could see two of him looming before my view, and not knowing exactly where he was, I cut with my right and then my left. I made contact with both blows. Blood splattered two directions and he went down. I fell to one knee with the movement, gasping for breath, trying to recover my senses. I was praying for Pistol Stewart to come and drag me away. I sucked a gulp of wind and stood up, ready to swing again if necessary.

"Who the hell are you?" My opposition asked, trying to stagger to his feet. He seemed tired and plenty willing to talk peace. I was relieved, for I'd never been in a tighter scrap with Stan Tomkins or anybody else.

"My name's Wesley Gallagher. I'm from Gallagher Springs, Utah. Howahkan Greathawk sent for me, and he is my friend. He told me to ride the horse here and use the phone and I did. Now who are you?"

"O'Rourke Greathawk—and I only wish old Grandfather would have told me he was borrowing my horse."

Chapter Eighteen

Of course I blinked stupidly. We'd drawn a crowd by then and they laughed at our mix up. O'Rourke spat a mouth full of blood into the dust of the road. He grinned, shaking his head. He stuck his hand out. "You can call me Rouree, for my friends do."

"You can call me Wesley. I'm sorry there was a misunderstanding over your horse. I would have done the same thing to any fool that tried taking mine back home, but I thought you were stealing Howahkan's mount and I couldn't let that happen."

Some of the crowd jostled nearer, slapping our shoulders and laughing at the mix-up. My right ear was ringing hollow tones and I wondered if it would ever be okay again. Rouree's nose sat sideways and I feared it was broke all to heck. A man stepped off the curb and straightened it, wiping blood from his hands when he was finished. Rouree's eyes watered but he didn't cry.

"I'm really sorry about that." I bit my lip, wishing I'd have just waited to talk to Grady after I got home.

"Let's be friends," Rouree insisted. "I don't want you for an enemy!"

I swallowed hard. "You weren't exactly my first pick for one, either."

A short, stout woman came out of the store. She held an ice pack out to Rouree's face. He accepted it, holding it at the bridge of his nose. "I'm a little dizzy," he admitted, taking a seat on the curb.

I sat next to him. "Gee, I hope you'll be okay." I must have been shouting and not realizing because the others laughed. I could hear them saying something about my lame ear. The woman came back out with some kind of tincture. She tipped my head sideways dripping a drop or two inside my ear. "Tip your head you sod-buster," she said gruffly, "So the oil doesn't trickle back out." Then she stuffed a little bit of cotton into my ear. There we sat. Bloodied and beat, winded and sore, humbled and apologetic...and amused.

The wicked banging inside my ear calmed quickly. I was amazed. "What is that stuff?"

"Willow oil, most likely," Rouree said.

"Yes, with lavender and yarrow," the stout woman offered. She seemed pleased with herself for fixing me so quickly.

My brows rose at the good knowledge. "Thanks, its helping. *Yarrow* is my sister's name."

"Yarrow is a powerful tonic."

I nodded. "That fits her."

"Yarrow should have been my sister," Rouree said glumly.

I turned sideways to look at him. His eyes were buried beneath the ice pack, but I studied him still. "Are you Gloria's boy?" The crowd got a kick out of that—they didn't think I should have known who Gloria was.

"No. Gloria's my dad's cousin, but we offered to take Yarrow, too. We would have been good to her."

I was quiet then. These people had an inherent claim on the child and yet Howahkan had given her to me! I knew just how powerful of medicine we made by the fire last summer. I didn't know what to say so I sat both deaf and dumb for several long minutes. The crowd wandered off, losing interest. Finally I said, "Yarrow is well, and I will tell her about you."

"Don't tell her about all of this blood," Rouree implored. "It would give her nightmares."

"No, I won't. But someday she'll get a kick out of our scrap over *your* horse."

Rouree's head nodded slightly. "You must be the kid old Grandfather calls Little Shoshone."

"Yes."

"Please accept my apologies for calling you some rough words. I didn't know. I would never have greeted the Little Shoshone that way."

I thought that was curious. "Well, no offense taken."

"That's a damn lie. You hit me like there was a lot of offense taken."

I laughed. "Well, I guess you're right then. At first I was a little sore."

"And now?" Rouree pulled the ice pack away so he could look at me.

I rubbed my ear and my knee. "Now I'm a lot sore," I goofed.

"So do you know the Big Irish?"

I smiled. "Yes. I was just talking to him on the phone."

"Jump back."

I choked, for that's what Wyatt usually said. "No—really."

"I thought he would be dead."

"No, and compared to your old grandfather, mine is still in his prime at ninety-two."

Rouree grinned beneath the agony of his broken nose. "What's he like?"

"Why don't you come and stay with me so you can meet him? And Yarrow."

"What would I do in Gallagher Springs?"

"I could show you the valleys of your people. I could take you to a high ridge where I saw your great, great, great grandfather leaning over me in a peculiar way."

Rouree pulled the pack off completely, staring at me. "Jump back—*way* back!"

"It's true. I saw Bodaway. He likes me, I think."

"You know," Rouree stated, "I'm named after the Big Irish."

"Yes."

"Actually I'm named for my grandfather, Kell O'Rourke Greathawk. He was named after old Grandfather's brother-in-law, the Big Irish."

I nodded again, for this wasn't news to me. "You'll like the man you are named after."

"So...you really think I can come sometime?"

"Why not?"

He shrugged, considering things. "How old are you Wes?"

I fudged for a second, not wanting to own my age. "Thirteen in February."

Rouree spat another pool of blood from his mouth. "Hello mighty."

"Why?"

"You fight like you're my age, at least."

"How old are you?"

"Sixteen."

"So what...it's not the age that makes a friend—it's the way he swings his fists that counts."

Rouree laughed again. "I can't believe my nose got broke by a punk white kid."

"I have older cousins and they don't mind hanging with me a bit. So...you can still come sometime if you want to. You could at least meet them."

"Maybe I will sometime."

"So...can I take the horse back to Howahkan's or should I start walking, or what?"

"Take it. I have our truck." He motioned down the road. Amos's shiny red Dodge was parked in front of a building.

"Amos is your dad?"

"Yes.

"Can you make it down there?"

"Soon as the world stops spinning I will be fine."

The stout woman appeared on cue giving Rouree some tea to drink, and anointing salve against his face. She was tender but not overly sympathetic. "This will stop the bleeding."

I clicked my tongue to the roof of my mouth, amazed at her wellspring of knowledge. "She interests me! I'm a vetinary apprentice myself, and would like to know some of her tricks."

"Ask her."

I shook my head, feeling embarrassed.

"Hey Gloria!" Rouree yelled. "The Little Shoshone has got some questions for you."

She reappeared at my side, looking stoic, just waiting. "You're Gloria?" My tone was incredulous. "You're the nurse, right?"

"*Hmph!* Listen Sod Buster, I'm a doctor and don't you forget it!"

My eyes sprang wide and Rouree had a good laugh at my expense. "Gloria knows everything about healing people."

"I see. My Grandpa Gallagher is a vet and I'll bet he'd like to know what you know."

"I'll just bet he would," she said, then walked away without looking back.

That evening Howahkan took me to a big bonfire. Many people were there but I wasn't sure if it was all of the reservation, or just

Howahkan's family. Drums beat, and my senses took in every sight, sound, and smell, keenly soaking up the experience.

They called it hand-drum singing, A few men gathered in a circle, all thumping on hand-held drums and singing old-time anthems. Amos joined them. It sounded marvelous to me, and I understood Grady's draw toward the native people when he was a boy. I closed my eyes, and imagined him sitting beyond the trees that rimmed the clearing in Washakie Fork so long ago, eager to see shadows dance.

"Yah-ho- Ah hey, hey-hey-hey-yo, Yah-ho Ah hey, hey oh Ah-ah hey." The tenor voices rang on and on, haunting the air with calling music. The singers often broke into different parts and rhythms, but always came back together again, never missing a note or beat. Sometimes one would sing lead and the others would echo.

As the drums pounded, dancers immerged. Young girls with bells stitched to their skirts danced around the fire. I learned that this was called a jingle dance, and I was amazed how the girls could move with such rhythm, never losing their steps.

"Is this a powwow, Howahkan?"

He looked disgusted. "It's not a Boy Scout cookout, you green horn."

Shawl dancers, grass dancers, and traditional dancers all worked the twilight, making it feel delicious to me. Then three or four strutting peacocks came into view. Young men, some of them possibly my age, decked out in feathers and quills began moving to a young men's fancy. That's what Howahkan called it.

I recognized Rouree, although not at first. He was transformed with a headdress of porcupine quills sticking straight up like the proud peaks of a crown. I didn't know how he managed to fasten it to his head so securely. He wore an elaborate feather bustle—looking more like a wild, exotic bird than a boy. A bone breast plate covered his chest, and he wore fringed buckskin, tall beaded moccasins with flossy fringe, and ankle bells. Ornately beaded arm bands stretched around well-developed biceps, and little bells jingled from wrist cuffs. A strip of black face paint concealed his broken, swollen nose. He looked stunning and raw, and I was amazed at the intricate patterns of his feet as he danced to the pounding rhythms of the drums. I didn't know how he could stand the jarring movements for surely he still felt the rattling pain from my fists.

He danced closer to me, and I studied his headpiece, being stupefied by it. I wasn't sure if it was made out of quills or not. I asked Howahkan.

"Rouree's headpiece is called a roach. It's made from tied porcupine and deer hair. Usually there are several rows of each hair tied onto a woven base so that the hairs will stand upright and move gracefully with the dancer as he moves. The deer hair is laced outside of the longer porcupine hair. They are held on with a braided piece of hair, brought up through a hole in the middle of the roach's base, and then run through with a roach pin. That's how it stays on his head as he bobs around that way."

I nodded, never taking my eyes off the wild preening dancers. I felt small and insignificant here, and very appreciative of such ancient tribal customs. In fourth grade we were taught to square dance, and I couldn't even do that properly being half clumsy. Last Valentine's Day Mrs. Despain came into the classroom to teach us the finer points of waltzing and two-stepping, but I two stepped when I shouldn't have and waltzed right over the top of my partner, Cindy Sue McCann. She called me a clod-hopper and I was glad when that day was over.

We ate after the dancing and hand-drum singing. "This wasn't a bonafied powwow, just a little show-off affair that I threw together for your benefit," Howahkan said. "I figured you might as well get a good taste of what your great grandfather developed an appetite for."

Dinner consisted of hot crispy mutton strips, corn, and fried onions. Large Dutch ovens full of them tantalized my taste-buds. We also ate Indian fry-bread which reminded me of Grady's scones. Howahkan smuggled some of Mother's plum syrup in a little jar and he saturated his fry bread with it, smacking his lips with every bite.

Some of the men got talking about me and Rouree's scrape. Howahkan laughed again and again with every rendition of it. Truly it grew funnier with the telling, and I had to join in, hearing it from the eye witness accounts and everything.

One man named Yancy Good said, "The Little Shoshone jerked Rouree off the horse with one try!"The men hooted, but I was hoping this fun and sport wouldn't get things going again. "Rouree lunged, and the Little Shoshone smacked his windpipe, and down he went." More laughter. "He wrestled an arm around him and held on for hell's sakes!"

Another man added, "But Rouree got a leg under him, to his credit, and the Little Shoshone had to let go. That's when the fists flew. Rouree took the kid's head off with a blow to the ear. *Ka-bam!* I thought that would be the end of it, but it only proved to agitate the boy. With his eyeballs circling around in two different directions, he swung a couple of punches, like a quick one-two, and down went Rouree, blood spattered and defeated."

Rouree's feathers were beginning to ruffle, literally. I winced, not wanting to lose a friend. "But I've never had such a tiger by the tail," I said. "And someone came out and reset the broken nose, which must have been awful to bear, but Rouree never even hollered! Back home we'd have gone off to the hospital in the ambulance. I couldn't believe it when I saw him dancing tonight! He's tough."

Then the men guffawed about the punk white kids riding to the hospital in an ambulance over something as minor as a busted face. I didn't mind the talk, for to them I was the Little Shoshone, and I didn't have anything more to prove.

That night as I turned the lamp off near my cot, I heard strange choking sounds coming from Howahkan's room. I slipped from the cot and walked to the next room, hesitating at Howahkan's door. I feared he was dying perhaps, and I wasn't sure what to do if that happened. "Howahkan?"

"Yes."

"Are you okay?" I stepped closer.

Howahkan was wiping tears, crying I guess, and then I saw the book. It was tugging at every heartstring he had, apparently. "No, I'm not okay! The Big Irish has written things that have stirred my soul for home, and the old ways. I miss my sister. Good Lord, but Kell did love her! And I love Kell."

"I thought you only respected him."

"Sometimes there is not a difference."

"I see."

"The Big Irish is my brother, too."

I grinned. "Then that makes you my uncle, and I will call you Uncle Howie."

"By hello mighty, you will not!"

We both chuckled, and it was good, for it took Howahkan's mind away from bleeding memories of days gone by. "You're right. I won't. Goodnight…thanks for sending for me."

Amos and Rouree picked us up the next morning. We went to a field and watched some of the young bucks do horse tricks. I sat on top of a fence railing, just watching. Rouree ran next to his horse, wrapping a handful of mane around his hands, then in four or five easy strides he mounted the horse, enabling it to take out on a dead run. It was graceful and fluid and I watched close, aching to go home and try it out on Misty.

A tall kid named Kenny Tanaka also impressed me. He could bounce onto the horse, and bounce off the other side, again running in stride, then back on the horse, and again off the other side. It was poetry in motion, alright, as he mounted, dismounted, and ran with ease, never stumbling, never faltering. I gauged his skills were partly physical, and partly mental, as the timing had to be perfect in order master the feat.

Yancy Good's boy, Dover, could also mount easily, just as Rouree and Kenny had done. But he practiced switching horses as they barreled headlong on a dead run. He could dismount one, and mount another, weaving himself back and forth between the horses. I had a lot of respect for the boys' riding skills and their horses. They kept performing more and more difficult stunts while the men and I watched.

At one point Dover started two horses running, and then straddled the horses, standing with one foot on each back. I couldn't believe it! "I broke my pelvis doing that once," Howahkan said grimly. I couldn't help gawking at him.

"I remember that," Amos drawled.

"What? Amos is your grandson! How the heck old were you when you did that?"

"Sixty-eight. I was just a kid, really," Howahkan boasted smugly.

Yancy pulled a cigarette from his mouth. "One time I bounded off of my first mount, then caught the mane of the second mount, and swung myself too hard. I flew right over the top of the second horse, missing it completely, and rolled about twenty times. I'm not going to lie to you—that hurt."

Howahkan and Amos burst into rowdy laughter recalling the incident.

"Alright, that's enough showing off for one day," Amos called sternly. The boys looped their horses around, coming nearer.

"Does the Little Shoshone want to try?" Rouree asked.

"No. I already know that would be a disaster."

"Come on," Dover said. "We'll just teach you how to do a running mount."

They persuaded me off the fence to the amusement of Howahkan, Amos, and Yancy. Rouree showed me how wrap my hands in the mane of the horse. At first I only tried running with it, but I would get out of gait and fall. The horse was well trained, trying to help me match up, and when I faltered, she would slow down. If I fell, the horse would stop and loop back to my side. Again and again and again the boys put me through my paces with the horse.

On the thirtieth attempt at throwing my weight up onto the horse's back, and after several servings of dirt for lunch, I swung myself up and managed to half-way make it. There I was, running at a breakneck speed, and only on sideways. The ground whirred beneath me so fast that I didn't know what to do! My legs were kicked higher on the horse than the rest of me, and if I let go I was afraid I would break my neck. I hollered, "Whoa!" I noticed a wicked gleam in the horse's eye, and thought I heard her chuckle once. Then she hit the skids on a dime and I went flying sideways past her like a bullet from a barrel. I landed face first in a clump of grass. I'm certain that it was the only thing that cushioned my fall, but for a split second I wondered if the grass stalks had smacked right into my brain, for I saw red lights and then nothing for a few moments. I could hear great excitement from the others, could hear them running towards me, concerned. I knelt up on my hands and knees calling, "I'm fine," and then I knew I wasn't and fell back to the ground.

A minute or two later I came to, blood everywhere. I was seeing double and triple perhaps, because it seemed like a whole tribe was leaning over me. "You broke your nose, too," Rouree said.

"Oh shoot!"

"Hear that?" Kenny asked. "He wouldn't say shit if he had a

mouthful—and he's got a mouthful!" They all laughed raucously and I didn't think it was funny.

"Don't worry," Dover consoled. "Dad reset your nose while you were knocked out. You'll be fine."

I wondered if I didn't need an ambulance. After all—I *was* just a punk white kid, and all I could see was blood. "I can't believe I did this to you, Rouree! Did it sting this bad—because you didn't act like it."

"Yeah, not bawling when you need to—that's the tricky part," Rouree admitted. "For a split second yesterday, I thought your fist actually landed *inside* of my face."

Tears ran down my cheeks unbidden. "I'm not crying! My eyes are just tearing for some reason."

"Don't fuss about it," Howahkan soothed. "You smacked hard and anybody's eyes would water."

I was dizzy and I wanted to throw up, but Howahkan wouldn't let me bend my head down. He made me hold it straight up, squeezing against the top of my nose, even though it hurt awful bad. Amos ran into town to get the doctor. Soon Gloria was handing me a cup of bitter tea. "Drink it," she said. She wiped off my face and studied my nose, making sure it was lined up. She anointed my face with the type of salve she'd used with Rouree. Then she dabbed some peppermint oil on my upper lip.

"That will keep you from tossing your cookies," she said. She dabbed the cooling oil along my hairline, and again trailed a small, soothing swipe above each eyebrow. She felt a hand up the back of my neck. "Awe, not good."

I wanted to faint! I knew it must be broken. "It's bad?"

"It's crooked."

"Shoot! Double shoot…"

"Relax," she said. Her fingers worked up my neck, into my hair, feeling. Then she placed her hands firmly against the sides of my face and jerked my head to one side. *Pop! Pop! Pop* went my neck. My eyes sprang open. She turned my head the other direction; feeling with her fingers as she did so, then *crack!* She popped it again, and the dizziness subsided almost instantly.

"Are you a chiropractor or what?"

"More or less."

I didn't know what that meant, but I really was thankful for her help. "That was weird, I feel a lot better already."

"Now that your head isn't on crooked," she said dryly. She looked at my eyes, and then rummaged through her bag. She handed me a bottle. "Take a little bit of this throughout the day. It will help with nausea."

"What is it?"

"Listen sod buster, if I wanted you to know I would have labeled the bottle. Trust me."

She put an icepack over my face and told me to keep my nose iced throughout the day. Twenty minutes later I was back in Amos's truck and we were riding home.

"We're sleeping out tonight," Kenny said. "Wanna come?"

"Maybe."

"If you're up to it," Rouree added.

"How did you manage to dance last night?"

"I dunno."

"I might manage sleeping out—but definitely not dancing."

"I doubt you could dance anyway," Dover piped.

I nodded, for he pegged me like a ringer.

Howahkan made onion soup for our lunch. He claimed it would help me mend. It tasted good and stayed down which was a good sign. "You lay down, Little Shoshone." He settled me onto the couch in the front room. He covered me with a blanket. "Now I'll read the Big Irish's book to you. You just listen."

That's how I spent the afternoon, caught up in the tales of old men when they were young. Many times Howahkan choked up. "I'm not crying," he said. "For some reason my eyes are just tearing up."

"That's because you've fallen back in time. You hit hard, and anybody's eyes would water."

"You are wise Little Shoshone."

As Howahkan's voice painted pictures for my mind to see, I found myself falling in love with Awinita. It was a weird sensation…and I knew that any other girl would forever and always pale in comparison. I imagined her a thousand different ways, and each one was exotic and beautiful.

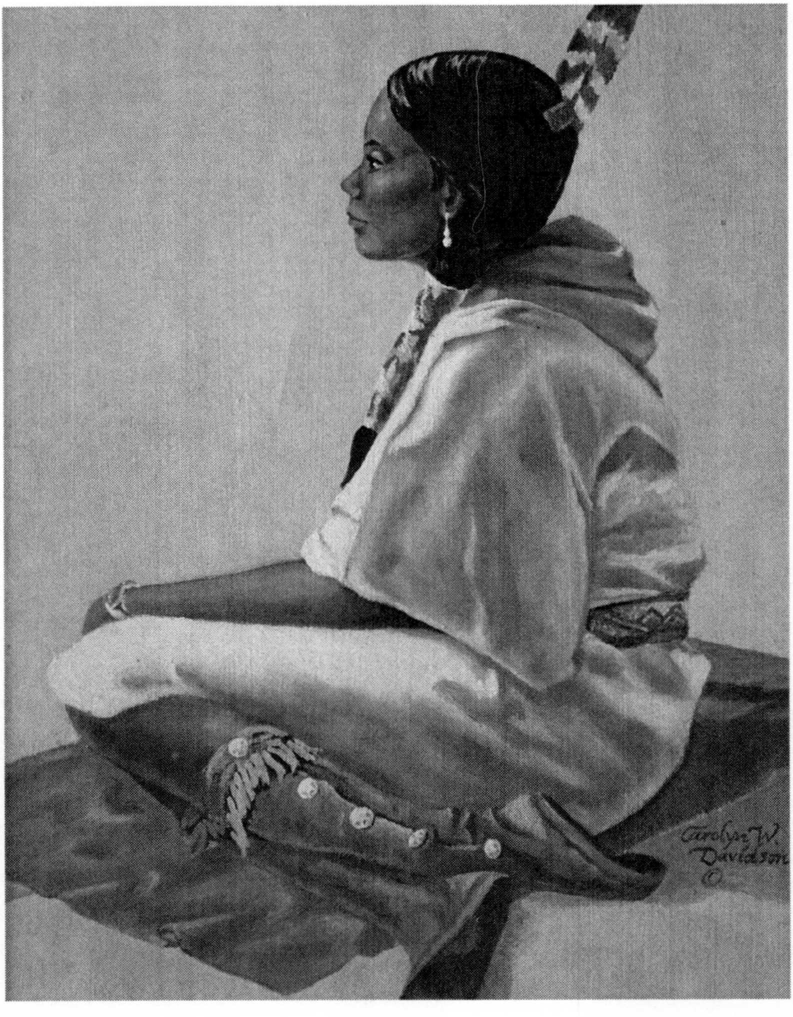

The teenagers came for me that evening at eight o'clock. Howahkan anointed my face with Gloria's leftover salve and made me take the medicine. "If that swelling hasn't gone down by tomorrow, I'm afraid your mother won't let you come anymore."

I took a bedroll and went out to Dover Good's fancy truck. I'm not sure where we went that night, not being familiar with the territory, but we set up camp near the river beneath a bunch of cottonwood trees. I kept quiet, being an outsider and all, but occasionally the boys reeled me into their conversation. They were curious about me.

"What was it like, rattling off different languages," Rouree wanted to know. "You know, when you made medicine with old Grandfather?"

"I dunno. I didn't really know I was. I just thought I was praying in my mind—but I do know that at one time, it felt like I was able to think and say many different things at the same time. Sometimes I wish I could feel like that again, because my mind was unbelievably clear, and expressing myself was easy. It was a free feeling—a high, maybe."

The boys laughed. "Like weed?"

"How would I know about that? No, it was a spiritual high."

"Cool."

"But afterwards I was really drained and didn't have any strength at all."

They nodded. Kenny lit a cigarette and dragged on it, passing it off to Rouree. Dover took a turn and they passed it on to me. I wanted to impress my new friends who were all older than me, but Mother's words kept circling in my mind, asking me to remember who I was. I shook my head and the boys went back to passing the smoke back and forth without any questions.

We roasted marshmallows which seemed like camping back home, and the boys talked about girls. Rouree had a thing for Marsha Brady. That was funny to me, but I don't know why, for my cousin John had a hopeless crush on her. Kenny bragged about making out with a girl from Riverton after a powwow, and Dover admitted to making out with Kenny's sister. That's when trouble started.

Kenny took a wild swing at Dover, and they grappled each other, wrestling and shoving, punching and swearing for a couple of minutes. Rouree grinned at me, and I grinned back. We both had broken noses and didn't want any part of the action. After Dover's lip was cut and bleeding, Kenny felt better about things, and they lit another cigarette and shared back and forth, making peace, apparently.

"What about you Wes?"

I was surprised at the question, for we hadn't had a conversation for several minutes.

"Do you have a girl?"

"No. I'm not thirteen yet."

"So what—I started girling when I was eleven," Dover boasted.

"*Girling?* What does that mean?"

"You know, liking them—chasing them."

"Well…I'm not there yet."

"No? You're missin' out." Kenny said. Dover agreed, for their fist-a-cuffs and shared cigarette seemed to mend their differences concerning Kenny's sister and all girls in general.

"How do you spend your time, Little Shoshone?"

"I help out on our ranch, and at the Big Irish's resort. I made a lot of money cooking hotdogs this summer. I like to fish and shoot, ride, and swim. I like to boat and read Phantom Flynn novels."

"Phantom Flynn, you know his books? We read *The Big Irish Secret* in school this year," Kenny drawled. "It was pretty good."

"*Beneath Washakie Moon* is my favorite," Dover claimed.

"Phantom Flynn is actually my great grandpa, Kelly Sheehan O'Rourke. Rouree is named after him."

The boys looked crazy eyed at me for a minute. "Are you kidding me?" Rouree asked.

"It's true. His new book is about him, Howahkan, Awinita, and all of your people—and mine."

"What's it called?"

"Feathers Flutter, Say Goodbye."

"Sounds good!"

"You guys will definitely need to read it. Personally I can't stop thinking about it."

"I do want to meet the Big Irish." Rouree's eyes were black and firelight danced patterns in them.

"Come and stay then."

He smiled and nodded and the others invited themselves to come when he did. I wouldn't say anything to Mother. I'd let it surprise her when it happened...

We kept the fire going all night for the October moon provided no warmth. I never woke up with any strange ghosts peering over me and I hoped that if they were there they were friendly. My dreams shilly shallied from here to there, but always ended with Awinita's perfect features looming before mine. I was jealous of Grady's memories when I awoke, for his reward was waiting for him and I was yet to find such a prize. I was sad to see the sun, for I must go back to Gallagher Springs today and I wasn't ready.

I packed my things and studied Awinita's photograph before wrapping it carefully between the folds of my shirts. I left Grady's book with his brother-in-law because I knew where I could get another one. He thanked me, saying, "*Feathers Flutter, Say Goodbye* is my new favorite book!"

Howahkan's lips quivered as I boarded the greyhound. He waved goodbye, calling, *"Tsaan dai neesungaahka."* All is well.

For some reason the return trip seemed much faster, and my family was waiting for me when the Greyhound pulled to a halt in Eisner. Yarrow came running and squealing, "My boy! My boy!"

"What's wrong with your face?" Mother asked before anything else was said. I laughed inside, for Gloria's ointments had worked wonders, and I was grateful she hadn't seen me yesterday.

"I broke my nose."

"What!"

"Howahkan says he's sorry, but it wasn't his fault. He says I'm a bonafied warrior now, riding as the young bucks do."

"What did the doctor say?"

I thought about Gloria, the nurse/doctor/chiropractor person, and hedged a little. "The doctor called me a sod buster and said I'd be okay," I answered vaguely.

Mother's eyes blinked rapidly, trying to process things. Dad shook my hand and we got into the car. I passed out souvenirs as we drove, for Howahkan made Amos take me to the store before leaving for Lander that morning. The moccasins were a hit with my sisters, and Mother thought it was sweet of Howahkan to buy a pair for Yarrow. I gave mother a necklace and Dad a pair of fringed, beaded gloves.

"These are for show only," he said, studying the workmanship. "No working in these!"

I filled them all in on my trip, leaving out my fist fight with Rouree of course, and the boys' smoking by the campfire. Mother would have pitched a fit about my new friends if I'd told.

News travels faster than lightning in a thunderstorm in our town, for new signs were going up on the outskirts of town. *"Welcome to Gallagher Springs, home of famous author, Phantom Flynn."* Beneath the letters were the words, *"A.K.A. Kelly Sheehan O'Rourke"*

"What do you think about that?" I asked Dad.

"I don't know what to think. Not one of us knew. Grady called us all together Friday night, since the boys had found out, and we had a family meeting. He gave us all complimentary copies of his book, and asked us to read them."

"And?"

"I am all a wonder," Dad said simply. "And I couldn't put it down once I began."

"Me neither," Mother said. "Reading about the young, handsome, and swaggering Howahkan made my heart race a little—and I had a hard time realizing you were with him."

"He is still handsome," I said. "Howahkan kept my book. He loves reading about himself."

"I'll bet."

"Mayor Spinnaker must be a real Phantom Flynn fan because it has only been four days since the release of the books, and he's got signs already made."

We unloaded the car. I gave Mother my dirty laundry with the exception of my bloodied shirt. I threw that away at Howahkan's so it didn't upset her. I spent an hour playing with Yarrow, and then I wrapped Awinita's picture in some tissue paper and drove up to Grady's. I knocked on his door, but didn't wait for him to answer. I walked in, smiling.

"Wesley! Ho, the president of my fan club!"

I hugged the man, looking down on his snow-topped head. "I'm proud to know you, Grady."

"And I'm proud to own you!"

"How did you ever keep it a secret for so long?"

"Well…I didn't want to set the world into a commotion, but that's just what I've done now, I'm afraid."

"Did Grandma read your new book?"

Grady nodded solemnly. "Yes, and she was here this afternoon asking more questions. My Cora's a good girl, and loves her old dad, bless her heart forever."

"It's finally time everybody learned about you."

"I suppose. I'd have told them long ago, but their ears weren't inclined to listen."

"I have a present for you."

The bushy white brows rose expectantly. "From Howahkan? Oh dear, let me guess—"

"You'll never guess."

"No?"

I shook my head. "No, and you'd better sit down while you open it."

Grady did as I requested, then his aged fingers tore away the wrappings. He gasped and his eyes were round like full moons. He stared, lifting the frame in trembling hands. "My Awinita!" He touched her picture to his lips and tears streamed unashamedly down his face. "My beautiful, gentle, Awinita! My love." He hugged the photograph to his chest and closed his eyes tightly. Then he pulled the oval frame away to study her likeness some more. I watched silently, lost in the moment.

After several long minutes, Grady rubbed a finger over the glass and a smile touched his face. "You know when this was taken?"

"No, but Howahkan told me how it happened." I shared the story of the green horn photographer and his fascination with Awinita.

Grady listened, nodding. "This was taken after they left here, that first autumn—you know, and my father whipped me, refusing to let me follow after her."

"How can you tell?"

"Look right here," Grady said, pointing to the photograph.

I studied the photo where he showed me, and I smiled, for I hadn't noticed it before. Awinita's right hand was clenching an object—a hairbrush. My heart panged at the sight! "Oh Grady, I have a secret to tell you."

"Yes? Out with it boy, for secrets can't be kept without a certain level of distress."

"I'm in love with your Awinita, myself."

"That's the greatest compliment you could pay me! I wanted her to live through the power of words in the book. Apparently she has." The eyes smiled at me and Grady nodded. "Of all my grandkids, you are the most like me. If I wasn't still here, *I'd* think you were me, in some reincarnated state—if I actually believed in such things. You soak in details, Wesley. You feel things in a sensitive way. You capture smells, and sounds, and sights, and catalog them away. You will be a writer, too, for it is in you. You will share with others what you feel, making them smell what you smell, and see what you see, and hear what you hear through the magic of words."

I gulped. "You really think so?"

Grady led me into a bedroom closet. He opened it up, and there were stacked white boxes, dozens of them. I'd seen them before, always wondering what they were, but had not been curious enough to ask. Grady reached up and turned one around. The spine of the box was labeled, *Pacific Wind*, and he flipped another one around. *Shadows Call after Dusk.*

"These are your manuscripts?"

"Yes, all thirty-eight of them—they are yours. I have willed it so."

My eyes teared again, and I smiled blindly, not able to read the other titles as Grady flipped them around. "This means a lot, Grady."

"I know. I expected you to figure me out first, too, and you didn't disappoint me."

"I was just dumbfounded when Howahkan started reading your book. I was dazed, like pious Peter Pellingham after Wicky Wacky McCracky shot his fine prancing stallion out from under him."

Grady got a kick of that. "See? You've hung onto every word I've ever said! I leave you my written works, and also my unwritten words, and may you make them all immortal."

Chapter Nineteen

When my nose was sufficiently healed I spent a lot of time with Misty. I was determined to nail a running mount, but first I had to train her to let me run with her, holding her mane. It took lots of tedious hours, and I practiced after school. I wasn't working at the resort in evenings now as things had slowed down and Mark needed the hours.

Misty thought I was plum loco at first, I'm sure, but she was a good mare, and patiently tried to learn what I wanted her to do. I carried apples and carrots in my pockets, and rewarded her when she paced herself to my gait, or when she learned to halt and loop back when I fell. One Saturday near the end of November I was in the corral, running with her and finally our movements fell into synch and I mounted her successfully. I think Misty wondered what took me so long, and she whinnied merrily, and we shared an apple. After that day, it felt easy and so I started practicing my dismount. I knew it would take a lot of work.

Wyatt often came to the corrals with me and watched from the fence rail, offering encouragement and sometimes criticism. The fresh air was good for him and he said he thought he could do a running mount easier than me, but it wasn't worth another broken nose to find out. I remembered the wincing pain and had to agree.

Thanksgiving dinner was held at Aunt Aura Leigh's house that year, and delicious aromas permeated the home as women cooked and

bustled around in the kitchen. Celia set the table, lingering over the napkin placement purposefully to avoid any more tasks in the kitchen. The dining room light illuminated her long blond hair. She was fast becoming very noticeable, and was super popular at school. She was a nice quiet girl though, and the attention didn't to go to her head.

We heard a stir at the door and Uncle Rob opened it grandly. Standing in the doorway, in full decorated uniform, was Uncle Aiden. John got to him first, nearly knocking him backwards off the step. The women came running from the kitchen to see what caused the fuss. Aunt Aubynn burst into a strange tangle of sobs and laughter. Uncle Aiden wrapped his arms around her and spun her around and around. He sobbed against her hair, proclaiming his undying love for her. Wyatt's body began flinching and shaking uncontrollably at the happenings, and Grandpa Gallagher quickly gave him a shot so his body could adjust to the excitement of the moment.

"Wyatt? Is that my Wyatt?" Uncle Aiden asked, seeing the action. "What's wrong with my boy?"

"Where to start?" Aunt Aubynn cried. "Where to start telling you about us—for there's been no way to communicate with you at all."

"I felt your prayers, though." Uncle Aiden walked briskly to his youngest son. He knelt in front of him, taking him in his arms. "I am home, Son! I am home! And I have brought you a medal."

"I don't need a medal." Wyatt's arms wrapped around his father's neck, and he cried and clung to him, saying, "I need *you*, Dad," over and over and over again.

"Where's Mark?" Uncle Aiden asked.

Aunt Aubynn smiled. "He is eating with his wife's family today."

"Wife?" I detected an exclamation point at the end of the question.

"Yes. He married a nice girl, Michelle Voss. They will make us grandparents in the spring. The world is their oyster, I should think."

"Do you dare interrupt their dinner?" Uncle Aiden asked, sounding hopeful.

"I already have," Aunt Aura Leigh chimed from the kitchen. "I called and Mark is on his way right now."

In point five seconds, the blue Dart screeched to a halt in the driveway, and Uncle Aiden reacquainted himself with his oldest son. He met his new daughter-in-law, taking it all in with a grain of salt, for fatherly scolding, or fatherly advice, was not called for at this point of the game.

"I want the Finnegan's to come to my house and stay for a week," Grady said. "You all need to be alone, and have privacy together. I will bunk with Cora and Riley."

"It would be easier," Grandpa Gallagher disagreed, "if they stayed where they are and Cora and I moved in with you."

"Well...so let it be written," Phantom Flynn said mischievously.

So that's how the best Thanksgiving *ever* happened in our family.

We scarcely ate with so much excitement, yet no feast had ever tasted better.

The Christmas season was fun with Yarrow! She prattled away, asking a million questions while we decorated the tree. She was fascinated with the idea of twinkling lights and shiny balls. Her little fingers couldn't resist touching the glimmering icicles, saying, "Myself isn't touching it *too* much."

She was all lit up over the Montgomery Ward Christmas Catalog as well. She lay on her stomach for hours looking through the pages with Allyson and me. Her heart was set on a Baby Tender Love doll. "This baby will wet if I give her a bottle."

"I'm glad I don't have to feed my toys!" I said emphatically.

"Myself doesn't mind it."

Her very favorite thing though, was our nativity set. She would stand and look at it for long stretches of time, trying not to touch.

"This is Baby Jesus," she said to anyone who passed by. "He's cold."

One afternoon Mother noticed something strange on the coffee table. She stooped to see what it was. Baby Jesus was wrapped up in an ace bandage. "What in the world?" she asked, unraveling the little porcelain figure.

"Oh Mommy," Yarrow cried. "He needed more swaddling bands so I wrapped him up. He's warmer now."

On a different day the baby Jesus came up missing altogether. Mother looked under the coffee table, and beneath the sofa, wondering if it had possibly rolled away. She couldn't find it anywhere. She asked Yarrow about it, and finally the little girl confessed to taking Him. "Where is He?" Mother asked.

Yarrow led Mother into the girls' bedroom and pointed in the dollhouse. "He's having a sleep-over," Yarrow said. The baby was wrapped up in paper towel and lying in a small plastic bassinet. That added a new twist to the Christmas story.

Several other incidents were similar. "Why am I always searching for Jesus?" Mother asked one day, wondering again where Yarrow had taken the babe.

Dad chuckled, "That's the whole idea, isn't it dear?"

The week before Christmas Mother got out an old-fashioned pop-up book of *The Night before Christmas*. It was a tradition at our house. Yarrow was smitten with it, and she requested us to read it again and again. "Does Santa stop at Jesus' house?" She asked one evening while Dad read to her.

"I suppose so."

"Oh good! For my Joni didn't know about him before!" She clapped her hands, delighted to share all she was learning about Christmas with her Joni.

Christmas time found the Finnegan's living in a new home. It was on the north end of town, and not next door, which cramped my time spent with my best cousin, although he was busy doing things with his dad anyway. None of us were sure how long Uncle Aiden would settle in Gallagher Springs, or if the family would pack back up and head for San Diego.

Uncle Aiden walked with a limp, and he was shorter than he was before the war, suffering from rickets and severe torture during his stay in the Hanoi Hilton. Occasionally he seemed confused, and Wyatt confessed that his dad drank on occasion, but I refused to judge him. We looked the other way when his footsteps were stumbly or his speech was slurred. He was home, and God bless him forever, for he had endured things beyond our wildest, most horrific imaginations. He started working with my Dad and Uncle Rob, and the ranch provided plenty of chores for them all.

Naturally, with another man around, my time was freed up, and so I had more opportunities to practice with Misty. I was eager to show my reservation friends what I had learned to do. Yarrow and Allyson bundled against the biting December winds to watch and clap when appropriate. "My boy's a cowboy!" Yarrow said. I liked to strut, and boast, and show off. I was the very opposite of Wyatt, and a perfect synonym of Howahkan Greathawk.

"You're not as cool as the Fonz," Allyson informed me after one especially athletic dismount, "but you'll do."

1974 rolled around, and Wyatt came back to school. He was doing better and still held the attention of Avery Anne Applewhite. They studied together in the library without being teased. Wyatt's mild manners and fragile health condition somehow earned him a pass from ridicule. The kids liked him, accepting him for who he was. Stan Tomkins steered clear, never getting close to him.

My birthday came. I was officially a teenager and ready to cause a ruckus somewhere. I didn't know what kind of mischief to stir so I minded my own business and just kept riding, no matter how cold the winds blew. On Valentine's Day I opted out of the school dance and went home to ride. Grandpa Gallagher, Dad, and my uncles watched me. They whistled and slapped my back after I nailed a graceful, running dismount.

"Monty's right," Uncle Rob crowed. "You're a pistol!" He shook my hand and told me to keep up the good work.

Feeling confidant, and happy with my audience, I said, "Watch this." I took Misty to the end of the corral, and copying the practiced skill of Kenny Tanaka, I ran by Misty's side, then mounted, rode to the count of five, then dismounted, running again to the count of five, and then mounted again. I did the switch eight times, each time mounting and dismounting from opposite sides. When I was finished, Grandpa Gallaher handed me twenty bucks saying that was the best show he'd seen in awhile.

"Boy you keep practicing like that and I'll make sure you never lack for horses. I can't believe how you've trained this one."

"How do you ever lift yourself on the horse?" Uncle Aiden asked.

"I don't. Inertia does it for me. I get running and when I'm ready to mount I simply set my feet, and the action jerks me off my feet and up onto the horse. It took me awhile to get it figured out."

One night after a long day at school, and a cold night's workout with Misty, I felt restless and lonesome, although I didn't know why. I took out my notebook, pondering Grady's admonition to write. My mind felt blank, and I stared at the page, but I forced myself to relax and I started jotting a few lines. I worked at it, scrubbing out entire sentences with my eraser until I coaxed the words to obey.

Tsaan Dai Neesungaahka

Voices whisper up the hill from times when life was simpler still—
drums beat softly and I hear them say, "All is well, is well today."
I want to sing with mournful chant, in ancient tongue, and yet I can't
but my heart soars high on sun's bright ray.
My spirit sings what I can't say!
Aspen rustles in the glen, whispering tales of times and men
I listen to the raspy sound, "Be still upon this hallowed ground."
My mind reflects the words again; I wish I might have lived back then.
Embers burn just down the hill, remembrance comes, a sudden thrill
for smoke curls upward with my plea, a sacred signal just for me!
My heart races and blood runs chill while Heaven listens to my will
The chanting cries are sung for me, guiding well beyond what I can't see.
I will listen as they say, "All is well, is well today."

I didn't know if the poetry was good or bad, but I was satisfied with it and hoped it would make sense to someone besides me. I would show it to Grady sometime. I decided to write to Howahkan and I included my poem, copying it precisely. I told him about my Uncle Aiden coming home, and about my attempts at riding like Rouree and his friends. I asked him if he got the case of plum syrup we sent him for Christmas, and thanked him for the knife he had sent to me.

Springtime came and the world was in blossom. Mr. Mulligan purchased a jukebox for the cafeteria, rewarding the student body for a year without pranks. I smiled at that because Monty had been gone for two years, and Mark had mellowed beneath the bonds of matrimony.

I was trying to keep my broken nose clean, for the most part, and so who was left to think of it? I was certain there were plenty of pranks still to come, but for now I rested, using my energy to become a trick pony rider.

Lunchtimes became noisy with high school kids dropping quarters like money grew on trees. Glen Campbell serenaded every meal with "*Rhinestone Cowboy*" while I daydreamed about starring in a rodeo with my new riding tricks.

"Eat your spinach, Wesley," Mr. Mulligan said, stirring me from my thoughts.

"Give it to Popeye, I'm strong enough already."

Mr. Mulligan winced at my lippy talk, but didn't press the issue. He usually tried to keep peace with me, as his most obstinate nephew, and the natural born leader of the seventh grade. Steve, Scott, Ross, Wyatt, Stan, and the others laughed at me, but copied my lead. I didn't have a bite of my spinach, and so the rest didn't bother with theirs either. Mr. Voss scowled slightly in my direction, wanting me to step up to the task of greatness, somehow. I figured that as long as nobody went over a cliff, I'd led the pack quite well.

Mark was eating alone, for Michelle had to quit school when their daughter was born. They named her Kelly Michelle Finnegan, after Grandpa Grady, of course, and I thought that was nifty. The five-generation photograph of Grady, Grandma Gallagher, Aunt Aubynn, Mark, and baby Kelly made the front page of the *Three Lakes Beacon*. The caption read, "Phantom Flynn Strikes Again" since more than a dozen stories had materialized about him since the disclosure of his identity as the well known author.

I scraped my tray in the garbage can. "*Rhinestone Cowboy*" started blaring again, for the third time during lunch hour. The whole student body dropped their forks to sing along.

"Like a rhinestone cowboy,

Riding out on a horse in a star-spangled rodeo

Rhinestone cowboy

Getting cards and letters from people I don't even know

And offers coming over the phone..."

I held my spoon to my mouth like a microphone, joining in our spontaneous concert. Miss Pell clasped her hands over her ears and Mr. Henry shook his head. The more chagrined the faculty seemed, the louder we all sang until the decibel level reached unhealthy volumes. *Like a rhinestone cowboy*...just then a tremendous idea burst into my mind. I would step up and lead—just as Mr. Voss had urged me to do. I grinned and left the cafeteria. I went to my classes that afternoon, listening quietly but not hearing a word. My mind was circling round and round.

I called information that afternoon to get the number of the Fort Washakie store. A voice answered.

"Hello. This is Wesley Gallagher from Gallagher Springs, Utah."

"Hey sod buster, how's the schnoz?"

"Gloria?"

"Who else?"

"Hi, um...thanks for fixing me so good last fall."

"State your business; I haven't time for small talk."

I bit my lip and furrowed my brows. "Of course not. Um, well... could someone give Howahkan a message to call me? Or Amos, or Rouree, perhaps? If you don't see one of them, I'd settle for Yancy or Dover Good, or else Kenny Tanaka."

"Anybody else on the whole damn reservation you'd be willing to talk to?"

"No Mam." I told Gloria my number, hoping the message would be delivered to *one* of them.

Before I hung up Gloria asked, "How's the girl?"

"Yarrow is wonderful—she got royally spoiled at Christmas and insists Santa Claus must be some kind of Grandpa."

Gloria clucked pleasantly. "Well if she becomes any trouble you can always ship her this way."

We had TV dinners in the front room that night. Yarrow was excited about the change and pretended her TV tray was a little table at Maggie's at the Point. She produced a small notebook and took our orders before *Happy Days* came on at seven. Allyson had a serious crush on Fonzie and she smiled and pinched her lips together every time he swaggered into Al's Diner on the program.

"Allyson likes the Fonz," Yarrow said comically, "But I think my boy is handsomer."

The phone rang and I scrambled to answer it. Howahkan's voice sounded in my ear. "Is everything alright, Little Shoshone?"

"Everything is good! How about you?"

"I get better looking every day."

I grinned, shaking my head at the beauty of such an attitude. "I figured."

"How is Kell?"

"The Big Irish is well."

"And our dazzling little Yarrow?"

"She's good. She's got her moccasins on as we speak." Just then Yarrow hollered something at me from the front room. "Oh, Yarrow says for you to come see her soon, and bring your long braids with you."

"What a little darling! Well, you're making me miss *Happy Days*, so what is it you wanted?"

"I wondered how you'd feel about bringing everyone to Gallagher Springs for a show, a giant show-and-tell—what do you think?"

It was silent for a few moments. "Sort of like a powwow? Why?"

"I wanted to do it for Grady's ninety-third birthday. I thought we could honor him for all of his writing, as well as being the oldest living resident of our county. I couldn't think of anything better than inviting the Shoshone back to where they started, either."

"And if it's Kell's birthday he will give a speech."

I considered the possibility. "I guess he could—"

"And since I am older still, I will also speak."

My brows shot high. "You would speak?"

"Yes. And all of the people will want to meet me because I'm a main character in Phantom Flynn's last book."

I bit off a chuckle. Howahkan was nothing if not proud and ready to strut. "Yes, of course! I want my whole school to meet you. We could do this thing up right during Memorial Day weekend since it's a time for remembering. I think I can get all of Grady's cabins reserved and there's plenty of space for camping."

"My people haven't been back to Three Lakes for many years. It will do us good to come."

"But you must bring the drummers and the dancers! Bring the riders too—and..."

"And you will show off with them, eh? Haw! Howahkan can read your thoughts, Little Shoshone! Yes...we will come in fine feather ready to show the Irish how to have a celebration, alright."

"So you can do it? Can you get the horses here?"

"Can I get the horses there? What do I look like, a helpless dude? Of course we can manage it! I will send the boys out a week before so that you can all practice together and choreograph your performance."

"Then you come too, Howahkan, please? I miss you, I think."

"I will stay at Kell's, for we are brothers."

"Yes, of course!"

"It is my birthday soon, too."

"When?"

"June first."

"Then this will be a double celebration for the both of you!"

"I will have our people bring trinkets, huh? The white Irish will snatch them up like tourists in their own town! "

"Do that...I'm sure it will be a hit."

"Haw! The trinkets will pay for our trip, no doubt."

"Thanks Howahkan."

"Thank you, Little Shoshone. Maybe while I am there you will take me to Washakie Fork so I can say hello again before I say goodbye."

"Yes—we could have the powwow there, but...I want to keep it a secret, sort of."

"It's too hallowed isn't it boy? No, we'll powwow in town, and then you and I will slip away and make medicine together away from the crowds."

We said goodbye and I went off to my room to draw up a plan. I would have to convince the town to go along with this, but I knew I could do it. I thought about riding with Rouree, Dover, and Kenny before the envious eyes of my school chums and teachers, and the people of Washakie Fork as well. My mind turned the details like a rock in a polisher while Glen Campbell's song echoed around in my head, serenading my thirteen year old dreams.

A couple of days later I went into Mr. Voss's room before school. "You know that class fundraiser we haven't done yet?"

"Yes."

"Well I've got an idea."

"I'm listening."

"I am organizing sort of a powwow. My Indian friends from Fort Washakie are coming. It will be a very good cultural experience for both them and us. There will be traditional dancing, grass dancing, jingle dancing, shawl dancing, and fancy dances, as well as hand-drum singing, trick riding, and lots of booths for food and to buy authentic Shoshone souvenirs."

Mr. Voss was staring at me strangely. "Go on."

"I thought our class could use my ten-prong hot dog cooker and sell them. It might seem like a simple thing, but actually I made quite a bit of money off of hotdog sales this summer. I thought we could make up a couple of milk cans full of homemade root beer because those Shoshone really like the *shoog*, if you know what I mean."

The grey eyes narrowed. "*You* are organizing a powwow?"

"Well Grady is turning ninety-three, and his brother-in-law, Howahkan, who just so happens to be the oldest elder in his tribe will be turning ninety-nine. They remember life in the olden days when the Shoshone still camped here so many months out of the year. Howahkan actually made medicine with Chief Washakie *himself*—and that's really neat, don't you think? So I think that before these guys die we should honor both of them. I called Mayor Spinnaker last night and he was crazy about the idea. He is organizing a parade and is also overseeing all of the ads for our big event. I talked to Mr. Mulligan and he wants to coordinate a school assembly."

"*You* are doing this?"

I nodded, "Yes sir."

"Without any persuasion from others?"

"No sir. It's alright with you isn't it?"

"Yes—yes! Of course," Mr. Voss stammered. "It's a capital idea, Wesley, but you're a little young to be calling Indian reservations and organizing community events."

"I hope I didn't overstep my bounds or anything."

Mr. Voss shook his head. "No—it's just odd, that's all. I would have never dreamed up calling all of the natives into town."

"That's because you haven't seen them dance and sing! I went to a powwow last fall and I'm telling you! It is neat, and I wanted to share that culture with others."

"Wesley, Wesley, Wesley," Mr. Voss shook his head. "You do beat all…"

"I suggested that we could have a community dunking booth too. A lot of money could be raised by letting the town drown Mr. Mulligan, the mayor, and especially the bishop. Those are the main ones I thought of, but there are probably some others, like the county commissioners and the water master. The Shoshones might want to dunk some of their people too. It could be funny."

"Where would we get a dunking tank?"

"Couldn't the FFA boys build it in shop? John said they needed to raise money for state competitions or something."

"I don't know—this is a pretty big undertaking."

"Yes, but if the *school* takes care of the assembly, and the *town* does the advertising and the parade, and *I* take care of the Indians, and the *Indians* take care of the powwow, and the *church* cooks a breakfast, and the *Lion's club* oversees the booths, and the *classes and organizations* host booths, then I don't think it's too bad."

"Wait a minute; *you* are taking care of the Indians?"

"Yes, I've booked reservations for them in Grady's cabins, and also called Three Lakes Campground and got them to donate camping spaces on Eisner Beach."

"How did you get them to do that?"

"I told them it used to be *their* beach. Once they understood the simple concepts of our local history they were eager to help. Of course I had to promise them that their hospitality would be mentioned at the assembly and printed up on the town's advertisements."

"That was using your head!"

"Yes and so then I realized that other businesses might be willing to donate in order to get their names mentioned and printed up as well, and that's how I got McCarthy's Market to donate all of the supplies for our class hot dog booth. We won't have *any* overhead, and clear profits smell even better than electrocuted hotdogs."

"You are not a normal young man."

"Yes sir—I mean, no sir."

"What is in it for you?"

"I just want to show off Grady and Howahkan, and let my friends see some of the things I've seen. I want them to hear what I have heard, and feel what I felt. Oh…and I was also hoping to perform some trick riding with them."

His lips twitched, and he bit off a smile, forbidding it from taking over his face. "I see. I didn't know pony tricks were part of traditional powwows."

"This will be a special kind…with some riding tricks. Think of this event as more of a giant show-and-tell."

"Where on earth will this *giant show-and-tell* be held? The rodeo grounds are down in Lakeside—and the park isn't big enough for powwows, people, *and* vendors. There's not enough parking, either."

"We are going to do it in the field behind the Protestant Church. It's perfect, as the ground naturally slopes, and people can bring their chairs and have a good view."

"How did you convince them to let you use the ground?"

"I mentioned the Mormons were cooking breakfast."

Mr. Voss smiled again. "I see."

"*Naturally* they wanted to help."

Mr. Voss rubbed a hand across his eyes. "Wesley, you do beat all… and it still bodes well for my son-in-law to have you for a cousin."

"Thank you—and Mr. Voss?"

"Yes?"

"Well, I just think that little baby Kelly is something special, and worth having, you know? Even if her parents *did* put the cart in front of the horse, or whatever."

Mr. Voss seemed to choke a little bit at my statement. "Yes…well, I am a proud grandfather," he blustered.

"So thanks for not killing Mark or anything. He was afraid you would." Mr. Voss's eyes closed, and an amused smile snuck up on his face. "John lost two bucks to me on a bet."

"What bet?"

"I bet that you wouldn't kill Mark completely dead, and John bet that you would. Just proves what a nice guy you are."

The eyes shut again. "Thank you, Wesley."

"Yep. Now, don't you think we need to have a special student council so we can talk about the upcoming event and each class and organization can decide if they'd like to take part?"

Mr. Voss nodded. "Yes, as student government advisor, I do think that's important.

"Good because I already scheduled it for fifth hour. I hope that's alright with you."

"Wesley!"

I'd pushed my luck as far as I'd better go. "See you later, Mr. Voss. Don't worry; I'll steer clear of those cliffs."

Chapter Twenty

The doorbell rang late in the afternoon in the middle of May. I answered it, happy to see Rouree Greathawk, Kenny Tanaka, and Dover Good. We shook hands and I invited them inside. The three boys seemed curious about our house, and their eyes swept around, taking it all in. "Geez, are you rich?"

"No. If you don't believe me go look in the garage. Our car is ten years old."

Yarrow peeked into the front room, smiling shyly. "Hi my boy."

"Come here, Yarrow." She walked over to me, grinning at the older boys. "Yarrow this is your cousin, Rouree Greathawk."

"Hi there," Rouree said.

"Myself is cousins with mostly everybody around here," Yarrow said. We had all been working with her, trying to get her to say *I* instead of *myself*, and she got it right half of the time now—just not this time.

Rouree smiled, looking somewhat enviously at me, for I had the little girl for a sister and he did not. I introduced the guys to Mother and Allyson. Allyson blushed awkwardly. "Hi," she mumbled.

"You're sister is cute, man," Dover said.

"She's eleven so back off," I grumbled.

Kenny and Rouree laughed at that and they followed me out to our corrals. We unloaded their horses. "I don't think you can do what Howahkan claims you can," Kenny said.

I cocked my head off to one side and clicked to Misty. She came over and I wrapped my hands in her mane. She took off running with me at her side then I set my feet and up I flew, right onto her back. I dismounted and mounted several times while the boys watched. "Good job Little Shoshone," Rouree called. "I knew you could do it!"

"Sorry for doubting you," Kenny said.

"No prob. Where's Howahkan? Didn't he ride with you guys?"

"Yes, but he had us drop him off at the Big Irish's house."

"Did you meet him already?"

"Yes, and had him sign all of our books," Rouree explained. "That guy is really little! But cool—I mean, we all like him."

I smiled, nodding. "So…you guys wanna go swimming, or what?"

"I'm game," Kenny said.

"Then we are staying in one of the cabins so that should be fun," I announced.

Mother was fretful about me having fifteen and sixteen year old friends. I was more worried that one of them would light up a cigarette in our house, and so I told Mother that I got along with Monty, Mark, and John okay and asked her to relax. Dad took my side, and she consented, saying it might be fun for us to stay in the cabin.

I grabbed my duffle bag and strutted out to Amos Greathawk's fancy red truck feeling a little full of myself. I was a big fish in a little pond and I hoped everyone saw me with the older Indian boys. I had bragging rights on having them for friends, and couldn't wait to show them off.

"Any cute girls in this town?" Kenny asked.

"Yeah, I guess so."

"I like a little white bread," Dover chimed in.

"You guys have girls on the brain!"

"Don't tell me you haven't started girling yet?" Rouree asked incredulously.

"I've been busy doing pony tricks."

"Man, you've gotta get a life," Kenny persisted. "Pony tricks are what you do to pass the time if there aren't any girls around."

"I wanted to impress you guys."

Rouree looked at me strangely. "We're already impressed, you weirdo."

"What will *really* impress me is if you can find us some cute girls in this town."

"I'm sure that you won't have any problem with finding girls," I assured them. "Aren't they fickle, and always wanting what's different and exotic? Don't they flutter and swoon over the tall, dark, and handsome types?"

"I sure as hell hope so," Dover said, lighting a cigarette.

We parked at the resort and I checked in for us at the desk. Mark was working. I introduced him to my friends and they all shook hands. We got lockers and met up in the pools a few minutes later. The guys loved the naturally warm water and swam athletically. "You ought to try some chicken fights," a voice called. We all looked up, seeing Mark grinning boldly from the poolside.

"Oh yeah?" Kenny asked, eager for some sport.

"You wanna join us?" Dover inquired.

"No, but Wesley can handle you all."

Kenny snickered but Rouree seemed convinced. He called to be my horse first, and Kenny climbed on Dover's shoulders. I smiled at Mark, tickled to think he thought I could best the Shoshone boys. I knew they were wild and tough clear through and feared the ridicule if I lost. Kenny started talking smack, and the boys knew how, every one of them. Even Mark's eyes opened wide at some of the comments.

"Come on, white boy. Come on kid, bring it," Tanaka challenged. He stretched his long arms forward and I quickly wove mine around his, pinning his elbows backward. I caught him by surprise. His face looked startled just before he toppled backwards and into the water.

Mark licked a finger and made a tally mark in the air. Kenny surfaced, muttering excuses and a few insults. "You cheat," he cried.

"How? How does a person cheat in a chicken fight?"

"Well...you caught me off guard."

"Climb back up there then," Mark ordered. "I've got three dollars that says he'll throw you again!" Kenny did, and this time he claimed he meant business. His face was surly as he grappled toward me. I didn't make any movement; I just watched and waited for him to get near. When he came close enough, he reached out, trying to push me off balance. I locked his upper arm with mine, pinning it. He swung with his other arm, and my left arm tied it up, again cranking his elbow backwards. I leveraged him down until both he and Dover crashed beneath the surface.

Mark chalked another point for me on his imaginary scoreboard. Rouree was laughing, having great fun with our sport. Dover and Kenny traded places. I threw Dover in no time, and had a sneaking suspicion Wyatt could probably have done as well. Dover assumed the secret was in the pushing. The secret was in the leveraging, and no mistake. Dover wouldn't go at me again, and Rouree refused flatly. "The Little Shoshone is more than I care to spar with, even for fun."

Mark went back to work and we climbed into a smaller pool, talking and laughing the way boys do. The sun was rapidly sinking low, and the steam was becoming more visible as the night crept up on us. We were making plans for the show, each of us expressing our desires for the performance. I let them do most of the talking—I was just pleased to be included. Suddenly Rouree's face lit up and he howled at the moon like a lunatic coyote. I looked over my shoulder to see what caused the ruckus. Celia Quinn was blushing at the bold boy.

"Hey Celia," I said, grinning.

"Hello Wes."

"Glory hallelujah, but you *do* know a girl," Dover crowed.

Kenny howled as well and then all three boys wolf-cried together. Celia's brows shot up and she gulped. "Um…I just came to tell you that your cabin is ready, whenever you want it. It's number eight—on the end."

"Thanks Celia."

"Woof! Baby you are a fox," Rouree said. I was certain the boys were only bold because there was safety and bravado in numbers. "Don't tell me you're the one who has just made the bed I'll sleep in?"

Celia blushed again and her eyes opened wide. She stammered, "Um…I guess I am."

"Well that just does certain mysterious things to me," Rouree answered bluntly.

I laughed, getting a big kick out this boy-meets-girl demonstration. I studied Celia's face to gauge her reaction. She was eyeing Rouree closely, mindlessly chewing on the inside of one cheek. Suddenly she ran a hand through her hair, looking confidant, just the way Monty always did. For crying out loud! Celia was my own cousin and she bewitched even me with her feminine wiles. I could hear Rouree's heart speed, and Kenny and Dover were mooning over her.

"Well, have fun Wes," she called, turning to leave.

Rouree grabbed my arm, bidding me to make her come back. "Celia!"

She turned around. "Yes?"

"These are my friends." She smiled at me and winked. She walked closer to the pool, seeming sort of pleased that I'd summoned her. "Guys, this is my cousin, Celia Quinn."

"Hell-ooo mighty," Rouree said lowly. "And how do you do, Celia?"

"I do well, thank you."

"Celia, this is O'Rourke Greathawk. He's named after Grady, but we all call him Rouree."

Celia smiled, sucking in one cheek again, appearing aloof, but oh so interested at the same time. "And this is Kenny Tanaka and Dover Good. They are going to trick ride with me at the powwow, and they also perform the Men's Fancy, which is unbelievably entertaining."

"Right on." Celia sat herself by the side of the pool. She kicked off her sandals and lowered her feet and legs into the water. "So what exactly is a Men's Fancy?"

"It's a dance," I explained. "They dress in amazing costumes and move to the craziest drumming patterns you can imagine. They really know how to strut their stuff." I paused. Celia didn't really seem to be listening. She was busy studying the three buff, tough, and broodingly handsome teenage boys. A coy smile teased against her mouth.

"Go on," she said, feigning an interest. Her eyes returned to Rouree and I felt a zap of electricity from where I was standing. I needed to be wearing a welder's mask to avoid vision damage from so many flying sparks.

"Well, you'll like to see it," I said, sounding young and lame.

"Are your girlfriends coming to cheer for you?" Celia pressed.

Dover snorted. "Yeah baby, but we'll make room. Why don't you join us?"

Kenny slugged Dover's arm. "No, no girlfriends."

"What about you?" Celia asked, looking directly at Rouree again.

"I was hoping that *you'd* show up," he answered cockily. "And then I guess you can cheer if you'd like to."

Celia blushed, showing her pretty smile and straight white teeth. "Well, it was nice meeting you all," she said again, and swung her legs out of the water to go. "In fact, it's been blazin'." Blazin'. That was Celia's nifty word and the guys liked it. Rouree moved past me in the water, hoisting himself from the pool with the strength of his arms. He followed her as she made her way toward the lockers. Dover and Kenny laughed lowly, intrigued. I was too.

Rouree reached out gently snagging Celia's hand, tugging her to a halt. Her eyes were wide, and she was genuinely surprised by his action. He did not pull his hand away from her hers, but kept holding it, studying her face. I could see color rising into her cheeks, but returned his gaze, smiling shyly. "I'd like you to join us," he said. "It would be as you say, *blazin'*."

Celia's mouth opened and shut, and she shifted her weight from one foot to the other, "Well I—I," she stammered.

"Please tell me you're not working."

"No, I'm finished, but..."

Rouree smiled at her. His left hand reached out and touched a strand of her hair. That apparently was the magic trick, for Celia looked as smitten as I'd ever seen her. I made a mental note for future reference: touch the hair, they like it. "I have my truck and would gladly take you home for your suit," he said smoothly. His voice was purring and creamy and I rubbed my eyes, wondering if he was the same Rouree who I'd been laughing and goofing with a few minutes before.

"Celia keeps a swimming suit here," I called. "We all have permanent lockers."

Celia shot a sideways glance at me, scowling, probably wishing I would go away. I didn't know why, for I'd practically gift wrapped this Romeo and handed him to her. Rouree's hand moved from her hair to her chin. He tilted it towards him, saying, "Please?"

"Sure," she said, not playing hard to get. "Totally copasetic. I'll be right back."

"Hey Honey," Kenny called. "Call some friends! Dover and I want in on the action!"

Rouree waited near the locker exit, casually leaning against the wall, talking easily with Mark. I had to hand it to him; he was a very attentive suitor, for when Celia immerged from the dressing room, he was right there, grinning. His eyebrows rose expectantly, looking happy with the results of Celia in a bathing suit. They sauntered back to the hot pool. I couldn't help smiling at my cousin, and she grinned back, looking a little bit giddy.

"Staci and Veronica are coming," she said pertly, making Dover and Kenny happy.

"And who are Staci and Ver-r-r-r-onica?" Kenny asked.

I glowered at him. "When did you start talking like Tony the Tiger, Tanaka?" He ignored me, opting to smile stupidly at Celia's generosity. The talk of girls was making my friends drunk with stupidity.

"My friends," Celia said, smiling smugly.

"That's gr-r-r-r-eat!"

And then I was disappointed because girls were going to ruin my fun night. I scowled and slapped the water. This was not *copasetic* with me! I'd waited since last autumn to bond with these guys and what happened? Girls! I climbed out of the pool and went into the boathouse for a Pepsi Cola. I jerked the cap off and took a chug.

"Hey you got a beer in here?" Dover asked.

"Nope."

"No?"

"Welcome to Utah," I said curtly.

"Well do you know where we can get some?"

"Absolutely no idea," I lied belligerently. "Besides, Celia's friends wouldn't be impressed by that."

"No?"

"Trust me...but I'll buy you a soda if you'd like."

Kenny grabbed a Tab. "So which one's cuter, Stacie or Veronica? Because I'm calling dibbs."

"I dunno...they're both okay, I guess. Don't you guys want to go boating in the moonlight or something? We could have canoe races. Our families have moonlight canoe races sometimes. They are fun!"

Kenny didn't pay any attention to me, for he heard female voices and went to inspect. I was now annoyed that I'd bought his pop. I didn't need his Tab on mine! I phoned Wyatt, wondering if he wanted to come up and soak with me or something.

"Hey Wes," he said.

"Hi—would you like to come up to Grady's? My friends from the reservation are here."

"Uh, well, I dunno Wesley. Avery's coming over in ten minutes and we're going to work on that Eiffel Tower puzzle. You know—the thousand piece one she gave me for my birthday."

"Well hell, I'd hate for you to miss out on that!" I was mad at my fellow man beasts at the moment and decided that since I was thirteen I would swear a little if I felt like it. It seemed like such a minor thing compared to smoking cigarettes and drinking beer…and girling.

"Don't be hissy," Wyatt complained. "You're my best cousin and everything, but you really need to get a girlfriend—or else go ride your horse or something."

"Okay," I said sarcastically. "Goodbye!"

Veronica O'Brien was laughing with the boys. She was miles ahead of her little sister, Judy Brynn, but *still* not interesting enough to hold my attention. "I'm sweet sixteen," I heard her giggle.

"Yeah?" Kenny asked. "Sweet sixteen and never been kissed?"

Oh brother! I dove into the biggest pool and began swimming laps, working off my agitation. What had been fairly entertaining at first suddenly felt dull. Who cared about girling? I wanted to talk horses and guns! I wanted to talk about fast trucks and motorcycles, Indian chiefs, outlaws, fist fights and pocketknives. I wanted to reminisce about broken noses and Howahkan Greathawk. These guys wanted to play patty-fingers in the swimming pool! I had half a mind to stuff my Pepsi bottle up Rouree's tailpipe, and fill Kenny's shorts with stinking cheese bait. I wanted to run Dover's clothes up the flagpole.

The madder I felt the faster I swam, back and forth, back and forth. I zoned my mind onto our upcoming riding event, mentally running through my routine. I must have been on my twentieth lap when I felt a soft flutter reach out and touch my arm. I jumped, completely startled, and I surfaced. A girl stared at me. It wasn't Celia, Staci, or Veronica. She had green eyes and auburn hair. Her mouth was full and pretty, and there were apples in her cheeks. "Do you swim competitively?" she asked.

I shook my head. "No…why?"

"I just wondered. You were really going at it. I've never seen anyone swim so fast."

"No?" I grinned. Whoever this girl was, she seemed plenty aware of athletic prowess when she saw it. I admired that quality in a girl.

"I'm Shonnee O'Shea."

"Yes you are," I said, and then felt stupid because the others laughed. I looked sideways, surprised to see they had all come into the big pool. Celia grinned and winked.

"Where were you swimming to so hard?" Dover asked. Staci Spinnaker stood near him.

"Just doing laps," I said.

"Yeah, but you looked like you actually wanted to break the pool down," Rouree quipped.

I shrugged. "I'm surprised you could take five minutes away from the Romance Follies to notice."

Rouree's black brows shot up. "Why are you so lippy all of a sudden?"

"I think he wants a race," Kenny suggested. "And I'm happy to give him one."

Well, that was progress. At least the boys were interacting with me again, not just making googly eyes at the girls. "You're on."

We lined up and Dover called "Go!"

I swam as fast as a fish, but I could feel the frothy movements of Kenny Tanaka at my shoulder. He was a good swimmer and it was all I could do to edge him out on the other end. "No fair," he protested. "You were warmed up."

"Worn out, you mean." I swam to the edge and took another swallow of Pepsi.

Dover and Rouree lined up and that was a dead heat, a tie. The girls smiled appreciatively at the bronze physical prowess that had recently blown in from Wyoming. And they could thank me! I was getting set to challenge Dover.

"Let's play Marco Polo," Veronica suggested. Figures, as that seemed like a dumb girl game. I would have expected as much from her idiot sister, Judy Brynn. Perhaps the whole O'Brien Clan was a bunch of dwebes and lame-Os.

"Alright," Dover agreed. I couldn't believe it!

"No thanks," I said. "I'm not in the mood for playing hopscotch or school, either." I climbed out of the pool and went to the lockers.

Mark was swabbing the floor when I got dressed. I grabbed another mop and helped him. An older couple registered for one of the cabins. Mark gave them the first one, careful to space them a good distance from us. Mark stepped back inside. "Wesley, why aren't you still swimming?"

"Ah," I said. "It's turned into a girly festival. Not really into sitting around and discussing which one's better, *The Brady Bunch* or *The Partridge Family*, salon perms or Toni home waves. Ugh!"

Mark grinned. "I guess that's not your thing, huh?"

"No! Honestly—after the chicken fights were over with our night went south."

"Looks like Celia's scoring points with that one kid."

"Rouree? Yes, he thinks she's a fox and she thinks he's *blazin*.'"

"Hmm…maybe it's a good thing Monty wasn't working tonight."

I grinned. "Maybe we should call him!"

Mark chuckled. "Let's give Celia some space. She's a good kid and if Rouree gets fresh we've got her back."

"So…how's the married life? It's still weird to me that you have a wife. And a kid."

Mark nodded. "It's still weird to me, too, but…it's good. I do get my fair share of girly talk, though."

"I'll bet!"

"But just for the record—I *am* happy. I think our little Kelly is the most beautiful, smartest, best baby in the world. I don't mind going home to that a bit. And Michelle is great! She's not a nag at all. Of course I'll like it better when she learns how to make good gravy, but..."

"Hey Wesley?" Staci Spinnaker was shivering near the locker door.

"Yeah?"

"Um...don't you want to come and play with us? Shonnee is my cousin and she *likes* you."

I felt my cheeks flush. "Um...well, I'm already dressed." Just then I saw Grandpa and Grandma Gallagher pull into Grady's driveway. "And I've gotta go talk to my grandparents," I lied. "I'll be out in a little while."

"We close at eleven," Mark quipped. I gave him the evil eye, scurrying away from Shonnee O'Shea's cousin and the curtain of rising steam.

"Little Shoshone!" Howahkan was happy to see me. Grandma gave me a hug and then I watched as Grady introduced Grandma and Grandpa Gallagher to the ancient.

Howahkan shook their hands pleasantly. He and Grandpa ran a silent assessment of each other as their hands pumped up and down congenially. I had tons of respect for both of them. "Howahkan Greathawk," the oldest man said.

"Doc Riley Gallagher," Grandpa nodded. "Great to meet you. Wesley's entertained us with the low-down on you."

Howahkan smiled. "You are Errol Gallagher's grandson?"

Grandpa seemed surprised. "Yes." His mustache twitched beneath a smile.

Howahkan grinned smugly. "The best horse I ever had came from Errol Gallagher."

"Oh really?" Grandpa was genuinely interested. "I didn't know you bought a horse from him."

"I didn't say that," Howahkan said. "But it sure was the finest horse I ever had!"

The room exploded with laughter at the comment. It *was* humorous and Grandpa conceded as much. "Well, as long as you appreciated it, I guess."

"I did, I did! Rode the shoes right off that mount and then I let him lope around barefooted. I bagged my last buffalo on Errol Gallagher's legal property. I'll thank him one day."

Grandma Gallagher seemed quite taken with the man. Her eyes narrowed whenever he spoke, careful not to miss a word. It made me happy to see that. Grandma was finally learning the things that she should have always known about her dad, and the old Indian's stories were colorful and held us spellbound. It was *miles* better than playing Marco Polo.

Grady's phone rang. I answered it for him but it was for me anyway. "Wesley?"

"Hi Mark."

"The kids want you to come back out."

I bit my lip. "Did the girls go home?"

"No, but they're dressed and going to have canoe races."

That was more like it! I would suggest boys against the girls. The competition would be healthy for the females, and I was certain they would find the arrangement to be *copasetic*. I hung up and said my goodbyes to the older set. They were the coolest bunch of senior citizens in the world.

Mark was locking up the boathouse and lockers. "See ya," I called.

"Goodbye Wesley. Be a good sport…and—be a good kid, okay?"

"I won't do anything you haven't done," I goofed. Mark looked grim. That was funny to me, and I stepped into a wall of steam and lost sight of the world behind me. I wound my way around the pools, then exited the pool gate and jogged across the grass to the docks. I could see the kids climbing into the canoes. Lantern light jittered in dizzy patterns on the water. Inish Lake was post-card pretty, and Grady had installed lanterns all along the north end, and again near the cabins on the west side. The moon was full and painted a path, inviting us out for night games.

"If you don't wear your life jacket I won't go," Celia said belligerently.

"I don't need a life jacket," Dover argued.

"I'm not going then, and neither are you. Its Grady's place, and Grady's rules, and Wesley and I both work here. We're not going unless you wear them."

"Fine," Dover muttered. He climbed into a canoe with Kenny, Staci, and Veronica. I was annoyed again, for my plan would have been a lot more fun!

"We could race boys against the girls," I suggested hopefully, but nobody jumped all over the idea. I said it again.

"We *could*, Little Shoshone, but this is more to our liking," Rouree trumped. "Climb in. Celia wanted to be on your team."

So I saddled up with Rouree, Celia, and Staci's cousin, Shonnee O'Shea. Sure, she was cute enough but I smelled a rat. Kenny Tanaka rattled off the rules to the race, and I wondered who died and made him the boss of Grady's lake, but I didn't toot off about it.

"Got all your oars in the water?" Dover asked us. He laughed at his query then shouted, "Go!"

We began rowing, with Rouree calling right and left, so we could paddle together. Dover and his bunch didn't start off with that system, and their canoe paddled in a circle because the girls were rowing opposite from the boys. The funny sight playing out over my shoulder was worth the strain of looking. Kenny was blustering orders, trying to solve their circling problems. Dover was out-shouting Kenny, and Celia's friends just seemed confused about what they were supposed to be doing.

I loved winning, and we worked together well. "Look at those wussies," Rouree howled. We silenced our oars and waited for the competition to actually start. "What's the problem?" Rouree called back to the shore.

"Too many chiefs and not enough Indians," Shonnee said just loud enough for us to hear. That was clever. I studied her as she sat in front of me, for surely there could be no harm in it. Moonlight gleamed against her wet, auburn hair. She had brushed it back into a simple ponytail and it looked sort of neat for some reason.

"Our team is definitely better than theirs," Celia said. "We're blazin' and they're bogus."

"*You're* blazin,'" Rouree whispered, grinning over his shoulder at her.

I don't know why I wasn't disgusted. Perhaps because we were winning by so far that we had to stop and wait for the others to catch up in order to call it a race. Perhaps it was the fact that I liked competition, or maybe it was just because I was on the best team all the way around. I always liked boating at night. I liked the moon on the water, and the fairy lights twinkling near the shore. I had always enjoyed these things. I liked the smell of the water, and the sight of steam rising in the distance. For all these reasons I was in good spirits again, and I was positively certain that Shonnee O'Shea's neat looking ponytail had nothing to do with it.

"Wesley?" Shonnee was looking at me, jarring me back to whatever.

"What?"

She smiled. "I just asked you how old are."

"Oh, sorry, I was…just thinking about stuff—um…I'm thirteen."She nodded, smiling pleasantly, but turned back toward the front of the boat.

"How old are you?"

"Fourteen."

She didn't turn around to face me again so I was at liberty to scowl. How lame was that? I finally met a fairly cute, clever, and sensible girl, and she was *older* than me? Talk about dumb! It bothered me that she turned her back on me so completely just because of our age difference. When I ignored her earlier it was justified because she was a *girl* and I'm not girling yet, but her attitude of ignoring me just because I'm a year younger was a low blow.

We didn't have time for anymore races that night. Staci and Shonnee had to be home by eleven thirty and so they left with Veronica. Celia loitered, hedging against a departure. I was wondering when Uncle Rob or Aunt Aura Leigh would appear, searching for her. I mentioned it to Celia and her bottom lip jutted out. She stepped into the cabin and called on the phone, begging for another half hour.

Each cabin had a fire pit and a picnic table near the water's edge. Rouree built a fire and we sat around talking. Celia sat near Rouree, and her smile was bright, and her cheeks extra flushed. Her hand rested on the log bench near his, and he gradually inched his hand over, interlocking his fingers with hers. They thought they were so sneaky, but I was catching all the action. They seemed plenty twitterpated.

Near midnight Kenny fingered a cigarette from a pack of Marlboro's in his jacket pocket. Celia's eyes were large as he took a puff and handed it off to Dover for a drag. He threw the pack across the fire in Rouree's direction. Rouree caught it in midair with his left hand, not releasing Celia's hand with his right.

"I don't smoke and I don't date boys who do," Celia said bluntly.

"Who smokes?" Rouree asked, tossing the pack right back at Kenny in one fluid motion. "I don't smoke."

Kenny and Dover were dumbstruck, both of them muttering about the sudden saint sitting across the fire. "I didn't know this was a revival meeting," Dover grumbled.

I grinned at Celia, feeling proud of her spunk and standards, for that began the reformation of Rouree Greathawk. There's nothing like a cute girl to help a man repent! That's what Grady always said, and I agreed.

Chapter Twenty-One

The next morning Rouree came to church with me. He was in the same Sunday school class as Celia, and I was certain that he was suddenly getting religion, alright. Dover and Kenny stayed in bed until noon but came to our house for Sunday dinner with all the rest of our relatives. Uncle Rob looked fairly curious about the looks passing back and forth between Celia and Rouree, but Aunt Aura Leigh didn't seem to notice. Grady smiled in their direction having the most sympathy on their situation. He would be Celia's excuse for dating outside of her race and religion, for he had. How could anyone fault them now? Hadn't society ebbed forward enough to accept whatever? I kind of had to smile, for Uncle Rob was in a tight spot.

Howahkan and Grady were seated in the end chairs of our long, long, long, dinner table. The family listened to their tales and banter and it was a pleasant meal. The Mulligan's were out of town for the day, and so that was a nice break, and Mark and Michelle were dining at Voss's. Monty was with Shaylin in Lakeside, and so our numbers were fairly manageable. Dori Jo and Allyson clung to every word the Shoshone boys uttered, seeming smitten beyond all ability to properly swoon. Grandma Gallagher, Mother, and my aunts, were fascinated with the ancient Howahkan. He was as old as the hills, but still cut such a striking figure, and Grady had immortalized him in his book. It was sort of funny to me that mothers and grandmothers of decent sense could still develop crushes on characters in a book! I dare say it was an entertaining meal.

That afternoon John and Celia invited Rouree, Dover, and Kenny to go riding around and see the town. I wasn't invited, and felt painfully too young, and miffed, but I needed a break from the older boys anyway. Wyatt and I tossed a baseball around in the backyard, making ourselves scarce and out of harm's way during dishes and clean up.

Yarrow came out into the yard, dragging three baby dolls in a buggy. She struggled down the back steps. I ran to help her. "Thank you my boy. These kids have got to git a bit of fresh air."

"Oh, they'll like to go for a walk, Yarrow."

"Yip. Myself is their mommy."

"What are their names today?" I asked because Yarrow's babies' names changed more often than their clothes.

"Heather, Rose, and Pete…aint they great?"

"Heather, Rose, and Pete?"

"Yip. I know you like Heather and Rose, that's who you wanted myself to be."

I peered in the buggy. Heather and Rose were wearing frilly pink dresses, but I feared Pete was sporting ruffled purple. "Pete's wearing a dress?"

"Pete has to. Pete don't got pants."

"Well for Pete's sake," I goofed. "Maybe you'd better let Pete be a girl."

"Pete can be a girl tomorrow. Today he's Pete."

"She's so funny," Wyatt said as Yarrow bounded around the house, pushing her children and singing loudly to them.

"Yes she is. How was the puzzle last night?"

"Good," Wyatt answered. "Really good."

"Avery's quite a girl, huh?"

"Yes. She's good at puzzles."

"I can't believe she hasn't gone flitting off to some other guy yet."

"She's not as fickle as you think. I'm going to marry her someday."

"Hmph! Don't be lame…by the way, you didn't miss out on much last night. The guys were too googly-eyed over Celia and her friends."

Wyatt nodded. "Sorry about that."

Howahkan stepped out the back door. "Little Shoshone, take me for a ride."

"Where to?"

"Wherever the hello mighty I want to go. It's our agreement, remember?"

"Alright. Can Wyatt come?"

"You're the driver."

I went into the house and told mother I was taking the car. Her lips pinched together. "You're not old enough, Wesley."

"You agreed. That was Howahkan's stipulation when we took Yarrow."

Mother scowled, but how could she argue with that? "Wyatt's coming with us, just so you know."

When I got back outside, Howahkan and Wyatt were seated in the car already, and Yarrow was buckled into the backseat with Heather, Rose, and Pete. I turned on my heel and ran back into the house to tell Mother that I had her. Suddenly she was all the more concerned, and barked orders up one side and down the other about my driving and how to stay safe.

I climbed in the Buick and turned the key in the ignition. "Where to?"

"I want to see where J-O-N-I went into the water." Howahkan spelled the name to keep Yarrow out of the loop.

"That's in Lakeside," I hedged.

"Well tootle-dee-doo. Off to Lakeside, then."

If Mother found out about this I would be creamed tuna on toast. I had only been allowed to drive on the dirt road up Gallagher Canyon, mostly. This would be my first highway experience and I was both eager *and* nervous. We backed out of the driveway, and I hit the blinker, turning from Gallagher Street to Main Street, and again from Main Street to the highway. We waved as we passed Rouree, Celia, John, Kenny, and Dover. They seemed surprised to see us motor by, and I hoped they wouldn't rat me out.

My grip on the steering wheel was white knuckled. I prayed that Pistol Stewart was home eating pot roast and enjoying the day with his family. We passed a northbound car full of tourists. I waved coolly because folks all waved to each other in Three Lakes Valley. I might not be legal, but at least I wasn't a snoot. I saw Monty's red mustang and sat tall. I waved with gusto as he went by and noticed a dust stir in my rear view mirror, as he'd nearly run off the road at the sight of me and my car full of various assorted passengers.

The drive was actually quite pleasant, despite my fears, for Howahkan pointed out places he'd camped as a boy. "I used to steal eggs from that old barn right there," he said at one point. "They had a bunch of good chickens."

"That wasn't nice of you," Wyatt protested.

"I let them keep their chickens," Howahkan argued. "It was very nice of me, I'd say."

Yarrow could barely peer from the back window, but she said, "That's Maggie's at the Point. That's where my boy took me for foods. We get to have supper there one time every month, and myself likes it! My daddy lets me order whatever I want."

"I'm glad you found your boy, Yarrow," Howahkan said tenderly. That comment made me feel tall enough to drive the car, and I relaxed my death grip on the steering wheel and actually enjoyed the remaining five miles of the trip. Stevie Wonder crooned *"Don't You Worry 'Bout a Thing,"* from the radio.

Lake Washakie was the smallest of the three lakes, and the deepest. It was faced on two sides by sheer granite cliffs. Two long fishing piers extended over the water on the west side. That's where the clacker had zoomed to its death. I refused to drive up on the pier, for my skills in reverse might not have been adequate to get us back on the road. I didn't want to end up in the lake. I wasn't ready to clack with butterflies.

I held onto Yarrow's hand and we walked onto the pier. Water lapped around the rocks, and I could see minnows flitting between the crevices just below the surface. Several fishing boats bobbed along the lake. I recognized Grandpa's cousin Archie, and waved. Yarrow lay down on her stomach to peer at the tiny fish. "I see somethin' down there. Look my boy—fish sticks!"

Howahkan laughed heartily, and Wyatt and I joined in. "Those are minnows, Yarrow," Wyatt explained.

"Yip! That's what they make fish sticks out of."

I put my foot on Yarrow's legs to keep her from toppling in head first. She was content to study the goings on in the water.

Howahkan became very quiet as his old eyes studied the rippling deep. He spoke in Shoshone. Yarrow pulled herself upright, fascinated by the chanting words. Her little hand clasped mine while we watched Howahkan pray. Wyatt was wide-eyed and reverent. We all were.

Howahkan wiped tears from his cheeks without shame. When

a man is nearly a century old, he's allowed to show emotion. "These waters are haunted with those poor, troubled souls," he said. "If only J-O-N-I would have realized who and what she was. We all loved her! She was my youngest granddaughter, and for her I would have given all that I had."

Just then a breeze stirred from the south, sweeping between granite cliffs. It blew goose bumps against my arms and neck. Yarrow giggled and she reached up with her free hand and waved. I looked to see who she was waving at, but saw only waves stirring choppily. Wyatt and I exchanged wary glances. Yarrow waved again, and her feet danced in exited patterns. I tightened my grip on her hand to keep her from falling off the edge.

"What is it?"

"Oh my boy! Myself is so happy that you brought us to Jesus' house!"

Even Howahkan scowled, trying to make sense of the riddle-talking child. "This is Lake Washakie, not Jesus' house."

"Nope, nope, nope," Yarrow squealed. "Because my Joni just waved and smiled at me."

Chills tripped in a haywire manner all along my spine. My heart pounded and my eyes watered. "Where, Yarrow?"

"Right there. See her?" She pointed again, and blessedly I did not see her. "She's so funny today; she's dressed like an Indian. She has moccasins just like mine, and feathers fluttering in her hair. My Joni looks *so* pretty today! She is smiling so much at me!"

Howahkan raised a leathered hand to the spot where Yarrow was looking. "Old Grandfather loves you, Joni." He then wiped the hand across his eyes. "Feathers flutter, say goodbye," he whispered hoarsely.

"Myself loves you," Yarrow cried in agreement. "You are my Joni!" Then Yarrow clapped her hands and whirled around and around. I had a time keeping her from spinning off the pier altogether. "My Joni is so clean, and my Joni is so clean and clean and cl-eeeee-ean," she sang.

"Isn't she standing there anymore?" Wyatt asked.

"Nope. My Joni had to go back inside Jesus' house, probably. I bet that's what."

Wyatt, Howahkan and I looked back and forth from one to another. What could we say? Wyatt's eyes were brimming with tears, and I only hoped he wouldn't start into a fit. I asked him if he was okay, and he said, "No! Weird, spooky occurrences follow you around, Wesley, and I don't like that kind of thing so much."

Howahkan's hands rested against both of our shoulders. "Let's go. Our Joni is resting easier now."

It was a quiet trip back to Gallagher Springs. Only our thoughts were loud. Yarrow hummed happily from the backseat, *I am a Child of God*, and her spirits were bright, and she seemed unaffected by the spiritual manifestation. I decided little kids were special that way. I peered in the rearview mirror at her. Yarrow kissed Pete on the head and told him he was almost home. "If you are a very good boy, myself will get you some pants on another day."

We pulled into the driveway. Yarrow bounded out of the door with her arms full of babies. "Hi Grady," she called, seeing her great grandfather in the back yard. "My Joni is an Indian, too!"

"She is?" Grady's eyes were merry, completely ignorant of the happenings of the afternoon. He bent down and kissed her dark head. He asked her about her dolls.

"These are myself's children. Heather is the oldest. Then this one with the bad eye, that's Rose, and the little fella is Pete."

Grady marched around, clapping his hands at the introductions. "Some grandpas are good, and some grandpas are great, but I'm so good I'm greaty great! Now I see I'm a great, great, grandfather again!"

Yarrow twirled around, singing, "You're lots of great and great and grrr-ea-t, Grandpa Grady!"

"She's special," Howahkan observed.

Wyatt nodded, and I agreed. "Yes, Howahkan."

"Do you know the best part about today?"

"What?"

"*Joni is dressed like an Indian*. She's wearing moccasins, Yarrow said. She remembers who she is now, and that makes my old ticker feel happy."

"Your old ticker? You sounded like Grady just then."

"Damn fool's rubbing off on me."

We'd been parked for several minutes, but none of us felt compelled to get out of the car. "Why don't you drive, Howahkan?"

"Never learned how."

We stared at the proud relic. "Why?"

"Never really needed to. Back in the day when autos were introduced I made fun of my friends as they learned. I called them all white dudes. Well—actually I called them a little bit worse than that, but you get the picture. The more the old ways disappeared, the more and more driving looked good to me, but I was too proud then. Life was changing fast, and I was resisting it."

"Why don't you learn now? You're never too young to try. Look at Wesley."

"I'm nearly ninety-nine! That's too old!"

"You can't learn any younger," Wyatt persisted.

"I'll teach you," I offered.

Howahkan laughed belligerently. "That'll be the day! Me drive, haw! Dream on!" He opened the door and stretched his long, lean legs onto the cement. "Maybe tomorrow... maybe."

Chapter Twenty-Two

Mr. Mulligan made arrangements for the three Shoshone boys to attend our school for a week as part of the educational, culturally inspiring experience of the upcoming powwow. I thought I was big stuff introducing them around. Rouree's eyes fired all along the jostling hallways until he spotted Celia Quinn. She smiled but made no sudden motion to seek him out. She was a quiet girl, old fashioned, and good—but she was plenty interested, too. When we finally made it down to the high school lockers, Celia took the initiative to introduce the guys to her other friends. Of course Veronica was mouthy and loud, letting everyone know she had an inside track on Rouree, Dover, and Kenny. Staci's nose wrinkled pleasantly in Dover's direction, but she too, was soft-spoken and not overbearing.

All of the girls in my grade twittered about the three hunky beef cakes, and my seventh grade buddies seemed half ticked off about it. I figured as much. It seems to me that the opposite sex is always drawn to what's a little different. The new girls were always popular in our school. I figured the same rule applied here. Grady claims that as humans, the grass is always greener.

"I hope Avery doesn't become enthralled with them," Wyatt whispered between first and second period. I was glad I wasn't girling so I didn't have to worry about it.

At lunch time Rouree broke all the rules, pulled out all of the stops. He asked to sit by Celia! That set the cafeteria to buzzing, for even Mark and Michelle had continued eating with their friends at their separate tables after they were married.

"Where I come from you do what you want to," Rouree crowed. "I want to eat with Celia Quinn." Of course Celia's cheeks pinked with pleasure. Kenny and Dover followed suit, saddling up to the table among Celia's friends. Lunch looked like a feeding frenzy that day. Rouree, Kenny, and Dover were mere scraps of meat in a viscous pool of hungry female sharks. The crazy thing was the fact they enjoyed the devouring process, offering themselves like willing, sacrificial beasts.

"It's time I start doing what I want!" John Finnegan cried. Everyone was shocked since he was always so quiet. He strode to the girls' table as well, looking like a cool cat all on his own! Jesse McCarthy, Rip Siskin, and Roger O'Reilly followed suit while Olivia Newton John blared, *"Let Me be There,"* from the Jukebox.

After school Wyatt, John, and I ditched the bus, opting to ride in the back of Rouree's dad's pickup truck. Kenny, Dover, and Rouree were piled inside the cab…with Celia seated next to the driver, of course. John was excited, talking two hundred words per minute. Apparently he had a secret crush on Staci Spinnaker. I didn't know that…which is excellent proof of just how secret the crush. Over the course of the day, Dover had developed a keen interest in Jenny Doheny and wanted to ask her out, but didn't want to hurt Staci's feelings, so he persuaded John to ask Staci to the movies in Eisner. All four couples were going to go see the adventure flick, *Earthquake*. But first we had to practice riding.

Howahkan, Dad, and Grandpa Gallagher sat on the top rail of the fence helping us set our choreography for the performance. We would begin with a running mount by Rouree. After Rouree mounted his horse, he would continue to ride in a circular pattern. I followed suit, launching into a running mount. I followed Rouree, loping around in the circle, and then Dover came barreling into the action, followed by Kenny. After all four of us were in the ring, Rouree led out in a figure eight, and I followed him while Kenny and Dover began the pattern from the other direction. That motion kept us constantly passing each other with precise skill at the intersection of the 8 pattern. It took us awhile to get the timing down, but I felt confident that it would look really good, and Dad kept calling, "Yes! Yes! That's it!" After we completed the pattern ten times, Dover and Rouree traded mounts by dismounting on the run and switching. Kenny and I did the same. I was nervous about doing the stunts with another horse, but Tanaka's horse was fine with it, and Kenny didn't have any trouble with Misty.

"Impressive!" Grandpa called out.

"The Little Shoshone's trained his horse well."

I was now on Kenny's horse, but on the next rotation we traded back, and so did Dover and Rouree. We changed up the pattern, and I traded mounts with Rouree while Dover and Kenny made the switch. Once we were all back on our own horses we broke out of the figure eight pattern and stretched into a single line. We all charged evenly, with Rouree and me dismounting simultaneously at the count of ten. Our horses kept running next to Dover and Kenny. The boys managed to stand up, stretching one leg on the backs of our horses and theirs, riding straddle-backed. I held my breath while I watched; hoping Misty would pace herself well to Kenny's mount since he looked quite vulnerable at the moment. It was almost like water skiing on horseback! I cheered at Misty's performance and vowed to give her a whole sack of apples. I also vowed to practice that stunt until I mastered it.

Grandpa Gallagher shook his head at the stunts for it was a marvelous sight! When Kenny and Dover drew their legs away from our mounts, again riding solo on their own, we clicked to our horses and they loped back for us. Rouree and I made running mounts, and we rode in the circular pattern again, with Rouree dodging out first, followed by me, Dover, and Kenny. We exited the way we began.

I heard shouts of praise coming from the men, and then I noticed Stan Tomkins looming near, peering through the fence rails of our big corral. He smiled at me and gave a little wave. I waved back, panting, for the routine was work and no mistake. I gave Misty an apple from my pocket and stroked her nose, lavishing my gratitude.

"That was something else again," Grandpa called. He walked over to us, reaching out a hand. My friends were happy to shake with him, and I felt proud all around. Dover fingered a cigarette between his lips and started smoking, not caring a hoot about the watching men. He was winded and needed the tobacco to help him catch his breath. Grandpa's brows shot high but he let it pass. Kenny was also out of breath from the vigorous workout and took a few drags on the cigarette. He offered it to Rouree, who flatly refused, and I was pleased to see that he was good for his word.

"Celia doesn't smoke and doesn't date boys who do, you numbskull," he said.

I noticed Grandpa's mustache twitch and he winked at me, patted us all on our shoulders one more time, then announced he was going home for supper. My Shoshone friends were in a hurry to go get showered, shined, and ready for their dates and left quickly after taking care of their horses. Dad shoveled out the stalls, whistling while he worked. He kept grinning, excited by the fancy riding, and me being a part of it.

"Hey Stan," I called. The boy was still leaning against the fence taking it all in.

"You're lucky."

"Think so?"

"Yeah. I wish I had a horse…and neat friends. I wish I had me a dad that cared." He hacked up a wad, spitting sideways. "See you around, Wes. You really are the hero type." He shuffled away, hands shoved in his pockets, lost in a swell of thought.

"Is that kid the one you fought last fall?" Howahkan asked.

"Yes."

"I figured. He respects you a whole damn lot. It's a shame he has to be so sad." I didn't know what to say to that so I just shrugged. "You know—some of us go through life thinking we just hit a homerun when actually we were born on third base."

I scowled, letting Howahkan's words sink in. "So what? What can I do for Stan? I've already been nicer than I've wanted to be."

Howahkan shrugged. "I'll be damned if I know but I wish that was my boy. I'd give him a reason to feel young and glad. We only get one shot at this old life. One."

"Yeah."

"So—you gonna teach me how to drive, or what?"

"You're game?"

Howahkan flipped a long braid behind his shoulder. "I was born ready to die stubborn...but I'm getting soft, so I guess it's time to learn a few things before I go, huh?"

"Let's do it," I grinned.

Howahkan climbed in the driver's seat of the Buick. He was careful to listen to my precise instructions. He turned the key in the ignition and backed out of the drive with a big smile on his face. "These mirrors are handy," he said.

I nodded, giving him instructions once we hit the street. Howahkan found the right gear, then clicked his tongue and the Buick lunged forward. I laughed at the clicking part. "This isn't a horse, Howahkan! The car can't hear you!"

But Howahkan was panicked because of the lunge forward, and jammed his foot into the brakes calling, "Whoa!" The car jerked to a halt and I careened right into the dashboard.

"Easy now, Howahkan, it's okay—try again."

"No, hello mighty no! A man could get into a run away in this thing."

"You'll be fine. Just don't *all or nothing* it this time. Easy on the gas, then easy on the brakes, it's a piece of cake." Again we lunged forward and Howahkan was sitting tall, looking petrified. "Good, keep going," I encouraged. "Don't get nervous, look we're doing fine! No need to panic—no need to hit the brakes."

"Oh my, oh my! Look at the fence posts speed by!" Howahkan was thrilled at the experience of driving the car all by himself, but I had to laugh again, for the speedometer only read seven mph, and I was certain Howahkan had ridden a horse lots faster than that before.

"Okay, now ease your foot into the gas pedal, easy—that's the key word. We need to go a little faster."

Howahkan clicked his tongue again and the car sped up a notch. We were really going to town now, and the world zoomed by at twelve mph. "Who-ee!" Howahkan whooped. We were coming up on the intersection of Second and Gallagher when I saw Delma Jean's station wagon coming up the road. I was certain she was seeing two of us and her cross eyes were wide open.

"Okay, Howahkan, you've got to stop at the sign."

He gripped the wheel, hollering "Whoa!" and sailed right on through. Delma jean's brakes screeched black marks but she missed the back of the Buick by six whole inches or so. Howahkan cussed insulting words at the car. "Damn thing won't stop when I tell it to," he yelled.

"It doesn't have ears, Howahkan! You've got to use your foot to hit the break."

"Oh yeah," he remembered congenially then buried his boot in the brake. Once again I found myself kissing the dashboard. Once again I scraped myself off and fastened my seatbelt.

"Okay, let's try again," I called.

"How far away from home do you want me to get?"

"Well, more than two blocks…come on, easy now."

Howahkan clicked and we lunged forward. I couldn't do anything but chuckle at my antique, determined friend. "Who-ee!" he called again. He urged the car up to great speeds that time, nearing fifteen mph. I saw Delma Jean's station wagon coming back down the hill on the corner of Fourth and Gallagher. She had the right of way, but I saw her looking all crazy-eyed at the Buick gunning for her once again.

"Slow down, Howahkan!"

"Whoa!"

"Hit the break!"

"Whoa! Whoa! Whoa!" We sailed through the intersection and I heard Delma Jean's station wagon squeal to a halt, with the rear end skidding around sideways. I think blue puffs of smoke were rising from all four of her tires. Again she missed us by inches but she climbed out of the car and shook her fists at us.

"Damn car just won't do what I tell it to," Howahkan explained while checking Delma Jean's angry tantrum in the rearview mirror.

"Howahkan! This is not a horse! You have to touch the brakes in order to stop."

"Oh yeah," he remembered and slammed a boot into the pedal just for good measure. That's why we careened to a stop a half a block past Delma's sideways station wagon. That's why the seatbelt hugged me so tight I got a belt-burn around my middle.

"Really Howahkan? I know you can do better than this! You are an intelligent man who's seen everything from wild herds of buffalo to rocket ships launching to the moon. Surely you can learn how to stop the dang car when you come to a stop sign!"

His brows furrowed into a sulky scowl. "Get out, Little Shoshone!"

"No. This is my car."

"Get out. I'm the driver. Go on!"

"No! You'll never make it back without me."

"Then mind your tongue. I'm doing great!"

What could I do but laugh? I laughed and laughed. "Oh Howahkan! You are something else," I cried. "Okay, let's go."

Again we lunged forward to the urgent clicking sound. We drove the half a block and Howahkan nailed the stop. I cheered. He smiled. "See, I'm great," he said. "Driving is easy."

"Okay, hit your blinker to the left. We'll go up the hill and turn back to the south." Howahkan hit the blinker first, driving all the way down the block with it going. "You don't have to signal that far in advance," I explained.

"Be still, Little Shoshone! I wanted to make sure I was ready." He stopped again and then we lunged ahead with Howahkan cranking on the wheel. It was a little tight, the corner, but we made it, and I was relieved there were no other cars to maneuver through. "Howahkan is good at this. Kell will need to see this to believe it."

"Okay, now hit your blinker again. We are going to turn again, see?"

Howahkan hollered, "Whoa!" and his boot pushed the brake. We stopped right in the middle of the road.

"Why are we stopping?"

"Because I'm supposed to."

"No, there aren't any stop signs on these up and down streets, see? The stop signs are on the through streets in this town. Delma Jean wasn't supposed to stop both times we nearly wrecked her. It was our stop, but now look, no sign for us so you can just keep turning."

"Driving is complicated," Howahkan muttered. He urged the car forward, clicking to it, but we didn't go anywhere.

"The gas," I said as patiently as possible.

"Oh yeah, I forgot." Howahkan gave it the boot. We lunged forward again and I was thrust against my seat, certain I had whiplash.

"Easy, easy," I soothed.

"Look now, Little Shoshone," Howahkan urged. He pointed to the speedometer. He had clicked his way clear up to eighteen mph.

"Good job, but you've got another stop sign coming up so be careful."

"Oh?" Just then we blew right through the intersection and once again I saw Delma Jean Conner's station wagon squeal sideways in a cloud of dust. I groaned. Howahkan chuckled at the sight in his rearview mirror. "Damn women drivers," he said, not even trying to stop that time.

"Now get ready to stop at this one," I warned, well in advance. He started slowing down and nailed a beautiful stop. Mr. Mulligan and Aunt Lace zoomed in front of us. Aunt Lace's head nearly craned backward to study the sight of us—an over confident, ancient Shoshone elder at the wheel, and an overconfident, thirteen year old driving instructor belted into the passenger's seat.

One more block and we were home free, and Howahkan turned into the driveway. Personally, I'd never been so relieved in all my life to be home. "Good job, Howahkan. You're a natural," I lied.

"Oh, Little Shoshone! Driving is so fun—I've been missing out! Tomorrow I will take you to Eisner with me and we will buy a truck."

"Um…let's sleep on it first. Okay? And when we go we'd better take my Dad along. He's good with salesmen and stuff."

"But I am going to buy a truck."

"Well, what kind?"

"I don't know. A really fast one."

I laughed outright at that. "A really fast one, huh? Like the Buick?"

"No, hell no—I'll get one that goes even faster than that."

"Come on, Howahkan, let's go eat supper."

"Yeah, I'm hungry and ready for more of your mom's cooking. She's good and uses just the right amount of shoog in everything."

Grady was at the house reading to Yarrow in the front room when we walked in. "Kell! Listen Big Irish; I'm going to buy a truck! The Little Shoshone just taught me how to drive."

Grady's lips smacked together, "Well my, my, my," he said. "Isn't that a thought? Howahkan Greathawk soaring on wheels. Next thing you know the roosters will come home, and Agatha Duffy's henhouse will be back in business! It's enough to make me shake with laughter."

"Don't poke fun at me, Kell. I'm going to drive back to Fort Washakie like a pro, and I won't have to sit on a stack of pillows like some little white fart I know."

I washed up and helped Allyson set the table. She was sulking that the boys weren't coming to dinner. "Those girls are soooo lucky," she said wistfully, "especially Celia."

"What makes Rouree so dreamy?" I thought I'd get the low down from an actual girl.

"Oh my heck, let me tell you," Allyson rushed. "His eyes are smoldering and dark. He's tall and lean, and his arms have these *rippling* muscles. He's the best looking of the boys, I think. Rouree's face lights up when he smiles. His hair is thick and perfect, just long enough, you know? We all like how it falls over his collar and on down his back a ways."

"Who's *we*?"

"Dori Jo, me, and every other girl in Gallagher Springs, that's who *we* is."

"Gee, what did you do, take a vote?"

"Actually…yes—Rouree's the cutest but Kenny and Dover are miles ahead of the other boys in this town."

"Oh brother," I mumbled.

"You asked."

"What about Fonzie? Does he pale in comparison to Rouree Greathawk?"

"Yes! A thousand times, yes."

"Oh for crying out loud! You need an Oscar for such a worthy performance."

Allyson's lip jutted out. "I'm serious!"

"Have you turned boy crazy?"

"No…just for certain ones."

"What if I told you those boys all smoke, then what?"

"I don't care."

"And drink."

"Doesn't change a thing! They're beautiful…just like Howahkan in Grady's book."

Oh, so that was it! Grady had romanced foolish ideas into the heads and hearts of all the women around here, young and old. I shook my head disgustedly, but then I remembered my own blazin' crush on Awinita and decided not to ride Allyson too hard.

We watched television after supper and Howahkan took notes during all of the car commercials. He was now having second thoughts about the truck—wondering if he wouldn't rather buy a Dodge Charger. "Looks spiffy," he said. Dad was amused by the first time car shopper and promised to let him drive more in the morning *to practice*.

"Don't get in a hurry Howahkan. You've waited this long, and you might as well look around and know exactly what you want before you rush into anything."

"You're dumb, Bill. I'm nearly ninety-nine. How much time do you think I have left?" Howahkan smiled, not meaning to give too much offense.

Yarrow was snuggled on Howahkan's lap, tickling her neck and face with the ends of his braids. "Daddy, you should grow your hair like Grandfather Howahkan's." We had a hearty chuckle at the mental image. Dad would look ridiculous with long braids! "Myself likes them so much," she persisted, twirling the end of one braid around and around her little hands.

Howahkan kissed her head. "You remind me of my sister," he said.

Grady's head snapped up, eyes narrowing at the mention of his beloved. "She does?"

"Yes. She looks like Awinita, and acts like her too, with her gentle heart and happy ways."

I spent the night with the guys at the cabin although it was ten o'clock when they came for me. They were all full of stories from their fun night with the girls, and proud that they managed to get them all home at a decent hour since it was a school night and everything. Kenny and Dover lounged out on the cabin's deck sharing a smoke and talking.

Rouree rolled over in his bed and looked at me. "I've got it bad, man."

"What?"

"I'm in over my head with that cousin of yours."

"Celia is cute, I agree."

"Man, cute doesn't even cut it. Celia is top to bottom sexy, and smart, and *good*. I've never met anybody like her in my whole life. I kissed her tonight."

"You did?" I was staring crazy-eyed now, even though it was dark and I couldn't really make out Rouree's features.

"I did. We got out to the truck from the movies before the other couples, and while we were waiting for them, I cupped her chin in my hands and kissed her smack on the mouth."

"How did she respond?"

"She kissed me back. Holy hell-oooo mighty, did she kiss me back!" He laughed thickly and I gauged he was replaying it over and over again in his mind.

Celia Quinn! I couldn't wait to razz her, but in some goofy way, I felt really triumphant for Rouree. I liked the kid a lot, and if anybody should get to kiss Celia I figured it might just as well be him.

"Are you feeling weird inside?"

"Yes! In fact I'm not sure how I can handle going back home again. It's gonna sting, saying goodbye."

"You're sort of like Grady and Awinita, only reversed."

"Yes."

"Really? Do you feel that strongly about her?"

"Yes."

"Celia has an older brother. He's pretty protective."

"Monty? Yeah…tell me about it! I met him tonight."

"You did?" I was all questions wanting to know how that shook down.

"Yeah. I went into the bathroom to wash the butter off my hands, you know—from the popcorn, and this guy suddenly pins me up against the wall by the collar. I knew it was Celia's brother because she'd pointed him out to me, or else I'd have knocked him on his can. Anyway, he says, '*What are your intentions with my sister, Chief?*' I said, '*Back up, you sod-buster! My intentions are as honorable as yours are with that chick you're snuggling with.*' He stared me down for a few moments and then he let go of my shirt and smiled at me. '*If you try anything I'll break your neck,*' he said pleasantly, and Little Shoshone, I believed him!"

I laughed. "At least he didn't slap you forty times."

"No, thank goodness."

"What if he would have?"

"One of two things would have happened. I would have sucked it up and born it, the way the Big Irish did when Old Grandfather cuffed him about, or, I'd have hauled off and knocked his head off. Either way...I still planned on kissing his sister tonight."

Kenny and Dover came back inside the cabin, stumbling in the dark until they found their beds. We lay still, listening to the loudness of our own thoughts while frogs sang lullabies outside. When I finally dosed off I dreamed that I was riding in a big time rodeo in Cheyenne, or somewhere. My horse was running fast, and just as I dismounted, my feet slipped inside a hole and down, down, down I fell, completely out of sight. It was dark underground and I struck a match. There in the haze and the din, looming in front of me, stood lovely, beautiful, Awinita. She smiled at me, and there were real embers in her eyes. I leaned forward to kiss her, placing my hands on her chin. The experience was sweet, and sumptuous, and I pulled away, saying, "Voluptuous, V-O-L..." I opened my eyes to study her but nobody was there and I was alone in the dark. Only feathers fluttered, reminding she had been. I spent the rest of the night trying to climb out of that sad, lonesome hole while the sounds of distant drums reverberated in the darkness.

Chapter Twenty-Three

The next morning Rouree grinned broadly. I was feeling weird myself as the kiss in my dream felt undeniably real, almost making me change my mind about girling. But the sad, lonely feeling of having the girl disappear was awful, and I didn't know if saying goodbye could ever be worth it.

School started good that day. We played a fun game in Miss Pell's class. We got spaghetti for lunch, and Mrs. Harris made the best bread sticks to go with it. Avery was ill so I had Wyatt all to myself and we tossed a football back and forth after lunch.

"Did John have fun last night?"

"Yes! He was in a really good mood when he got home. Apparently he kissed Staci when the others weren't looking."

What? My, my, my, Cupid was certainly busy target practicing last night! What a well-stocked quiver the little cherub must carry. "That's good."

"Yeah. He likes Kenny and Dover a lot. Everybody does."

"I guess. I like Rouree best, myself."

"Yeah, well…so does Celia."

I noticed Stan Tomkins leaning against the corner of the school. I tossed the ball in his direction. "Catch, Stan!"

He looked dumbfounded, but recovered his senses in time to save his face. He seemed unsure of what to do with the football for a second, but Wyatt clapped his hands together, "Here, Stan."

Stan threw it to Wyatt, and that's how we started tossing the ball in a triangular pattern. It was the first interaction between Wyatt and Stan since the beating, and that had been fourteen months ago. I was proud of Wyatt for adapting to this situation and he seemed to be taking it all in stride.

Just before the bell rang, Stan made a wild pass and Wyatt couldn't reach it. He scurried to pick it up. "Sorry, Wyatt."

Wyatt retrieved the football, holding it against his hip. "What?"

Stan's personal dam broke. "Sorry, Wyatt…about everything! I'm sorry about it all. It was so *bad* what I did to you!"

"Let's just not talk about it." Stan nodded and hurried inside the school. Wyatt stared at the place where Stan had been.

"Are you okay, Wyatt?" I was worried.

"I dunno."

"Wyatt?" He shrugged and suddenly his shoulders looked puny and his face was pale.

"I just wish it would have never happened that's all."

"Me, too, but maybe things can be better now. Stan's been a jerk to you since the day you moved to Gallagher Springs, but I think he's genuinely sorry now. He's left you alone pretty well lately."

"I know. Wesley, I don't feel good."

I walked over to him. His eyes were dilating kind of funny. I took the football. "Come on; let's take you down to Aunt Lace."

We walked briskly through the jostling halls, away from the junior high commons and into the elementary. I knocked on Aunt Lace's door. I hadn't really spoken to her since she squeezed me to her bosom after Wyatt had been hurt more than a year ago. I was purposefully aloof, but I thought the lamb could use a shepherd at the moment.

Aunt Lace stepped to the door. "What's wrong, Wesley?"

I motioned to Wyatt who was leaning against the wall. "Wyatt needs some help, I think."

Aunt Lace darted around me, crouching to look him over. "Wyatt, are you okay?"

"My head hurts, and I just don't feel very good. I *was* fine and then it just sort of hit me."

"Let's take you home. Come on. Wesley, run down and tell my husband to come cover my class, *now*!"

I did as she directed, and watched out the window while the Oldsmobile rumbled to life in the parking lot. I felt shaky inside, and upset. My whole day went south. It was hard to concentrate on my school work. I didn't understand why Wyatt couldn't just be well. Had I overdone it, tossing the football with him? Was it all emotional, and did talking to Stan set it off? Either way, I felt I was to blame.

A note hit my desk. I flinched away from my thoughts. I looked around warily, wondering where it came from. I opened it slightly with one hand. *"Dear Wesley, I have a big crush on you. If you like me, circle yes, if not circle no. Love, Margo"*

I grimaced and circled no. Then I added an exclamation point and tossed it back to the dumb girl, wishing she wouldn't embarrass me with her attentions.

"Wesley? Did you want to share that with the class?" Mr. Henry asked.

I shook my head no.

"Wesley?"

"No, sir. I didn't even want to share it with myself." The kids laughed.

My eyes trailed momentarily to Margo, and her cheeks were crimson. I gave her a mean look, wanting to injure her with my eyes for further complicating my day. I didn't count on her face clouding up and her eyes watering so instantaneously. Soon big crocodile tears were running down her cheeks. Mr. Henry glowered at me and held his hand out for the note. Margo gave it to him reluctantly. He read the note and then glared at me some more.

"Class time is not *the* time."

"No sir," I said, wondering why he didn't say something to Margo. She started it.

Mr. Henry went back to the board and suddenly I was being assaulted by note wads from every direction. "Wesley, you're a big fat jerk!" Judy Brynn O'Brien wrote, "You made Margo cry!" And a jagged note from one of the nine Cindy's read, "I thought you were nice, but I was wrong!" I rolled my eyes. For Heaven's sake! For this purpose I refused to go girling for the rest of my life! Another note shot into the back of my head like a little missile. "You're rotten!" I don't even know which female it came from.

"Wesley?" Mr. Henry was glaring at me again.

"Sir?"

"Do you insist on being a problem today?"

"I started getting pelted with notes! It's not my fault." I held out my hand, wanting to show him the evidence, but he was being a crank and wouldn't even look at them.

"You're on your last warning," he hissed.

"Send me to the principal's office, then!" The classroom gasped at my sass. I hadn't been in trouble all year, not since the first day of school when I'd gotten hauled away in the sheriff's car.

"Fine! You're on your way."

"Good," I said, belligerently. I gathered up my books and slammed out of the room. I went down the hall to the elementary, and stopped at Aunt Lace's door. I poked my head inside. Mr. Mulligan was reading to the class. "I'm going to go check on Wyatt."

He seemed surprised, but I dodged back out before he could tell me otherwise. I then walked back into the high school and asked Mrs. Clark to page Rouree Greathawk out of class. She did.

"What's up, Wesley?"

"I need you to give me a ride to the Finnegan's. Wyatt didn't look very good to me, and I'm leaving." He nodded and we left with no other questions asked.

Amos Greathawk's truck turned onto the highway, and from the highway onto Main Street, following it to the very north end of town. Rouree was concerned about my cousin; claiming Celia too, had been worried about him. He dropped me off then headed back toward the school. Apparently Rouree Greathawk was suddenly very interested in his education. The Mulligan's car was still in the driveway.

I knocked twice on the back door and then walked in. That's what we all did at each other's houses. We were on the *two knocks and enter* system. Aunt Aubynn seemed surprised to see me. "Wesley? What are you doing, dear?"

"I just wanted to make sure Wyatt was okay. He was perfectly fine today, and then bam! It hit him kind of fast."

"I know. That's the way his migraines come on. He's down in his room."

I walked down the hall and pushed the door open. "Wyatt?"

Aunt Lace was standing at the foot of his bed talking in soothing tones. She was puzzled to see me as well. "Wesley?"

"I just wanted to come see him."

"He'll be fine," Aunt Lace said. "He's had his medicine and now he'll be able to sleep it off. Did you just *leave* school?"

"Mr. Mulligan excused me, that dear, dear, blessed man."

Her brows shot high momentarily then her lips pinched shut. I wondered what was circling in her head, but I didn't wonder bad enough to ask. Aunt Lace patted Wesley's foot again, and then scurried away, remembering the principal was covering her class.

"What's wrong, Wyatt?"

"I dunno." A cold cloth was covering his eyes, and the windows were blacked out to prevent light from irritating his them. Ever since the beating, his eyes had winced against bright light, and it was magnified ten times in a migraine.

I pulled a chair close to his bed. "Was it my fault, you know, because I threw the ball at Stan and sort of included him?"

"I dunno."

I wished I could see Wyatt's eyes while I was talking to him. It would have helped me discern more than he was giving me. "Because I don't know what to do, Wyatt! My allegiance lies with you. I nearly went to jail trying to choke Stan Tomkins to death last fall. It was all for you."

"I told you not to."

"I know, but…I love you, man."

"I know."

"And…then I look at Stan and his life is a zero. He looks like a poster child for Alcatraz! He's a walking time-bomb just waiting to go explode somewhere. He's hurting and he's alone. He looks at me sometimes and it makes me wince because he wants to be me."

"I know."

"So, it kills me to be nice to him, but I'm trying to. Howahkan said something the other day that really made me think. He said, *'Some of us go through life thinking we hit a homerun, and we were actually born on third base.'* Wyatt, you and I were born on third."

"I know it, Wesley. If anything happened to our parents, we've got grandparents, and aunts, uncles, and cousins who would take over. Stan's got dirt."

"Yeah, that's my point. So—when I threw the football at him I was just trying to do the right thing, and not send you home with a spell."

"I know. I don't think that hurt me any. I think I wrenched my arm trying to stop his wild throw. That's all it takes, you know. Wrench one little muscle and my body flinches into a spasm and fit."

"How long do the doctors think this is going to last?"

"Probably always."

"I hope not. Well…maybe I'd better be more careful and not make you do things, like throwing and stuff."

"Wesley, if I can't do a few things I'd rather be dead! Compared to the things I was doing a year and half ago I already feel like I'm in a nursing home."

I scowled and nodded even though he couldn't see me. "I'm sorry, Wyatt."

"I'm sorry too, because you've had to solo lots of things that I would like to have been doing with you."

"Such as?"

"Trick riding."

"I wish you could have been learning these tricks with me. It would be a ton more fun. But sometime maybe you'll be stronger, and then I'll teach you, and we'll train ole' Whip just like Misty."

"Whip's too old to learn new tricks."

"Grandpa will get you a younger horse then. He promised me I'd never lack for horses as long as I was willing to ride and work with them so much."

"Is it fun?"

"Yes."

"Real fun?"

"Yes."

"Because it looks fun. I'm glad you're riding with the Indian boys."

"Yeah, they're pretty amazing. They are just so athletic. They can do stuff that I probably will never dare try."

"I'm not jealous of them."

Wyatt's comment stopped me short. "Why would you be?"

"Because you're running with them. It's okay, just so you know. You've been alone pretty much since I've been laid up and you're a loner now."

I didn't consider myself a loner! I was the leader of the seventh grade! "Don't feel sorry for me," I said. "I feel sorry for you."

"But I've had Avery to lean on. She likes doing quiet things and its okay. When I'm with her I don't mind taking it easy."

"Well…what are you saying?"

"That I'm not jealous that Rouree Greathawk is turning into your best friend."

I scowled again. Was he? "Well…you're my best cousin for always."

"I know."

"And Rouree Greathawk is turning into Celia's boyfriend. I'm soon to fly solo again. Maybe I *am* a loner."

"You are."

"Oh."Gee, this conversation was bringing me down. "Well, Wyatt, what can I do for you?"

"Nothing. Just…keep being good to Stan. The day he beat me, he just snapped."

"Obviously."

"No, I'm serious. You were gone, and Steve, Ross, Paul, Scott, Miles, and the other guys and I were playing soccer at recess. Stan went for a goal and missed, 'cuz the ball went A-wall and flew sideways over the school yard. He didn't mean for it to go that direction."

"And?"

"Paul said, '*Gee, Stan, you're a loser. No wonder your ma did herself in.*' That was an ugly thing to say, Wesley. I slugged Paul in the arm and told him to shut his mouth, but then Ross said, '*Yeah, you're a screw up. No wonder your old man can't stand you. I'd be a drunk if you were my kid, too.*' I told Ross to apologize because the statements weren't said in fun. The kids were just being cruel, and I'd never seen them so awful, not really."

"I'm glad you got in Ross's face! His brother's a lush so he doesn't have any room to talk."

"I know, but then Paul told me to shut up, claiming you weren't at school to fight my battles. I said, *'So what? Looks like I'm doing fine on my own'* and I knocked Paul back a step. That's when the negative comments started whizzing in my direction. Paul said something mean about my Dad in Viet Nam."

Now I was mad and Paul Siskin was going to get it right I the chops! Ross was next on my list. "What?"

"He said he was a coward, and a Commie, and a Red, and a spy for the Viet Cong."

"All of those things? That's stupid!" Gee, when I caught up to Paul there wouldn't be anything left of him! He was a dimwit and a poor reader, anyway. The bin full of bolts in his father's hardware store had more character.

"So, Stan swings over to their side, glad to not be standing alone and taking it."

"Stupid, idiotic, oh!" I was too mad to go on.

"The bell rang and everybody went back inside. Mr. Despain made us work on penmanship before the bus came. Some of the boys were jeering in my direction, though. They were still mad that I'd defended Stan. Stan was happy because he thought, for once, he was in with them. We grabbed our stuff when the bell rang, and I realized my jacket was still out on the playground. I ran back there to get it."

"And then what?" Although I really shuddered to ask. This was the first time Wyatt had ever talked about it.

"Stan followed me instead of going to the bus line. He started talking crap about you being the hero and me being the sidekick. I just listened to him rant for awhile, but then he kicked me and I dove at his middle, ready to take him down. He winced awful badly, and I pulled back. His shirt was knocked up and his ribs were black and blue. I asked him what happened to him. He started going off, talking dirty and calling me names, saying his dad *wasn't* a bad guy and his dad *didn't* use a crowbar on him. I tried to calm him down, but he snapped. He snapped big time, and jerked me by the arm, dragging me into the bushes along the north fence. He said, 'My dad never used this crowbar on me in his life,' and then he picked up a crowbar to show me. I said, 'He must have, you're all black and blue! Stan, we've got to get you help.' And that was it. He started swinging it at me. I tried to fight back and I tried to get away, but he was swinging a powerful advantage."

"Dirty, dumb, son-of-a—" I was mad all over again, and I planned on cleaning out the lot of them. I always tasted blood when I was angry.

"No, Wesley, don't you see? Stan's in a bad way! When I say he snapped, I mean he completely S-N-A-P-P-E-D! Aldean had nearly done him in, and he'd taken the crowbar and hidden it where his dad couldn't lay a hold of it again. He hadn't planned on beating me with it, but that's just how the day ended up. Paul and Ross didn't mean to start anything either, but I've heard the psychiatrists, and the doctors, and the department of social services all talking together over my case. They all said kids can be cruel, and I believe it. Stan was treated poorly on a day when he just couldn't take it."

"Yes, but it doesn't make any sense that he took it out on you! You were the only one standing up for him."

"Well...he's the only one that sticks up for Suzy at home, too, and she's cruel to him."

"Suzy's not so bad."

"She's nice to her other kids and mean to him. Don't believe for a second that she's the Mother of the Year."

"I don't think that. She's unconcerned at best, but she's always been nice to me—and she makes sure Stan has clean clothes to wear and something to eat."

"And I suppose she's nicer to Stan than Aldean is, yes, but does anybody really *love* that kid?"

I thought about it...and couldn't say that anyone did. "Why doesn't the state get involved?"

"I dunno. I don't understand adults and how they think. The whole town sorrows for the situation, but nobody does jack to help out. I wasn't mad that you threw the ball to Stan. I was going to on my next turn."

I let out a heavy sigh. Wyatt's words seemed settling to him. He needed to let these things out for a long time, way too long. We sat in silence for several long minutes. "You need anything?"

"No. My medication is making me drowsy now and my head isn't hammering as bad."

"I'll leave then so you can rest. Thanks for talking with me."

"Thanks for being my best cousin."

"Thanks for being my best friend."

"Have fun with Rouree today. Have fun riding…and Wesley?"

"Yeah?"

"Do me *one* favor?"

"Yes?"

"Go cause some mischief somewhere and then call me up and tell me about it. You've been painfully quiet for much too long."

I promised I would. I closed his door quietly and walked back into the kitchen. "Thanks for coming Wesley," Aunt Aubynn said. She was chopping vegetables at the sink. "You're a good boy."

"How's everything going for you guys? I'll bet you like having your own house."

"Yes, it's wonderful. It's good to be away from the fray just a little bit, too. Aiden needs a little space once in a while."

I nodded. "Well, bye Aunt Aubynn. I've got to go practice riding with the Shoshones."

"Would you like me to drive you home?"

"No, I'll walk."

"See you, Wesley." She handed me several cookies. I love Aunt Aubynn!

The screen door banged shut and I jogged up Main Street, doing double time. Rouree and the kids were just turning onto to Gallagher Street when I hit the intersection. He stopped and I piled in the back with Kenny and Dover. Celia, Staci, and John were in the front.

The wind blew through my hair as we pulled up to our corrals. Apparently we would practice today with an audience of Celia, Staci, and John. "Hello, kids," Dad called, leading Misty out of the stable. He had arranged his day to be able to watch us again. Yarrow nipped at his heels like a puppy dog.

"Hi my boy. Myself is Daddy's partner today. Mommy took Allyson to the dentist." Yarrow peered at the group of teenagers behind me. "Hi all my cousins. You guys been missin' me?" Celia picked Yarrow up and gave her a love just to prove how much, and Rouree patted her head like a faithful dog—not really sure of the whole cousin protocol, but deeply enthralled with the little girl just the same.

"Celia," Yarrow said, "Allyson is jealous!"

"She is? Why?"

Yarrow pointed a tiny finger toward Rouree, and I had a sneaking suspicion Allyson would have fainted dead away from the embarrassment. Dad was chagrined with the little tattler and gently reprimanded her. "That's enough Yarrow. We don't tell tales out of school."

"I'm not in school," Yarrow persisted, and Kenny, John, and Dover got a big kick out of it.

Practice went smooth and Celia watched with eyes of wonder, marveling at all of us, but seeing only Rouree. John and Staci cheered from the top rail of the fence, and I noticed John held her hand. He was getting pretty bold! Just last summer he had refused to dance at Aunt Lace's wedding, and now he was holding a girl's hand right in front of my Dad! I assumed the Wyoming boys had helped him swagger right up to speed, for he seemed to be making up for lost time, easily overcoming his shy years.

"Are you guys going to decorate your ponies for the performance?" Celia asked.

"Yes," Kenny answered. "We will paint them like we are riding into war."

I was all a wonder over that. I'd never painted my horse before. I was kind of excited about the prospects of it.

"Are you going to dress like natives then?"

"Yes," Kenny said again. "Breech cloths."

I shook my head, "No way! I'm out. I'm out right now."

"You'll ruin the routine!" Kenny fired back.

"Tough crackers. I'm NOT wearing a breech cloth!"

Then they laughed for they'd only been making sport with me, but it did start me fretting about what I *would* wear, for I didn't have any native attire hanging around in my closet. I supposed I could always be the cowboy, but I knew Howahkan would shake his head disgustedly and call me Hollywood, for he mostly thought cowboy and Indian productions were a botched job.

The teenagers left so Rouree could drive John, Staci, and Celia home. Dad and I would see to their mounts and feed and curry the horses.

"Where's Howahkan?"

"He rode to the dentist in Eisner with your mother and Allyson," Dad said wryly.

"Why?"

"He wanted to stop and look at new cars and trucks."

"That's so funny! How long will he get to drive it before he's gone?"

"I imagine the truck will still smell new when he's pushing up daisies, but I suppose he should experience the thrill of it if he wants to."

"I don't think he has enough money."

"No, I don't think he does either."

"No bank is going to lend a ninety-nine year old man money for a new truck."

"No…I suppose I'll have to sign with him."

"You would do that for Howahkan?"

"Son—look at *this*," he said, motioning toward Yarrow. The girl was dozing gravel into a pile with a little stick. "How can I not?"

That was one less worry for me, too, for I'd wondered if I could stand seeing Howahkan be dashed with disappointment since his heart was so set on a vehicle.

The boys were soon back at our house. Dad fried hamburgers for our supper and then told me to do the dishes before leaving with them. Rouree helped me dry them and put them away, and I appreciated his help. We talked about cars and trucks ourselves, and it was a pleasant conversation.

Just as we were wiping up the counters, I asked, "Are you and Celia going out again tonight?"

"No—I wanted to, but I don't want to risk getting her in Dutch with her folks. I'd like to stay on the good side of them if I possibly can. Celia probably shouldn't be out every night with the same boy." I nodded, thinking Rouree was incredibly sensible.

"So what do you guys want to do tonight?"

"Something good," Dover said.

I grinned. "How does mischief sound?"

"Suits me fine!"

"The Little Shoshone makes mischief?" Rouree seemed surprised.

We drove around Gallagher Springs in Rouree's truck looking for mischief. Of course we couldn't get serious about finding any until the sun went down. While we were waiting, we skipped rocks on Eisner Lake and practiced shooting a tin can with my .22. The boys liked my gun a lot. Then we got to shoving each other into the water, and Eisner Lake is still icy cold in May, but the scuffling was healthy and good for our circulation. I heard a familiar honk and waved at Monty's red Mustang heading south to Lakeside. I wondered when wedding bells would start ringing, for he'd been dating Shaylin Parks for three years.

"I hope he noticed I *wasn't* with Celia," Rouree said.

By seven thirty we were frozen and shivering with wet pants and sox from our scuffles in the water. We lit a bonfire and dried ourselves off, telling stories, and spouting dreams. Of course the conversation turned to girls, and I didn't mind talking about them—not so much. Kenny bragged about an Arapaho girl named Feather.

"Feather?"

"Yeah, she really knows how to tickle a guy."

We laughed at that, and I wondered what her name really was, or if such a generous girl really existed, because Kenny liked to crow.

"Did I ever tell you about the time Tisha Tanaka tickled me?"

Whoops. Didn't Dover remember the last time he talked about making out with Kenny's sister? Suddenly Kenny charged, knocking Dover end-over-teakettle, and back into the icy clutches of Eisner Lake. Rouree and I didn't stir from our places at the fire, but we were plenty amused by the butt kicking our friends were giving each other. Kenny was tall and lanky while Dover was shorter and stockier. Kenny could reach farther, delivering cuffs and barbs, but when Dover connected it packed a wallop.

"I hope they don't bust their noses. Gloria's not here to help them."

"Ah…they'll light up a smoke in a minute and feel better after a few drags."Rouree's words rang like a prophecy, for soon Dover Good and Kenny Tanaka were sharing a cigarette and trying to get dry near the fire. They seemed easy to anger and quick to forgive so I assumed their friendship was very balanced.

Dover wiped his hand against a bloodied lip. "Alright Greathawk, what about Celia?" Apparently he wasn't done talking girls.

"Celia's a lady and not campfire fodder for foul mouths or dirty minds." Rouree's eyes were firing, and truly, truly, he looked blazin'. If only Celia could see him now!

"Yeah," Kenny sassed. "Saint Rouree has spoken; go write it in a holy book somewhere."

Rouree looked annoyed, and his chin pulled against his neck, making him seem proud and cocky—just like I'd seen Howahkan do. "You want a fight? 'Cuz I'll sure as hell give you one if you really want it."

"Relax, man," Dover drawled. "We're just funning with you."

I changed the subject to Claude Walsh and his marvelous raspberry stained lips. The boys were interested and their curiosity piqued. They decided they wanted to go take a look at this guy. That's where the real mischief started…

We drove down Sixth Street, parking well up the hill from the Walsh residence. I was mad at Margo for complicating my afternoon already. It wasn't going to hurt my feelings any for the guys to get a good look at her ridiculous father! It was dark outside and street lights didn't run as far up the road as the Walsh place. We shuffled along in the darkness chuckling softly amongst ourselves. The lights were off in most of the house, but we could see a television set from the front room window, and several lamps were turned on in that room. We loomed on the porch, peering through the lace curtains the best we could, but Claude's back was to us.

"What are we going to do if they come out here?" Rouree whispered.

"We'll tell them we've come to invite them to the powwow, which is totally believable," I said.

Plain old Mavis was darning sox on the sofa. I could see Margo laying on her stomach, wearing plaid pajamas and coloring in a Barbie coloring book. Allyson had the same one at home. Fifteen year old Melinda's hair was rolled in spongy curlers, and she was filing her nails from an armchair. Kenny was getting a kick out of spying on her. "She's cute. What's the deal with her dorky dad?"

"Search me," I said. "I've always wondered. He's mostly normal except for is lips, but his sideburns are copasetic." I was using words from Celia's vocabulary a lot these days.

Kung Fu was blaring from the television set. I noticed their antenna wasn't on top of their roof; instead the antenna pole was mounted to the side of the house with sturdy brackets. I remembered Margo saying that every time the wind blew they lost reception and had to go out and wiggle the antenna to finish watching their favorite programs.

"Hey guys, hide in the bushes a minute."

They scurried into a small forest of lilac bushes and I tiptoed to the antenna and twisted the pole. I could see the television go snowy, and then I hightailed it around the house, finding a little pine tree next to the fence. I hid there, listening to the door open. Heavy steps clomped down the porch stairs. I saw the tall antenna turn, then footsteps on the porch again, followed by the thud of the door.

I snuck back around the front and saw the bushes shaking with laughter. "Do it again," Dover whispered. It was pretty funny the first time, so I did it again, running pell mell back to the pine tree to hide.

Creek! The door opened and footsteps sounded on the porch. *Clomp, clomp, clomp* went the boots. I saw the antenna spin from the rooftop view, then *clomp, clomp, clomp*, and the door creaked shut. Why was this so funny? Search me, but I was laughing my innards into turmoil.

I interrupted the program seven times. And every time got funnier.

"Did you guys see him in the porch light?" I whispered.

"Yes," Kenny roared quietly, holding his side. "He's silly."

"The family is normal, all but that one thing," I said in defense of Claude's kin.

When we were certain that we'd haunted the Walsh residence enough, we wandered down the road in search of more unsuspecting victims. We were just past the Walsh's barn when Rouree snorted. "I've got a great idea!"

"What?"

He pointed into a pasture. "Are those Walsh's bum lambs?"

"Yes. They own quite a few sheep."

Rouree climbed through the fence. We followed. He tromped into a nearby shed, spying marking paint. Sheep ranchers brand their stock with paint. Claude Walsh happened to use red paint, and had recently numbered his lambs by the looks of the fresh markings on the backs of the fleecy white babes. The numbers helped the Walsh's identify each baaing lamb.

Rouree grabbed a paint marker and stepped out of the shed, snagging a darling, white-faced lamb. He painted big red lips around its mouth. The poor lamb looked ridiculous and we howled with laughter. We began catching lambs, painting them all with sexy smackers. There was no harm in it, surely. "Hot Lips Hoola-lamb," Rouree goofed.

"Claude Walsh's livestock should definitely wear his brand," Dover laughed. I couldn't leave well enough alone, and after painting lipstick on my lamb, I changed the number on its back from six to sixteen, just by adding a one in front of it. The boys liked the idea and we renumbered all the lambs. We colored on twenty-five of Margo's little pets and then hurried down the road.

Agatha Duffy's house loomed ahead. I remembered Grady's funny statements concerning her and shared them with the boys. They were delighted with the prospects of helping her out of her financial difficulties. "This is no time to be out of business," Kenny quipped. "Inflation's high...gas is soaring—we should help her."

Rouree zipped back up the hill, again rummaging in the Walsh's lambing shed. He returned, carrying a painted board which read, "Cock-a-doodle-doo! Henhouse Back in Business!" He had obviously used the lamb marking paint for the sign. I squealed inside, it was so funny. Rouree pounded the sign into the front lawn. I had to laugh at the difference in my ability to process and understand Grady's jokes concerning Agatha Duffy. Two years ago I had actually believed her poor chicken coop was washed up!

"We need a rooster. We'll tether it to the post."

That's when Rouree jogged back up the hill for the second time. Apparently the Walsh farm provided any number of resources. A fine red rooster was in his arms when he returned. He had thrown his jacket over its head to keep it calm in the transport. We tied a baling twine around one foot and hobbled it to the post in Agatha Duffy's front yard. Surely when he was cut loose, he'd run back up the hill to his home in the chicken yard, and I justified our actions because all's well that ends well.

We wandered around the block aimlessly until Shamrock met Fifth Street. That was Mr. Henry's house, and Mr. Henry was not my favorite person at the moment. We noticed a television antenna similar to the Walsh's set up. *The Streets of San Francisco* was dancing from the television in the front room. Mrs. Henry was knitting an afghan from her rocking chair. Mr. Henry was watching from a recliner, drinking a glass of prune juice. The boys hid, and I wiggled the antenna and then made a beeline around the corner of the house to wait in the shadows.

I was disappointed not to hear the door open right away. Rouree whispered loudly from his post in the front yard, "He's pounding on the set, trying to make the picture come in…ooh, here he comes. Quiet everybody."

Creak. This town needed a healthy squirt of WD-40. Everyone had really squeaky hinges. Brisk footsteps sounded and then the antenna wiggled back into place. *Creak.* The door shut.

I studied the situation. Little hooks fastened around the door frame, and I figured the Henry's strung Christmas lights on them in the holiday season. I still had some twine in my hand and stretched the line from one side of the door to the other, about seven inches from the bottom, securing the string on the hooks. Kenny, Dover, and Rouree were doubled over with the anticipation of the cranky science teacher running out of his house and catching his feet on the string. When I was satisfied, I twirled the antenna out of position. The sound of the door knob turned before I was ready and I dove into a Fitzer bush near the steps.

Creak. "Damn television!" Mr. Henry grumbled.

"Now Lou, there's no need to use the devil's language," Mrs. Henry called.

"The hell there's not," Mr. Henry muttered. I was expecting a fiasco of flying body parts at any moment, but the slippered feet padded past me on the steps. I felt disappointed. The antenna turned, all the while Mr. Henry muttered. I noticed he was wearing a robe and pajamas when he clopped back up the stairs. I wondered if the prune juice was a nightly routine, forgetting *myself,* about the baling twine trap. And then *Ka-bam!*

Mr. Henry's slipper clipped the twine and he launched himself headfirst into his own house. I poked my head up to see where he landed, and he was still flying like a human cannonball toward Mrs. Henry. He hit *smack*, right into her middle, laying Mrs. Henry, her rocking chair and all, right over backwards. The whole display was visible from the street. It looked so peculiar!

"Well," Kenny said. "They really should shut their curtains—I'm embarrassed, myself!" That was funny, for it truly was a mass tangle of arms and legs and rockers, all tussling together in the middle of the room! We scrambled from our hiding places and ran like crazy out of the yard and up the street before Mr. Henry could investigate. We did notice plenty of the devil's language streaming out the open door, and most of it came from sweet Mrs. Henry.

We panted back to Rouree's truck. We pulled away from the west side of the Walsh residence very casually. We drove up and down the backstreets looking for an easy target. I noticed Aunt Lace letting her wee dog Jester out for a potty break. "Stop just up the road, here."

"That's a good looking woman," Kenny noted.

"Aunt Lace? Yeah, but she's snippety."

"Good looking women own the right to be."

"I don't like her very much."

Rouree's eyes turned on me. "Man, that's cruel! She's your own aunt! You can't say that."

"Oh yes I can. She was too snippy to even get married for a long time. She only married Mr. Mulligan last summer and she's my mom's age. She's thirty-four and her biological clock is ticking. That's what my Aunt Aura Leigh said when Aunt Lace wasn't listening. Aunt Lace thinks my dad is lame because he's a cowboy, and she thinks my mother is lame for marrying my dad."

"Gee...that *is* snippy."

I surveyed the Mulligan's property, regaling my friends with all of the shenanigans Wyatt, John, Monty, and I had perpetrated against them in the last two years. Kenny was game to reenact our past crimes, but that would be too suspicious. Aunt Lace whistled to the spoiled Chihuahua and the little scrapper scurried back inside, and the door shut. In several minutes the lights began shutting off all through the house.

"Maybe they're working on getting you a cousin," Kenny suggested.

"Shut up, Tanaka. My mind doesn't want to go there."

The boys laughed. At that moment I noticed two things, one being a very large chimney jutting out of the Mulligan's roof. No smoke wafted from it, and it was late in the year for a fire, anyway. The other thing I noticed was a pair of cats going at it in Delma Jean's yard.

"What?" Rouree asked.

"Let's go catch those cats and drop them down Mr. Mulligan's chimney."

"What?" Dover was dumbfounded.

Rouree cleared his throat. "Those cats are busy making kittens at the moment. The Tom cat will stink up the house."

"Exactly." I thought of the stinking cheese bait in Aunt Lace's purse and the decaying worms under the Oldsmobile's seat, and I laughed wickedly. There was a big difference in me from eleven years old to now. I no longer thought about being a good boy, for being a rascal was so much more fun! I could only hope that someday I would live to be very old, and then I would repent and hope I still got into Heaven, but for right now Salvation just meant not getting caught.

"Let's tie a note on the Tomcat that says, *'For you, Mr. Mulligan, a free demonstration because your wife's biological clock is ticking. Tick, Tick, Tick, Tick, Tick.'* Huh?" Kenny hooted at the suggestion and we seconded the motion. Dover scrambled in Amos's glove compartment for a slip of paper and a pencil. We then found some gloves under the seat and set out for another adventure.

The cats were yowling and Delma Jean stuck her face out the back door, eyes traveling every direction at once. "Quiet you beasts! Ernie's trying to sleep. Behave yourselves!"

The door shut and we abducted the cats. The stink was strong and the scratching intense, but we were set on our course. We snuck out of the Connor's backyard and into the Mulligan's. Kenny and Dover maneuvered like Hollywood Indians staging an ambush. They were athletic and skilled, balancing nimbly on the rooftop, each one clinging to a scratching feline.

Dover crept to the chimney hole and released the hissing cat. "Don't worry," he promised. "You'll land on your feet, alright."

Kenny finished tying the note to the nasty old Tomcat's hind leg and dropped him down. Rouree and I were set to run. It took about fifteen seconds, and then the darnedest clatter I ever heard broke out inside the newlywed's lair! Howling and hissing and moaning, and then…the Chihuahua went ballistic! Lights began donning all over the house, from room to room.

Dover and Kenny were trying to dismount the house as agilely as they did their horses. Meanwhile a circus unfolded inside. I saw the female tabby dodge into the front room window, skidding along the sill, catching Aunt Lace's sheers with her claws. The hefty Tomcat was on her heels and tangled in the drapes and jerked them from the windows altogether, revealing a better view for the entire town to see. Uncle Melvin was herding the cats, flailing his arms up and down, and hopping around in only his underwear. He was doing his best, yet his best was typically ineffective. The dog was spazzing out and Aunt Lace was trying to round the little pooch up, tripping along in a long flowing penior set. *Lime green*. She reminded me of a character in a soap opera. She wore matching feathered scuffs on her feet and the sight was a gas!

We were too enthralled to dash away, and the Mulligan's were engaged in battle so there was no sense in hurrying. The light in the kitchen turned on just in time for us to see two cats skidding across the table, knocking a plant upside down on the floor while a little stack of mail fluttered like confetti. Jester bounded onto a chair and leapt on the table as well. Of course, just after he'd set himself into motion the cats bounded elsewhere with Mr. Mulligan riding herd. Jester skidded down the length of the table trying to stop, but he sailed right off the end of the highly polished walnut finish and smacked into the glass patio doors with a yelp. He slid down the glass in slow motion, reminding me of a cartoon. Aunt Lace's feathered heels clipped along the linoleum floor. "Oh my poor darling Jester!"

I was doubled in two by this time, howling louder than the cats. Tears coursed down my cheeks and I couldn't draw wind. Rouree was on the ground, rolling and watching, and I didn't know the status of Dover and Kenny, for I couldn't draw my eyes away from the unfolding spectacle. I could hear them laughing though, and knew they'd need to smoke a lot to catch their breath after this abdominal workout.

Jester whimpered pathetically, drawing lots of sugary sympathy from his mistress. She cradled him to her bosom, inspecting him for damage. The little dog wasn't really hurt, but he sure was milking the system and wailed forlornly.

"Help me, Annelaise!" Mr. Mulligan bellowed from the front room. One cat was leaping from the bookcase to the top of the piano. Crash, down went a vase. We could hear it shatter from clear outside. The other cat leapt from the floor onto the piano keys and a thunderous melody ensued. *Beethoven's Last Symphony* couldn't have compared in musical grandeur.

The pussycat sprang from the piano top to the back of the couch and the Tomcat gave pursuit. "Melvin!" Aunt Lace shrieked. "Don't let that stinking thing lay on my couch!"

"What do you propose I do about it?" He thundered back.

"Don't yell at me! I didn't let these animals in here!"

"You must have done it when you let Jester back in."

"I did not! Don't you accuse me, you big oaf!"

"Put that dog down and help me herd these cats outdoors, dearest." The affectionate name didn't sound affectionate.

"Oh no! Melvin, these maniac cats are tracking soot all over the carpets and chairs! Did they fall out of the fireplace?"

"Now how in the deuce would they have gotten in there? Do you suppose they tumbled down the chimney? That's absurd! Cats have unbelievable balance!"

"I've seen them fall out of trees before so don't you insinuate I'm stupid!"

"What's on that cat's hind leg? Here, kitty, kitty, kitty…" Uncle Melvin switched tactics, trying to deduce the meaning of the madness. He pinned the cat against the wall and read the note. He looked crazy eyed and started blustering, but we couldn't understand him. Just then Jester squirmed from Aunt Lace's grasp and the ruckus started up again. I saw cats fly in two different directions, noticing one leaping again for the piano while the second one hissed and popped along the kitchen table.

Voices were rising under the strain of the moment. The front door opened in an attempt to set an escape route. We dove for the shadows in the perimeter of the yard. Just then I noticed lights donning next door and Delma Jean came bounding down her front steps like a mad hornet. Her hands were on her hips and her legs were thrust into Ernie's work boots, making terrific stomping noises. Her night gown was knee length and a tatty robe was jerked around her shoulders. Curlers poked beneath a scarf.

She barreled up the walk just as Mulligan's were herding the first cat through the door. The tabby hissed and popped at the intruder stomping up the walk, dodging back behind the sofa to hide

"What in the deuce are you doing?" Mr. Mulligan yelped at the unsightly neighbor.

"What the deuce are *you* doing?" Delma Jean bellowed back. "Godfrey! Put some clothes on, man!"

"This is *my* house!"

"What kind of a damned ruckus are you folks causing, anyway? Ernie's trying to sleep! The noise coming out of this house is ridiculous!"

"Well, we're sure sorry about that!" Aunt Lace huffed. "Poor pity you can't sleep and all! What about us? Did you think we wanted *your* stinking, mangy cats in our house?"

"I didn't let my cats in your house! My cats are in my back yard, or they were a few minutes ago."

"Well, then would you mind explaining this?" Mr. Mulligan shook his fist in Delma Jean's direction. The crumpled note waved like a hanky beneath Delma Jean's nose.

"I don't know what you're talking about, man! Godfrey, you're a complete lunatic!"

The tomcat was slinking past, trying to make his way outside. Mr. Mulligan snagged the raggedy animal. "Is this big fella yours?"

"Well, he's just an old rogue," Delma Jean explained. "Tomcats don't belong to anybody, really. I do feed the smelly old thing once in awhile."

"Ah-hah! That makes him *yours*!" Mr. Mulligan walked to the door and threw the fat cat out.

"Then why did you cat-nap him?"

"Why did you send him over here with an ignorant note tied to his hind leg? Was this your idea of a joke?"

The female snuck from behind the couch and leapt into Delma Jean's arms. "Oh Fluffy," Delma Jean whimpered. "Little Fluffy, what's happened to you? You're all sooty!"

"You know darn good and well what's happened to her!" Uncle Melvin blustered.

Jester began yapping at the excitement, lunging from Aunt Lace's arms. Fluffy hissed and climbed her owner's frame, scratching her way over the top of Delma Jean's head. She leapt out the door and ran yowling for home where the tomcat was waiting to pounce, that homeless old rogue. Jester followed suit, rushing between Delma Jean's clodhoppers, knocking her off balance. She tipped over backwards and her nightgown went flying up over her head creating a sight I never wanted to see. Aunt Lace rushed to her side, trying to help her up.

"Don't touch me, you cat-napper!"

"Get out of my house, you trespasser!" Mr. Mulligan hollered.

"Be nice, Melvin! We don't need a feud with the Connors!" Aunt Lace snarled. "And for Heaven's sakes, stand up Delma Jean!"

"Don't tell me to be nice. Read the note!"

Aunt Lace's finger pointed at her husband hotly. "Don't you tell me not to tell you to be nice, you big oaf!"

We skedaddled like flashes in the night, running up the road toward Amos Greathawk's fine red truck, but Aunt Lace's shrill notes cut the night with a chill. "What a pity," I said. "I was hoping they were happier together. Perhaps a new cousin isn't in my future after all."

"Marital bliss *is* hard to find," Dover agreed.

It was midnight before we unlocked the cabin door. Kenny and Dover sat outside to smoke and giggle over the night's mischief raids. Rouree and I were chuckling too, but he sobered when he saw a note on his bed in Celia's handwriting. "Awe," he lamented. "I wish I'd have been here when she came." His eyes shone as he read the letter, and a wonderful smile lit his face like a roman candle.

"I'm certain your note is better than the one I got today. What does it say?"

He gulped once, considering his option of telling me to buzz off, but since he was a generous boy he read, *"Dear Rouree, you're so blazin my heart is on fire. I can't wait to see you tomorrow. School is better with you around—so is everything. Love Celia"* She dotted the I with a little heart.

Celia Quinn was falling in love. Rouree Greathawk was already there! Celia was old fashioned and good, but still felt compelled to write a bold note. I thought about Awinita then, sneaking into the Big Irish's house and brushing his hair in the middle of the night, and I smiled, willing myself to see it in my dreams.

Chapter Twenty-Four

"So you see," Miss Vincent said, "Girls mature lots faster than boys—socially, emotionally, and sometimes even physically. You girls are more like fourteen year olds, really, while your male counterparts are still behaving as ten year olds."

"Yes," Coach Mills agreed, "So you girls can't feel badly that the boys aren't as ready for boy-girl relationships at this stage." I rolled my eyes. Instead of getting to play kickball for P.E. today, we ended up getting some kind of puberty and maturing lecture from the teachers. Mr. Henry was sitting in on the class, and I figured my refusal to have a crush on Margo Walsh had instigated this meeting. I was annoyed! This was America, and I was free to crush or not to crush at my own discretion! I couldn't wait to vent to Grady about it all for surely he would get riled on my behalf.

"So that's why they just act so dumb most of the time?" Margo asked primly. The girls looked down their noses in our direction, and my fellow man-beasts and I scowled back. Adolescent pep talks weren't really our thing.

"Yes, Margo. Just be patient with them. Boys usually catch up about their freshmen year, and then you can enjoy more meaningful friendships with them. Until then, you mustn't let their common disinterest get you down."

"By then we'll be swooning *elsewhere*," Judy Brynn O'Brien sniffed arrogantly.

"By then we will too," I retorted. Just maybe I'd convince a certain fourteen year old named Shonnee O'Shea to take a second look. Haw! That would show these snippets. Mr. Henry scowled at me and I wanted to ask him if he'd tackled his wife lately...but I let it pass. I saw Avery make the shape of a heart in Wyatt's direction, indicating he was plenty mature for her already.

That afternoon the student council set up chairs for Friday's big assembly. The natives would be coming to town en mass that afternoon, and the whole school was eager for it. A dance was scheduled for Friday night at the school and the hallway was buzzing with anticipation. The boys were blustering about finding some cute Shoshone girls, claiming it would be a big fat payback for the girls' attentions to Rouree, Kenny, and Dover. Being Memorial Day weekend, the city council expected a whole influx of folks from Salt Lake City, and elsewhere, to descend for the goings on. Town would be bustling and brimming to maximum capacity. I smiled, realizing I'd started it all.

Mr. Voss didn't mind that I wasn't post pubescent yet. He didn't' seem to fault me for being a thirteen year old seventh grader. He liked me, and I liked him because of it. He was definitely my favorite teacher. He kept encouraging us. The older student council kids were hanging red, white, and blue bunting all along the stage. Old Glory waved from the corner of the stage on one side, and the flags of Utah and Wyoming were posted on the opposite end. Mr. Voss was careful to include both state flags out of respect for our Wyoming friends.

John and Mark were instructed to take Mr. Voss's truck down to Eisner and pick up two plush armchairs on loan from the Three Lakes Furniture Company. They would be arranged on either side of the podium for the guests of honor, Howahkan Greathawk and Kelly Sheehan O'Rourke. I knew the men would be happy that so much effort had been made to pay homage to them. As a final touch, Cindy Murphy, a senior art student, displayed a beautiful depiction of an Irish shamrock and a Shoshone rose.

"John and Mark were lucky to get out of school this afternoon," I said to Mr. Voss as we finished the last row of chairs.

"Good kids, those boys."

I grinned, happy to know things were okay between Mark and his father-in-law, and I said so. "It's neat you trust Mark with your truck."

"Why wouldn't I? I trusted Mark with my daughter and my beautiful granddaughter. My truck is nothing compared to the treasures he is responsible for already."

I pondered the words while I walked to my last period class. History was a great way to finish the day, but Mr. McGill was out of the classroom on an errand and kids were involved in pockets of conversation all over the room. I walked past the mature and overly developed girls of my grade. "Excuse me, I'm looking for the nursery," I said, heading for the boys.

"Ha ha, Wesley!" Cindy Sue said sulkily. "That's where you all belong, alright."

"If you're so developed why is your chest just as flat as it was last year?" I asked, inciting an angry hiss among the girls.

"Actually we need to talk to all of you *toddlers*," Judy Brynn called. "You're *so* immature, but I hope you can keep up." We were grimacing, but lent our attention to the bossy girl. "Margo has been very upset all day!" Oh no…not this again! I don't *have* to have a crush if I don't want to! "Because somebody *vandalized* her lambs last night."

Oh…yeah, that.

"What?" Wyatt asked incredulously. "Vandalized her lambs, you say?"

"Someone scribbled big ugly red lips all over my lambs, and they messed up their numbers. Feeding them this morning was very difficult! I had two number sixteen's, two elevens, three twelve's, two tens, two thirteens, and a fifty nine. I've never had a number fifty-nine lamb, EVER! Which one of you blockheads is responsible?"

"Don't look at us!" Miles piped. "We have better things to do than go around painting the number line on your dumb lambs."

Wyatt's electric blue eyes focused in on my face. I knew he was looking at me and I nodded ever so slightly. I hadn't yet had a chance to regale him with the details.

"Red lips?" I asked. "Are you sure? Maybe your lambs just need some chap stick or something."

"Why would my lambs need chap stick?"

"Maybe the Avon lady gave them free samples." The guys laughed at my jest.

"Yeah!" Steve McCarthy trumped, "Like your dad!" That did it. Margo clouded up and rained all over the classroom.

"Zip it, Steve," I said. "There's no reason to get personal. Sometimes you guys go overboard on saying mean things." I looked directly at Paul Siskin and Ross Moore, trying to make my stare sting a little bit.

"You were talking, why can't we?"

"I was talking about the lambs! Margo's dad didn't need to enter into our conversation. I think you owe her an apology."

"I didn't paint their mouths red, you jerk," Steve muttered. I already knew that. I knew who the culprit was, and it was really funny at the time, but Margo didn't need to be razzed.

Suddenly Margo's tears dried up and she smiled at me again, beaming happy vibes my way. I let out a big sigh for there was no winning! I was certain to be handed another note tomorrow, and then what?

"But I'm not the only one who had trouble last night. Someone pounded a sign in our neighbor's lawn that said she was a hooker."

Wyatt's neck snapped sideways, and his eyes were huge. His facial expression was no different than my own, for we certainly did NOT call Agatha Duffy a hooker! We simply put an OPEN sign on her front lawn, and Margo had things all twisted up. To hear her tell it, it sounded really nasty. For Pete's sake! No wonder rumors fly at lightning speed in this town.

"What!" Half of us cried in unison.

"Well, not in so many words, but…"

"Now Margo," I said gently. "I can't imagine that anyone would say something like that."

"It's true, Wesley, and if you ride the bus to my house I'll show you."

Oh no! She was not tricking me into going to her house! "No thanks, I'll take your word for it. You know, there are some real jerks around here."

Wyatt kept grinning wider and wider, and his cheeks looked healthy. He started laughing and his shoulders rolled beneath the bellows until the whole class joined in, even Stan Tomkins.

That night Grady and Howahkan came to our house for supper. Mother was getting good at feeding a crowd. The Shoshone boys ate heartily. Allyson peered at them whenever they weren't looking, especially Rouree. Yarrow kept singing songs about fried chicken and Pete's new pants, for Mother had brought her some boy doll clothes home from Eisner.

"I went scouting for trucks," Howahkan told me.

"Oh yeah?"

"Yes, its highway robbery what those crooks want for one, but I guess I'd better have one anyway."

"What are you going to get?"

"I thought I'd take you and Rouree with me, first of next week. I'll let you choose."

The black eyed boy across the table grinned at me expectantly. This sounded like lots of fun to us! "Right on, Howahkan!"

Grady smiled in my direction. "Everything ready for tomorrow, Wesley?"

"I think so. We set up for it today."

"How was school in general?"

"Dumb! Instead of P.E. we had to go into the gym and have a lecture on girls maturing ahead of boys and I'm mad about it. I didn't see any of those big grown up girls spearheading this project!"

Grady rubbed his hands together. "No, by Jingo Jones! What about it my boy—you'd better blow off a little steam before you bust a vessel."

"Well…I think it all got started because stupid Margo Walsh dropped me a note yesterday, telling me she had a crush on me. She asked if I liked her back and gave me a yes or no option."

Howahkan started laughing before I even got to the good part, and so did Dad and Grady. "Multiple choice!"

"I circled *no* and put an exclamation point behind it. I handed it back to her, but Mr. Henry confiscated it and then got hissy about it, hence the lecture this morning."

"Oh *Wesley*," Mother groaned wearily. "Haven't I taught you *anything* about being nice?"

"Boys *are* immature," Allyson said. "They have to be fifteen *at least* before they're worth much."Her eyes slid to Rouree, Dover, and Kenny. All three boys grinned at her and her cheeks flushed and she ducked her head and didn't say anything more.

"It's America! I don't have to force myself to like anybody I don't want to," I persisted, hoping to push the start button on one of Grady's best tangents, but he merely winked and said, "Someday you might take a look at Margo Walsh and kick yourself in the pants."

Mother set slices of spicy apple pie on the table. "Are you two ready for your speeches tomorrow?" She asked the old men.

"Oh, perfectly ready," Grady chirped enthusiastically. "What an honor!"

Howahkan shook his head warily at his brother-in-law. "Haw! By the time Kell rattles on and on, there won't be any time left for me. I've prepared a brief statement, just in case—two words the crowd will be happy to hear, *The End*." We laughed at Howahkan. What a proud, interesting, stubborn man he was!

It was still light after supper and we went back out to the corrals to practice riding. Our time was getting slim for rehearsals. Yarrow insisted on taking Pete with her so he could learn how to be a cowboy when he grew up. Allyson's heart pitter pattered again and again as she cheered for the Shoshone boys, and not so much for me, but still she was proud and happy that I could compete with some of their skills. "Good job, Wesley," she called.

"Man your sister is so cute. Let me give her one little flirt," Kenny begged. "Just one to set her heart in motion."

"You're a dork," I said, but grinned to see what he'd come up with.

"Hey Allyson, this is for you." Kenny took off riding, and then nailed a hand stand on the horse's back as it barreled at breakneck speeds. He launched into an acrobatic dismount, spinning twice in the air before landing on his feet right in front of her perch on the fence rail. He bowed before her while she looked wide eyed and thunderstruck. Not only Allyson, but Mother as well—for the stunt was incredible.

"Show off," Dover grumbled.

"Allyson won't sleep tonight," I said. "Geez, that's somethin'. Just like a cat down a chimney."

Rouree laughed. "I wonder if Celia would like that?"

My brows shot up. "You can't do that can you?"

"Who do you think taught Tanaka?"

"Do it then," I challenged.

Rouree hollered, "This is for you, Allyson!" And he thundered through the corral, mastering the same stunt, but he held his weight with only one hand before pirohouetting athletically to the ground.

My chin dropped and so did everyone else's. "Why aren't we doing that for the show?"

"Don't wanna show off too bad," Rouree said.

I saw movement against the north side of the corrals. Celia and Dori Jo Quinn were leaning against the fence. "Hey Rouree," I motioned in their direction and Rouree broke into all smiles. He rode over to where she stood.

Rouree motioned Celia to join him in the corral, then reached down with one hand and pulled her up behind him on the horse. Her arms wrapped tightly around his middle and they loped around the arena. Dori Jo scurried around the perimeter. "Oh my heck, Allyson! Did you see *that*?"

Grady and Howahkan watched Rouree and Celia ride together. The wind stirred in Celia's long blond hair like a golden flag. "Well Big Irish, there's nothing like young love, even when you're old."

"That's the truth, Howahkan."

"When we were young, who would have wagered we'd have great grandkids falling for each other?"

"Nobody. When we were young we couldn't see the future for the stars in our own eyes."

The small audience disbanded. Dori Jo and Allyson went into the house to giggle over the older boys, and hopefully work on a math assignment. Dover and Kenny shared a smoke behind the barn, and Howahkan left with Grady to see if any of his friends and neighbors from Fort Washakie had arrived. Mother took Yarrow into the house for a bath. "Can Pete have a bath too?"

"I suppose."

"But you said boys don't bath with girls."

"Well, you can bath Pete because you are his mommy."

"And Pete will be so clean, and clean and clee-ee-an!"

I led Misty into the barn and fed her some oats and curried her. She hadn't worked up lather or anything, but she enjoyed the pampering. I looked out of the stall window. Rouree and Celia had ridden into the north pasture. My heart panged in a weird way at the sight of them. Some day when I decided to go girling I hoped I could find one that looked at me the way Celia looked at Rouree. I hoped to find a girl who liked horses and a show off rider because I would learn to do a handstand and acrobatic dismount if it killed me.

"Before you can do a handstand you've got to stand on your feet, first," Dad said, reading my thoughts. I nodded. It would take a lot of practice, but I was thirteen years old, and time was on my side.

When we finally drove up to Grady's place that evening, I noticed lots of Shoshone vehicles parked near the cabins, and bronze people were paddling in canoes on Inish Lake. A few Tipis were being erected. "That's just for show," Kenny drawled, sucking his cigarette until the ash flickered red in the gathering twilight.

"You smoke too much," I observed.

"I know. I'm not a saint like you and Rouree Greathawk, and I don't intend to be."

"Well…you're an amazing athlete. It's too bad you can't suck air 'til you take a puff."

"I've been smoking since I was nine."

"Tobacco is used for prayer, isn't it?"

"Yeah." Kenny's head bobbed.

"Because I thought the smoke carried the prayer to Heaven. That's what Howahkan said when we made medicine together."

"And, your point is?"

"You pray more than anyone else I know. You are the biggest saint of us all, perhaps."

Dover grinned. "He got you Tanaka!"

"Next time I see you light up, I'll be quiet so I don't interrupt your holiness."

Kenny muttered obscenities at me, but they were mostly in fun.

Celia persuaded her folks that she needed to help Grady with the incoming crowd. I don't think Uncle Rob believed her for a moment, but he gave her permission to stay out until closing time. Grady had personally seen to it that Maxine Flanders was on board to help Mark with the extra bodies, and so Celia was free to sidle up to Rouree. His arm was around her back and he introduced her to his dad.

Amos grinned at the couple, whistling lowly between his teeth. "I see you've had a good week, Son."

"This is Celia Quinn. She's the Little Shoshone's cousin."

Amos shook Celia's hand congenially. "I can't blame Rouree for being smitten." Celia's cheeks pinked prettily and she ran a hand through her hair, thanking him shyly.

Kenny and Dover went in search of their families, full of tall tales to tell. Yancy Good shook hands with me, and so did some of the others.

"How's the schnoz, you swaggering sod buster?"

"Hello, Gloria."

She eyed me thoughtfully. "Where's the girl?"

"She's home...but, I can take you to see her if you'd like."

"No. I'm too tired tonight, but I would like to see her. I brought her something."

"That was nice of you!"

"Nice hell! Don't try to polish my apples, you cocky little rooster. You just make sure I get to meet my niece."

I hurried away from Gloria before she could extend anymore of that warm, loving, Wyoming hospitality on me. I went into our cabin and called Mother. "Steel yourself up for meeting this woman. She's as soft as a cement pad, as tender as a cactus, and as sweet as a mouthful of horse radish."

Many of the Fort Washakie citizens had never been to Three Lakes Valley, and Howahkan had a little group of interested people walking around the hot pots, listening to stories. We suited up and went into the steamy pools to soak. Rouree kept his arm around Celia, making sure the other guys took note. Some of the Indians nodded my direction, recognizing me from my stay in Fort Washakie last autumn.

A girl with long thick hair stepped into the water. Her eyes were dark and her looks were brooding. She wasn't as pretty as Awinita, but then again, no one was. "Hello Little Shoshone," she said.

I was surprised, for I didn't recognize her. "Hello."

"You don't remember me?"

I shook my head briefly, and then looked at the water, feeling uncomfortable. "Sorry."

"It's okay. I was a jingle dancer at the dinner last fall. I guess you didn't pay much attention."

"No, I did, I mean, there was just a lot to take in. Mostly I noticed Rouree dancing the Men's Fancy and wondered how he could do it with a broken nose."

Celia smiled at Rouree, and then snuggled closer, laying her head against his shoulder.

"I'm Callie Halfmoon."

Callie Halfmoon? What a cool name! "I don't know why I didn't remember you," I said, and then I blushed because I heard Celia giggling in the background.

Callie smiled and I noticed a dimple in one cheek. I liked it. "So… I'm going to be dancing tomorrow at your school. You'll have to smile at me so I'll know I have at least one friend."

"Yeah, no problem. Don't worry, though. I'm sure it will be blazin'."

A black brow arched with interest. "Blazin', huh?"

I nodded and saw both Rouree and Celia smile again. I stepped a couple of feet away from them, casually drawing our conversation further from my audience. "I do *like* jingle dancing," I persisted. "All of those little bells stitched to your dress sound really cool when you dance."

"Mine are made out of Copenhagen lids."

"What?"

"The little tin tops off Copenhagen containers, you know, my mother rolled them into the shape of the cones and stitched them on. There are three hundred and sixty five bells stitched onto my dress."

"One for everyday of the year." I sounded lame and Callie sounded normal. She made conversation easier than I did, that's for sure. I thought about our stupid discussion in P.E. and decided it was all true. I was ten in my social skills and this girl was at least fifteen. "What grade are you in, Callie?"

"I just finished eighth. I'm fourteen."

Doomed again. I was cursed, and now I knew why thirteen was considered an unlucky number.

I changed the subject, talking about the resort, trying to impress her with Grady's empire. "Everyone says I'm a lot like the Big Irish," I boasted.

"He's really little."

Doomed. Doomed! Doomed! I changed the subject back to dancing. "I can't wait for all my friends to see you guys perform tomorrow. It's like a fun sneak peek before Saturday's powwow."

"Tomorrow I get to help Rain Washakie teach Joni Whitecliff's daughter how to dance."

"What?"

"Yeah, the little girl will be dancing in the powwow with the girls."

"Yarrow? She's my sister."

"Yeah, I know. She's Rain's cousin, but Rain has never met her."

"Who *is* Rain Washakie?"

"Gloria's daughter. Don't you know Gloria? She was Joni's oldest sister."

"Yeah, I know Gloria." I winced, for I didn't get the happy vibe from the short, stout woman, and I feared Yarrow would be black and blue from the verbal cuffing if she didn't dance correctly. "Well…huh!"

"What?"

"I hope Yarrow can learn all in one day."

"She will. Joni was an amazing dancer."

"You remember her, before she ran off?"

"Yes. I used to wish I was just like her."

That was an interesting revelation. I thought back to last summer and my opinion of the dirty hippie chick. She hadn't made a smashing first impression and I was reminded about the significant choices we make in our lives, choices that either build us into better people or tear us down. Then I thought of Yarrow seeing Joni at Lake Washakie, and remembered she was now clean, and dressed as an Indian. She was wearing moccasins and feathers fluttered in her hair.

"Hey Wesley," Rouree called. "Want to race?"

"Not at the moment," I said, needing to ask Callie Halfmoon some more questions.

"Whoot! Whoot!" Rouree tooted. "The Little Shoshone is catching on!"

I scowled, wondering what had come over me…perhaps I was just tired, for we had put in a late night of it, and then school and riding practice had taken it out of me. Yeah, sure…that was it.

Chapter Twenty-Five

The doorbell rang before school the next morning. Allyson ran to the door and opened it. Gloria and Rain Washakie, Amos Greathawk, and their ancient patriarch, Howahkan stood at the door. "Hello Allyson," Howahkan greeted.

Mother stepped into the living room, greeting the visitors with as much grace as she could muster. I was just grabbing a notebook of mine, and Rouree, Dover, and Kenny were waiting in the driveway. I was happy to skip out and not be in on Gloria's pleasantries, for I doubted if she had any.

"Yes," I heard Mother say, "Yarrow is in the tub, but I will hurry her along."

I knew Yarrow would win and woo them all, but I couldn't be late for school. "See you this afternoon," I called to Howahkan.

Rouree and the others would only attend school until ten o'clock, and then they would go back to the cabin to get their costumes and make ready for the afternoon. I was as nervous as a cat, hoping it all went down okay. This whole weekend had morphed into a huge thing and it had all started as an idea of mine. Of course nobody would remember that fact, but I hoped the event was successful anyway.

I scurried into Mr. Voss's room first thing to make sure everything was in order. "Ready or not, Wesley, this is it."

"The Shoshones rolled into town last night."

"I know. I went up and sat with Mark in the boathouse for a while. It was fun to watch."

"Oh, you did?"

"Yes, and I noticed you were most congenial and making friends easily."

"Well..."

Mr. Voss winked. "It's amazing, Wesley! This whole ballgame is your brain child. Really, all of this work, just to showcase a new found skill in pony riding?"

I took a deep breath, considering the question. "It might go further than that."

"Yes?"

"Last fall when I went to stay with Howahkan Greathawk, I heard Cher's song, *Half-Breed*, come on the radio. I listened to the words for the first time. Howahkan said*, 'Sounds like your new little sister to me.'* That bothered me, and I asked, *'Yarrow?'* Howahkan said*, 'She's a half-breed.'* Well, Mr. Voss, you know I just love Yarrow to death—we all do. I never saw her as anything but perfect, but I started to wonder how other people might see her. I decided the best thing I could do was educate this town about how cool of a heritage Yarrow really has. I love those Shoshone people. I'm hoping Yarrow's little friends will see some neat things this weekend, and then remember. When they look at Yarrow I hope they will see the beauty there."

Mr. Voss nodded thoughtfully. "I don't know what kind of a kid you are, Wesley...on one hand you're a normal, mischief making thirteen year old, and on the other hand you're are wise beyond your years."

"Haw! Tell that to Mr. Henry, Miss Vincent, and Coach Mills. I'm still prepubescent and wet behind the ears. I'm a ten year old, apparently."

"Prepubescent?" Mr. Voss croaked. "Oh Wesley!"

I opened my locker and a little note fluttered out. I closed my eyes, dreading the reading of it. *"Wesley, hey! This is a funny note because I'm just tricking you...I had Rouree stuff it in your locker, never expecting it would be from me, eh? Thanks for the fun time last night. See you around, probably."* It was signed *Callie Halfmoon*, and she drew a symbol of a half moon near her name. That was a neat thing to do. I was relieved that it wasn't from Margo and nearly let out a little "Whoop!"

"Hello Wesley," a familiar voice said.

I whirled around, grinning too big from Callie's note. Margo Walsh was looming before me. My heart sank down around my ankles like a pair of baggy pants in the bathroom. "Hey," I said, trying to collect my jubilant smile into containable, prepubescent non-interest. "How are your vandalized lambs? Are they still vandalized?"

"You should come see them, they're so awful! I cry every time I look at 'em."

"Gee, that's too bad. I'm sure the lambs don't care."

"Well...I'm not so sure. Frankly, they seem embarrassed to me."

"They're acting *sheepish*, huh?"

Margo giggled at my dumb pun and I wished she wouldn't have. "You're a wit, Wesley!"

"Ah," I shrugged it off. "I'm a twit not a wit."

"See...you're funny."

"Well, um—guess next Wednesday is the last day of school. I'm sure ready."

"I like school."

"Well, yeah, you girls would, being more *mature* and everything."

"Don't feel bad about that."

"Oh I don't. I totally agree with Coach Mills. I am *way* too immature to handle a girlfriend. I'm too busy thinking about horses and grass stains and stuff." I tried my darnedest to talk her out of liking me. "I'm not ready for anything as neat as you girls are, that's for sure. I still like the sandbox."

Wyatt walked behind me. "You're so full of it your eyes are brown," he whispered.

Margo switched her weight onto her other leg. "Oh Wesley, don't think so poorly of yourself. You are leagues ahead of the other boys in our class."

"Not so much, and well, I'm kind of allergic to acting my age."

"Oh Wesley, for pity's sake! You're not *that* bad!"

I sucked in a deep breath wondering where to go from here. Being mean got me in trouble with Mr. Henry and Mother, and half the class. Being nice got me in trouble with myself. "Hey, you know what? I know somebody that's got a thing for you, Margo!"

"Really—who?"

"Promise not to tell."

"Cross my heart, hope to die, stick a nee-dle in my eye."

"Well…it's not necessary to do all of that."

"Who, Wesley? I've just gotta know!" Margo stomped her scuffed saddle shoe against the hall tile, and she was half cute when she did it. What's up with all these females, anyway? They never used to do cute things!

I remembered how I was going to let him have it. "Paul Siskin."

"Paul?" Margo seemed disappointed.

"Sure, and you know how he's a year older than us, you know, from flunking first grade and everything. Well, surely he's ready for a girlfriend."

"Paul Siskin?" Margo half shuddered, seeming undeniably repulsed by my juicy, made-up scrap of information. "Oh Wesley, anybody but him! Promise me that if he asks me to dance tonight, you'll tap him off. Oh please, Wesley! I've just had such a bad week already—my poor lambs and now *this*."

This wasn't going the way I thought it would. "Well, gee Margo… Paul's okay."

"Yuck! He's not either. He has the personality of a—a—cucumber! Promise me!"

"Now Margo, I'm not much of a dancer. How about I buy you some nice sudsy shampoo and you can scrub your lambs up, huh? I'll bet my Grandpa has some super duty vetinary shampoo that's really good for washing lambs with. That will make your week go better."

"Please Wesley."

"Well…I'm not sure I'll be at the dance," I muttered. "But I will if he asks you."

Margo squealed and headed down the hall, disappearing in the girls' bathroom. I leaned against my locker and rubbed a hand over my eyes. It was eight fifteen in the morning, and they felt tired. *Now what?* I saw Paul and wasted no time beating a trail to him.

"Hey Paul! Guess what?"

"What?"

"There's a ten dollar bet on you."

"For what?"

"Well, there's a ten dollar bet that says you can't stay away from Margo Walsh at the dance tonight."

"I don't get it."

"I didn't think you would…listen, man! I heard that somebody is betting against you. They said you would dance with Margo tonight, but you will get their ten dollars if you leave her all the heck alone."

"Really? Somebody will pay me to *not* dance with Margo?"

"That's right."

"I feel richer already!" A drippy looking smile covered his face.

"Good, so do I." The bell rang and I scurried off to my first hour class. What a morning! My plan to get Margo to like Paul didn't work. I didn't realize he was so personally offensive to her. Her plan to get me to tap him off if he danced with her was personally offensive to me. Now I didn't have to worry about that, but I'd be out ten bucks, and Margo still needed a decoy away from me. Hmm…some problems are complex, and no mistake.

Miss Pell had us write essays on our school year since the last day of school was next Wednesday. She wasn't too strict while we worked, and so we visited quietly amongst ourselves, jarring each other's memories of things that happened during the past nine months.

"You should write about the first day of school," Judy Brynn O'Brien said to me. "It was so memorable, seeing you get hauled away in the sheriff's car."

"Thanks, I hadn't remembered that," I remarked snidely. I peeked across the room to Stan's desk and saw him smiling. The expression looked good on his face. "Did you remember that Stan?"

"Nope."

"I'm going to write about the worst day of my life," Margo lamented.

"When was that?" Cindy Sue asked.

"Yesterday, after I saw my lambs had been vandalized!"

"I'm writing about the jukebox for the cafeteria," Steve mumbled.

"I'm going to write about basketball," Paul Siskin started to say.

"Shut up, Paul! We don't care about *what* you have to say," Margo sassed cruelly.

Miss Pell scowled at the girl. "Margo, mind your manners."

Paul blinked a few times, wondering where this sudden hostility was coming from. I shook my head, realizing Margo was trying to provoke Paul into *not* liking her, which she didn't have to work too hard to achieve since I'd made up the lie in the first place. She was now treating him ten times worse than I had treated her, but I doubt if she realized it.

Paul continued, "I'm going to write about our game against Lakeside when we beat in overtime."

"You didn't have anything to do with the win," Margo seethed. "I'm surprised we didn't lose by a hundred points with you on the court! You dribble the ball off your shoe every chance you get."

Miss Pell scowled again. "Margo! That's enough. Keep your mean-spirited comments to yourself or you'll all have to stop talking."

"I'm writing about doing homework with Wyatt when he couldn't come to school last fall," Avery said. "We had a lot of fun doing lessons together."

Whatever Avery Anne Applewhite said seemed to be okay. Whatever Wyatt now said was fine too, and he answered, "And we played a lot of chess, huh Avery?"

"Yesssss....and you're the king of the chessboard!"

"I like checkers, myself," Paul said.

"You *would*," Margo snarled, as if there was something wrong with checkers. "And no doubt *Uncle Wiggly* is your favorite game."

"I do like the Skeezics," Paul admitted.

"You're so lame," Margo whispered so Miss Pell couldn't hear. "You're so lame you are a Skeezics!"

Paul tapped me on the shoulder. I turned around and he was grinning stupidly. "I can't believe some guy is going to pay me ten bucks NOT to dance with her. Ha! I wouldn't dance with her if somebody paid me to!"

So much for a lousy investment.

I wrote about practicing with Misty every night after school. I enjoyed writing it, and felt a little smug knowing my great grandfather was a famous author. He said I would be a writer too, so maybe my essay would be good. I tuned the other students' voices out, concentrating on my work.

"I fell a hundred times—no maybe a thousand. I fell and fell, but my goal of riding as the Shoshone boys did kept me staggering back onto my feet. Misty kept wondering what I was doing, and why the sudden interest, and I think her curiosity kept her willing to go forward, too. I rewarded her with apples from my pocket and we became good friends. One day it finally fell into place. I wrapped my hands in her mane and we began running and I set my feet and actually launched myself onto her bare back. It was a triumph for both of us! I cheered and raised my hands above my head

while Misty ran a victory lap. We shared an apple after practice that day, for Misty wanted me to have a bite, too. She had trained me well."

"Wesley?"

I looked up. Miss Pell had been walking up and down the aisles, reading over our shoulders. I never realized she was standing above me. "Yes?"

Miss Pell tapped my paper. "This is good."

I grinned at her. "Thank you."

"No, I mean, this is *really, really* good. Are you going to be a writer, too?"

"Yes Mam."

"Have you been writing in your spare time?"

"A little bit."

Her eyes studied me thoughtfully. "I'll expect more out of you from now on."

"Yes Mam."

"Your ability to organize your thoughts is very developed for one so young…and I have a feeling that more is scooting through your head at any one moment than most thirteen year olds ponder on in a week. Put it to good use, Wesley."

I nodded and she moved to Paul's desk. "No Paul—you can't write in all capital letters. You're trying to take up tons of space with a few minimal sentences, and I'm not falling for that trick. Now erase your paper, and start again, in *cursive* this time."

Miss Pell snaked up and down the aisles. She picked up Stan's paper. "May I share this with the class?" Stan turned red and ducked his head, nodding. Miss Pell read, *"The best day of my life happened this year when Wesley made friends with me, even though he beat the crap out of me the day before, and we got hauled off to Lakeside in the Sheriff's car. I deserved everything he gave me, but that didn't mean I wasn't really, really sorry for what I did to Wyatt Finnegan. I will be sorry all of my days about what I did to him. My next best day this year happened when Wyatt and Wesley played football with me after lunch. I also liked watching Wesley practice riding his horse every day after school. When I grow up I will get a good job at the mine, or the railroad, or someplace like that so I can buy myself a horse. I will always keep apples in my pocket."*

Miss Pell looked up from the paper. "Wesley, Wyatt, and Stan, please come with me. The rest of you keep working."

We followed her out into the hall, wondering what she wanted. "I just wanted to do this," she said, hugging all three of us. "You are good kids, dang it! I hope you will continue to work on your differences and problems in a positive way. Stan—keep your chin up! You have so much potential, young man! And Wyatt, thank you for having a gentle heart. Wesley—people are watching you. Dang it! Lead right."

We looked bewildered, but we all promised to do what Miss Pell asked. She hugged us one more time, and we filed back into the classroom. I finished working on my paper, realizing I had two favorite teachers now, and I think both of them worried about me running for a cliff.

By the time the student body filed into the auditorium for the assembly, the room was packed, and Mr. Voss and Coach Mills were raiding the classrooms for more chairs. I smiled to see so many townspeople and Fort Washakie friends, as well. The Superintendent and School board members were seated on the front row. The big regal chairs from the Three Lakes Furniture Company were still empty and moved toward the ends of the stage, near the flags, and the podium had been scooted off to one side. Obviously Howahkan and Grady had something else in mind.

My eyes scanned the rows until I located my family. Yarrow was dressed in a smashing white buckskin dress and matching headband with feathers in her hair. The dress was beaded with red Shoshone roses and it was a masterpiece. She was curled up on Gloria's lap, and the gruff woman seemed so matronly with Yarrow seated there. Yarrow saw me and pointed. Her mouth said, "Hi my boy!" But I couldn't really hear her voice. Gloria turned to see what Yarrow was pointing at and she actually smiled at me. My chin dropped. Gloria's head bent close to Mother's and they looked like real, genuine friends. I thought it was curious.

The Quinn's were seated in the same aisle as my folks. Monty and Shaylin were both here for the show, sitting next to Mark, Michelle, and their new little baby. Shaylin and Michelle were good friends, and I knew the two couples hung out a lot. Uncle Aiden and Aunt Aubynn motioned toward Wyatt and I, and we waved.

Avery asked me to slide down one chair so she could sit by Wyatt. I was a little annoyed, but what could I say? I slid down a chair and that put me sitting right next to Margo Walsh. Margo kept turning her head to look at me—I could feel her eyeballs studying my ear and neck. I fidgeted uncomfortably in my chair. I leaned around Avery, "Hey Wyatt, switch me places, would you?"

"Why?"

"Just do it."

He did, and I was resettled between Avery and Stan. Stan grinned like the Cheshire cat, thinking I had traded to be good buddies.

Mr. Mulligan walked up to the front and tapped on the microphone. "Welcome to a special assembly, without further ado, we will begin."

A hush swept across the audience, and the lights dimmed. Stage lights lit with illuminations of muted red and green. A drum beat softly and a Native American flute wailed hauntingly. Howahkan stepped onto the stage. He played the flute, making interesting bird calls and trilling notes. It sounded eerie and sad, and goose bumps trailed along my flesh. He wore fringed buckskin leggings and moccasins. His shirt was a red tunic, and a beaded sash tied at his waist. The tunic was open at the throat and a bear claw necklace was strung around his neck. A beaded headband circled his head and matching beaded bands secured his long braids. His copper bracelets jangled from his wrists as he played, and his rings twinkled beneath the red stage lights. His haunting melody warbled like a lonesome bird, forlornly calling out for a friend.

"Ta toodle-dee-tootle-dee-doodle dee day, ta toodle-dee-tootle-dee-doodle dee day," a Celtic whistle replied, and Grady stepped onto the stage from the other direction. The green stage light revealed western

style clothing. His pants were tucked into tall leather boots, and spurs jangled as he walked. A holster was strapped around his waist. He wore a black shirt and leather vest, and a neckerchief was tied around his throat. Both men played their different tunes at the same time. Slowly they stepped toward the center of the stage, getting closer together, and their notes morphed into a harmony, and then they played the same song. All of the stage lights lit and the men shook hands while the audience erupted into rapturous applause. It was the most effective opening I had ever seen at an assembly.

I wondered whose idea it had been, to start that way—and couldn't believe the old men could have gotten along well enough to coordinate the effort, but obviously they must have. I was expecting Mr. Mulligan to stand up and welcome everyone, and then we'd ramble off the Pledge of Allegiance and then proceed with regular talks and stuff, interspersed by some historical facts and Native performances, but I could see that the we were in for a treat! The old men had a few tricks up their sleeves.

Howahkan's voice boomed over the speakers, "For many generations the Shoshone people camped near the waters in the Three Lakes Valley. We hunted and fished and foraged native berries and grasses. The deer and elk were plentiful here, and the skies painted diagrams for us to follow. Night times found us celebrating our successes near the fire." I couldn't see a microphone in his hand, and then realized he was wearing a tiny microphone clipped to his tunic.

The drumming became louder and Yancy Good, Amos Greathawk, and Charlie Tanaka walked onto the stage. They stood on the right rear corner, and the hand drum singing began, "Hey yaw-yaw hey, hey hey hey-oh, Hey yaw yaw hey, hey oh-aah ho!" Their voices were clear and chilling, and the chanting and beating invited more characters onto the stage. Grass dancers moved to the drumming rhythms. Different men and boys, all adorned with draping fringe flowing from long tunics, attached to their arms and backs, danced in patterns which illustrated the successful hunt. As they swayed and moved, it actually looked like breeze stirring tall grasses on a prairie plain or in mountain meadow pastures.

Grady's voice said, "There were more than nine thousand natives camped in these mountain valleys when white settlers arrived in 1854, founding Lakeside. Irish settlers came in 1864, colonizing Gallagher Springs and Kilkenny Point. My father was fifteen years old then, and he said his eyes had never beheld such stirring sights."

I heard the bells and knew the jingle dancers were making their way onto the stage. My eyes shot around until they rested on the features of Callie Halfmoon. She grinned at me and I waved a hand. Five girls danced rhythmically with the jingles making music. The crowd was enthralled. The girls' feet stepped to the chanting rhythms of the men and drums, and when the men's voices halted so did the girls. Not one millisecond of difference occurred, which told me they were very familiar with the music. The dancers held fans in their hands, always positioning them with poise. When the men's voices rang again, the girls stepped in unison with bells jangling merrily. They danced off the stage and the drummers were quiet, but stayed in place.

Grady's narration continued, "The Irish settlers were new to America, and were filled with wonder and fear. Brigham Young, the first territorial governor of Utah, and Chief Washakie were determined to work together for both were men of vision. Washakie's people protected many settlers and wagon trains bound for Oregon and California. Of course there were dissenters, and also frequent skirmishes with enemies, sometimes leaving both the settlers and natives vulnerable."

"And who counsels great men?" Howahkan asked. "Who bestows vision and foresight? My grandfather was Bodaway. He counseled Washakie many times. In 1842 the men made medicine by the fire after a war party returned victoriously against our enemies. Bodaway cast a prayer to the Father above the Clouds as he smoked the pipe. The smoke carried the prayer upward and Bodaway was carried away on the wings of a great hawk. He soared above the trees and rocks. His eyes beheld the coming of the whites. Droves of them stretched across the lone prairies, and their numbers were more than the mighty buffalo. Bodaway soared above our lands and streams seeing white men's' houses and villages springing up before his gaze. He saw fractions of our brothers ride to battle against them, and many fell. Bodaway soared until he saw the mighty herds of buffalo fall. He witnessed the changing of our people. He wept to see us dwindle as the buffalo, but saw that we would do well to embrace change more than resist it. Bodaway became Greathawk, a visionary; and the powerful warrior, Washakie, listened to the seasoned voice. He had not yet been made war chief for the Shoshone people although he was revered as a pillar of the nation."

The hand drum singing began again, and I heard bells raucously jingling and knew the fancy dancers were soon to appear. The auditorium gasped to see the marvelous costumes worn by their new friends, Kenny, Dover, and Rouree. With their feather bustles, erect roach head pieces, painted faces, cuffed wrist and arm bands, tom-toms, and flossy moccasins; they began spinning and gyrating in terrific patterns. I thought Celia Quinn would jump right out of her seat at the sight, but her reaction was more subdued than some of her friends! Elvis never created a stir like this one! Howahkan smiled smugly as his eyes scanned the audience reaction. Truly the sight was beautiful and breathtaking, and the crowd hadn't seen the last of the amazing talents of these three young men.

The narration continued, going back and forth from Howahkan to Grady. They told of the treaty which allotted lands for the Shoshone in the Wind River Valley of Wyoming, and the mighty changes which the Shoshone faced, learning to live with agency regulations and rules while still maintaining their identity as native people. Washakie had tip-toed a fine line in leading his people to adapt to the new "civilized" ways while still maintaining the ancient traditions of the Shoshone. Modern day powwows are celebrated out of reverence for ancient customs and ceremonies.

"I was born in 1875," Howahkan said. "The following year Washakie led many warriors into battle against the Cheyenne, joining forces with U.S. army campaigns. My father fell in battle—dying as a patriot to the very government who made and broke promises with our people. Washakie pled for honest men to deal with us, and hated the forked tongue which promised lies and delivered empty wagons of hope, but he continued to pray for peace and a good outcome for our people."

Traditional dancers came onto the stage, and although it was anticlimatic from the fancy dancing of my athletic friends, we were well entertained and wide-eyed. One darling girl in white buckskin danced with the group. It was my sister, Yarrow Whitecliff Gallagher, and she watched Gloria's lead, stepping carefully, and her moccasin clad feet were nimble and light. Unbidden tears streamed down my cheeks and I tried to mop them up before my friends saw. I turned in my chair and saw my mother and father both wiping tears. Brewing tears also gleamed in the eyes of Grandpa and Grandma Gallagher. Joni Whitecliff might have forgotten at one point, just who she was, but her tiny daughter was discovering their heritage, and I just couldn't swallow the lump in my throat.

"I was born in 1881," Grady's voice cut in. The Shoshone were settled in the Wind Rivers by then, but different groups would leave for hunting trips. Some came each year to the Three Lakes Valley, and I was fascinated with them. With my own eyes I have looked upon the features of Bodaway Greathawk, the ancient visionary who sat in wondrous counsel with Washakie. With my own ears I heard him proclaim a blessing over the healing waters of Gallagher Springs."

With my own eyes, I too, had seen the ancient man, as his spirit leaned over the top of me while I slept on Gallagher Ridge! I twisted in my chair to see Monty, and his eyes were wide, taking it all in. He flashed a thumbs up at me, acknowledging our shared experience, and a shiver splashed down my arms in recollection.

Grady laid out the old history of his resort, talking about the hot pots before the land was developed. He told stories right out of his last book, and the townspeople clamored for his words. Everyone was now familiar with the beautiful tales of Awinita, the spectacular Shoshone maiden. Rain Washakie fluttered onto stage, dancing a fancy shawl dance while Grady spoke. Long fringe draped from her colorful shawl and she pranced gracefully, just as gracefully as a butterfly flutters and flits. She was beautiful—but not as exquisite as the original Awinita, of course.

Howahkan took over the narration, colorfully telling us of slapping and cuffing *"Kell, the Big Irish."* Laughter rustled along the rows of chairs, but Howahkan paused. "The Big Irish was a man while other whites were still boys. The Big Irish earned my respect. Bodaway Greathawk approved of Kell and now he is my brother forever."

Reverence replaced laughter, and Howahkan told of several decades of silence which ensued after the death of his sister, as well as stricter agency control over the education of his own children. "We were not given the same liberties to travel about, hunt and camp, as we had always enjoyed, for my children were taken to agency schools on the reservation where they were punished for speaking their native tongue. The government thought they could punish the Shoshone blood from their veins, and I was sick at heart to say goodbye to the old ways. We stopped coming to Three Lakes, and for many decades I did not see my brother."

Grady said, "But one lovely girl changed all that. Last summer one little great granddaughter of Howahkan's became a beloved great granddaughter of mine." The hand drummers began singing again, and tiny Yarrow reappeared on stage, walking between Rain Washakie and Callie Halfmoon. She was now wearing a jingle dress, and she bobbed up and down as the older girls did, making happy music and grinning widely as the singing melodic voices of Yancy Good, Amos Greathawk, and Charlie Tanaka, chanted to the beating of their drums.

Lots of school kids turned around, mouthing, "She's so cute," in my direction, but I already knew that. I was her boy, and finders' keepers.

The stage lights came on and the podium and chairs were pulled back into place in the center of the stage. Howahkan and Grady took their places. The superintendent, Mr. Mulligan, and the school board carried their chairs onto the stage where they were joined by a spiffy guy I'd never seen before.

Mr. Mulligan strode to the podium. "Let's hear it for these great pioneering men!" And the place went ballistic. Folks leapt to their feet, clapping and stomping. Whistles and cheers rang enthusiastically and some of the elementary kids covered their ears. Mr. Mulligan waited until the ruckus quieted and then he nodded toward the wing of the stage. Yarrow entered again, only this time she was all alone. She carried a couple of plaques in her arms and her skirt jingled as she walked. She handed one plaque to her Grandfather Howahkan, kissing him on the cheek. She handed the other plaque to Grady, lifting her arms to him, and he picked her up. She was content to grin at the audience from his lap.

"As you all know," Mr. Mulligan went on, "Kelly Sheehan O'Rourke is soon to celebrate his ninety-third birthday and we wanted to present him with a plaque recognizing him as a cherished pioneer of our community. He has been a builder of our youth. He champions the cause of young people, and I don't suppose there are any in our town who hasn't received encouragement from Grandpa Grady O'Rourke. I was lucky enough to marry a granddaughter of his, and so I can legally call him that, now." Folks chuckled, as the comment was mildly funny, even though I wouldn't deem the principal to be a great wit.

Grady stood up and waved to his neighbors and friends, and Yarrow skipped over to Howahkan's lap, where she settled in, wrapping his braids in circular patterns around her hands and wrists. Howahkan seemed pleased. The sharp dressed man then stepped to the microphone.

"It's my privilege to be with you today! My name is Michael Vander-Smythe, and I am here representing Avondaire Publishing Company, the western United States' *premier* publisher. To date, Phantom Flynn has sold more books for us than any other western author, and I am pleased to give him the prestigious *Writer of the Century Award.* Mr. Voss carried a large crystal and gold trophy onto the stage. It was at least four feet tall, and when Grady went to receive it folks chuckled, for it looked to be almost bigger than he was. "I present this trophy for superb literary genius and dedication to preserving the history of the American west."

Audience members leapt from their seats and the auditorium roared with applause. Allyson, Dori Jo, Wyatt, me, John, Monty, Mark and I all made eye contact with each other. We were so proud of our great grandfather!

"Mr. O'Rourke has published thirty-eight books with our company since 1955—a marvelous feat!" Mr. Vander-Smythe then called for Grandma to go up on stage. "Avondaire Publishing wanted to present the daughter of Phantom Flynn with this token of our appreciation. It's obvious that you are a generous and giving daughter, and may you find joy in the fruits of your father's labors for many years to come." Mr. Vander-Smythe presented Grandma with several dozen long-stem roses and her eyes were huge at the presentation.

We thought this portion of the assembly was finished but we were wrong. Mr. Vander-Smythe smiled sincerely, and said, "I have been moved with the performances and inspired words of the assembly today. My personal favorite work of Phantom Flynn's was his last novel, *Feathers Flutter, Say Goodbye,* and as you all know, in that book Phantom Flynn discloses his true identity as Kelly Sheehan O'Rourke. Howahkan Greathawk is also in this story." Mr. Vander-Smythe raised his arm toward the ancient. Howahkan smiled proudly. "In fact, he immerges as somewhat of a literary celebrity. We have received many reader reviews all screaming for more. I am prepared to offer *you*, Howahkan Greathawk, a contract book offer. Avondaire Publishing wants your *personal* story."

A crazy hiss swept through the aisles in the auditorium. Howahkan looked proud and regal, pulling his chin towards his throat, appearing tall and straight in his chair. Grady clapped his hands in an amused manner, shaking his snowy-topped head with pleasure. "Come on," Michael Vander-Smythe persisted. "What will it be?"

Howahkan stood with Yarrow in his arms. He stepped toward the podium, strutting with each step. "I say, what's in it for me?"

The man from Avondaire Publishing Company seemed shocked by the question, but quickly recovered. "What would make you happy, Sir?"

"Don't call me Sir. It makes me sound like a little white fart." The crowd laughed at the comment. Mr. Vander-Smythe withered visibly, cowering somewhat before the tall, proud, Shoshone elder. "What then?"

"Why do you stare at me so? Am I a haunt, an enigma, or a pleasant threat?"

"I don't know, Mr. Greathawk—but I am prepared to sign a book contract for your story. You are undeniably interesting!"

"Haw!" Howahkan honked into the microphone. "I am as rare as the lone buffalo, but I don't type."

"Avondaire Publishing was counting on you partnering with Phantom Flynn—he is incredibly skilled in typing, grammatical structure, and manipulating words into intriguing tales."

Howahkan nodded. "Well, after all little man, he *is* the Big Irish!" We laughed again.

"Well…what is your answer?"

"Kell and I are brothers. We will write your book, but there's something I want."

"Yes?"

"A new truck."

"A new truck?"

Howahkan nodded. "Yes, and I'm nearly ninety-nine so we'd better hurry."

Chapter Twenty-Six

Blue Swede sang, *"Hooked on a Feeling"* and couples crowded the dance floor. I watched Rouree wrap his arms around Celia. She closed her eyes, resting her cheek against his shoulder. It was weird to think they'd only known each other a week—for they were plenty crazy about each other. Kenny and Dover were dancing with lots of girls—feeling very popular after the frenzy created from the assembly. They were wild, different, athletic, and swaggering—and the girls were flipping over them. They broke into the gyrating rhythms of the fancy dance upon request.

Paul was good for his word, avoiding Margo like a bad dream. I slid him his ten bucks early on, for there was no worry of him slipping up and asking her—not after her shoddy treatment of him in school. Margo gazed wistfully at me a few times, but I quickly looked elsewhere, feeling itchy and fidgety. Wyatt and Avery danced every dance not caring what anybody thought. They were truly best friends and had forged some sort of engagement; possibly the longest one in recorded history.

Judy Brynn O'Brien was dancing with some stocky Shoshone kid I didn't know. She was tripping along like a cat in cream, and I wondered if someone shouldn't warn that poor Wyoming boy. *Icky*...I shuddered at the thoughts of having to touch her.

"Are you ever going to dance?" Miles asked me.

I shrugged. "I don't know. Not really the right music for me," I hedged, although I didn't know what type of music worked for me. I had two left feet on the dance floor.

"Fine, I'm just going to get brave and do it," Miles said.

"What?"

"Ask her."

"Who?"

"Margo."

My brows shot high. "You're going to dance with *her*?"

"Look how cute she is!"

I scowled in Margo's direction, biting my lip. Her hair was curled and a big blue bow clipped on the side of her head. She was wearing a blue pleated skirt and a white sweater. It looked like she was wearing a tiny bit of makeup, but it was too dim in the gym to really tell.

Miles took a deep breath and sauntered across the floor. She nodded and stood, but the song ended. My buddy looked uncomfortable for a moment, but another song began, *"The Most Beautiful Girl,"* by Charlie Rich. Miles grinned at Margo and they began dancing stiffly. It looked like rigor mortis had set in.

Dover went scooting past me, guiding Margo's sister, Melinda. He winked as they glided by, saying, "Why don't you dance? You can do everything else."

That was a good question, excellent in fact. I just didn't really know how, and I didn't like doing what was uncomfortable to me. I decided to go out to the hall for a soda pop. Just as I was scurrying out the door I bumped into a huddle of kids. Callie Halfmoon turned around.

"Hi Callie! You did great today."

She rolled her shoulder at me and that made me mad. Why act snippy now? "What did I do?"

"Nothing! I've been here for twenty minutes, and have you asked me to dance?"

"Well…I didn't know you were here."

"Where did you think I would be?"

"I dunno—but I did look for you, I swear."

"And?"

"Well…um, do you wanna dance?"

She smiled and that dimple of hers was still there. I liked it. We danced, but the music was loud and we couldn't talk very much and I liked talking to Callie, so we dodged outside to the playground.

We saddled up on the teeter totter and I'd never had a better time at recess. Callie was an interesting person. Her dad worked on a big cattle ranch and she helped in the hayfields so we had a lot in common. Callie's brother had a motorcycle and her little sister played the cello. We talked about Yarrow and what a good little dancer she was.

"She's a fast learner," Callie said, "And so incredibly funny!"

"I know. She cracks us up all the time."

"She asked us if Pete could be a jingle dancer today."

"Oh yeah?"

"But Gloria said he didn't have the right costume, and Yarrow said, 'Pete sometimes wears a purple dress, what's wrong with that? We can sew my mommy's Christmas bells on it.' It was so funny. Gloria kept crying today, watching Yarrow dance—I suppose she was thinking of Joni."

Callie asked me about the day we got Yarrow, and how all of that went down. We talked and teetered, and talked and tottered, and I was surprised when the dance was over. We strolled back toward the school to catch a ride with Rouree, but his truck was already gone, and I suspected he and Celia had slipped out to go smooch somewhere. Kenny Tanaka was mushing it up with Veronica near the gym doors and I didn't know where Dover was.

"Need a ride?" Mr. Voss asked me.

"Let's just walk," Callie whispered.

"No thanks, Mr. Voss."

"It was a successful day, Wesley, and you can feel so proud."

"Thank you."

Callie and I shuffled along the sidewalk. We weren't walking fast because it felt like we had a lot to say, and there wasn't any hurry. The two miles would eat themselves up fast enough. We talked about the differences in our two schools, and our favorite subjects and teachers.

"I like English," Callie confessed.

"Me too because I'm going to be a writer."

"Really? Like the Big Irish?"

"Pretty much," I boasted confidently.

"Will you write something for me sometime?"

"Maybe."

"Come on, Wesley—you can do better than that! At least promise to write me a letter."

We traded chit chat as we dogged along the side of the highway, near the shore of Eisner Lake. Callie wore her jingle dress and each step sounded merry. The twinkling lights of town were getting uncomfortably close and neither one of us wanted to stop talking.

"Do you like to skip rocks?"

"Sure, and I bet I can beat you," Callie challenged.

Of course I'm always game for a game, so I accepted, and we walked closer to the lake. Callie stumbled once, and her hand flew out to steady herself. Instinctively I reached out to break her fall and her hand grabbed my wrist. "Whoa, don't get in a run away," I said, sounding like Howahkan.

Callie giggled softly. "Thanks!" She drew her hand away and we both picked up flat stones to skip. I threw one and it skipped along the glassy surface seven times. We counted the hops together. Callie's stone flipped six and she smiled brightly. "You win!"

The next round her rock bounced farther than mine and I found myself congratulating her which wasn't like me. Usually I would *have* win, no matter what. "That was a good one, Callie."

"You're fun to do things with," Callie said, skipping a doosy. The rock tripped fourteen times before sinking beneath the moonlit depths.

"You too," I conceded, counting only four bounces and one big hop. We laughed at the stunt.

"You couldn't do that again if you tried!"

"Let's see," I said, finding another rock and trying to make it take a big bounce. It plopped twice and sank. "Oh that was impressive," I muttered.

Callie sat down in the sand, hugging her knees to her chest. "It's really pretty here."

"Yes. All my ancestors, from both sides, are from here."

"Mine too, if you go back far enough."

I grinned at Callie. "I guess you're right."

"Bodaway is my great, great, great grandfather, too."

"So you're a cousin to Rouree?"

"Yeah, third or fourth cousins—not too close. Rouree's the most popular kid in our school and it looks like Celia has claimed him. There will be weeping in the streets of Fort Washakie."

"Well...I guess they'll still be free to date anybody they choose. He'll soon go back to Wyoming and she will be here."

Callie sighed. "I think it's kind of sad."

"You do?"

"Yes...kind of like the love story of the Big Irish and Awinita."

"I guess."

Canadian geese honked overhead and I noticed several fish jump, telegraphing ripples on the water.

"Is it true, Wesley? Have you really seen Bodaway?"

"Um—where did you hear about that?"

"Howahkan told my dad and some of the other guys about you before you came to Fort Washakie last fall. It made a big impression on us, you know."

"Oh, well—yeah, I did."

"What was it like?" She laid her cheek against her knees, listening closely. My heart did a weird thing and sort of skipped a beat.

I lost my train of thought, "Um…what?"

"What was it like, seeing Bodaway Greathawk?"

Oh that. "It was scary!"

"Yeah?"

"I mean—I didn't know who it was at the time, and I wasn't expecting it."

"And?"

"Well, I'd just drifted off to sleep and I startled awake, hearing faint drumbeats. I thought for a second that I was still in a dream or something, but goose bumps were racing on my skin. I sat up and there he was, Bodaway Greathawk, leaning over me, studying me. He was smiling."

Callie shuddered with shared emotion. "That gives me chills, Wesley."

We sat for several minutes in silence, just watching the wonders of the night. "I wonder what time it is? You probably need to get back."

"You too then?"

"Well, I've got it easy this week. I've been staying at the cabin and so my folks don't know what time I've been coming and going."

Callie nodded. "My folks are not really strict, and mostly I do what I please."

What is it with these Indians? I remembered Rouree saying, "I do what I want," in the lunchroom. I wished I could be more like that, and I said so. Callie shook her head, seeming plenty amused. "What?"

"You do already."

"What?"

"You do what you want already. Howahkan said you drive wherever the *hello mighty* you want to—and you do. You paid for Yarrow's adoption because you *wanted* to. You ride like a wild man, because you *want* to, and I happen to know this whole shindig was your idea, so don't tell me you *don't* do just as you please!"

Was that true? Was I willful and independent? My mind wandered back, trying to decide. I thought about me just leaving school on Wednesday, and I had to laugh. I thought about the mischief I made, and about teaching an old man how to drive. I thought about driving all the way to Lakeside, and about breaking Rouree's nose last fall while trying to protect Howahkan's' horse. I thought about adopting a little hippie girl, and paying for it with my own money. I thought about a lot of things and decided Callie Halfmoon was probably right.

"You are very good looking, Wesley."

I'd never given my appearance much thought, and the comment threw me for a loop. I didn't see it coming at all. "Um..."

She giggled again, shaking her head. "You set every girl's heart to racing last fall when you came to the reservation, and yet you didn't notice us *at all*. No fair! You're sort of clueless."

"You must have me mistaken for someone else."

Callie's black eyes rolled. "You're *so* oblivious to girls it's painful."

"I'm not oblivious to you." I don't know why I said it—and my heart clipped at an unhealthy pace because of it.

"You were last fall and you were tonight—for half of the time."

"Not really...I just always have a lot of things on my mind."

"Yes, like how to avoid girls, for one..." Callie was funny with her observations of me! I ran a hand through my hair, nervously. Callie let out a big sigh. "You make me nuts when you do that."

"What?"

"When you do that thing with your hair."

"Why?"

"I don't know—I don't even think you know you do it."

"Maybe it's a bad habit," I stammered, wondering now, and feeling concerned. Monty and Celia both did the hand through the hair thing, and it looked sort of neat when they did it, but I wasn't aware of doing it myself. "I'll work on it."

"Why?"

"So it's not bothersome."

Callie's nose wrinkled and her dimple popped. "You are so funny, Wesley! It's a *good* nuts not a bad nuts, you goofball."

"Oh."

"So you're thirteen?"

"And a quarter—which is half way to half."

Callie grinned again. "You seem more like fifteen to me."

That was a good thing, right? "In that case I hope you like older men."

Callie giggled and I *felt* older, somehow. For this girl I would be fifteen if she wanted me to be. For the other girls, I might remain ten forever.

"We'd better go." I extended a hand to Callie to help pull her from the sand. She brushed herself off and we sauntered back up the highway.

We had a big bonfire that night. Dover and Kenny had a couple of girls a piece, and I wasn't sure why the situation was copasetic with them, but that was the arrangement. Rouree and Celia roasted marshmallows and then we all took the canoes out for a moonlit paddle. I *felt* fifteen, hanging out with my friends. In fact, I kind of felt bulletproof and euphoric and I nearly held Callie's hand. *Nearly.*

I didn't sleep well that night—I was too wound up over the day, I suppose, and my mind kept spinning the events in rewind; Yarrow dancing with the Shoshone, Howahkan's book offer, Grady's trophy, the excitement of the assembly, the dance, skipping rocks with Callie, and that one blazin dimple in her cheek.

I was apprehensive about my upcoming performance, still worrying about what to wear. I was so restless that I finally climbed out of bed and stepped outside. The air was brisk at two in the morning, and the celestial glow was breathtaking. I lay down on the deck and studied the sky. Stars glistened like flecks of diamonds and gold. I remembered Howahkan's words about our valley, *"The sky painted diagrams for us to follow."* I closed my eyes and prayed for everything to turn out okay.

The door knob turned and Rouree stepped outside as well. "What's wrong, Wes?"

"Too much excitement for one day. I just needed to see what the stars said and unwind a bit."

He stretched out beside me, clasping his hands behind his head for a pillow. "I couldn't sleep very well, either. I can't believe Old Grandfather got a book offer today—*unbelievable,* the things that have happened since we met you."

Gee, that was a heavy statement…I had nothing to do with it—but I listened while Rouree expounded.

"I told Celia I loved her tonight."

"Oh yeah?" I was quite interested in this juicy scrap of information and I leaned up on an elbow to look at him while he talked.

"We left the dance because I just wanted to be alone with her—ya know we just needed some space from the crowd. I was tired of everybody asking me to dance crazy when I was busy dancing with Celia! Kenny and Dover were eating it up, the attention, but I wanted to be left alone. We drove to your corals and took my horse out for a jaunt. I like riding with her—I like doing everything with her."

I took a deep breath, nodding. Celia was special—I had always gotten along with her. She never treated me bad even though I was younger. We'd worked together a lot last summer, and actually became genuine friends, not only cousins.

"And?"

"We rode up to those cottonwoods on the south end of the big pasture. We dismounted, and walked along the side of the creek, just talking. Celia told me about catching fish out of the creek when she was little, and the moonlight was glistening on her hair, and I just said, "Celia Quinn, I love you!"

"How'd she take the news?"

"Pretty good, actually. Her eyes filled with tears and she said, *'Rouree Greathawk, I love you, but if you break my heart, my brother will dismantle your face.'* I promised her I wouldn't."

"How?"

"I kissed her, hard and tender, soft and crazy."

"Hard and tender, soft and crazy? I have absolutely no idea how a kiss can be all of those things."

"Search me, but it curled my toes and then some...*I'm telling you...*"

"Was it wet?"

Rouree's chin bobbed at my ridiculous question. "Yes."

I started giggling then, there wasn't another word for it. "You're tripping me out, man!"

"Your cousin tripped me out."

"So, you're glad you stopped smoking—she's been worth it?"

"Yes! She's been the funnest excuse for breaking a bad habit I've ever heard of..."

"And, what about religion? Have you talked about that?"

"Yes."

"And?"

"I'll be whatever she wants me to be."

"Rouree, that's something personal. You've got to want it for yourself."

"That's what Celia said, but that hunger has got to start somewhere, doesn't it?"

"I guess."

"Well then—mine has started with her! Wes?"

"What?"

"If we don't get some sleep we'll be zombies while riding tomorrow."

"I know. Rouree, what am I going to wear?"

"We all have buckskin pants and tunics."

"Even me?"

"Yes."

"Where did they come from?"

"Howahkan and Gloria."

I grinned and we went back inside the cabin and slept.

Chapter Twenty-Seven

"What about your class booth?" Mother asked while she quickly braided Yarrow's hair.

"I assigned Wyatt and Avery to be in charge. They made a class schedule, assigning everyone a time slot, but me. I did my part by donating my cooker for their use, and by arranging things with the market. I told them I wouldn't have time to fuss about it since I needed to get my horse painted and everything. Mr. McGill is our class advisor, and should be milling around if they need anything. He's already got all the groceries from McCarthy's Market in a cooler."

"Please be careful today! No broken noses, Son."

I smiled. Mothers worry about stuff too much. "Okay."

"Myself is dancing today," Yarrow piped.

"I'm so proud of you, Yarrow."

"Myself will teach you and Pete on another day."

"Oh, I get to have lessons with Pete?"

"Yip. Pete's wants to learn. He's been bothering me about it. Myself has not had time to hardly put up with him lately!"

"What about Heather and Rose?"

"They're girls. They already *know* how to dance."

"Allyson's rubbing off on you, I'm afraid."

Mother smiled at me. "Wesley, I'll be glad when today is over, and you move back home with us. I don't like having you gone so much!"

"Yes, and then you can help out around here," Allyson scowled from the sink where she clanked dishes around in hot soapy water.

"Yes," Yarrow agreed. "It's time you stayed home and tended my kids!" We laughed at the little girl. I promised I would do my duties better once the powwow was over.

We painted our horses before the parade. There was no time for us to make the pancake breakfast at the park.

"Circles around the horse's eyes and nostrils indicate alert vision and a keen sense of smell," Rouree explained.

I painted red circles around Misty's eyes since I thought her eyes were really good and everything, but I refused to draw around her nose, feeling like it was over-kill on the circles, but Kenny drew linking circles on his horse's shoulders. He loved circles apparently—for they rimmed each ear, eye, and nostril.

"You mark the horse's front legs with thunder stripes to please the God of War." With purple paint I drew a snazzy thunder symbol. It resembled a double lightning bolt. "Arrowheads on all four hooves make the horse swift and nimble footed." I definitely wanted that for Misty so I drew four bright yellow arrowheads above each hoof.

"But a handprint on the horse's right hip is the highest honor," Dover explained, and all four of us marked our horses that way. I wanted Misty to be honored everywhere so I also put two handprints on her chest.

"That means your horse just knocked down an enemy," Kenny pointed out.

"Oh, well…we knocked a couple of cats down Aunt Lace's chimney, and that's pretty much the same thing," I said laughing. "I'm good at justifying my behavior."

"Crooked arrows bring luck to the rider," Rouree informed me. I took note and put several on Misty's side.

"And your horse's battle scars are always marked with blue handprints," Dover informed me.

"Misty doesn't have any battle scars, but I'll give her one in honor of my broken nose."

"Hey you were on *my* horse when that happened," Rouree said. "I'll give Thunder one too, in honor of the Little Shoshone's bloody wounds."

For one special Irish touch, I put a green shamrock on Misty's left flank. The Shoshone boys laughed. "What does that mean, Little Shoshone?"

"That this is a fine Irish horse," I goofed. When they weren't watching I drew two small half moons near Misty's ears. That touch was in honor of Callie, of course. We fastened feathers into the tails and mane of our horses and Misty pranced around feeling dressed up and ready to show off.

We ran into the house to paint our faces. Rouree took care of me. He painted a four inch strip of red across my eyes, rimming the strip with a narrow line of black. I looked menacing and squinted at myself in the mirror. Nobody better mess with me today. War paint made feel tough and ready to fight. I guess that's why they call it war paint.

Kenny's face was painted with vertical black and red stripes and Dover's cheeks sported lightning bolts of blue and black. Rouree painted his typical black strip across his eyes and called it good.

Rouree braided a section of my hair and attached a roach with two feathers secured to it. I had been resisting haircuts since my birthday, much to Dad's chagrin, but I was glad now, as my hair fell over my tunic collar and looked more convincing than a military haircut would have. Townspeople would actually have to know it was me to know it was me. "What do you think?"

"I think you're pale," Rouree said wryly. "But you look good, too."

The VFW provided a color guard to begin the parade, and Uncle Aiden marched in full uniform. The citizens of our valley were proud patriots and showed respect as the soldiers presented the colors. I was certain Grady would have something pertinent to say about that later on.

Howahkan Greathawk and Kelly Sheehan O'Rourke were the grand marshals. They were riding in the car of Michael Vander-Smythe from Avondaire Publishing. He was driving a sporty convertible, some rare and expensive model, and the old men waved and smiled to the crowd. The marching band followed behind them, and then the mayor and city council followed. Most of the Shoshone opted to walk or ride in the parade, showing off their native costumes. Of course the fancy dancers weren't showing off their costumes, for they were riding with me, looking stern and ready for war. I got a tingle down my spine when I realized that Howahkan had actually worn war paint before, and for the real purpose of riding into battle against enemies and my respect soared even higher.

A few local businesses put floats in the parade. The FFA drove an old tractor, and the volunteer fire department sported their oldest engine. Miss Dairy Princess, Staci Spinnaker and her attendants wore gowns and tiaras, representing the Dairy Council. It was a decent parade for a small town.

The crowd at the park was jostling and the individual booths seemed to be doing well. Our class was making a killing on hotdogs, and Wyatt and Avery Anne had things well in hand. They included Stan Tomkins by assigning him to keep the condiments in order. He seemed so happy to be involved. I saw Grady give him five dollars, saying, "A reward for spiffy service. Buy yourself a souvenir of the day, my boy."

The eighth graders sold snow cones and the freshman fried doughnuts, selling a dozen for two dollars. The FFA's dunking booth was a hit, and Mr. Mulligan looked like a drowned rat after the first five minutes. Monty Quinn paid for twenty-five throws and had unseated the man twenty-one of those times. A line of fifteen or twenty kids streamed behind Monty. The FHA girls offered homemade loaves of bread and other baked goods. I watched Howahkan buy himself a whole nut-covered chocolate cake and he smacked his lips, saying, "Just a little shoog does me good."

Gloria had half of her stores' merchandise set up, and by Jingo Jones, it was a hit! She sold everything from Indian dolls to beaded gloves and moccasins. Little boys purchased play tomahawks and little bows and arrows. Girls clamored for beaded Indian necklaces. Dori Jo and Allyson poured over the items for most of the day. Grandpa Gallagher bought them matching beaded purses and bracelets. The girls smiled triumphantly.

Rouree and Celia walked around the booths together, and when they approached Gloria's booth, the stout woman handed Celia a smashing pair of moccasins, saying Rouree had paid in advance. Celia was thrilled, crying, "They're too pretty to wear!"

Gloria gave Yarrow an Indian baby doll and suddenly Heather, Rose, and Pete lost their luster, I'm afraid. Yarrow danced around, clapping her hands. "Myself has a new child! Myself is so happy so much!"

I turned from the Shoshone booth. Callie Halfmoon was grinning at me. I was glad to see her, "Hey Callie!"

She smiled, and the dimple popped. "You're making quite a splash in your buckskin."

"I am?"

"Yes! See that group of girls over there?"

I looked in the direction Callie was pointing, and I was surprised to see several older girls clustered together. Shonnee O'Shea was standing in the huddle. She was laughing with the girls, tossing her head, and that neat looking auburn ponytail swished back and forth with the motion. "Are you sure?"

"They think you're amazing *today*."

"Only today? Then I certainly won't notice them *tomorrow*."

Callie's smile spread jubilantly. "Good one, Wesley."

"What can I spoil you with, Callie? Would you like a genuine child's tomahawk, or a pair of beaded earrings, perhaps?"

Callie's head bobbed as she laughed with me. "I've got my fill of tomahawks just lately," she goofed, "but I was thinking that something Irish might be kind of fun."

We strolled to the junior class booth. They were selling pennants, and I shelled out fifty cents for one that said, "*The end of the rainbow begins in Gallagher Springs*." Callie got a kick out of it, but then I noticed jangly charm bracelets being sold by the Pep Club, and I slipped two dollars to Jenny Doheny for one. It was full of lucky charms and shamrocks and I clasped it around Callie's wrist. "This will help your Jingle Dance jingle even more."

"Thank you!" Callie really did like it and she couldn't wait to show it off to Rain Washakie and her other friends. She grabbed my hand and jerked me toward the Shoshone girls. I saw Mother's eyes on me, and she seemed very amused. I would have blushed, but the red war paint was camouflaging my reaction so there was no point.

"I almost didn't recognize you," a voice called behind me.

Again I turned, and saw Shonnee O'Shea smiling at me. She was quite stunning with the sun shining on her, but I remembered her shoddy treatment of me once she realized I was a year younger than she was. "Hey," I said. "I'm surprised you tried."

"What?"

"Oh nothing. It's nice you could come this weekend. Well, see you around."

I reached for Callie's hand. It was bold and not really like me in the least, but I, Wesley, was wearing war paint, and I do what I want, apparently.

Callie seemed both shocked and happy and came when I tugged. I took her over to the seventh grade booth and introduced her to Wyatt and Avery. Stan was surprised and Wyatt blinked stupidly.

"Wesley?"

"Hey, this is Callie Halfmoon. She's blazin', huh?"

Avery choked and her strawberry blond eyebrows arched high. "Yeah, blazin'—"

Just then a soft quavering voice asked, "Wesley?"

"Hi, Margo."

Margo's face dashed to pieces and her eyes clouded up. She started crying before I could get away. "My life is over," she wailed to Avery.

Callie's hand pulled away. "Don't cry. Wesley's just goofing off. We're just friends."

The tears dried up and the sun came back out to play in Margo's face. It was weird, really I'd say. I wondered about Callie's comment myself. I finally got enough nerve to hold her hand, and she said I was just goofing off? I didn't know how to process it and quickly retreated away from everyone, claiming I needed to go get ready for the powwow.

I crossed the street and headed toward the Presbyterian Church. Misty was tied up in the large open field behind the building. I had an apple for her. Her ears stood up and she leaned toward me, happy for her treat. My thoughts were loud and distracted. *Was* I just goofing? Did Callie just say that to make Margo feel better? Was I acting erratic and strange because I wasn't really myself today? Was I masquerading beneath the strip of red paint? I wished I could replay the last ten minutes over again so I could see for myself what happened. "I don't get girls," I muttered to Misty.

The powwow didn't begin until four o'clock, but people began sauntering over the field by two thirty, setting up chairs and throwing blankets down on the grass. The big area sloped upward, creating a natural amphitheatre. The crowd was even larger than the mayor predicted, and I was relieved we hadn't tried to hold the event at the park.

Rouree, Kenny, Dover and I took our ponies and loped around the field, warming our horses and minds up for the performance. The boys had never done trick riding in front of an actual crowd either—this was a new phenomenon for each of us. This kind of thing wasn't part of traditional powwows.

"My hands are sweating," Dover said.

Mayor Spinnaker asked us if we would be willing to carry the colors at the beginning of the event, and we had practiced that way only twice. When Rouree mounted his horse upon entering, he was to reach out for Old Glory, and it would wave and flutter as he rode. I was next, and would grab the Utah flag, and follow Rouree's pattern. Dover would carry the Wyoming flag, while Kenny carried the one specifically designed for this occasion. It had Cindy Murphy's depiction of the shamrock and Shoshone rose. The mayor's request would change our choreography just a bit. Now I was feeling jittery about actually grabbing the flag, and not missing it as I sped by.

Stan Tomkins watched enviously as we loped by him. "Good luck, Wesley!" I turned around and gave him a little salute. He grinned and I decided I would teach him how to ride and share my horse with him so he could learn.

We slowed our horses to a walk and continued to ride around the field although the grassy slopes were filling up quickly. "There's got to be five thousand people here at least," Kenny mumbled.

"It's hard to tell," Rouree said, eyeing the crowd.

The mayor was setting up speakers and electrical cords were plugged into extensions running all the way back to the church. I immediately began worrying about Misty or me getting tangled in cords, and loped up to the Mayor and asked if he could run the cords on the very perimeter of the grass so we wouldn't get twisted up in them.

"Oh yeah, that would be a good idea," he agreed.

Rouree rolled his eyes at me and we shared a quiet chuckle. "He's like most politicians—daft."

At quarter to four my heart was pounding in my ears. We dismounted and led our horses to the area where we'd begin. Kenny and Dover shared a cigarette so I assumed they were quite nervous as well— and joining together in prayer. Uncle Rob and Aunt Aura Leigh stepped over to where we were. Celia was with them and grinning at Rouree. Uncle Rob thrust a hand out to each of us, "Just wanted to say good luck, and thank you boys for quality entertainment all week."

Rouree shook first, "Sir," he nodded, respectfully. Rouree then shook Aunt Aura Leigh's hand, quite congenially, and my unemotional aunt smiled broadly and gave him a quick wink. "Young man, I don't blame Celia, not one little bit."

Celia beamed at the alliance and so did I. I loved my Aunt Aura Leigh at that moment, for not cowing, harping, or crowing contrary to good will. Rouree's head cocked sideways. "Mrs. Quinn, that's quite generous of you, Mam, and I will again be seeing you at church in the morning."Aunt Aura Leigh's smile was genuine, and her laughter rang like merry bells. Perhaps she noticed more than I gave her credit for.

A disturbance broke out just then, about ten feet from where we were standing. Aldean Tomkins cuffed Stan up the side of the head, swearing. "I know you've got money boy," he rasped.

"I spent it," Stan said, eyes watering at the humiliation of the public display. "I bought a pocketknife with the money."

"Damn you," Aldean spat, cuffing him again. Stan flew backwards and Aldean grabbed him by the hair, jerking him back up so he could slug him again.

My pleasant, good natured, Uncle Rob moved past me in a flash, grabbing Aldean Tomkins by the shirt collar. "Don't you hit that boy again," he hissed. His face was red and he looked like a mountain holding the drunken man up like that—the crowd shushed, straining to listen.

"Now Rob, this aint your concern," Aldean sputtered.

"The hell it's not! I'm not putting up with you treating this kid poorly anymore!"

"Put me down, you *blankety blank*!" My ears filtered the nasty stream of polluted obscenities.

Uncle Rob's head pulled back and he let Aldean go, alright. He released his collar, but his fists doubled persuasively, and he connected against Aldean's jawbone with a powerful blow. "No more, Aldean! No more beating your wife and your children!"

Pow went the fists, *Wow* went the crowd. The powwow was now the *Pow Wow*, at least by my way of thinking.

"Aldean, you could have been kind to your family, but you've bellowed and fussed, and hurt and abused until they all hate you. A big man doesn't force a woman to cower and quake! A real man protects his kids, and makes them proud! *What have you done?" Pow* went the fists, *Wow* went the crowd, once again. "Now how does it feel to have someone bigger and tougher lay into you, huh? How does it feel?" Aldean's head flew backward with every blow, and blood spattered from his lips and nose.

Pistol Stewart soon pushed his way through the throng. "Sheriff," Aldean whined from the ground, "Sheriff, this man's assaulted me, throwing the first punch."

"He's beating that kid again, and I'll be damned if I'll stand by one more minute and watch it," Uncle Rob thundered. "I can't bear seeing this kid become another *Cipher in the Snow*!"

The sheriff nodded and threw a pair of cuffs on Aldean's wrists, not caring a hoot about the protests. "That's right," Pistol said, "That's right, Rob. We've had enough. It's G—D time we all had enough."

"You can't cuff me! Rob Quinn assaulted me!"

"You're drunk and disorderly, and this here's a community party, you damned infernal puke! Now shut up or I'll conveniently turn around and let Rob finish what he started."

That was it. Pistol led Aldean to his car, cuffing him inside, and then he skedaddled back to his place on the grass to watch the show.

Rouree was impressed with Celia's dad, and I'll tell you what—we all were! And although Aunt Aura Leigh had been squealing, "Rob, no fighting," she was now gazing starry eyed at her husband for protecting that poor, dang, unloved kid.

Stan stirred uncomfortably from the grass, not sure how to act, where to go, or what to do. Uncle Aiden sidled up to him, "Wyatt and Avery would like you to come over and sit with us, Stan. You'll come, won't you? And tonight we're going up to Grady's place to swim and boat and eat with the Shoshones. We'd like you to come with us—you won't disappoint us, will you?"

Stan seemed surprised, but shrugged, "I guess I can."

"Sure, it will be lots of fun. You can stay with us tonight. I'll talk to Suzy if you'd like."

"She'll be gone."

Uncle Aiden put his hand on the loner's shoulders, herding him over to our families' spots on the grassy slope. A few townspeople looked bemused since Stan Tomkins had put Wyatt Finnegan out of commission for a good portion of the last year. Mouths gaped dumbly at the goings on.

Wow—I was proud of two uncles in the same five minute stretch, and I wanted to laugh and I wanted to bawl! I wanted to howl at the moon, but I suppose that was the war paint talking. Just then I saw Aunt Lace and Uncle Melvin make their way down the hill toward the rest of the family. Every three or four steps Mr. Mulligan paused, pounding a hand against one ear while kicking a foot, trying to get the water out. Our cat fell into the bathtub once, and that's just what he reminded me of! I laughed out loud at the spectacle, drawing comparisons between all three uncles at the same time. "Two out of three's not bad," I croaked.

Soon everyone was shushing and Mayor Spinnaker addressed the crowd. He announced our names and music bellowed over the loud speakers. I closed my eyes for one quick prayer, and then Rouree bolted forward nailing a running mount. He reached out and grabbed the American flag, looking fluid and graceful.

I clicked to Misty, "Come on girl, this is it." We took off running with my hands wrapped in her mane. When the timing was right I set my feet and the force launched me in the air and onto her back. My hand made contact with the flagpole, and *blessedly* I lifted it, feeling the air whip the fabric as I rode. Following those amazing stars and stripes, a lump the size of golf-ball settled in my throat and I couldn't swallow it. We rode around the make-shift arena, carrying our colors, letting the wind whip them about, and then we broke into a line and a fat lady from Eisner sang the National Anthem. I couldn't sing, but my hand was on my heart, and my eyes scanned the crowd—several thousand were on their feet and goose bumps trailed along my neck. *I had done this!*

My eyes connected with a kind pair of hazel ones. My mother was wiping tears, smiling at me. I smiled back, even though I knew the expression was in direct opposition to my fierce war paint. Dad gave me a proud nod and Allyson wasn't looking at me. Her eyes were trained on Rouree Greathawk of course, and that was okay, for he was carrying our nation's banner, and that's where she was supposed to be looking.

After the song, Rouree led out and we handed our flags off to members of the city council, riding again in the circular pattern until we broke into the figure eight. Again and again I heard applause and whistles, particularly when we dismounted our own horses, and switched mounts. And the applause was deafening while Kenny and Dover rode straddle backed, for it was truly incredible to see. We finished our routine the way we had begun, and I felt absolutely euphoric, riding high on the energy of the moment. When we were done riding, we yip-yip-yipped like warriors, and then we broke into coyote howls to the audiences' delight. I took the horses and Kenny, Dover, and Rouree scooted into the church to change.

I gave all four mounts apples and rubbed them all down during Grady and Howahkan's performance with the native flute and Celtic whistle. They decided to use the same script as they had at the assembly, by popular request. I walked around the perimeter of the grounds and settled myself among my family. Monty Quinn clapped me on the shoulder. "Kid, you really are a champ."

Stan sat between Wyatt and me, and we shared a package of Cracker Jacks while we watched the grass dancers move and sway. "Dad's going to jail," Stan whispered.

I shook my head, "Naw, Sheriff will just keep him overnight again."

"Nope. That was his last chance. The state's been watching and he had one last chance."

"So then what?"

"Suzy will leave and take the little kids. I'll sure miss Jamey." Tears spilled down his cheeks, and he covered his face with his arm and cried. "I'll be alone because Suzy doesn't want me."

"You can stay with us then." Stan shook his head, unable to believe my words.

"I adopted Yarrow and I'll adopt you too if something better doesn't work out. Don't cry, Stan! I promise you won't be alone."

Wyatt was trying to console him as well. "Maybe you're dad will get another chance. Maybe he'll straighten up."

"I hate him," Stan cried. "I hate him, but he's still my dad! I don't want him getting hauled away."

"I know, and if you hadn't kept everything such a secret for such a long time, he'd have ended up in the big house before now. This isn't your fault, Stan! He's made his own decisions."

"What if they put me in a foster home—and it's worse than what I've already had?"

"Well…I'll go get you."

Stan scowled at me. "How?"

"I do what I want!"

Wyatt glared at me. "You'd better go wash your face so you're not so braggedy." I grinned at my best cousin, plenty ready to admit that I was being a heady hot-shot, alright. I spied the prize sticking out of the Cracker Jacks and offered it to Stan. It was a miniature metal airplane, and Stan shoved it in his pocket for luck.

"If all else fails you can stow away in our barn and I'll sneak you apples and carrots every day."

Yarrow did well with her dances. The traditional dance was a bit easier for her than the jingle dancing, but she was so cute it didn't matter if she was right on or not. Her moccasin clad feet were nimble and light and her smile beamed brightly.

Once again the young Men's Fancy stole the show. The athletic dancing of my fine, feathered friends, was hard to trump. Bold girls from Salt Lake City catcalled raucously, and Celia's lip jutted out in a jealous way, but I saw Rouree wink at her while he spun. Aunt Aura Leigh caught it as well, and patted Celia on the back. "See? He didn't wink at those other girls!" She sighed, "Oh what a brilliant boy that one is..."

The event drew a standing ovation, and Grady was surrounded by city people all seeking his autograph in their books. Dad and Amos Greathawk took the horses back to our place to feed and curry them. The Shoshones formed a receiving line, and those who were interested filed through, asking questions and shaking their hands. Yarrow stood in line for a little while, sandwiched between Rain and Callie, but soon she tired and went in search of old Howahkan.

"Hey there, my little Shoshone Rose," the ancient said, lifting her in his arms.

Yarrow laid her cheek against his shoulder, immediately reaching for his braids. "Myself is so tired, and I need to tickle my cheek with your braid, Grandfather." Howahkan grinned proudly, letting his little Shoshone Rose do whatever she wanted to. She was fast asleep within minutes and mother took her from his arms so he could shake hands and autograph *Feathers Flutter, Say Goodbye* with Kell, his brother, the Big Irish.

The family of Kelly Sheehan O'Rourke, and the friends and relatives of Howahkan Greathawk, enjoyed a barbeque and private party at the resort that night. Stan came with the Finnegan's, alright, for the poor kid had no place else to go. Suzy had already packed up and gone without even saying goodbye to the stepson she'd lived with for eight years. Stan kept lamenting, "What will happen to them, Wesley?"

I couldn't answer his questions—none of us could. "Suzy will take care of them, you know that."

"But who will care for Suzy?"

"Where was she headed?"

"Back to her folks' house in Whitehall, Montana."

"Then that's who will help her."

"They're old and doddery."

"Harmless then, surely."

"I guess," Stan muttered. Every so often tears trickled down his cheeks that night. And just every so often he smiled, forgetting his troubles, too.

The night became very humorous when Amos, Charlie, and Yancy challenged their sons to a round of water ballet. The men and boys were downright silly and even Stan had to chuckle. Yancy Good was an especially funny guy who made us laugh many times throughout the evening. Rouree and Celia took a pedal-powered boat onto Inish Lake and pedaled slowly, lost in deep conversation. John, me, Stan, Wyatt, Kenny and Dover canoed out to the island just for fun. I wouldn't let Wyatt paddle, but the rest of us made good time, and the boat sliced the water's surface like a sharp knife with so many of us rowing together.

When we pulled the canoe back to shore a happy commotion was sounding near the hot pools. Shaylin Parks was flashing an engagement ring around. My unemotional Aunt Aura Leigh once again became very emotional. I shook Monty's hand and his Paul Newman good looks seemed fairly radiant to me. "I wanted to wait until I graduated from the U, but if I don't step on it, I might end up like Mark—in trouble."

"Yeah man, because those bee-stung lips are sexy," I droned, and Monty laughed, agreeing wholeheartedly with my comment.

Gloria lavished her attentions on Yarrow, and I had to keep reminding myself that she wasn't really that nice in real life. She caught me looking at her and scowled at me until I quickly shifted my gaze elsewhere.

"That's my boy," Yarrow piped.

"He's a strutting, crowing, cocky little sodbuster," Gloria grumped.

Yarrow seemed surprised to learn all of that. "Oh, myself only thought he was my brother."

Later in the evening Mother held Yarrow, wrapped in a quilt near the side of the pool. The little girl was sleeping. Gloria ventured into the hot pool where Kenny, Dover, John, and I were goofing off. Wyatt and Stan sat along the side watching us. After ten minutes, Gloria's voice said, "What's wrong with you?"

"Me?" Wyatt and Stan both asked at the same time.

"Well hell yes, what's wrong with the pair of you?" Gloria's eyes narrowed and she stepped closer to Wyatt. She held his chin in her hands and then ran her hands up the side of his head toward his ears. Wyatt's eyes were huge at this unsolicited intrusion into his space.

"I nearly beat him to death," Stan confessed soberly.

"Pipe down, green horn! I'll get to you in a minute." Gloria scowled, reaching her hands behind Wyatt's head, feeling his skull and running her fingers down his neck. Uncle Aiden and Aunt Aubynn watched curiously as the nurse/doctor/chiropractor/storekeeper stared at Wyatt's eyes, peering at him from different angles. "What's wrong with his adrenals?"

Many brows shot up, and now Grandpa Gallagher stepped closer, intrigued by this woman and her strange healing intuitions. Aunt Aubynn explained, giving the short version of the story, no doubt to spare herself the discomfort of being called a green horn—or worse.

Gloria nodded, listening carefully. She cleared her voice and said, "Adrenal glands help the body handle stress. The produce energy too, and this kid does not have any. Look at him! See the dark circles beneath his eyes? The ligaments in his neck and back are incredibly loose. The adrenals also maintain ligament integrity. He doesn't have any of that, either."

"No, his adrenals are hypo-functioning, that's for sure," Aunt Aubynn agreed congenially.

"His lips are discoloring, see this?" We all looked, spying Wyatt from the lantern light. We nodded, having noticed that symptom before.

"He needs help, this boy." Wyatt's face paled significantly at the diagnosis from this blunt woman. "I can help him."

"How?" I asked first, because I had to know.

"Hush up," she glowered at me. Her face softened while she talked to Aunt Aubynn. "First of all, his jaw is dislocated."

"Well—gosh, it was broken and wired shut for a good part of last year, so..."

"Well, they might have glued it back together again, but it aint in the right place, just sayin'."

"Um," Aunt Aubynn asked curiously, "So how do we go about getting back in place?"

"Do you mind if I show you?"

"Go ahead," Uncle Aiden said.

Gloria hefted her stout frame from the pool and pattered around the side. She knelt down behind Wyatt." Now boy, you just relax and pretend I'm not back here," she said. Wyatt looked petrified and couldn't relax, despite the nice warm water he was soaking in. "Boy, I said relax, not stiffen up like a corpse! Now you do what I say, or old Gloria will—" And just as she was scolding, and Wyatt wasn't expecting it, Gloria moved her hands in a precise way and we all heard a loud crack as the jaw slid back into socket. Wyatt's eyes sprang wide and I feared he might pass out. "There now, kid, you just lay your head back a minute and let the world stop spinning." She leaned over him to study his face. She was smiling. "That kind of makes you woozy for a minute, doesn't it? You did really good, boy."

Why the tenderness? I had a hard time processing Gloria Washakie.

Howahkan's chin pulled against his chest in a proud way. He said to Grady, "That's my granddaughter, Gloria. She's a nurse."

"I'm a doctor!"

"It's the same thing."

Gloria's eyes rolled and we all chuckled. Gloria leaned over Wyatt again, studying him. "Are you okay?" Wyatt nodded. "Good." Gloria placed her hands along his neck and suddenly we heard more popping sounds. "Haw!" She blasted, "Your head wasn't even on straight. You're as crooked as a dog's hind leg. You're as crooked as Nixon saying he wasn't a crook!" She laughed at herself, and then felt further down Wyatt's backbone. She manipulated the boy here and there, lining him up and straightening him out. "Now that's going to swell, and you are going to need several treatments, but you'll notice the pressure in your head will dissipate with each treatment. You need to get ice on that neck and jaw right now."

Uncle Rob hurried into the boathouse and came out with a bag full. Aunt Aubynn helped Wyatt position the ice packs.

"Now this kid's *got* to get some adrenal strengtheners in him, and I don't mean maybe."

"Okay, and what are adrenal strengtheners?" Doc Riley Gallagher asked.

"Haw! You're a doctor, you figure it out."

"I'm a veterinarian, not a quack, so I *don't* know."

Gloria scoffed, treating Grandpa as abominably as she did me. She was one big sulky mood, if you asked me. "He needs some astragulus, winter cherry, and ginseng, lots of ginseng. He needs raw adrenal too, and I order some special pills that have the glandular in them. It's essential to him ever mending. We've got to strengthen up his adrenal glands or his back and neck will never stay aligned, and he'll just be plagued with round after round of headaches, migraines, weakness, dizziness, fatigue, and misery."

Gloria was a hard personality, and no mistake, but she seemed pretty accurate about Wyatt's condition. "You'll have to send him home with me for awhile so I can treat him."

Aunt Aubynn's mouth opened and shut, but she didn't know what to say. "Well, I don't know—"

"Do you want him to get well or don't you?"

"Yes, of course!"

"Then why are you sputtering?"

"Because Wyatt's my baby."

"All the more reason to trust me."

"Okay, but let me pray about this." Aunt Aubynn was sincere and Gloria couldn't argue with that.

"You do that, lady. You pray about it because just as sure as Heaven hates Hell, I'll be taking this kid home with me."

Wyatt's eyes teared up and I knew he was scared spit-less.

Gloria then climbed back into the water, walking closer to Stan. "You are a mess!" Stan's eyes teared, looking like the lamb's bum twin. "I don't know who the hell you are, or where the hell you've been, but it's been a combat zone in more ways than one." She stared at his eyes for several minutes. "It's none of my business, but you are all scarred up and beat to smash, kid." She looked back at us, trying to locate a mother, but of course, Stan had dirt. Pretty much all Stan Tomkins had in life, was *us*—just neighbors.

"He needs adjustments and treatments. I don't want this kid getting within ten feet of a head shrink, either. There wouldn't be anything left of him. His whole face would be the size of a shriveled little pea after a shrink finished with him! He needs emotional therapy though, and I've got just the ticket."

"I imagine so," Mother said warmly. Gloria had taken a shine to her on Friday morning, and she beamed in Mother's direction.

"What happened to your nose, kid?" Gloria rubbed a finger along Stan's face. He pointed at me, and Gloria looked disgusted. "Oh for mercy sakes, I should have known! That damn roughneck is the famous nose breaker of the west! He even managed to botch his own schnoz, the dumb lummox."

I was getting ready to stuff a stinking tomcat in Gloria Washakie's trunk and see how she liked it. I was getting set to chain her bumper to her bum and see which one broke first. I was getting set to—

Uncle Aiden interrupted what I was getting set to do. "Could you treat these boys at the same time?"

"Can I treat these boys at the same time?" Gloria asked snidely. "What do I look like—a helpless, impotent, one-patient quack? Of course I can treat them both at the same time, and I can fix what ails *you*! By hell I'd say you're a walking catastrophe your own self!" She waded over to the hollow veteran, studying him thoughtfully. "You've got demons of your own, I'm guessing. You've been to Purgatory and danced with the devil, haven't you man?"

We were surprised by the revelations of Gloria Washakie! How did she know all of this stuff? "Have you been in Nam?"Uncle Aiden nodded, tears collecting in his own eyes. "I knew it. I think you are a good man, with a good heart. You only survived because of the spiritual strength in you, but what you have suffered has a taken a toll on your physical person and on your mind…but the flashbacks are haunting you until you drink them into non-existence."

"How can you tell all of this?"

"Because I am Gloria, and that is short for glorious." She sounded so funny trumping away about her marvelous healing virtues that we all laughed. "I am not all mean, you see. Come to Fort Washakie for awhile. I'll get you stronger, and I'll help those two boys."

"You folks can stay at my place," Howahkan volunteered. "I'm staying here with the Big Irish. We're authors, you know. We have a book deal, and we've got to hurry the hello mighty up on getting it written."

I stepped away from the crowded soaking pool, walking closer to the lake, thinking about the odd goings on. I watched as Celia and Rouree pedaled lazily on the moonlit waters. Monty and Shaylin were also snuggled up in Grady's motorized fishing boat. The motor was off, and they seemed content to bob on the waves, going nowhere in particular. As Aunt Aubynn said of Mark and Michelle, *"The world it their oyster, I should think."*I figured Monty and Shaylin had plenty to talk about.

"I didn't mean to make you mad today."I skittered sideways at the unexpected voice. Callie was sitting on the shore, looking sad.

I didn't say anything.

"I just didn't want that pitiful girl to cry anymore, that's all."

I chewed on the inside of one cheek. "You're kind to strangers, are you?"

"I'm a kindhearted person, usually—but you took off so fast I knew I hurt you, and then I felt terrible. I've had a lousy day ever since."

"Well, don't lose any sleep over it."

"I liked you holding my hand—but I wondered if you were sincere about it or merely being crazy…"

"I do what I want."

"And so…what does that mean?"

"It means there's no way in heck that I'd have ever grabbed your hand if I didn't want to."

"Oh."

My jaws were clenching and unclenching and I felt a trifle bit ill. All around it had been a huge day, and a strange one at that. I didn't know what to say so I didn't say anything more.

"Wes, please come sit by me."

I looked at Callie. Her eyes were large and liquid, and tender trepidation was playing across her features. I wanted to hurt her for making me feel like such a dude earlier, and yet I wanted to talk to her as well. She was leaving Monday, and who knew if I'd ever see her again?

"I don't know."

"Please?" I gazed at her eyes again, and they were sincere and pleading. I gave in and settled into the cool grass, which was a shock because I was still wet from the hot pools. "Here," Callie offered, tossing a blanket around my back.

"I'll get it wet."

"So? I don't care."

"I think my cousin and another kid are going to end up in Fort Washakie so Gloria can doctor them for awhile."

"Really? Rain's mom is pretty groovy about stuff."

"I'm a little jealous, I guess."

Callie turned to look at me, and her eyes were really studying mine. "Why?"

I shrugged a shoulder. "Oh, you know—I was just getting to know you and maybe I'd like to go to Fort Washakie instead of them."

Her hand slipped over mine and I didn't jerk it away. Instead I thread my fingers through hers and felt a hot rush of blood tingle up my arm. Surely hand holding was a circulatory tonic! My heart pounded loud in my ears and I didn't care if she heard. "Thank you," she whispered.

I nodded, but didn't trust my voice to do anything but squeak, so I remained quiet, just enjoying the moment. I knew that I was growing up, and my perceptions were definitely changing. It wasn't age that mandated feelings, but people and experiences. Coach Mills and Miss Vincent were wrong about it all! Maturity is a personal thing. I might be ten years old forever where Margo Walsh and Judy Brynn O'Brien were concerned, but sitting here by the shores of Inish Lake, holding Callie Halfmoon's hand in the full moon's light, I said goodbye to boyhood. It was time to move on.

Chapter Twenty-Eight

May waved goodbye and June greeted us warmly. Mark and Michelle graduated, and Rouree and I helped Howahkan pick out a luscious, blazin' red truck before Rouree returned to Fort Washakie. He and Celia were writing to each other at least three days a week, and I could always tell when Celia received a letter! Her cheeks glowed and she wafted around in a dream-like state, cleaning cabins, and renting boats and lockers. She looked like a walking love song.

Monty and Mark were working for Grady as much as they could that summer, overseeing and managing things, and he desperately needed them to because he was busy tutoring Howahkan's writing career. Celia and I worked the boathouse and cabins together. I cooked hotdogs until I was sick of the smell, and I cursed Oscar Meyer on occasion, taking his name in vain. I was making money though, and I was glad for that. When Dad or Grandpa Gallagher needed me, Avery Anne Applewhite often helped out at the resort as she had nothing better to do with Wyatt gone.

After careful consideration, Uncle Aiden and Aunt Aubynn packed up Wyatt, John, and Stan Tomkins, and went to live at Howahkan's snug home for several weeks, or until glorious *Gloria the doctor* released them from her care. Dad missed Uncle Aiden and John in the hayfields, and I never had a spare minute to myself. Grandpa Gallagher claimed it would make a good boy out of me.

Aldean Tomkins sure enough went away to jail for awhile. None of us knew how long he'd be gone, but Sheriff Stewart had worked with the state to grant temporary custody to the Finnegan's. Gloria had explained to Pistol Stewart how she thought she could help the kid, and Pistol said, "The good Lord knows he could use some help, but I'll never understand why the Finnegan's are so goodhearted as to take him in! He's the one that nearly killed their boy."

"Well If you knew as much about the good Lord as you say you do, I'm surprised you don't know the answer to that, you big long-legged lummox!"

I grinned just replaying the conversation back in my mind. I was renting boats and a voice said, "Hey, Wesley!" Shonnee O'Shea and Staci Spinnaker were grinning at me.

"Hey, what can I get for you?"

Shonnee's bottom lip jutted out. "Is it always business with you?"

"Pretty much, I guess."

The girls bought a couple of Pepsi Colas and I went back to my duties, pretending I was busier than I really was. Celia came in and gave me a break while I ran into Grady's. He'd made a whole tray of Grady Specials and I knew the summer people would quickly scarf them up.

"How's it going out there?" Grady asked me.

"Good. How's it going in here?"

Howahkan waved a hand. "Good, Little Shoshone! Kell is learning about me." He went back to his work and Grady winked.

I got a letter from Callie the last week of June, and I went into my room to read it. I smiled, for the return address had a picture of a tiny half moon.

Dear Wesley,

I see your cousins sometimes, and wish you were here too. I miss Gallagher Springs and the pretty sights and good company. I'm helping my dad on the big cattle ranch this summer, and so I'm guessing we are doing lots of the same things. I don't like mosquitoes, and fixing fence isn't my favorite chore. I like riding horses, but I don't do that often enough. Someday we'll have to ride together, huh? I think your friend Stan is getting well. He has been riding with Kenny Tanaka and Dover Good. He has good color in his cheeks and the other day I saw him laughing. Gloria is making him do new things and meet new people. I think he and Rain are becoming great friends. John and Rouree hang out quite a bit. Rouree is faithful to the memory of Celia Quinn and her l ong flowing hair. He doesn't know any other girls are alive on this whole planet!

How is Howahkan Greathawk doing on his book? Did he get the new truck he wanted? And what kind did he buy? Has he let you drive it? How's Yarrow? Is she practicing for the autumn powwow? How's Pete?

Well, I guess I'd better go. Have a great summer and don't forget me. I think of you every day, after all, you are the king of blazin'!

Love,

Callie Halfmoon

P.S. You are my favorite trick rider, EVER!!!

I tucked the letter inside of the envelope. I would write her back when I had a minute. I had to pack a few things into a bag for Dad was sending me to Washakie Fork to fix the fence.

"Oh Bill, he's just a boy," Mother argued from the kitchen.

"He's more of a man than you give him credit for."

"He's only thirteen!"

"I've gotta have him, Shannon!"

"Send Rob..."

"Shan, come on! He'll be fine. Let's give that kid the benefit of the doubt."

I listened pensively. I would be alone in Washakie Fork, riding the perimeter of the property, fixing fence. I'd be gone for three or four days. This was big responsibility for me, and I wanted to prove to Dad that I could do it.

Mother wiped tears from her cheeks. "Be careful, Wesley!" She finished packing my cooler with food.

"I will, Mother. I'll be fine." I patted my pistol in its holster and she cried again.

"This isn't the Wild West, you know!"

"It's not?" Dad asked. "Since when?"

"Honestly! This is 1974 and my son should be out delivering newspapers or something, not riding around in the mountains, packing heat, and camping alone!"

I grinned at Dad, and in the end, he won out. I carried my bedroll and stuff out to the truck. Misty was saddled and loaded in the back. I called for Old Blue, too. He was a good dog, and I felt safer having him around.

"Oh my Boy!" Yarrow wailed, wiping tears from her cheeks. "Pete's lonesome for you and so is myself."

"Goodbye Yarrow. Be a good girl and I'll be home soon. Help Mother tend Allyson."

I started the truck and headed up Gallagher Canyon. The trust my father placed in me was a little unsettling. I stopped on top of Gallagher Ridge to survey the scene and utter, "Tsaan dai neesungaahka."

I drove the pickup truck as far south as the fork allowed, and then I loaded fencing supplies on Misty, carrying staples, wire cutters, and pinchers in my saddle bags. I rode along the fence line, mending the wire where it needed it. We'd soon turn our cows out for summer pasture and the fences needed to be secure. Blue trotted next to me, but occasionally he was lured away from guard dog duty by a darting bunny rabbit or taunting squirrel.

My thoughts were a spin cycle of activity, thinking about everything I possibly could, being alone on a quiet mountainside. I thought about new pony tricks and new trucks. I thought about Monty getting married, and how weird that would be, having two of us grandkids hitched. I thought about Mark and Michelle and darling baby Kelly having to live above Mrs. McCracken's garage. I wondered when they would ever afford to get something of their own.

I reached the far end of the south fence line by the time the sun was setting over the western horizon, and decided I'd better call it a day and head back for the truck before nightfall. The shadows were growing dense and a cool breeze rattled the aspen leaves and left chills upon my back.

I pulled the saddle off Misty and curried her. We were friends, my horse and I. I talked to her and she listened, sometimes replying with a whinny. I didn't even hobble her, as she always came when I clicked and so I just let her graze the tall mountain grass near the truck. We were near Washakie Creek and she could eat and drink to her heart's content.

I arranged some kindling into a pile and struck a match, blowing on the flame to encourage it to take a hold and burn. Soon warm licks of yellow and red grew higher, consuming the tinder. I put more substantial pieces of wood on the fire then, and settled in, eager for warmth. I spread my bed roll out and Old Blue curled up next to me as I ate a sandwich for supper. I gave him my crust and he snarfed it down without tasting. A notebook was packed into my duffle and I wrote letters to Wyatt and Callie while the fire flickered and crackled, providing warmth and light. I told Wyatt all about the common everyday stuff happening at home, knowing he would be interested. My letter to Callie was somewhat more poetic, and I wondered if I was really skilled in writing, or just a goofy sap.

Dear Callie,

I'm camped about fifteen miles from home tonight, writing by the glow of a campfire. I've been riding our summer range fixing fence. The pine trees smell like Christmas and the aspen rattle and talk all day long even though I'm too busy to answer them. The sagebrush is potent, generously sharing pungent fragrance like a department store perfume counter. I like it, the smell of sagebrush. I will ride again tomorrow, crossing the gushing waters of Washakie Creek, and try to repair the fence along the southwest rim of our property. I am alone, except for Misty and Old Blue. Both of my companions let me be the boss so we are getting along very well, the three of us.

I sometimes sense I am not really alone, and then chills creep along my flesh and I force myself to think of boring things like mathematical equations and structure of atoms and molecules to keep from getting spooked, although this valley is alive with voices from the past, chanting, whispering, and yearning for recognition. I've decided that the words we say never go away. They do not fade into nothing, but echo and reverberate into eternity, cycling forever, with life of their own. I guess that's why we should speak kindly, for our sentiments live on and on. That's why silence sounds so loud sometimes.

The beauty here is unbelievable. Our cows will flounder on the green carpet of feed! Wild geraniums, bluebells, and dock flowers are in bloom, dotting all along the hills. Clover is in blossom near the creek, and today I sucked on a stem of mint all afternoon, thinking about my great grandpa and his young Awinita. I feel like a character in one of his books as I ride through the brush and rock.

I am happy to know Stan is getting help, and I hope Wyatt and Uncle Aiden are too. As gruff as I personally think Gloria Washakie is, there needs to be more people like her. She is probably the only person in the entire world who Stan could truly bond with. He's used to gruffness, but not kindness. Gloria's curt words will make him feel right at home, while her tenderness heals and soothes. I'm glad Rain is his friend.

Howahkan's new truck is nice, just ask Rouree about it.

He let us pick it out! Yarrow is good and persevering in teaching Pete and I how to dance. Pete's a faster learner than I am.

Well Callie, my fire is sending a trail of white smoke curling toward the Heavens, and so I guess I'll make medicine my own way, and say my prayers. If they require smoke to rise upward, then surely they will be heard tonight. Thanks for being a cut above the rest.

Wesley

I read through the pages, hoping my words weren't just friendly fodder, but I had a feeling Callie would appreciate them. I slid the notebook back into my bag, and decided to make good on my words, and I began praying. I thanked the Lord for the blessings of the past year. It had been nearly a year since I'd come to Washakie Fork with Grady and Howahkan, and it now felt like I was realizing the blessings from every petition I had uttered then. I needed to thank Heaven for it. I didn't ask for much, only that life could go on being good for us. I did ask for protection and courage while I was away from my family, and also prayed for Mother, that she wouldn't feel anxious over me, or remain too mad at Dad. Like most prayers, nothing spectacular happened, but I felt peaceful and soon kicked off my boots and settled beneath the covers to sleep. I clicked to Misty and she clopped near, easing herself to the ground near Blue and I. Life was good and I stared at the brilliance of the night sky before sleep stole the sight from my eyes.

The next day was a repeat of activity. I rode along fixing fence where necessary. Several times I had to ride back to the truck for more wire or stays. I was sweaty and tired when evening came, but I had progressed well, and my campsite was near Grady's cabin. I washed up at the creek, and then took Blue and climbed over the gate that rimmed Grady and Awinita's house. I walked back to the headstones. No feathers fluttered today. I felt a sense of melancholy press upon me, knowing that sometime I would stand over Grady's headstone as well. He couldn't live forever.

I pressed my face against the old glass pane of the window, spying the cook stove and rocking chair. I looked at the bed, studying the skins and blankets draped across it. My eyes rested on the cedar chest while I reminisced about the antique treasures inside. I looked at things until I felt sadder, and then chided myself sternly and left without looking back. I made camp on the south end of the familiar clearing. I felt jumpy being so near the place where the phantom campfire burned in the night. My eyes swept from place to place, and I was tempted just to jump in the truck and head home, for I was only a few miles away now—but I didn't want to let my dad down. He sent me out here to do a job, thinking I was man enough to handle it.

I built a fire and ate another sandwich, sharing the crusts with old Blue. I stretched out my bedroll, but felt so uneasy I climbed into the cab of the truck for awhile. I started the engine and listened to the radio, hoping for some settling music. I couldn't get anything very clear, mostly just a lot of static rattled from the speaker on the dash.

Outside my window I noticed Blue crouch low, and his hackles rose. I turned the radio off. I couldn't hear anything so I stepped warily from the truck and looked all around. At first my eyes didn't see the dark form riding toward me, as it blended with the looming cottonwood shadows on the opposite end of the clearing. It materialized slowly into view. I jerked the strap away from my holster as the mounted silhouette rode closer. My eyes were having a hard time discerning fact from fantasy in the waning hues of twilight. Adrenaline sped at heart attack speed, and I felt tingly and numb.

Was Bodaway playing me for a dude? Or was this some other spook? Did phantom warriors ride phantom horses? Why not? Misty's ears picked up and she called merry whinnies toward the other pony. To my surprise the ghost horse answered back, and then I did wonder what I was looking at! Was this rider from this world or the next? I leaned toward the unfolding spectacle.

"Don't shoot!"

I closed my eyes at the relief flooding over me like a born-again baptism. My breath wavered shakily. "Howahkan, what in the Sam Hill are you doing?"

I heard the proud ancient laugh, but he didn't reply until he was closer. "What's wrong Little Shoshone? Did you think the goblins had you?"

"I didn't know for sure."

"What am I then—an enigma, a haunt, or just a pleasant threat?"

"Tonight you were a haunt."

"I see. Well, your imagination wouldn't happen to be running double time, would it?"

"Well, it's just this particular place..." My thoughts trailed off. Howahkan grinned smugly, knowing he'd nearly caused me to wet my pants.

"You're white, Little Shoshone!"

"I know I am!"

"No, I mean you're really white—like a ghost."

"I thought *you* were the ghost!"

"What in the hello mighty were you going to do if I was?"

"Blast you to hell for the second time, I guess."

Howahkan's laughter scraped the night. He slapped against his leg then slid from the back of good old Whip. "This horse is as old as me, I reckon. I meant to get here sooner."

"Don't you know you're too old to ride all over the place? You're ninety-nine for crying out loud!"

"Yeah, but I won't collect retirement for another year so stop blustering about my age. Don't I still look young and virile?"

I shook my head, exasperated with the beautiful, ancient relic. "You look good enough to be resurrected already, but I think you should still be more careful."

"Yes, I nearly got my head shot off by a green horn kid! That would've made a sad end to me."

"Why are you here?"

"Awe...I was thinking you'd be getting the heebie jeebies about now. I thought I'd ride out to lend some much needed company. I can see I was right."

"You're the one that caused my distress in the first place!"

"Nope! You were already feeling faint and rickety before I came into view." I scowled at Howahkan, wondering how he knew. He read my thoughts. "I was having an early supper with Kell, and a quiet voice that nobody could hear but me said, "The Little Shoshone needs you, Howahkan." I told Kell I was taking one of Doc's horses and not to send the posse after me."

I grinned and nodded quietly. "I'm glad you came then."

"I wanted to make medicine anyway." Howahkan pulled a Catlinite pipe from his neck where it hung with a burlap strap. He also untied a bed roll. I helped him spread it near the fire. He sat down and filled his pipe with tobacco, cedar and sage. I struck a match and offered it to him while he puffed it into a smolder. "Thank you Little Shoshone. Did you make medicine last night?"

"In my own way, I guess. I prayed."

"You are a wise kid. Your mother gets a lot of credit for you if you turn out."

"What do you mean *if* I turn out? I'm already turning out."

Howahkan laughed, pulling his chin against his throat, sitting proud and straight. "You do my heart good, Little Shoshone."

I stoked the fire and settled the dog. Howahkan began puffing on the pipe, enjoying the ancient custom. With one hand he fanned the smoke, encouraging it to rise higher. I hunkered down, feeling reverence for Howahkan's prayer time. "You pray, too, Little Shoshone."

"I prayed pretty good last night," I said again.

Howahkan's head bobbed. "You need to pray more than once a

year, you stubborn dunce." He passed the pipe to me and nodded, prodding me. I puffed on the pipe, not feeling as anxious as I had done last summer. I handed the pipe back to its owner and Howahkan puffed some more. He again motioned the smoke upwards and passed the pipe back to me, trying to coach me in correct procedure. I puffed again, trying to guide the smoke as he had done. His eyes narrowed and his head bowed. He spoke in the ancient Shoshone tongue. *"Yei nanisundehai hubia,"* he began. I didn't know what he was saying, but didn't want to interrupt. I just listened with my heart. *"Daa Ape 'a, enne dammen usen tsa 'i, mai nemmeen niikwi."*

My head was bowed in reverence, listening to the strange melodic words. I felt Howahkan nudge me again with the pipe. I took a bigger puff this time, trying to make the smoke rise to please the praying man. Howahkan smiled at me, nodding his head. *"Dammen Newenahape, andebichi u nangasumbaaduka."* Howahkan paused, translating that line for me. "Our Indian traditions, a stranger understands them..." I nodded, listening. Again the pipe came my way and I tried again to please the old man. My hand worked the smoke, helping it curl and waft upward. He smiled and nodded again, continuing his plea to his Father above the Clouds.

The last puff was a lulu, and I felt somewhat dizzy and lightheaded. At that point I prayed for redemption of a sick feeling coming on! I prayed, begging God to forgive me for my errors, and asking that my prayers could be received in whatever custom I prayed them in. My mind spun further and I heard a hawk scream. I cracked an eye open, expecting to see a manic bird diving toward me, but I didn't see anything but smoke in the night, and Howahkan Greathawk.

I redoubled my efforts, trying to pray more fervently to avoid these distractions, but the harder I concentrated, the noisier the world became, and I heard drums pounding, strange voices, and the crackle of many fires. Again I cracked one eye open, wondering if I were hallucinating, seeking more information to my sudden delusional world. I saw only the red glow of our fire and my eyes closed, crying out with all my heart in prayer, out of respect for Howahkan's wishes.

The curious face of an old man loomed before me, whether in

my mind or in reality, I could not tell. He smiled and I knew it was Bodaway Greathawk, the visionary who counseled Chief Washakie. He spoke to me, at first in Shoshone and I did not know what he said. He nodded, seeing I was trying to comprehend, and his tongue shifted into English. "You know me?"

"You are Bodaway, who became Greathawk."

The black eyes danced upon my utterance and he nodded. "You are drawn to us." This time I nodded, not sure of a proper response. "You are drawn to us because I have seen you before."

Now I was confused, and still feeling quite dizzy. I did not understand the riddles he was talking. I wondered where Howahkan was, and if he too was seeing what I was seeing. "When?"

"I flew above the earth. I saw the white man come to this place. I knew they would outnumber my people. I saw the destiny of this American land, but I also saw you."

"Why?"

"My vantage point above the ground gave me broad horizons. I saw my people confined to the Wind Rivers, but I was born in Three Lakes. My father fell in battle here, as well some of my sons. I wondered if the change that was coming for us would fence us forever from this place. I saw a strange alliance between the one who looked like you and a Shoshone maiden, yet unborn."

"Yes, that was Kell. He is my great grandfather."

"I knew he would come. I spent many years waiting for him. I knew he would be drawn to us, too. One night as we celebrated a successful hunt my spirit took flight and I sought him out. He sat beyond the shadows, watching. He came again and again, bringing gifts, leaving them in the still of the night."

"Yes."

"But our world was changing. My people no longer had liberties to roam. My spirit groaned with this knowledge, but as I hovered, circling on a high air draft, I saw you. You were the likeness of the other one. You would be led to our people. You would arrange an alliance between the Irish and the Shoshone. You would love them enough to invite them back. You were the hope of things to come."

How could my powwow and assembly have been foreseen? "It was just a simple event."

"You are teaching them."

"Who?"

"My grandsons and my granddaughters—my family."

Was he talking about Rouree and Callie? I didn't teach them! Or did he mean something else?

"Yarrow?"

Bodaway loomed nearer. "She was sent to you. She was the test for you."

"What test?"

"Would you care about her?"

"I love Yarrow!"

The ancient face nodded and the eyes narrowed. "You have been a friend to my grandson, Howahkan. His hair is white but there is much work for him to do before he can lie down to the rest of his fathers'. Your fire, your interest, your ability to listen to the whispers in your heart has given him a voice. He will write the story of our people. He will write the story of our family. Howahkan is a bridge, connecting the old ways to the new ones. "

"Yes."

"The most important work we do for ourselves comes through the honoring of our dead."

I wondered at the words, not fully understanding their meaning. "What was I doing when you saw me in vision?"

"Washing the face of a dirty child."

"That was foreseen in 1842?"

"Yes."

"What does it mean?"

"You are on course."

The hawk screamed and suddenly my spirit lifted into flight, soaring on its wings. We sailed over the top of the ridge and the twinkling lights of Gallagher Springs illuminated various specters. I saw Yarrow tucked into bed and Allyson was reading to her. Heather, Rose, Pete, and her new doll were nestled all around. I saw Celia sitting on the dock, staring at the moonlight dancing across Inish Lake. I saw Grady talking to Mark and Monty by the side of the hot pools. I felt the warm steam rising upward as we soared above them. I saw Grandma Gallagher step onto the porch and look up at the starry night, calling Grandpa to come and take a look.

We lifted higher and higher until the waters of Eisner Lake and Lake Washakie swirled beneath us, and the mountains and plains blurred beneath our view. In a matter of seconds we hovered, circling over the Wind River Mountains, and then I saw Stan Tomkins. He was looking through a telescope and Gloria was helping him adjust the focus. He was smiling. I sensed a peace about him that I'd never felt before. Still, the hawk soared, carrying me with it. Callie Halfmoon was laying out in her yard near a bonfire, and Rain Washakie was with her. They were giggling together, reading *Teen Beat* magazine and eating popcorn. I saw Rouree and John driving around in Amos Greathawk's truck, no doubt looking for mischief. Kenny Tanaka and Dover Good were in the back sharing a cigarette. I saw my best cousin Wyatt. He was sitting on Howahkan's steps petting the cats, and his color looked healthy. Uncle Aiden's arms were wrapped around my Aunt Aubynn in a soft embrace just inside the opened door.

We swooped close to the earth skimming Washakie Cemetery. I saw feathers fluttering from the great chief's monument. The hawk cried and then we swooped past the marker of Bodaway Greathawk. I also gazed at the headstone of Joni Whitecliff. She might have run away from her life and family, but the fates drug her back to where she belonged, and she rested next to her parents. All of this I saw within a minute's time. I wanted to ask questions, but the vision faded from my mind. Again I heard the piercing scream of a hawk and then nothing more.

I came to, noticing the rising sun. I was as weak as a kitten and it took great effort to raise my hand to shield the sun from my eyes.

"You are alive, Little Shoshone?"

"Good morning Howahkan."

I felt a hand touch my forehead. "You are powerful at the medicine."

I swallowed and my throat was dry and scratchy. I felt Howahkan lift my head and my lips met with a cool drink from my water jug. The liquid soothed and revived me somewhat, although my head was heavy and I still felt exhausted. "Why am I so weak?"

"Because you are spiritually strong and it drains your body—just rest for awhile, Little Shoshone." Howahkan pulled a quilt around my head until it shielded the sun and I fell back into a spiral of unconsciousness.

When I finally awoke the second time, the sun was higher in the sky and I felt ashamed for sleeping so late. I had a lot of fence to fix, and I stirred beneath the covers. "I've overdone it now," I lamented.

Howahkan shoved a cinnamon roll in my direction. "It's okay. I will help you and nothing will be lost."

I would have never dreamed a ninety-nine year old man could be so much help fixing fence, but Howahkan worked alongside me and our work progressed and then some. We kept moving the truck so that it would be near us when we needed more wire or fencing stays. We ate some roast beef and cheese slices for our lunch and then it was back at it until suppertime. We had progressed well, nearing the north rim of our property now.

"Grady took us target shooting a couple of years ago to this same spot," I said, remembering the fun.

"I once killed a nice elk while standing on this same rock," Howahkan reminisced. "I cut a handsome figure while doing it, I'd say...and I wasn't much older than you. I was wearing red beaded chaps, and oh my hell, was I proud of them!"

I listened, begging him to talk. He did. Fantastic stories unfolded. "These have all got to be in your book, Howahkan!"

He nodded. "Yes, I needed to come here. I needed to jumpstart my memory huh?"

I shook my head, laughing to myself.

"What is so amusing, Little Shoshone?"

"I just remembered something. The day we came here shooting targets, Wyatt asked me if I thought any Indians had ever sat on this rock...and now I have found out the answer. It chills me a little bit. I will have to write him a letter and tell him about it."

Howahkan nudged Whip to walk a little faster. We were nearly back to the truck. "We'll make camp down here," Howahkan said. "And we will finish your job tomorrow."

"You don't have to stay with me if you don't want to. I'll be fine."

"I like being here," the old man said, and the words settled in on me. I had been reflective all day, feeling very hallowed at the experiences of last night. Howahkan had respected my sober mood, willing to hold the peace.

We lit a fire and Howahkan smoked his pipe, but did not pass it to me. I did not need to make anymore medicine for a long time, for I had more than plenty to ponder on and he knew it. I wrote another letter that night, a letter to Stan Tomkins. I told him I was glad he was getting well.

"Little Shoshone, why are you here?" Howahkan's words stirred me away from my writing.

"What?"

"What did you see last night?"

"I saw your grandfather and he took me soaring. I saw my family and my house. I saw Grady, and most all my loved ones. I soared above the Wind Rivers, and I checked on your house, for one thing, and everything's fine so don't get nervous about it."

He smiled, deep lines cutting into his face. "But why did Bodaway seek you out?"

"Because he saw me long ago."

Howahkan nodded. "I figured you were the one."

"What do you mean?"

"Grandfather used to tell stories around the campfire. He prophesied about a boy that would call us back."

"And?"

"I knew it was you. I knew it was you the first time I saw you and you overcharged me for a stinking hotdog." I nodded, laughing with my ancient friend. "But when you made medicine last summer I was plum amazed at the things you said. You shook my spirit up a little."

"What *did* I say?"

"Live long enough and you'll remember. It's not for me to repeat, for the some things are too sacred, too marvelous."

"And what happened from your perspective last night?"

"You prayed like a warrior does before riding into battle. You spoke in Shoshone again. You spiraled into a vision and lay as if dead upon the ground for many hours."

"I spoke Shoshone? I don't think so—I remember Bodaway switching to English."

"Haw! I doubt it. You're the one that switched. It fills me full of wonder."

"Me too, *everything* did, but I don't understand a lot of it."

"It doesn't matter. All you need to do is remember who you are and that you have a purpose in this life. You will see things unfold in this nation that will make you quake with horror, but the good times, the happy times; the *peaceful* times will outweigh the darkness. Remember who you are, Little Shoshone, for bless your heart, you have a purpose!"

Chapter Twenty-Nine

Summer sped by. I was too busy to count days and before I was ready for it, school started again. Monty and Shaylin were married in August and happily settled in Salt Lake City for another year of college. Grady offered Mark a job as manager of the resort, and I don't suppose a college degree could have landed him a more prized position. He was only eighteen and the grand duke of Grady's empire. Grady hired a contractor to build Mark and Michelle a new home up Gallagher Canyon, near his house.

"That way you can watch things after dark," Grady said. I supposed Grady was getting things in order before old age really settled in.

I climbed on the bus and made my way back to Wyatt. "Hey," I said casually.

"I can't believe school's starting again."

"Me neither." The bus stopped and Avery Anne climbed aboard and I was kicked out of my seat. I slid into the one behind them and decided I should probably get used to taking a backseat to Avery. Their heads bent in happy conversation.

Wyatt was looking better, and his headaches were coming a lot less frequently now. The Finnegan's hadn't returned home until just before Monty's wedding. Gloria sent them home with tinctures and oils for both Uncle Aiden and the lamb. They had already made one trip back to Fort Washakie for a treatment before school started.

A body slid into the seat next to me. "Hello Wesley."

"Hi Margo."

"It's going to be weird not having Stan in our class, huh?"

"Yes, but I imagine he'll enjoy his new school. He's the new kid—and probably popular."

"I just can't see it."

"How are your lambs?"

Margo smiled pleasantly. "They're good! Number fifty-nine earned me a grand champion winner at the fair last month."

"Oh, I saw that. Number fifty-nine, huh?"

Margo nodded. "I still don't know who painted that ridiculous number on his back, but I really should thank them. I probably wouldn't have noticed him so much, and he really is a special animal."

"Grand champion material, at least. Well, all's well that ends well, that's what I always say."

The bus chugged to a halt in front of the school and we piled off, excited and reluctant at the same time. I compared today to last year. Stan and I were being lugged off to the Sheriff's office in Lakeside, and now Stan was gone. Gloria had requested temporary guardianship of him not long after he went to Fort Washakie, and it was transferred from the Finnegan's without much fuss. I envied Stan, for today he would be attending the Washakie School with Callie Halfmoon and many of my other friends. I smiled because it was probably the only time I had ever envied him. I would write another letter sharing my jealousy. That would surely make him crow.

We had an opening assembly and the cheerleaders danced and we heard pep talks from Mr. Mulligan and John Finnegan, who had been elected student body president. Celia was secretary and I was proud of both cousins. Mr. Voss announced a chess club would be starting and Wyatt was thrilled, as he wasn't exactly football material just yet. Of course he could compete with the chess club and I knew he would do well. Chess wasn't really my thing—I lacked the patience to tiptoe little pawns around the board, but I promised to watch Wyatt whenever a tournament presented itself.

"Chess clubs are being organized in Lakeside, and Eisner, and of course they've existed in other schools before now. We will host a chess tournament within our own school, and the winner will represent our school as captain."

So even though Wyatt's health was more robust, after school time found him playing chess instead of fishing with me. Several nights I took Howahkan and Grady and we motored out to the island.

"The Three Musketeers ride again," Howahkan crowed one evening. There was no insult about Grady being one of the Three Stooges and I had to smile, for Grady and Howahkan were the oddest pair in the world, but they relied on each other and had truly formed a very tight bond. When Grady spoke, I noticed Howahkan sneered less and listened more. Phantom Flynn nurtured the fledgling writer with patience and Howahkan loved him for it.

"Look at that! Look at that!" Grady chirped, reeling in a dandy trout.

"That's a good one, Kell! You are the shortest man I've ever looked up to!"

Life was good.

Autumn colors were vibrant and rich on the first Thursday of October, and the school was geared up for an all-day chess tournament. All our relatives came to watch Wyatt participate. It was a long day, by my way of thinking, for some of the matches dragged on, and were only called after a timer sounded. Twenty four students were finally narrowed down to twelve, and then the twelve became six. The six names were written on a bracket, heading into the finals. Wyatt was one of the six, and so was Avery Anne Applewhite.

The matches were strategic and aggravating. Pawns moved and brows furrowed. The clock ticked and soon there were only two names remaining on the board. Wyatt and Avery faced each other soberly. Uncle Aiden shook his head, finding a lot of humor in the situation.

"They've been practicing together for the last year and a half…they definitely should know their opponent!"

The clock ticked as the final round had only been allotted sixty minutes and Wyatt and Avery looked like Robert E. Lee and Ulysses S. Grant, both trying to position their troops into the best strategy. The eight graders were loud in cheering for them as it was exciting that two from our class beat the older high school kids.

With one minute remaining on the clock Wyatt grinned at Avery and moved stupidly, leaving his king vulnerable. We all knew he was conceding to her.

"Checkmate," Avery called with five seconds to go. She shook her head at the boy. "You are in so much trouble with me!"

"Why?"

"Because I was going to do the same thing and let you win."

Oh brother…these two had it bad.

I kept riding after school, and also spent plenty of time on the ground, practicing handstands, tweaking my balance. I did sixty-five chin-ups a night, hoping to increase my arm strength and stamina. I was also religious about pushups, trying to do at least fifty before bed. Dad challenged me to try one handed pushups and I got pretty good at them. I wanted to eventually try Kenny and Rouree's tricks, but Dad was right, first I needed to stand.

Howahkan was driving better and better, and one night he and Grady came for supper. Mother was used to feeding the men, and always tried to have a good dessert on hand, just in case. Howahkan bit into a piece of hot apple crisp and said, "You make me miss my Anna. She was sweet and full of shoog."

"How long as it been since she died?"

"Forty-one years." Howahkan was tough and eternally young and beautiful, but his jaw waivered slightly as he said it. Suddenly he looked his age, old, and weary, tired and lonesome.

"I've been without my Addie for twenty-six," Grady mentioned, and for some reason the words just felt so sad.

"It's good you've got each other," Dad said.

Howahkan grinned at my dad for a moment, and then said, "Bill, it's just not the same."

"No, by Jingo Jones, it's not quite the same!"

"I'm going home next week," Howahkan said. That caught us by surprise.

"Why, is your book done?"

"I'm homesick, I guess. And I need to drive around and look at the place there, for much of my story unfolds near the base of those mighty mountains. The Big Irish is going with me for awhile. He needs to see where the story of Awinita began."

Dinner became very quiet at that point. None of us had ever experienced life without Grady being just up the road. Anytime we needed anything, it was up to Grady's we went. We had become accustomed to Howahkan, too, and now we would say goodbye for awhile. Surely it was practice for what was to come, but I didn't want to think about it.

I didn't fight tears while I did the dishes that night. Nobody was in the kitchen to see me.

"Don't mourn, Boy," Grady said from the door.

I quickly rubbed my face against my arm and shook my head, feeling awkward and foolish. "I just—I guess I'll miss you, that's all."

"I'll be home before you know it. I need you to go up at nights and check on Mark—make sure he's got things well under control."

I nodded, knowing Mark was capable of handling things. Grady was just trying to make me feel important. "Well heck...tell Stan hello for me, and Callie Halfmoon—if you see her. Also, tell Rouree that Celia is still flipped for him."

"Okay, I'll say hello to them all. I'll dance a jig on every doorstep if you'd like me to."

"Oh Grady," I mumbled, shaking my head.

"Do something else for me, will you?"

"What's that?"

"Write."

"I'll write to you often, Grady."

"That's fine, but I'm not talking about letters. Write! Write every time you get a minute! Write your feelings, write you doings, and write about your family and friends. Write about your hopes and dreams, and write about Bodaway Greathawk, and those thunderous, wondrous visions! Write about your adventures with a couple of proud old men, and also record their tales just as you heard them. Write about your mischief—about dropping a pair of cats down Annelaise's chimney. Write about—"

"You know about *that*?"

"Yes, the whole town knows about that."

"Do they know I was involved?"

"No, probably not, but I, Kelly Sheehan O'Rourke, was not born yesterday."

I laughed then, and knew I'd be able to laugh about it later with my great grandpa. He would like to know the particulars!

"Write about painting juicy red lips on Claude Walsh's lambs. Write about Stan Tomkins and his trouble. Write about that darling, beautiful Yarrow, our miniature Awinita. Write Wesley! For Heaven's sakes, please carry on the stories."

I took Grady's words to heart and I wrote that night for awhile, although my words sounded gloomy and sad, for that was what I felt like.

October progressed, and we had planned on taking Yarrow to Fort Washakie to dance in the autumn powwow, but early snows fell on the rugged mountains of Wyoming, derailing our plans. Celia and I were both dashed, for we'd planned on taking her with us. Yarrow cried and so we let her dance for us in the front room while she paraded around in her native dresses, but half way through her second dance she began crying again, saying, "Myself is so disappointed. This isn't the same!"

November slid into place and still Grady stayed in Fort Washakie with Howahkan. He called Grandma Gallagher's every Sunday evening and we all got a chance to talk to him for a few minutes, but we were homesick for the old man and the phone calls only whet our appetite for his stories and charming wits and mannerisms. We missed Grady's words and Grady's ways.

Letters poured back and forth from Fort Washakie to Gallagher Springs. I corresponded with Grady, Howahkan, Rouree, Stan Tomkins, and Callie, of course. I looked forward to the mail and was dashed on days when the box was empty.

I was at Grandma's on the evening Grady called to say he would be spending Thanksgiving in Fort Washakie. Grandma's chin trembled and crocodile tears streamed down her cheeks. Allyson and Dori Jo tried to console her, but Grandma said, "I've never spent Thanksgiving without my dad. I guess I'm hurt to think he can spend it without me."

Christmas time came, and still no Grady. We decorated the tree and Yarrow pranced enthusiastically, but the sparkle of the holidays didn't glisten as brightly as it once had for Allyson and me. We were growing up and steering toward the *hard years*, at least that's what Mother called it. "You don't see the magic—it's hard for you to feel it."

"Will it ever come back?" Allyson asked glumly.

"Yes, when you have little children of your own."

"But what happens when they hit their hard years?"

"You cry every other day, I suppose. Thank goodness for Yarrow!"

"Christmas is about the birth of the Savior so focus on that," Dad counseled. Allyson and I rolled our eyes and I continued thumbing through the Montgomery Ward Catalog, hoping Christmas magic was waiting in the gun section.

"Focus on this, my boy," Yarrow said, placing the little porcelain Jesus on the catalog page I was staring at. I wasn't prepared for chills to spread down my arms, but they did.

On the eighteenth we got out of school at eleven for Christmas break. We rode the bus home and Yarrow met us at the door. "Myself has a secret, myself has a secret, and a see-eeec-ret!"

"What's your secret?"

Mother's hand clamped across Yarrow's mouth and she said, "Never mind about secrets now! Everybody scurry around and get your chores done and your rooms cleaned. When I'm satisfied about that, then we'll let you in on it!"

Adrenaline pumped, for I knew something must be up! I vacuumed and dusted and made my bed. I took a pile of laundry to the hamper and kicked the miscellaneous stuff under my bed where Mother couldn't see it. I ran out to the barn and fed and watered the stock. Just then a brand new truck pulled into the driveway, and I was stunned to see Dad behind the wheel.

"Who's truck?"

"Yours."

I pulled my head back knowing I didn't hear him correctly, "What did you say?"

"This is your truck, apparently."

I stared at the shiny blue Dodge, completely mystified. "I don't get it."

"Apparently Howahkan had enough money to buy his own truck! He said he knew I was willing to sign with him and get the loan, and even pay for it on his behalf, but he had his own money."

"Where did he get so much money?"

"That's what I asked him and he said, 'I saved it from what I would have spent on truck payments all these years.' And then he told me the truck was *yours*. I reminded him you weren't yet fourteen and still didn't have a license and he said, 'Haw! I want to give it to him before I am pushing up daisies.'"

"How did it get here?"

"A salesman from Logan delivered it this morning."

My chin fell open about as far as it could have and I inspected the unbelievable miracle with four wheels. "What the heck?" I whistled and blinked, then sighed and stared, but I just couldn't make sense of the offering. I was staring at a brand new 1975 Ramcharger! "I can't even wrap my mind around this. It's blazin! It's so blazin' I could cry." And I did.

"It's not the only blazin thing," Dad said wryly.

"What else?"

"He bought a pull-behind camp trailer to go with it. It belongs to Yarrow so we can travel around the countryside and let her dance at powwows."

"What?"

"It's over there." He pointed behind Grandpa and Grandma's house knowing it was hidden away to make the surprise even sweeter.

"What?" I was crying and laughing and the world was spinning with weird sensations. "That's crazy!"

"He said it was Yarrow's inheritance from Old Grandfather. We are leaving in it in one hour."

"What?" I cried again. Every *what* grew louder and more shrill.

"We are going to Fort Washakie so get a move on."

"Yippee!" I crowed. "Do they know we're coming?"

"It was part of Howahkan's terms. We *have* to, and we are to bring Celia."

"Is she part of Rouree's inheritance from Old Grandfather?"

Dad laughed, "Well, I think she's at least Rouree's Christmas present."

I showered quickly, wanting to spruce up enough to ride in my new truck. Allyson and Yarrow were excited as well. "Yip, that's the secret," Yarrow said. "Myself owns us a camper now." One hand perched on her hip, and her black eyes sparkled.

"Well, both of you need to realize that they are for *all* of us to use—and don't get smart about it." Mother scolded, but when she was out of earshot I pulled a face at Allyson and asked her what she got. Her bottom lip jutted out while she sulked.

"So, I don't *care*," she blustered several minutes later. "I get to go see *my* Grady!"

"He's ours and not *yours* alone," I argued.

"My Joni is mine," Yarrow insisted, just to be part of our argument. "Nobody else gets my Joni but me!" We nodded and Yarrow's eyes fired around, trying hard to think of something else to say. "Oh, and my boy is mine, too!"

Allyson's head tilted off to one side. "Ugh! You can have him!"

The weather was mild for December eighteenth, and it was still early in the day when we picked up Celia at the Quinn's. She grinned from ear to ear as she came bounding out of her house. "This is too much!" she said, eying the sudden windfall that blew its way into our driveway. "I can't believe you have a truck!"

"Myself has the camper," Yarrow reminded her.

"It is crazy amazing," Celia squealed. "I couldn't believe it when I got home from school and Mom told me. Then I completely *fl-ipped* when she said I got to go with you guys to Fort Washakie!"

Of course Dad was driving, and Allyson, Celia and I squished onto the narrow bench seat in the back, but we didn't care. Celia and I visited quietly all the way, and she kept getting more and more excited to see Rouree Greathawk with every mile. "I'm going to write this down in my journal as being my most copasetic Christmas, EVER!"

"Are we there yet?"Allyson asked in Kemmerer, Wyoming—just thirty-five minutes after crossing the state line. I had to laugh, because our trip hadn't hit the long part yet.

Dad winked into the rearview mirror. "Ask again in two or three hours."

In twenty minutes Allyson asked if we were there yet, and Dad said, "Ask in two or three hours." He answered her the same way until we turned onto the Old Wind River Highway. It was almost dark, and I guided Dad to Howahkan's house. We passed by Rouree's on the way, and I pointed it out to Celia.

"That's Amos Greathawk's place."

Celia's brows furrowed and she gasped. "Rouree lives *there*?"

"Yes, and you'll be impressed for they have two TVs."

Allyson's chin was hanging open as well. "I thought it was just a shed or something."

"Allyson, you watch your mouth and watch your step this trip," Dad counseled. "Don't you dare wrinkle your nose up at anything!"

"That goes for you too, Yarrow," Mother scolded softly.

"Myself didn't even say nothing about it," she whined.

Celia's head shook rapidly. "Wesley I can't believe that blazin' kid lives back there."

"Does it distract from his dazzle any?"

"No...it doesn't. I think it makes him shine even brighter." I grinned at my ultra cute cousin because she was definitely not snippy or snooty in the least.

We pulled into the driveway at Howahkan's cozy well-kept home and Allyson and Yarrow ran for the house. The door opened before we could knock, and two old men stood in the doorway smiling. Allyson nearly knocked Grady down, and Yarrow lifted her arms for her Old Grandfather, reaching immediately for his braids. Celia and I got untangled from the back seat and made our way to the door also. Grady was happy to see us, and wiped tears from his eyes. "I've missed you, oh how Grady loves his family!"

I shook Howahkan's hand, and tried to thank him for my truck. It was still so jaw-dropping to me that I couldn't quite say anything, let alone pay proper gratitude. "I know Little Shoshone. I know. You don't need to say a word, for I've seen your shock and joy a thousand times in my mind while I've planned this! Haw! Howahkan Greathawk is greaty great, too!"

"You sure are!"

We crowded inside Howahkan's house where he had a pancake supper waiting for us. Mother sent me out to the new camper for a case of plum syrup and Howahkan smacked his lips at the sight. "That's what I knew you'd bring me! That's why I cooked pancakes!"

We ate, some of us standing up, because there wasn't enough room around the table, but it was a joyful kitchen. "Unhook your trailer right by the side of the house here, Bill." Howahkan instructed. "You can plug it in and have heat and everything! Unhook your truck, though, for I'm sending the Little Shoshone and Celia to the dance at the school."

Our brows shot up and Celia blushed prettily. "You are?"

"Yes, and I bought the truck and I bought the camper so I can send you wherever the hello mighty I want you to go!"

We laughed at Howahkan, sputtering away like a king, mandating laws and edicts.

Mother looked closely at me. "Remember who you are, *both* of you." We promised and Celia slipped into the bathroom to freshen up while Dad unhooked the trailer.

Celia and I went to the truck. I felt ten feet tall climbing behind the wheel. Celia had changed into a skirt and sweater and looked fresh and pretty. Her hair was long and glossy, and it looked better than Marsha and Jan Brady's, combined. A tiny sprinkling of freckles skipped across her nose. "You look nice Celia. Rouree will be surprised."

"I hope so. I'm nervous though. I haven't seen him since the first week of June."

"Don't worry, Celia."

Celia stared at me while I pulled onto the road. "You look nice too and I hope Callie is at the dance." I shrugged a shoulder, for I didn't have any control over that. "Too bad your dad made you cut your hair."

I grinned. "He said it couldn't get longer than Donny Osmond's."

"You sure looked good with your David Cassidy hair. I like long hair on guys," Celia said, sounding rough and reckless.

"Well that's good since you're sweet on Rouree Greathawk and everything!" Rouree's hair was shoulder length and obviously Celia thought it was blazin.

We pulled up to the school and I turned off the truck. Celia and I looked at each other nervously and we both burst out laughing, not knowing what else to do! "This is awkward," Celia hedged. "I've never barged into a foreign dance before!"

"Foreign?"

"You know, at a different school."

"Is that your definition of foreign?"

"Yes."

We laughed again and I felt like having a stroke on the front steps, but forced myself to walk foreword.

The gym was decorated with twinkly Christmas lights, and it was dim and hard to see. Celia and I stood in the doorway for a minute, letting our eyes adjust to the shadows. I spotted Rouree. He was standing with a few boys and his back was to us. I grabbed Celia's hand, dragging her forward. Her cheeks were flaming crimson but she couldn't stop smiling. I tapped on Rouree's shoulder. He turned around, and his mouth gaped upon seeing me. I grabbed his face and turned it towards Celia and it was a great moment I was glad to be part of. Rouree's face lit up like a Roman candle and he scooped the girl to him, swinging her around, letting out a raucous wolf cry. Everyone turned to see what the fuss was all about. He held her at arm's length again and then he kissed her right in front of the gaping crowd! Applause broke out, followed by cheers and whistles.

Suddenly I was being thumped on the back, and I turned to see Dover and Kenny, both grinning broadly. "Hey man," they were happy to see me. They began talking my ears off while Rouree swept Celia onto the dance floor, holding her ever so close. I listened and smiled, but my own eyes worked the room, hoping to spy Callie. I did.

"Hey guys, I'll get back to you in a jiffy," I said, but walked away from them. An enormous smile broke across Callie's face as she realized I wasn't oblivious to her at dances anymore.

"Would you like to dance?"

"I would!" I held my hand out to her and she took it and tingles tangled, and I was a hand-holding junkie, for this was the third time in a year! I was stupid when it came to dancing and being romantic. I was a lame-o and no mistake, but I sure enough was happy to see Callie Halfmoon and so I wrapped my arms around her like Rouree did Celia. Surprisingly I didn't trip over my feet for I was too interested in talking to Callie as we danced, and it diverted my attention away from being a clumsy clod. Perhaps dancing is better while performed from a subconscious level.

"Thanks for the letters, Wesley."

"Thank you!"

"I really do think you're a talented writer."

"I only write weird if I'm talking to you—you know, to impress you and everything."

She leaned away, studying my face. "You seem so much older again."

"Well, I'm trying, you know."

"Your muscles have grown!"

"They have?"

Callie nodded and I was glad that I was trying so hard to get buff for more riding tricks. "I'm working at it."

"I can tell!" Her dimple popped and I liked it.

We were having a good time when I felt someone tap me off. I turned around and Stan Tomkins asked, "May I?"

"No you may not."

Callie thumped my shoulder, not wanting me to be rude, but I was annoyed as I'd ever been. "I was hoping we were becoming friends, Stan, but right now I feel like feeding you a little dirt!" I strolled back over to Kenny and Dover and then led them outside to see my truck while Stan danced with *my* girl.

"That jerk has got a lot of nerve," I muttered.

"Who?"

"Stan Tomkins! Couldn't he see I was dancing with someone?"

"Yeah, but he likes Callie."

I rolled my eyes, for the arrangement was not copasetic with me—not in the least.

"Relax," Dover said. "Stan's the man."

Oh brother! I was annoyed yet again. Since when was Stan Tomkins the type to tap off well-suited dance partners and hedge in on the merry trick rider's club? Forget me wanting him to be happy, for I desired to stomp back inside and make him miserable!

"Great ride!" Kenny and Dover went ballistic over the wheels and soon I was giving them a ride up one road and down another one. Kenny reached for a cigarette, but I said, "If you're going to smoke you can take your butt outside—literally! I'm not having you stink up my new truck."

Kenny made a hissing sound but put the smokes back in his pocket. I was annoyed again, and turned the truck right around and drove back to the dance. I felt edgy—like I had in May when they had come to Gallagher Springs and girls ruined our night. Now I was annoyed that I had been girling and Stan Tomkins ruined my night.

"You're moody and sulky," Dover said. "Are you pregnant?"

"Shut up!" I wasn't in the mood for their crap and I told them so, but they took it good and didn't seem offended at all.

We walked back into the school. Stan saw me coming and intercepted my beeline toward Callie by asking her again. I've never come so close to decking anyone before, not even him! I waited until they started dancing and then I tapped him off. "May I?" I asked in a surly way.

"No you may not," Stan said emphatically, but Callie shook her head at him and he stalked away.

"Sorry about that," she said to me, resuming our previous conversation.

"Do you like him?"

"Yes, Stan's a good friend. He's really popular here."

"Looks like it has all gone to his head to me…would you like to see my new truck?"

"*You* have a new truck?"

I nodded. "Yeah, I just got it today."

"Sure!" With my hand clasped in Callie's I led her outside. I smirked smugly at Stan as we walked by.

We climbed inside the truck and I turned it on and started the heater. We fiddled with all of the buttons and switches, and it was fun exploring my property with her. Callie fiddled with things until she pulled the owner's manual from the glove compartment and began reading it out loud like a storybook. It was funny and I was content to watch her face and listen to her read about four wheel drive in an animated way.

"I've missed you."

She looked up, seeming startled. "That's a good thing, right?"

"I guess it just depends if you've missed me too…or not."

"I liked seeing you look around for me tonight. You honed in on me and it gave me a little rush."

"Oh yeah?"

Callie nodded and I reached for her hand again. We talked and talked until the dance was over. Rouree and Celia came out and Rouree made a fuss over my truck. "Well, do you mind if I drive Celia home?" I shook my head knowing he would want to.

"Can I give you a ride home, Callie?"

"Sure."

I started the truck and began driving toward her house. She was scowling at me when I pulled into her driveway. "How did you know where I lived?"

I flushed then, feeling strange about it myself. Of course I had seen her house plainly, and Callie too, as I soared in vision with Bodaway, the Great Hawk, but how would I ever explain that?

"Um..."

"Um what?"

"I saw your house in a dream."

Her face scrunched up. "Huh?"

"I saw you and Rain Washakie lying by the fire eating popcorn and reading a *Teen Beat*, last June."

Callie shuddered. "How did you *see* that?"

"Bodaway showed me."

Callie's eyes narrowed and she shuddered again. "You are strange, Wesley."

I closed my eyes, fearing she was right—knowing I was different. I hadn't shared the experience with anyone but Howahkan, and this was why! It made me sound like a goofball. "Well, I know it. I'm sorry about it." Nervously, I ran my hand through my hair and puffed a breath from my cheeks.

"Oh, the hair thing again." Callie smiled.

"Oh, sorry..."

"You really are strange! You say sorry when you should say 'Thanks for noticing.'"

"Thanks for noticing."

We talked a few minutes more, and then Callie went into her house. I drove back to Howahkan's feeling strange and unsettled. Again, this had been a huge day. The excitement of everything was overwhelming. I really liked Callie Halfmoon, but so did other boys, and although she was friendly and genuine, I could not gage how much she *liked* me. She thought I was strange, and that was not a good sign.

Chapter Thirty

We stayed in Fort Washakie four days. It was a great vacation, and we enjoyed being with Grady and Howahkan. Howahkan took us to different sights and even showed us a flat-topped butte where the Shoshone people had gone into battle against the Crow over hunting rights in the Wind River Range.

"Fearing utter annihilation to both bands, Chief Washakie challenged the Crow's leader, Chief Big Robber to a contest. Their people had already fought for five days! The winner would be granted the range so the battle could mercifully end. Chief Big Robber accepted. It was a tough battle, and Washakie finally prevailed, but he was so impressed with the courage of Big Robber that he didn't scalp him. Instead he cut his heart out and placed it on the end of his spear. He raised it in the air and there it remained while our people celebrated with dancing around the fire that night. Little Shoshone, that's where this place got its name, and I want you to know that my father was there."

Allyson's nose was wrinkled up and Mother's lips pinched together. "That's *terrible*," Allyson croaked.

"No, it was wonderful, for Washakie prevailed and it meant the salvation of our people! Food was scarce and it was truly a battle for survival."

"I think it's kind of neat," I said while Allyson shuddered.

"You *would*," she grumbled.

Howahkan took us to Gloria's store, and Allyson looked longingly at many of the pretty dresses and moccasins. Grady bought her a snazzy white buckskin dress that matched Yarrow's; I think to compensate her for not getting a truck or new camper. She was all smiles about it. He also lavished her with new moccasins and jewelry—the whole set up.

Gloria held Yarrow, prodding her to dance. Yarrow pranced around enthusiastically and without a bashful bone in her whole body.

Stan came into the store and leaned against the counter, grinning at me. "We meet again."

"Hey." I didn't feel like over doing it. I wasn't feeling so friendly toward him since the dance, and I feared he was Callie Halfmoon's new crush.

"How's life back home?"

"Still there."

"Oh."

"Ever hear from Jamey?"

Stan shook his head. "I've never heard a word. I guess I never did matter much to any of them."

What a crummy life—I felt bad for him again, even if he was cutting my grass. "Sorry about it."

He shrugged. "Bud and Gloria are great! I love it here and *never* care to go back. *Ever.*"

"Well, I hope you don't have to then."

"I won't."

"You're positive?"

"The state called. My dad's dying of liver cirrhosis. He'll never make it out of prison alive."

I didn't know how to answer that. Should I say, "Oh great, because he's a big bad man," or should I say, "Gee that's too bad, I was hoping he would so you could go back to where you hoped to never go again." Which was best?

"Whatever," Stan shrugged not waiting for me to figure it out.

"Could Gloria help him, maybe?"

Stan shook his head. "He's too far gone. Gloria has made a petition to adopt me legally."

"Great, now I don't have to."

Stan smiled and nodded. "No hard feelings from the dance, right?"

"Who says?"

He shrugged again. "I don't play second fiddle to you here, Wesley." His eyes narrowed down while he studied my face, wanting to gauge my reaction.

"Maybe you should learn! I'm the Little Shoshone."

"Old men may revere you, but it all stops there. Go back to Gallagher Springs and boss the white kids around! Go back to your legendary stomping grounds where you're the natural born leader of...not too much."

I wasn't feeling sorry for him again, and I wanted to pound his face into the asphalt outside! I let it pass and left him standing where he was at. I went back to the rear of the store and waited with Howahkan until the others finished. Gloria was rubbing off on Stan Tomkins and no mistake. He used to want to *be* me and now he called me *the natural born leader of not too much?* Was that a slam against me or everyone else in Gallagher Springs?

As we left I sneered against the side of Stan's ear, "On June twenty-fifth I flew above Fort Washakie and saw you looking through a telescope on Gloria's porch. What did you see when you flew with the great ones? Don't tell me I'm the natural born leader of not too much, for I definitely have a purpose! I am the Little Shoshone."

I was silent in the truck and brooded for awhile that afternoon. Rouree asked me what was bugging me, and I told him. He laughed. "Let it go, Wesley. Stan's got it better now than he ever has, and he's just talking crazy because he can."

"It's stuck in my craw! *Old men may revere you, but it all stops there.*"

"I revere you, and so does Kenny and Dover. Our dads all love you! Stan never rides with us but what he doesn't hear about the Little Shoshone, so shake it off."

"And I think Callie is crushing on him."

"Oh. Well, I dunno about that. Is that why you haven't made an effort to go back and see her since the dance?"

"I guess."

"Coward."

My head cocked off to an agitated angle then and I remembered the first time I met Rouree, and plowed his face with my fists. "That's a good looking nose you've got there."

Rouree laughed. "Take it easy, Little Shoshone, take it easy!"

"Why is Stan fitting in around here anyway? I remember some of the mean things you called me when you thought I stole your horse. I'm amazed any white kid dares show his face around here—I mean, except for me, of course."

"Stan's going to be adopted by people who have ties to both Bodaway Greathawk and Chief Washakie. That's as prime as it gets—plus the guys and I have been protecting him, you know—as a favor to Gloria."

At two o'clock in the afternoon on our last day a knock sounded on Howahkan's door. Callie Halfmoon was bundled up against December winds, holding the reigns to a couple of horses. "Hey, would you care to go riding with me?"

It's amazing what that did to my mood. I felt bulletproof as I dodged out to the camper to get warm clothes on. Maybe Dover was right—maybe I was pregnant, for it seemed like my mood was quite subjective.

The snows had come early, and melted off before Christmas hit. The ground was barren and the temperature a lot more moderate than what we had at home, but the wind was still brisk. It didn't matter to me, though, and Callie and I rode through fields and meadows near the river.

"Weren't you going to come back and see me before you left?"

I looked at the dark-eyed girl riding next to me. "I wasn't sure if you wanted me to."

"Why?"

"Because I'm so strange and everything."

Callie rolled her eyes and shook her head, "Oblivious, you are still completely oblivious."

At four o'clock we stopped and built a bonfire to warm up and toast marshmallows. Callie was prepared for a real afternoon of it, apparently. We talked while the fire crackled and popped and life was good.

"Do you have a crush on Stan Tomkins, or what?"

"He'll soon be Stan Washakie, and he's crowing about it."

"You didn't answer my question."

"Some days I do."

"Oh."

"And then I get a letter from you and change my mind, so you'd better keep writing to me. Your words are pretty, Wesley, and they do interesting things to me." She pressed a hand against her heart. Callie's eyes were tender and she was very honest. I felt like kissing her but chickened out—guess I wasn't ready for that.

I returned back to Howahkan's after dark and Yarrow was curled up on his lap, sound asleep. Dad was grinning in the kitchen, turning the loose pages of a completed manuscript. Grady sat across the table from him, asking, "Well?"

"I can't believe you two have finished it. When will you hear from the publisher?"

"Oh, we already have. They asked for a few revisions, which they usually do, but Howahkan refused. He called them up, requesting to talk to Michael Vander-Smythe himself, and said, 'You enlisted me to do this job, now how about you don't make me mad? I'm not changing anything, for it's a hundred percent the truth!' and Avondaire Publishing complied, very quickly, sending a pre-publishing bonus and an apology letter for ruffling the proud Shoshone's feathers."

"Haw!" Howahkan called from the corner near the stove. "They don't mess with me, do they Kell?"

"Nobody messes with you Howahkan."

The ancient smiled and smirked proudly while he traced little trails on Yarrow's cheek with the end of one braid.

We were happy that Grady decided to go home with us. "It will be Cora's Christmas surprise," Grady chirped. "I'm glad she's missed her dear old dad!"

Howahkan grabbed him roughly, beating him on the back as a farewell. "I will miss you, Kell. We are brothers forever, right Kell?" The dark eyes were teary and I knew Howahkan would feel very lonesome after we left.

"We are a sad pair Howahkan, for we are too lonely now to be apart, perhaps. Come see me when you can."

Howahkan leaned into the truck. "Enjoy your truck, Little Shoshone. Remember I am Howahkan Greaty Great! And Celia, Rouree loves you so much it is killing me to watch! Be tender with my grandson, huh?"

Grady climbed in and it was a tight squeeze. Allyson smooshed in the front with Mother and Dad, and Yarrow sat on Mother's lap. It didn't matter! We were happy to listen to his prattle, and the return trip passed in a flash. Celia kept sighing and peered at a little ruby ring Rouree gave her for Christmas.

"What is the meaning of such a ring?" Grady asked.

"Oh, just friendship, surely," Celia said pleasantly.

"A friendship ring comes in a box of Cracker Jacks, and is usually devoid of little shimmering rubies. That boy has something more serious circling around in his mind," Grady answered.

"Perhaps."

Grady reached behind my head to pat Celia's shoulder. "Oh my lovely Celia Girl, Grandpa loves you so."

"I wonder how he ever afforded it?" Celia whispered, lightly fingering the tiny gem.

"He sold his pistol to buy it for you."

Tears brimmed instantly, clouding Celia's vision. She blinked rapidly, trying to contain them. "Oh Grady, are you sure?"

"Yes, but I'll let you in on a little secret."

"What?"

"I secretly bought the pistol back for him and it is wrapped up under his tree as we speak."

Tears flowed down Celia's face without restraint at the revelation. "I love you, Grady! You always do everything right! I just feel bad because I didn't have a gift for Rouree, too."

"Fear not, Celia Girl. I signed the tag on Rouree's pistol from you. He shall be quite delighted on Christmas morning, I should think."

We pulled into our driveway and secreted Grady to Grandma's house like a giant Christmas present. Allyson and Celia tied a big red bow around him and positioned him on the doorstep. I rang the bell. We heard Grandma's shoes clipping against her tile floors and the door opened. "Dad!" She melted into a puddle of happy tears, dragging the little man into her house, smothering him with kisses and hugs. Soon the rest of the family swelled into the house, the Quinn's, Finnegan's, and the Mulligan's. Our dear Grandpa Greaty Great had been sorely missed!

1975 said hello with fierce winds and blizzards and Dad was grateful for the new four-wheel drive pickup truck. In February I turned fourteen and wrote to Callie, crowing that we were now the same age until May.

Howahkan's six hundred page book was released in March. What a stir it caused! I squealed when I got my hands on it! *Shoshone Sun Rising* by Howahkan Greathawk and Phantom Flynn (Kelly Sheehan O'Rourke), I ran a finger across the words and smiled.

Many excerpts made me bawl, and parts of the book echoed *Feather's Flutter, Say Goodbye* but it was interesting hearing the narrative from Howahkan's perspective.

"I crept into the barn, watching the boy as he unsaddled his mount. He was good looking for a white, but was he suitable for Awinita? He turned around and his face grew pale at the sight of me. I slapped his head sideways, waiting to hear the cry of pain, but he held his tongue and I slapped again. Both of my palms burned and his cheeks ignited into flames, but he did not cry. I slapped and cuffed until blood rose to the surface of his skin and his eyes raged with anger, and yet he bore it, silently. What manner of white man was this? I remembered Bodaway's prophecy and I smiled at the Big Irish, for he was man enough for my sister. Without ever saying a word, I said no more."

Avondaire Publishing sent Grady and Howahkan on a book promoting tour and the men had a grand vacation. The publishing house stood the cost, and provided a chauffeur to drive them wherever the hello mighty Howahkan demanded to go. They also flew to several major cities and it was Howahkan's first experience on a plane. To hear Grady tell it, that first flight to California was one the other passengers would never forget— nor the flight crew or pilots, either.

In May our community received word that Aldean Tomkins was dead, and nobody was around to mourn. Townspeople could only whisper about it being a pitiful end to a wasted life. Mother sent Suzy and the kids a sympathy card to Whitehall, Montana, and also one to Stan Washakie, but never heard a reply from either place. The Tomkins' home was awarded to Stan, as Suzy's name was never on the deed, and neither was Aldean's. Instead the house was deeded in the name of Aldean's first wife, Irene Baker Tomkins. Stan was her only heir, and so the property was his. Gloria hired an agent to try and sell the property in her new son's stead, claiming the money would be used for Stan's education. She said the boy wanted to be a doctor. Knowing Gloria, I thought perhaps Stan wouldn't dare be anything else, for I remembered him once writing that he wanted to be a miner or else work for the railroad.

Howahkan hit the century mark on June first, and he drove into

Gallagher Springs, claiming he was bored. Rouree was with him, and my dad and Uncle Rob gave Celia's flame a job on the ranch. Rouree and Celia had both graduated, and I wondered how long it would take them to get married, for blazin' sparks danced in their eyes. John Finnegan went to San Diego to attend the university there, and Aunt Aubynn wept to see him go. Change happens.

Summertime came and went, and Mark's house was completed and the little family was happy to move in. Grady decided to spruce the place up a bit, and added three more cabins around the lake, bringing the total to eleven. "I can't keep up," Grady wailed, and we laughed at him, for he was ninety-four and going strong. He also announced plans for larger locker facilities and it really was necessary to keep up with the crowds. He hired Uncle Aiden to do the building and my Dad was thankful to have Rouree on board, or else he would have been terribly short-handed on the ranch.

In September Aunt Lace did not return to school to teach, for blessedly Mr. Mulligan made good on the tomcat's example. Aunt Lace was pregnant and expecting twins. Everyone was ecstatic at the news, and I overheard Aunt Aura Leigh whisper to Aunt Aubynn, "Now Annelaise will be forced to think of someone besides herself."

"Yes, *two* somebody's," Aunt Aubynn replied.

Grady was thrilled at the idea of receiving more great grandchildren. "I will build more cabins," he said. We laughed at that. As part of his renovation projects, he had named the cabins, Monty, Mark, John, Celia, Wesley, Wyatt, Allyson, Dori Jo, Yarrow, Kelly Michelle, and **?**. Now Aunt Lace's forthcoming babies would eliminate the question mark from that nameless cabin, and necessitate a twelfth. "Progress is good," Grady trumped enthusiastically. "Yes-sir-ee, progress is good and so is love, for it invites the propagation of the human race."

"Yes, but you can't keep building cabins for every grandchild that comes along," Grandpa Gallagher pointed out. "You'll end up with a city!"

"I'll start naming the lockers then."

Grandma smiled at her father. "That's a good idea, Dad."

Rouree was baptized in October and he and Celia were married in November. "They're so young," Aunt Aura Leigh sobbed after the ceremony. My unemotional aunt was becoming the most emotional one of all, perhaps.

"Aint it great?" Howahkan asked.

"The younger the better," Grady trumped proudly. "They can grow up together and train each other well!"

"Life's too short to wait until you're ready...for that day never really comes."

"And if you wait until you can afford it you'll die alone in the poorhouse."

"Kell speaks wisely," Howahkan crowed. "Me and Kell know a thing or two about it—by now we know a lot! Hell, we're smart."

Half of Fort Washakie came to town for the wedding and there was dancing at the reception. Yarrow was proudly stepping around in her jingle dress, grinning toothlessly, for she was now six and loved dancing to the hand drum singing of Yancy Good, Charlie Tanaka, and the proud groom's father, Amos.

So that's how Stan Washakie came back to Gallagher Springs. He danced the men's fancy to the shock of all the Gallagher Springs girls, and Margo Walsh tumbled head-over-heels in love with him. I wasn't jealous about that, but I noticed Callie Halfmoon winked at him between performances, and so while I was friendly and cordial to Callie, I did not let her light the sun for me anymore after that night. Our handholding days were over and I stopped writing letters to her.

While in Gallagher Springs, Amos Greathawk went to look at the property of Stan Washakie. Gloria was anxious to unload it for the boy. "Gee this is pretty nice," Amos said, looking around.

Stan, Rain, and Callie were up at Inish Lake boating together to avoid bringing bad memories to Stan, but I was with Amos for some odd reason. I thought the place looked creepy, for all of Aldean's things were still at the house, along with whatever Suzy hadn't taken with her. It felt morose, almost.

"See that closet right there?"

"Yeah?"

"Well that's where Stan's mom hung herself."

Amos considered my dour news momentarily and then shrugged it off. "Doesn't matter, for she's not hanging there now."

I shuddered. "You're not thinking about *buying* this place?" My tone was incredulous.

"Hush up you cocky little sodbuster! I'm prepping a sale!"

I glared at Gloria, for I hated to see her pawn something off on her cousin just because she was a pushy real-estate agent. "I'm just sayin.'"

"Well," Amos said, stroking his chin, "It's a whole lot bigger than my house now…"

I turned around to keep from busting a gut. The Tomkins' kitchen was bigger than Amos's whole place!

"Your TVs would fit," Gloria prodded hopefully.

"What will you do if you move here?"

"I'll be closer to Rouree and Celia."

"Well, yeah…but…"

"It's only ever been me, Tashina, and Rouree. My Mary Josephine died when Rouree was born. Tashina got married last year to that tall Randy Cantrell from Raymond, Idaho. It wasn't hard for me to see her marry a white man, but an Idahoan? Now that took some getting used to!" He chuckled, nudging me in the ribs at his joke. "Now it's just been Rouree and me."

We walked down the basement to take a look. Three bedrooms and a large storage room sprawled beneath the home. I pulled the light chain in the storage room, and a bare bulb revealed fifteen or twenty cases of beer on the shelves. Apparently Aldean Tomkins had taken to heart the church's counsel to be prepared. Amos's brows rose expectantly. "Does this beer come with the price of the house?"

"Yes," the doctor/nurse/chiropractor/storekeeper/real-estate agent chirped. "Of course!"

"I guess I'll take it then."

"Just like that?" I asked.

"Pipe down, you dumb lummox—he wants the house."

Well, that was weird to me. Amos Greathawk had just purchased himself a mansion, or so he thought, and he popped the tab on a beer to celebrate. He offered me one, but I said. "No thanks, I never drink before breakfast," and even Gloria had to laugh.

When Rouree and Celia returned from their honeymoon they helped Amos clean the home. Celia scoured that thing to Suzy's standards and Amos kept saying, "You are a darling, Celia Greathawk. My boy is lucky, lucky, lucky!"

Celia grinned and kept cleaning—and cooking. She cooked up a storm for Amos, making freezer meals that he could easily warm up for himself, and also promising that he could come to dinner with them anytime. I pushed a rented floor polisher around and Wyatt squeegeed the windows. Dori Jo and Allyson made up the beds, for Suzy had left most of the furniture.

"Gee, I could start a motel," Amos said.

"Run competition with the Fat Shamrock," Dori Jo suggested.

"I'll call my place the Chubby Clover," and he laughed and laughed. "At least I'll have room for company. Next time Charlie and Yancy need a place to stay, they can bunk with me! Grandfather could move in with me if he wanted to, although he'd have to drag Kell, the Big Irish along, for he's quite attached to the little man."

"No smoking in this house," Celia said, once she finished polishing the last cupboard handle.

"What? This is my place and I'll smoke if I want to! I do what I want."

Celia shook her head. "No Amos! I've worked myself ragged shampooing, scrubbing, polishing, and shining this place up for you, and I don't want it getting all stunk back up! No cigarettes and I mean it."

Amos scowled at his darling new daughter-in-law but went out to the back steps to light up. I walked out the back door and sat next to him. "So how old are you, Amos?"

"Forty-four."

"That's not too old."

"Nope."

"But you've been alone for awhile. Aren't you lonesome?"

"Maybe I will be now."

"My English teacher is kinda cute. I'm just sayin.'"

Amos blew smoke from his nostrils, laughing. "And who is your English teacher?"

"Miss Pell."

"Is Miss Pell pale?"

"Miss Pell is a fiery redhead."

Amos seemed interested. "Irish? Do tell."

"She's very pretty. She was engaged once, but apparently her fiancé knocked up her sister and so she called it off."

"I should hope so!"

"Her name is Pamela."

"Pamela Pell?"

"Yep."

"Well I'll be jiggered. That's quite a name, alright."

"Of course her parents named her Pamela Joy Pell, or else her initials would have been P.P."

"I don't suppose I know any females named Pamela."

"Well, mostly the town just calls her Miss Pell."

"I don't suppose I know any females named Miss Pell, either…but to be right darned honest with you, it just don't have the same ring to it as *Pamela*. Hell, that's kinda fun to say. Pamela. *Pamela*." Amos tried it out, repeating it several times.

"She's good at diagramming sentences, if that turns you on."

"Never diagramed a sentence in my life—is it fun?"

"Not necessarily, but she's good at it."

One lazy Saturday afternoon I took a boat to the island. I thought about Callie, trying not to let it hurt inside. I would always think fondly of her—she was my first real infatuation, possibly even my first love. "I did it to myself," I said to a flock of calling birds. "I made medicine in Washakie Fork…pleaded that something good would happen for Stan. It did…Callie Halfmoon is the best and greatest thing that could have *ever* happened to him. She is tender and genuine…and really beautiful."

Thanksgiving was more crowded than ever before. Grady brought Howahkan and Howahkan brought Amos and Amos brought Rouree and Rouree brought Celia, and Celia would have been there anyway, but Celia brought Dori Jo, and Dori Jo brought her folks, and they invited Monty and Shaylin. The Finnegan's came, including Mark and Michelle and little Kelly, and John flew home for the holidays. Wyatt took me, and I took Yarrow, and Yarrow took Heather, Rose, and Pete, and Pete took Allyson, and my folks and Grandpa and Grandma Gallagher brought up the rear. The Mulligan's were the only ones who couldn't make it, and I was at peace with that.

It was weird seeing Shaylin, Michelle, and Celia all in the kitchen fussing with the women, and I thought about Thanksgiving a couple of years ago when Celia had loitered over the table settings to avoid getting trapped in the kitchen. Allyson and Dori Jo were now the ones fussing over the table. They were close to thirteen and both of them were getting shapes and feeling apprehensive about it. No longer did their baby dolls crowd the dinner table, but both girls looked wistfully at Celia's new husband.

After dinner the whole family tribe came out to the corrals to watch me and Rouree ride. We had been practicing together all summer and fall, and after we showed off doing our regular stunts, Rouree called, "Hey Celia, this is for you!" He rode straight toward her, doing a handstand on the horse's bare back, and then switched his weight to a one-handed dismount, pirohouetting to the ground. Aunt Aura Leigh's eyes flashed and she boasted about her brilliant new son-in-law and Celia's good fortune.

I surveyed the crowd, wondering who in the hello mighty I was performing for. "Hey Grandma, this is for you!" Everyone laughed and I clicked to Misty and we lunged forward. I mounted, and then did a few crazy stunts, finally doing a one-armed handstand. With Misty flying at a dead run, I switched arms, which is something Rouree Greathawk couldn't do, and then I cried, "Whoa!" Misty stopped on a dime, which propelled me forward into a double somersault. I landed on my feet in front of Grandma and she grabbed me and kissed me like I was seven.

That evening Grady called a family council at the resort. "Mark is doing a fantastic job here," he said. "He really is!" We applauded and Mark took a little bow. "But I've decided to enlarge the pool area somewhat, you know, to match the swanky new locker rooms, and also put in a little drive-in. I can't keep up with the Grady specials anymore, and Wesley can't keep supplying hotdogs to the nation, for his dad needs him, and he's still Doc's vetinary apprentice. I've decided to split the workload from Mark's shoulders. I'll keep him overseeing the pools, lockers, and drive-in, but I'm going to assign Celia to be the manager over the lake, cabins, dock, and boathouse. She's taken care of all that for awhile and knows the business like the back of her hand! I've decided to build Rouree and Celia a home along the lake on the west side, you know, so she and Rouree can keep an eye on things after dark."

I was thrilled for the opportunity streaming Celia's way! Basically this was Grady's way of setting everybody up for a long and prosperous future, and we knew it. Celia and Mark both had crackerjack positions and no mistake.

"Dad, can you afford all of this building you've been doing?" Grandma asked.

Howahkan's chin pulled in proudly. "Haw! Can Kell afford it?

Let me tell you something—those Vander-Smythe's from Avondaire Publishing take good care of their investments. They've invested in Kell and me, and they know how to spread the butter. It just keeps getting thicker!"

Grady laughed. "Well, it's true that since my real identity has been disclosed, there's a new frenzy over all of my books. Everything's gone into second or third printings. Avondaire Publishing Company has treated me squarely…and I must confess that Howahkan has some news."

"*Shoshone Sun Rising* just made the New York Times Best Sellers list." We all went crazy clapping at the news. "I think America is starving to know where it came from. The people need to know they have a purpose." Howahkan looked directly at me as he said it, and I caught a little chill.

Later that night Wyatt and I drove around Gallagher Springs in my truck. I would soon be fifteen and I was so close to legal now that Pistol Stewart didn't even try to look the other direction. We talked about life and girls and horses and guns. The Eagles crooned from the radio. I don't know what we were looking for that night, or if we ever found it. We were young and restless and that's what life's like when time is on your side. We passed Amos Greathawk and noticed Miss Pell was riding with him. Our necks nearly cranked backward at the sight! Then we passed a shiny red truck and I saw tail lights come on in the rearview mirror, so I tapped on my breaks and shifted into reverse, backing up slowly. Howahkan and Grady were out dragging Main, too. We rolled the window down to visit.

"Where are you guys going?" I asked.

"Wherever the hello mighty we want to."

"Same here," Wyatt grinned from the passenger's seat.

"We're restless," Howahkan explained. "We don't know what we're looking for, but we are sure to know when we've found it."

So that's the difference, I suppose, between young men and old.

Chapter Thirty-One

Amos and Miss Pell were married on Valentine's Day. The whole town of Washakie Fork returned for another wedding, and Rouree and his friends performed again. Celia's eyes sparkled with the bedroom dancing in them while Rouree moved to the gyrating rhythms. At least that's what I heard Shaylin mention to Monty, and I suppose that was newly-wed talk for *hubba-hubba, zing-zing* and all of that good jazz.

Callie Halfmoon was friendly with me and I was always happy to talk to her. Her dimple popped in her usual blazin', amazin' way, but I wouldn't allow myself to be swept in. I had sealed myself off to anything more than friendship. Rain Washakie showed plenty of interest in me, too, but as sure as Heaven hates Hell, I would not have enlisted Gloria to be my mother-in-law, so I was somewhat skittish around her and basically all girls in general.

The community danced at the reception, and Miss Pell's high school students especially went crazy for Queen's *Bohemian Rhapsody*, and the screaming Eagles *Take it to the Limit*. It was 1976 and the music was worth cranking the radio over! I saw Wyatt lead Avery from the dance that night, and watched him actually kiss her behind the church. I wondered if our whole family was destined to marry young, and Grady was no help, for he encouraged us all to pair up.

"You think Grady will build you a house?" I asked sarcastically, and the sweethearts leapt apart, blushing. Wyatt grinned at me. He'd hit a growth spurt after Gloria's treatments, and now he was tall and lanky like John and Mark. I now had to look up to him and he was quite proud of himself over it.

I didn't feel too good so I went home and clicked to Misty. I did my usual running mount, but my side hurt kind of bad with the force of landing on her back. I rode gently then, not pushing myself into any of my typical routines. I sang Ray Steven's *Misty* as I rode. It was safer serenading my horse, and she was one gal I could count on. I dismounted easily, feeling somewhat achy. I curried her and gave her a few carrots and half a bucket of rolled oats before going in the house.

Everything was quiet and I sat down at my desk to write.

"You would arrange an alliance between the Irish and the Shoshone," Bodaway Greathawk said. The words echoed, tinged with shades of doubt. How could I be the hope of things to come, as he declared? Eighteen months to ponder the words, and eighteen months to see. It started the day Doc Riley Gallagher took his assistant to help a sick cow and we happened upon a broken down hippie wagon. A small black-eyed girl peered from the stinking din of the ramshackle interior.

"The kid's hungry," a lost soul said.

I took the filthy child in my arms and walked toward my greatest joy, unknowingly. I washed her hands and washed her face, not knowing the scene had once played before, like the preview to a great movie. The image had glared like a flame's reflection in the keen eyes of the Great Hawk.

Yarrow was like a rare jewel—or a bar of yellow gold. She was highly prized and our family's need for her burned like treasure's fever. I pled to the Heavens to keep her, and the phantom flame burned in the clearing, a flicker of encouragement, a signal of things to be.

Howahkan Greathawk came, the proud, ancient man. We made medicine together, and he gave her to me like a philanthropist bequeaths his riches, for Yarrow's worth was beyond a price and I would love the old man forever. He understood sacrifice and offered it.

Howahkan called me to the Wind Rivers and I met many, many friends. Rouree's life connected with me the minute my fist met his face. I never dreamed we'd be best friends, nor that he'd light the moon in Celia's sky, but life doesn't spill all its secrets in the first introduction.

The Shoshone boys were rough, and I liked them. We rode together and bled together and I came back to Gallagher Springs with big plans spinning in my brain. I couldn't have known that soon I'd invite all of them to Gallagher Springs, either, but my vanity got the best of me and back to Three Lakes they came.

I'll never forget the shivers that raced down my back and neck when Yarrow waved to her Joni at Lake Washakie! Howahkan's prayers were answered, and what was lost was found. The lost hippie soul was wearing moccasins and feathers fluttered in her hair. Howahkan found peace in telling her goodbye. Yarrow danced and sang to see her Joni was so clean.

I'll never forget the assembly, of the harmonious notes blending together, between the Native flute and Celtic whistle. The song plays itself into my subconscious thoughts, rocking me to sleep with a lullaby when I'm restless. My life has become such a blending of the two cultures, and I am proud to own them.

Stan Tomkins enters the picture here, a boy that I prayed for so much. He was lost and hurting and bleeding inside. His life was like a black vapor where not even a match could burn. Gloria the nurse, Gloria the doctor, intuitively studied that boy. Who would have known that Gloria Washakie came to Three Lakes to find a son? A new future soothed the boy like a cup of Yarrow tea. (No wonder Joni named her precious daughter Yarrow, for her presence healed us all!) Uncle Aiden and Wyatt got help and answers too.

Providence smiled grandly and Howahkan was invited to tell his tale. He and his brother Kell took a hold of one another for comfort, finding friendship and company in preserving memories of yesterday. Writing stories is like making plum syrup, I guess. You preserve today what you might not have tomorrow, and the taste grows sweeter with time.

Rouree and Celia were married and Amos bought Stan Washakie's house. Stan could count on a future and Amos could count on one too for his destiny danced in Miss Pell's eyes.

If my story ended here, the prophecy of Bodaway's words would surely be fulfilled, but I know it cannot stop now, the alliance of our people. For Rouree and Celia will have children, and Yarrow won't be the only half breed in town—not that it would matter, but I envision a beautiful race of Irish and Shoshone posterity decorating Grady and Howahkan's family trees, for their marriage linked the men's genealogy yet again.

If I never soar again on lofty air drafts beholding splendors, my eyes have at least seen the partial fulfillment of the Great Hawk's words, and I have a lot to ponder on for the rest of my days."

I stretched my arm because writer's cramp made it ache. I read through my words and then went to bed before my family came home from the reception. My mind was determined to dream about Awinita, but when I shilly shallied into dreams, I dreamt of being chased by Nazi's and my feet got stuck in mud. I got up at two o'clock and got a drink of water, and then peered out the window at the night sky for awhile, thankful that Nazi's weren't part of my reality.

The next time I dozed off, I was riding Misty along the highway.

A few cars passed by, and suddenly I was in the middle of a huge, congested city. The cars looked futuristic and strange, and the people were rushed and unfriendly. Misty's ears skittered back, for we weren't used to this many people, neither one of us. I looked up, somewhat startled to see we were in New York City. I recognized the skyline! I could see the Empire State Building, and the new Twin Towers of the World Trade Center, reaching high, tearing jags in the horizon. It was such a change from Gallagher Springs, and Misty and I were all a wonder. Suddenly I noticed a jet plane careen from nowhere, flying right into one of the towers. Commotion sounded around me and my heart sped at an unhealthy clip at the sight. I felt horrified and urged Misty through the traffic so that we could inspect the scene. We'd scarcely made any progress through the rushed morning tangle of traffic when another plane smashed into the second tower, and I knew things were not copasetic! Both towers collapsed beneath a billowing cloud of ash and debris. The angry black cloud rolled through the streets swallowing everything in its sight. It nipped at Misty's heels even though she was running for all her might. It overtook us before I could force myself awake.

My pajamas were sweat soaked and my heart pounded in my chest. The dream was a nightmare and no mistake. I'd never been to New York City, and didn't know why such insidious images should haunt my sleep, sending any peace of mind into the dark dregs of panic. I paced my room with the light on, wishing I could calm down, but the vision played itself across the stages of my mind again and again. I was fifteen years old and felt too sheepish to wake my parents. I went back into the kitchen and got another glass of water, and took an Alka-Seltzer just in case the *flop- flop fizz- fizz* really offered relief.

"What's wrong, Wesley?" Allyson peered at me from her doorway.

"Bad dream."

"Why does your bedroom smell like camp smoke?"

"What?" I squinted at my sister in the light, wondering if she was really awake.

"Your bedroom smells like a campfire."

I scowled at her and stepped back into my room. The pungent aroma of smoke was acrid and I felt slightly dizzy and sick to my stomach. "Bodaway?" I whispered the name, but of course nobody answered, and they didn't need to. I wondered if Bodaway Greathawk had once seen the horrors of my nightmare. I prayed that whatever was wrong, or whatever might go wrong someday, would somehow be okay. What else could I say? I also prayed for sleep, but the blessing was denied for the remainder of that night.

I was never as grateful for a sunrise in my life as I was the following morning. I was also thankful to go to church and sing hymns and say prayers and listen to the good word of God. Teddy Burke was my Sunday school teacher, and I'm positive I was more attentive than ever I'd been a day in my life. I needed some sort of feel good material to soothe myself with after the haunting dream which persisted to play itself again and again in my mind like a worn-out rerun.

We ate at the Finnegan's that day, but dinner didn't taste good to me. By that afternoon I was burning up with a fever and had bad belly cramps and diarrhea. I knew I was delirious, for I cried out, "For Heaven's sakes, please call Gloria!" The woman was still in town for her cousin's wedding and soon she came bustling into my bedroom.

"What's wrong little sodbuster?" I detected *one* tinge of tenderness.

I tried to tell her, but I was so sick I felt like I was spinning down a long tube. She felt around. "He's got a hot appendix."

"Are you sure?" Mother asked.

"Oh Shannon, you've got to get this kid to the hospital and I don't mean maybe. His appendix is hot and ready to burst!"

"But he only became ill after church."

"Have you been feeling alright the last couple of days, Wesley? You seemed pretty quiet at the wedding. You didn't show off once, and I never saw you slug anybody. No fuss, no ruckus, no broken noses, I believe you were ailing yesterday."

"He had a bad night," Allyson said. I leaned my head over the side of my bed and threw up in a basin, heaving violently. "Ooh!" Allyson whiffed, "That's sick!"

"Exactly," I muttered "*Ooh. Sick*. Bad sick."

"He kept rattling around in the kitchen getting drinks."

"Were you sick?" Gloria asked.

"I don't know. I just had a lot of nightmares and stuff, and they made my heart pound and I felt kind of bad I guess."

"Well, dreams are always nightmares when you're sick," Gloria persisted.

"And his bedroom smelled like camp smoke," Allyson said.

Nobody listened to the comment long enough to figure it out. Dad tried to help me up so I could go get in the car, but I passed out, and when I came to, I was laying in the back of the Buick. Mother was turned in her seat, studying me. "Wesley, please be okay."

I nodded, and closed my eyes against the realities of feeling too ill to actually die. I was dizzy and I tried to only focus on one thing to keep the world from spinning round and round. I realized the object I was staring at was a long white braid hanging over the back of the front seat. It donned on me that Howahkan was sandwiched between my parents. "Howahkan?"

"I'm here Little Shoshone. I wanted to make sure the doctors fixed you correctly!"

I passed out again as I was being loaded into a wheel chair, and that's all I remembered for awhile. A black stretch of time wrapped around my mind like a bandage. I came to, and I was staring at a bright light, feeling incredible pressure against my middle. I saw an army of masked faces hovering over me, and heard Doctor Hooper say, "Look at that abscess! Catch it! Get that *blankety blank* cup under there before it drains any more poison into him."

A sheet was up and I couldn't see what they were doing, but it didn't sound encouraging. "How's it going?" I asked feeling quite concerned. The nurses startled and old Dr. Hooper let out a staggering jag of language and someone clapped a mask over my face and gassed me out like a light.

When I came to again, I was in a shadowy room, and my mind refused to entirely check in, but my spirit didn't check out. I knew I was alive, but that was all. Drifting, drifting, I shilly shallied between unconsciousness and reality. My logic fluttered like a feather in the breeze.

Shadows moved beyond my eyelids, and I felt funny sensations like bubbles up my nose. My limbs were numb and tingly and I was so very cold. An image of a porcelain baby Jesus turned in my mind. It spiraled and spiraled with snowflakes and wind beating against it. Jesus and I were cold, so frozen. I wished for Yarrow to wrap the babe in swaddling bands and invite Him over for a sleepover. I wanted the baby to be warm, for I was so cold myself.

"Wesley?" Someone interrupted my spinning image of baby Jesus and that disrupted me. "Wesley, can you hear me?" It wasn't Mother's voice and so I blocked it out, feeling too cold and shivery to answer. "Wesley!"

"Mmm..."

"You are burning up! I'm going to cover you with a cold blanket, okay?"

No, no! Don't freeze me to death! I tried to scream and plead for warmth for I was rattling with chill already. I felt the shock of a cold, cold thing come against my flesh and then the mental image of the porcelain baby Jesus shattered like a falling icicle against the ground. As it shattered I cried out for mercy—a release from the icy blast of sadistic winter.

In answer to my prayer, someone lit a campfire, and I smelled the smoke and heard the crackle of flames licking against tinder. Blessed, wonderful fire! I was so thankful to know I would soon be warm! I lifted my hands toward the glow and waited for the heat to thaw me.

I don't know how long I hovered near the fire, but I breathed the comforting smell of rising smoke and tried to pin all my hopes on it. I wrote a letter to Heaven and tied it on a rising vapor.

"Wesley?"

"Hmmm."

"Can you hear me, Wesley?"

"Hmmm." Geez, didn't they hear me the first time?

"I'm going to pack some ice bags around your legs, okay?"

"No! I was just getting thawed."

"You're burning up with a fever reaching close to a hundred and six."

"No," I moaned. "No, I'm just thawing out." But an iceberg rolled over the top of Gallagher Ridge and squelched my fire into wet, frozen ashes.

Time in a vacuum doesn't tick. I had no idea how long I teetered with the raging fever. I was delirious and sometimes hallucinated about things that weren't really there. A hawk kept circling above me in the bed. I pointed it out to a nurse and she just said, "Oh Wesley, we aren't allowed to keep pets."

Whenever the pain got bad I smelled the campfire, and then I would quiet right down for a spell. "Thank you Bodaway," I groaned. "Thank you for my fire." For some reason my praise went to his head and the fire stoked hotter and hotter. The flames' glow singed against my hair, and my skin and lips were blistering against the raging heat like Hell's inferno. "Enough fire, Bodaway. Enough! I'm burning up."

I felt myself kicking, trying to dislodge heavy quilts. I was smothering beneath the weight of them, but as I flinched a pain seared my middle and someone touched my leg and said, "No, no. Don't kick."

"Get the blankets off me, I'm roasted."

"You don't have anything on, dear." My hands traced downward to verify the information, and I was utterly humiliated to find out I truly did not have *anything* on! "Wesley, we've undressed you dear, to cool you off, but your fever is breaking now." The voice did not belong to my mother.

Sometime later I felt like I was swimming in thick, oozy honey.

Sweat poured from everywhere. The fever had broken, but I was clammy and disgusting. The sweat made me chill again and I longed for a blanket and a hot bath.

Soothing cloths dipped into warm water and began wiping against my skin, giving me some comfort. I begged for my bather to wash it all away and make me comfortable. I heard a sympathetic chuckle and for the first time since the middle of my operation, I sort of opened my eyes. I saw a pair of hazel eyes looking kindly at me. "Mother?"

"Yes, Wesley."

"My appendix broke open."

"Yes, they did. You've been such a sick boy. Doc Hooper didn't know if you'd make it for awhile."

"He didn't sound encouraging," I agreed.

"Wesley?"

"I woke up during my operation and he wasn't happy about it."

"Oh, I see." The lovely face grimaced.

"Is it still Sunday?"

"No, Wesley, it's Friday morning."

"Friday?"

"Yes."

I was dumbstruck by that. "I've been so terribly cold and hot…and cold."

"Yes, it's been awful for you."

"Am I dressed?"

"You are decent enough for me to wash you clean."

"Was I naked once?"

"Yes, but I covered your private parts with a towel so you wouldn't die of shame, just in case you came to."

"Thanks. Have I had anything to eat?"

"No. You have a needle in your arm and a tube up your nose to carry gas out of your belly."

"Oh."

"Wesley, you've scared ten years off the end of my life, you know."

"Sorry…did you ever smell camp smoke in this room?"

My eyes were resting, but Mother hesitated and so I opened them to look at her. "It was very strange, Wesley. Every time Doc Hooper was afraid you were turning for the worst, we could smell the camp smoke and somehow you would do some better, improve a bit."

"Oh…really?"

"Why? Why is that?"

I wasn't sure myself, and didn't really know what to say. "I have an ancient Shoshone friend who watches out for me, I think."

"I know you do, and his name is Howahkan Greathawk."

"No—I don't mean him. I mean Howahkan's grandfather. His name is Bodaway, and that means *fire-maker*."

Mother's brows furrowed and I didn't pursue the matter. I would just let her think I was still delusional, and maybe she was right. "Howahkan has refused to leave. Grady finally persuaded him to go home and get some rest a little while ago, but Howahkan has kept a vigil and often prayed Shoshone words over you."

"That was great of him."

"He also got baptized, claiming he would own a religion if it meant that the Father above the Clouds would make you well."

"Howahkan was baptized?" I couldn't believe it!

"Both he and Amos—Mrs. Pamela Greathawk has reformed her new husband."

"When?" Amos' stash of beer was obviously gone or he would never have agreed to such a thing.

"Last night. I missed it to stay here with you, but your Dad said it was rather touching, and that Howahkan said, *'There's no such thing as something for nothing. I need to be willing to sacrifice in order to make such a request, and the Little Shoshone must live!'* They were baptized in the smallest hot pot at the resort. Howahkan said his grandfather—the same one you just mentioned—had been baptized by early church missionary Amos Wright. Howahkan's grandfather always encouraged him to be baptized too, but he was just pig-headed and stubborn."

"What else have I missed?"

"Aunt Lace had triplets."

"Triplets? You have got to be kidding me!"

"No, and they were *more* than surprised! Aura Leigh, Aubynn, and Grandma have all been busy, trying to help out. Me, not so much, for I was needed elsewhere."

"Well...what did they have?"

"Two girls and a little boy, Ainslie, Addie, and Aaron. The girls each weighed four pounds, but Aaron only two."

I nodded, thinking the little fella had it rough. He'd be outweighed by his sisters now, and outvoted later on.

The nurses gave me lots of morphine for the pain but the medication made me hallucinate. Once I thought I saw a wild mustang bucking right for me. I dodged a hoof just before it connected with my face, and the jarring action didn't do me any good. I decided to lay off the pain shots then, and just try to get well enough to go home, but I didn't see my own bed until the first of March.

Yarrow was happy to see me, proclaiming all of her days in Kindergarten were spent worrying over her boy. "I got to have lots of sleepovers at Grandma's, Wesley, but I was so worried, so much!" Allyson was extra meek and mild, trying her best to be quiet, and good, and helpful, and that was proof enough that I'd nearly died.

I was weak from being down so long, and my strength was a thing of the past. I didn't go back to school for another two weeks, and I dreaded the stacks of make-up work that came home with Allyson. The former Miss Pell, now Mrs. Greathawk, had the kids make get well cards for me which was really nice. I got a kick out of some of them.

Paul Siskin's wrote, "Get butter, kwik!" I knew the teacher probably winced at his creative efforts in spelling.

When I did return to school I felt pale and ugly. I felt puny and gawked at. "Hey," Miles O'Reilly called pleasantly.

"Don't start on me," I growled. I was really irritable for awhile. Wyatt was a lamb but I was a badger, I guess.

Wyatt came over one night to help explain a math problem. "Wesley, you've been really ornery."

"I'm sorry."

"Remember when you brought Avery trailing into my house?"

"Yes! You flipped me off and we had a hissy fight."

"We're about to have another one if you don't get nicer. Stop acting so cagey."

I figured my tall, lanky, best cousin was right. I needed to start living again, and stop being a boob. I threw my school books in the corner and went up to Grady's. I soaked in the hot pool since my incision was proclaimed healed and everything. Howahkan and Grady soaked with me, and just talking to them in the old way made me feel tons better.

Somehow we got talking about age and Grady said, "I'm so old I'm nearly young again! I'm stepping along, heading into my second springtime." I'd heard the words before, at least a dozen times, but they settled in on me and made me think of life, and seasons, and the meaning of it all.

"Wesley, you've been awfully mopey lately," Howahkan said.

"I haven't felt good, remember?"

"I think you're heart's been bruised. Aren't you sweet on Callie Halfmoon anymore?"

"She's not sweet on me. Her affections transferred to your new grandson, Stan."

Howahkan laughed sarcastically. "If she chooses Stan over you then I see she's as dim as her dumb old grandfather."

"Why?"

"Well, he wasn't bright enough to be a full moon...just a half." Grady, Wyatt and I laughed at the funny Shoshone man and instinctively I reached a protective hand across my stomach to shield it from the pain of merriment.

"There are plenty of cute gals around here," Grady piped.

"Ah," I said, "I'm not looking."

"Not every flower needs to be an Indian Paintbrush."

"What's that supposed to mean?"

"Not every girl needs to remind you of Awinita."

"Oh Grady," I muttered, wishing he'd drop it. What was I, an open book?

"My Addie was a spirited lovely redhead, and there was nothing wrong with her! My Addie was a rare beauty, too."

I lay back in the water, willing myself to float on my back to avoid the conversation. It wasn't so much to my liking. I thought about my riding pattern and set new goals to get my body back in shape.

The first Saturday of May I was sitting in the boathouse selling hotdogs. Celia was busy renting boats. Howahkan came into the building and bought himself a root beer. He pulled a chair up and visited with me while I worked. A city dude with a big beer belly and rude ways came blustering up to the window.

"Hey Chief, I want a dozen hotdogs so step on it."

Howahkan's head tilted back to a proud and ruffled angle. "I'm not your chief!"

I grinned, wondering where this would end up. I quickly thread several hotdogs onto the prongs, but the man couldn't see me for Howahkan.

"I said, hurry old man!"

Howahkan stood up, glowering over the dude. "I have the right to refuse service to idiots and assholes!"

I nearly choked to death at Howahkan's words. I leaned around Howahkan, "They're coming," I called. "Keep your panties on, Mister!" I stepped around the proud Shoshone, setting the hotdogs on the counter. "Do you want drinks and chips with that?"

The man nodded uncomfortably, feeling the shadow of Howahkan looming large above him. "Yes, please."

"Please?" Howahkan cracked. "The little Colonel has manners? I thought by hello mighty I would have to teach you some."

The man colored and cowered down, trying to quickly squeeze mustard and relish onto the buns. "I'm not your Colonel."

"Colonel *Custer*," Howahkan persisted, verbally bullying the squirming guy. "Do you know the pathetic end to his story?"

"That's twelve dollars," I cut in, interrupting the spat. I had an idea that Howahkan had a whole arsenal of taunting smack up his sleeve, and if his tongue really turned loose it could get ugly. The man flipped a twenty dollar bill in my direction and fled, looking over his shoulder several times as he retreated.

"Idiot," Howahkan muttered beneath his breath. "I've scalped better men than him before."

"Don't let him rile you. Most tourists are stupid. When they go on vacation they usually leave their brains at home in a drawer."

"I doubt if that guy has any, home or otherwise."

"Maybe not, but his twenty bucks spends as well as the next guy's."

"His pathetic bald scalp wouldn't make a suitable conquest for anyone's belt, but I wouldn't have served the green horn."

"I know. I heard! You can't go around swearing at the customers, Howahkan."

Howahkan grunted. "I do what I want. That guy was whiter than most…"

I was amused as ever I'd been at the exchange. "It's better just to get even."

"How?"

"He's parked over on the end of the lot. I saw him pull in this morning. The best I can tell, his brother and family are here on vacation, too. The brother parked right behind him, only he backed in, so there bumpers are close together."

"And?"

"Did I ever tell you about the time Monty Quinn chained Mr. Mulligan's bumper to the telephone pole in Grady's driveway?"

Mischief gleamed from the wise black eyes. "Are you planting delinquent suggestions in my old, renegade mind?"

"Just sayin, that's all. Sometimes us little punk white kids ride into battle too."

Howahkan looked around the boathouse, spying a chain in the corner. "I need to borrow this for a few minutes. Just sayin'."

Howahkan returned twenty minutes later grinning to beat the band. His eyes looked like glowing bits of ebony and his manner was smug and swaggering. He popped the top on another soft drink and started singing, *Why Can't We be Friends,* by War.

We had to wait until seven o'clock that evening, but it was worth it. The rude guy and his brother gathered up their wives and families and headed to their cars. I gauged they were on their way to the Fat Shamrock for the night. Doors slammed on the sedans and engines fired. Both cars lunged forward and a mighty spinning of tires ensued. The rude guy seemed annoyed and gunned his gas pedal impatiently, and sure enough, he broke loose…and his bumper clattered to the pavement, just before his brother's did. The other customers stared at the goings on. Both men climbed out of their cars, inspecting their broken bumpers, angrily hopping around and waving their arms.

I saw Howahkan peering from Grady's kitchen window, smiling smugly. I went back into the boathouse to belly-laugh in peace. Mark's head poked into the window. "Wesley, was that you?"

"No, I swear to you it wasn't!"

Mark grimaced. "I was hoping to be rid of those two demanding morons. They've hung around being big fat pains in the pa-toot all day long!"

"I know it."

Sure enough, the man and his brother came storming into the boathouse, demanding to use the payphone. I listened while they called the sheriff and I just wanted to howl at the moon. Sheriff Pistol Stewart hated having his evening coffee interrupted, and was probably clear down in Lakeside. I was right, for his car didn't' appear for at least fifteen minutes.

I walked with the vandalized tourists out to the scene of the crime, acting very concerned. Pistol Stewart seemed annoyed that he'd been summoned on such a silly emergency. "What happened?"

The rude man blustered, "Someone chained our bumpers together!"

His brother lamented, "My car is brand new!"

"What did you do that for?" Pistol asked belligerently.

"I didn't chain my car to his!"

"Did you think somebody would steal your car or what?" Pistol persisted wickedly.

"Huh?"

"Because I always see folks tie up their horses, and chain up their bicycles, but this is a new one on me…never saw anybody chain their car up before." The sheriff had a good sense of humor, but it was wasted on the ill-tempered men.

"We didn't do it! Can't you understand English?"

Pistol's jaws clenched and he said, "No, why don't you teach me?" The man quieted down, fidgeting nervously again. Pistol took out a notebook and made a report. "I'll be happy to give you the number to a good repair shop if you'd like."

"Well…won't you catch who did this? They should be responsible for the repairs."

"Sure thing, I'll go right to work on it, boys. No need to protect the peace or help those in need when I've got something *this* pressing."

By eight o'clock the excitement died down and the sheriff and the disgruntled brothers cleared out. Most of the customers trickled away, making a special point to check their bumpers before getting in their vehicles.

"Hi, I'd like to rent a boat."

"Be with you in a second," I called, straightening things. When I looked up I saw Shonnee O'Shea grinning at me.

"Hey Shonnee. Are you alone?"

"Yes."

"We have a policy, you know. No lone riders." I don't know why I said it, for there's no such policy.

"Oh. Well, are you busy?"

"I'm just ready to lock up the boathouse."

"So…"

"I'm feeling up to a good boat ride, myself."

She smiled. "Remember the night we beat those other guys in a race?"

"Yep." I finished sweeping the floor then propped the broom in the corner and grabbed my jacket. "That was the night you got kind of high and mighty because you are older than me."

Shonnee looked startled by my statement. "I did not! That was the night you were high and mighty because you didn't want to have anything to do with me."

"I did once we were in the boat…but you got smug."

"I didn't! I just didn't' know what else to say and I'm sort of shy. Staci was the only person I knew that night, and she was in the other canoe with those Shoshone boys."

Gee…had I dreamed that all up? I'd been avoiding this cute girl like the plague. "Well—how old are you today, Shonnee O'Shea?"

"I'm fifteen today. I don't turn sixteen until next week."

"Well I'm fifteen and a quarter, which is half way to half. Am I a suitable boating companion tonight?"

She grinned. There were no dimples in her cheeks, but they were rosy and pink, and her skin seemed creamy and smooth. Her lips were full and pretty and she was wearing a light layer of strawberry gloss over them. At least it looked strawberry and I wondered if it was flavored...

"Of course! You're funny, Wesley."

I led the way to the dock. "Which boat did you have in mind?"

"Don't I need to pay for it first?"

"Tonight it's on me. I get that perk around here, you know."

"A pedal boat?"

"Sure." I unfastened a pedal boat. Grady had named all of his boats after us, too. I chose the Addie, in honor of my great grandmother—who was a blazin', spirited redhead. "The Addie is loaded with Irish luck, Shonnee. How does that suit you?"

"Sounds great," she said, stepping gracefully into the small craft.

I climbed in and we started pedaling. "So, where do you live?"

"War Bonnet."

War Bonnet was a small place, just south of Eisner. It nestled midway between Eisner and Gallagher Springs. It was across the border into Idaho and so the War Bonnet kids went to school in Eisner.

"Oh really? For some reason I thought you were from someplace far away."

"No, I'm just a Three Lakes girl."

"Did you know I have my own truck?"

"Yes. Staci and Celia told me. That's great!"

"I'll bet it could probably make it to War Bonnet and back, what do you think?"

"You don't have your license though."

"No, but I do what I want. Pretty much."

Shonnee smiled and I noticed her teeth were straight and pretty. "I'm here for the weekend. My parents had to go to Idaho Falls for my mother's class reunion or something. Anyway, I came here to stay with Staci, but Staci got detained at college and isn't coming home."

"Are your aunt and uncle okay with you being out tonight?"

"Yes—they know I love the hot springs. They've actually gone to Lakeside for something."

"How were you planning on getting back to their house? Two miles is a long walk."

"I told them I'd hitch a ride with friends. They thought I was meeting up with some kids."

"And?"

"I did, didn't I?"

"Well, I'll give you a ride to the mayor's house too, and then you can tell me if you'd trust me driving clear to War Bonnet sometime."

She looked pleased and her pink cheeks flushed a little bit more. The sun was beginning to sink behind the western ridge and the splintering sunset glow lit her auburn hair into fiery shades of scarlet and deep crimson. We pedaled to the island. I pulled the craft ashore and we hiked along, finding a grassy spot.

"I fish here a lot."

"I've always wanted to come to the island, but never have."

We talked about Grady's books, and Shonnee admitted to being a big fan. "My favorite is undoubtedly *Feathers Flutter, Say Goodbye* because the romance is so delicious, you know? But my second favorite has got to be *Castles of Promise.* I just love the whole setting of that book!"

"Well now that we know that most of his books were talking about the mountains and valleys of Three Lakes, is it any wonder they appealed to us so much?"

"No, not at all, but that book would have appealed to me no matter where I lived, I'm sure of it."

"*Castles of Promise* was the first book Grady told from a woman's point of view. It's interesting he was able to do that."

"Maybe that's why I loved it so much! I really connected with Marianne."

"I own the original manuscript to all of Grady's books."

"No way?" Shonnee's eyes popped with excitement at the revelation. "That's impressive! You know we could start our own Phantom Flynn book club and discuss one book each week for thirty-nine weeks!" I thought that was a blazin' suggestion and this girl was making a huge impression on me.

I had a couple of matches in my jacket pocket and I built a bonfire. It was cozy and I found out more about Shonnee O'Shea, and she asked questions about me.

"How long did it take you to learn the riding tricks?"

"All fall and winter that year."

"Holy cow! Well, it was impressive."

"Thanks. It was a successful day and I was really stoked over the turn-out."

"I'll bet. My uncle is impressed with you."

"Seriously?"

"Yes…and so are lots of people."

"Such as?" I was good at fishing.

"Staci and all of her friends. Staci said she wished she was younger or you were older. She liked your cousin John for awhile."

I nodded. "He's in California now."

"Yes, I heard that."

I checked my watch, grimacing to see the hours of daylight fading away. "We'd better get you back to the Spinnaker's before your uncle isn't impressed with me anymore."

We let the fire burn out. "Wesley, I'm sorry you got so sick this spring."

"It's okay. I survived."

"I'll bet you got cabin fever, huh?"

"Oh man—did I!"

"One of my aunts is a nurse and she said Dr. Hooper didn't think you'd live through your operation—and then you woke up and talked to them right in the middle of it!"

"That was too crazy, I'm telling you! I *do* remember that, but things were sketchy for a while afterwards. I got pretty cagey after the second week of it."

"You probably missed riding and fishing and stuff."

"Yes, exactly! I learned some really awesome tricks, and I was just getting good at them, but my dumb appendix reversed my progress, I'm afraid. It will be awhile before I build my strength up. I got puny."

"You don't seem puny to me."

"No?"

She shook her head and her glossy hair swished back and forth. Instinctively I touched a wispy strand near her ear, and Shonnee's face registered both shock and pleasure. I remembered Celia's face when Rouree first touched her hair and I had to smile. "You have nice hair, Shonnee. It's blazin'." And it was—it reminded me of red embers, and a new flame flickered in my eyes.

Chapter Thirty-Two

Howahkan came to our house one evening. He held Yarrow on his lap and she fiddled with his braids until she fell asleep. "My little Shoshone Rose is growing up," he said. "It amazes me how much she looks like Awinita."

We watched *The Six Million Dollar Man.* Howahkan loved that program, and often commented on the particulars of bionics. "This is somebody's phony baloney dream, but someday you'll probably see bionic pieces going into people."

I took Yarrow from Howahkan's arms, for his legs had gone to sleep. I carried her into her bed and tucked her in. I stared at her in the shadows for a moment, loving her, that little sister of mine. As I stared at her, I sensed a strong whiff of mint...and clover. *Awinita?* Was Awinita the guardian angel to my sleeping sister? How often did she loom near, unseen, and unsuspected? Was Bodaway my spirit guide? I wondered, but the scent was undeniable. As I turned to leave I saw Howahkan standing in the doorway.

"Do you smell mint?"

"Yes. My sister has been with me all day today."

Chills crept along my neckline. "How do you know?"

"I know. I smell her and feel her."

"Well. . .huh."

"Little Shoshone, old Howahkan loves you. You know that, don't you?"

"Yes."

"Drive me to the top of the ridge, please."

"Right now?"

"Yes."

We walked out to my truck. It was late and the night was black with just a sliver of moonlight. I felt strange about things, fighting a sense of melancholy. The mint fragrance came with us, and it was strong in the truck. Howahkan talked about interesting things as we meandered up the road.

"It was my son, Kell O'Rourke Greathawk that first taught me to read and write English, and cipher in white man's ways. I can thank the Little Shoog for that."

"That's great," I said.

"And who would have known I'd grow up to be the author of a six hundred page book?"

"Maybe the Little Shoog knew it."

"Haw!" Howahkan blasted. "Haw—his old dad write a book? Not likely! It was my daughter Wyanet that taught me how to cook good pancakes."

"She was a good teacher, then. Your pancakes are the best!"

"It was the Little Shoshone that taught me to drive!"

"Yes, Howahkan, and you nearly put Delma Jean Connor into a fit while you were learning!"

"Haw! She's a crazy woman driver! It was the Big Irish who helped me learn to make a book." I nodded, agreeing with him. "It was my sweet Anna that taught me how to be gentle. She could break my proud swagger with a simple expression. Anna trained me like nobody could!"

"Yes. Life is one big lesson, isn't it?"

Howahkan nodded. I drove up the winding hillside, inching closer to the top of the ridge, careful not to scratch the paint on my truck. "Life is full of learning, but oh my hell, am I smart!" I nodded again, grinning at the proud old man. Howahkan drew a long breath, measuring his words carefully. "Little Shoshone, I have learned enough."

"No," I shook my head, trying to think of something witty to say.

"Stop the truck."

I did as Howahkan bade, but I didn't like the melancholy feeling pressing upon me as I did it. Howahkan climbed out of the truck, looking young and beautiful and fit as ever. He was tall and straight, not bent or broken! He began chanting in Shoshone. He laughed and motioned a hand across the valley of Washakie Fork. A campfire burned in the clearing. I was not surprised to see it, for it had burned before. "It lights the way for me," Howahkan said, laughing again.

"Let's go, Howahkan. It's late."

"You will do the temple work for me and my people. Get Rouree and Amos to help you with that. I wager you haven't seen the last of my posterity, either. You will live to meet more of them, and oh my hello mighty, you will be impressed! "

I nodded my head, "Of course—"

"Thank you Little Shoshone! Always remember who you are! You have a purpose. Every once in a while the Great Hawk may visit you—perhaps he'll drag me along! Take care of my Little Shoshone Rose!" He unfastened his bear claw necklace and handed it to me. "This will protect you and give you courage. I killed that grizzly in Washakie Fork when I was nineteen."

I reached for Howahkan's arm. He lifted it around my shoulders, hugging me to him. He smelled good and I didn't mind embracing my ancient friend. I buried my face against his neck. "Thank you for Yarrow!"

He started talking again, but it wasn't to me. I looked up, trying to discern his actions. "He looks like Kell, doesn't he Awinita?" Laughter scraped against his throat. His eyes were fixed on an unseen source. "Oh, my hell, there's my Anna!" His body trembled with excitement.

I couldn't stop the tears coursing down my cheeks. Howahkan Greathawk was dying, and it seemed as if Gallagher Ridge was the only juncture separating life from death. Drums sounded and the aspen rattled with a breeze. Howahkan began chanting again. He squeezed my hand and took a step toward the sounds. I suppose his spirit bounded down the hillside with all of the grace and ease of a spring buck. Yes, he was running, whooping cries of jubilation, for I heard them even though his body crumpled at my feet.

I knelt down, helplessly cradling his head on my lap. I touched his high cheekbones and ran a finger down his excellent nose. I touched the features of my beautiful friend, engraving his face forever in my mind. "Goodbye Howahkan Greathawk. *Tsaan dai neesungaahka."* All is well.

I was shaking inside and bawling like a baby. I couldn't lift Howahkan into the truck. He was heavy and I was too puny to leverage the dead weight. My mind spun around, wondering what I should do. I hated to leave his body lying on top of the ridge while I went for help, but at last that's what I had to do.

I stretched him out in a respectful position, even though I knew he was past caring. I laid my jacket over his face and climbed into my truck—the one Howahkan bought for me. I let the tears course freely as I sucked on the aching fire in my throat. I loved Howahkan Greathawk and he was gone.

I maneuvered the truck around, noticing dozens of fires now burning in the clearing. I cut the motor and rolled the window down, listening to the drums and joyful sounds of celebration. Of course there was cause for making merry! Howahkan Greathawk was reunited with his wife and children, his mother and father, grandparents, brothers, sisters, and friends. I wiped my eyes and drove toward home.

I wondered where I should go first. I didn't want to upset Grady—but what was proper protocol? Should I get someone to help me bring the body down, or was that the job of the officials? I wasn't sure so I went home.

The lights were off but I stepped into my parents' bedroom.

"Wesley?"

"I need some help, Dad."

A lamp switched on very quickly. "What's wrong, Son?"

"Howahkan's dead. I left his body on the ridge because he was too heavy to bring down."

Dad leapt from beneath the covers and pulled his pants on. Mother's face washed ashen and her eyes turned to liquid. "He was just *here*," she whispered.

"He spent his last evening in this life exactly where he wanted to be! He had me drive him onto the ridge so he could die, I know he did. He started telling me goodbye before we got out of the truck, basically."

Dad called the sheriff, and while we waited, I phoned Amos. It was a hard call to make, but he handled it very stoically. "I will come. I'd like to see where he breathed his last," Amos said. "Why don't you call Rouree?" I was kind of wishing Amos would have told him—it wasn't fun news to share, but I did what Amos asked and called my new cousin-in-law.

"Hey," Rouree said, hearing it was me.

"Rouree, I'm sorry…"

"Oh no!"

"Yeah, Howahkan died a little while ago."

"Where?"

"On top of the ridge." It was silent for a few moments. "Rouree, it was a celebration. I heard him laugh and holler as his spirit leapt into eternity. I heard drums and saw many campfires burning in Washakie Fork. Life goes on, Rouree! I wish you could have seen what I saw, and hear what I heard! It was sacred."

"I'm glad he was with you."

I knew I'd better go tell Grady before he saw lots of lights and commotion. I drove up Gallagher Canyon and knocked twice on his backdoor then stepped inside. He was curled up on the sofa watching the late movie. "Oh, Wesley, I thought you might be Howahkan. He's not come home yet." I turned the light on and Grady saw my blotchy face and he knew. "Howahkan?"

I nodded. Grady took the news pretty well—in fact I think he was relieved that he died on my watch and not his, but he was very reflective as well. "Howahkan Greathawk nearly drove me crazy some days, but—I really learned to love him too."

"I know."

Grady rubbed a tired hand across his eyes. "Oh, I've buried so many of my loved ones and friends over the years. You'd think that the white hot scorch of pain would soften over time, but it always stings the same."

"Yes. Grady, I'm not ready for you to go—just so you know. I haven't reached my summer yet so please don't get in a hurry."

"Me? I've got too much to do!" Grady embraced me, thumping me on my back. He was as short to me as I had been to Howahkan.

"Grady, Awinita helped call Howahkan home. My truck still smells like her if you'd like to take a whiff."

Grady's brows furrowed but he moved past me, swiftly making tracks for my truck. He opened the door and climbed in. He inhaled deeply, almost tasting the sweet clover and tangy mint. "I love that woman!" He filled his lungs one more time, wiped tears from his cheeks, and then walked slowly into his house. I leaned my head against the steering wheel and cried.

The rest of the night unfolded in a robotic way. By the time the sheriff and coroner made their way to the top of the ridge, the valley of Washakie Fork was dark. No smoke, no flames, no celebration, no fuss, just a regal man's lifeless body.

When I finally got to bed in the wee hours of morning, I noticed an envelope on my pillow. "The Little Shoshone" was written on it, and my heart panged and banged at the sight. I tore the envelope with a *schriippp,* pulling out a handwritten note.

Little Shoshone,

This is goodbye. I love you boy! Take good care of Yarrow and never forget who you are. I leave to you my pipe and my whole library of books. I also want you to take my old photograph of Bodaway.

I want Yarrow to have my photo albums and also the ceremonial clothing of her great, great, grandmother's. They are folded in the chest in my room. Rain can have the chest—she's always been so fond of it.

To Wyatt Finnegan, I bequeath my cats, Ned and Esther. Rouree gets my truck, and my home goes to Gloria. She can convert it into a doctor clinic if she chooses. I leave my other personal effects to be dispensed between my other family members at Amos's discretion.

My book royalties shall be split between my great grandchildren to be used for college. May they learn all they can! I want my family to be respectful, good citizens. Amos will oversee all monetary affairs.

To Kell, I leave the original manuscript, Shoshone Sun Rising, but after his death, the manuscript shall be given to The Little Shoshone. My headstone should read, Howahkan Greathawk, the Bridge. Of course you know what that means, Little Shoshone, and I don't care if anyone else understands it or not. Thank you for teaching an old man how to drive. I love you.

Howahkan

P.S. Every once in awhile a man must make medicine. I will always be with you when you do.

Most of Gallagher Springs packed up and went to Fort Washakie for the funeral. It was almost odd how connected our two towns were now. Howahkan was buried in the cemetery next to his cherished Anna, with his children and some grandchildren clustered about him. Tributes of eagle feathers fluttered goodbye.

Using Howahkan's letter to me, Amos directed the cleaning out of Howahkan's place while we were there. Uncle Aiden was a little chagrined at Wyatt's inheriting the cats, but he was a good sport about it. Wyatt seemed happily suited to the felines since he was now an only child at the Finnegan house. They would be good company for him.

"I will miss Old Grandfather so much," Yarrow stated emphatically. "Daddy, please grow braids for me to tickle myself with." She wrapped her arms around Dad's neck. "Oh please, Daddy!"

"You'll have to get a feather to tickle yourself with instead."

"It's not the same," she lamented. "It's not the same, or the same, or the sa-aaa-aame!"

June came, and we noted Howahkan missed his hundred and first birthday by only a week. The sun was unseasonably hot and we were in for a sultry season. The resort was jumping. I helped Mark and Celia all I could, and still traveled with Grandpa, doctoring sick calves and horses, bulls, sheep, pigs, and dogs. Whatever was wrong, Doc Riley Gallagher could generally help. One morning we went to War Bonnet to do a cesarean on a late-calving heifer. My eyes were peeled as we drove down the country lanes of the snug community. I spied Shonnee O'Shea out mowing the lawn, and my heart lurched just a little. It would be handy knowing where she lived, and maybe I could accidentally cruise by sometime.

We got back to Gallagher Springs at noon and I showered up and ran up to the resort to help out. I was surprised to round the corner to the boathouse and run smack into Shonnee. "What are you doing here?" I was quite startled since it had only been a couple hours since I'd seen her.

"Celia hired me to help out this summer." Shonnee smiled tentatively. "I hope that's okay."

"God bless Celia!" I couldn't contain my enthusiasm over my new coworker. "Welcome to Utopia!"

"Is it really Utopia here?"

"Yes. I think so."

"Well, that's what I was hoping for. It's hard to beat Utopia!"

"So...what are you doing right now?"

"I'm supposed to be getting orientation from you."

"Orientation? Awe, yes. I'm famous for my orientation courses, naturally."

"Wesley...I'm sorry about your old Shoshone friend."

I grinned at the girl. She seemed so softhearted and...well...perfect. "It's okay."

"Celia told me you were with him when he died."

I nodded, feeling reflective. "I was, and it was, um—hallowed."

Shonnee's eyes narrowed, studying me thoughtfully. "I'm glad I'm going to be working here."

I led the girl with the glorious auburn hair into the boathouse. I showed her how to do rentals, cabin reservations, and run the register for tackle, bait, snacks, pop, and food. Occasionally we were interrupted by customers, and I watched as Shonnee took care of them. One lady was snarly and impatient.

"I'm sorry you're having a bad day," Shonnee said meekly. "I hope the natural beauties of Gallagher Hot Springs will brighten your day."

"Hmph!" The buxom woman thundered off, not sure how to respond to the kindness.

"Wesley, is the customer always right?"

"No, Shon, they never are—but you handled her brilliantly." She flushed a little. "But if they get too cantankerous we just chain their bumpers to something and get even with them."

Shonnee bit her lip. "I rather like that idea!"

The afternoon passed quickly, and soon the sun was waving goodbye. We cleaned up the boathouse, sweeping, and scrubbing. I showed Shonnee how to count the till and it was pleasant being with her. We shared a candy bar and bottle of soda. Celia called to see how things were going. "Tomorrow I want you to show her more about the docks and boats, and then I'll give her the low-down on the cabins."

"Okay—and thanks."

Celia's voice giggled into the phone. "I knew you'd like that."

"Oh, you did?"

"Yes. You don't sulk about girls so much anymore."

"Especially this one."

"Right. It's all copasetic, isn't it?"

"Very! Goodnight Mrs. Greathawk."

"Argh!" Celia squealed, "That makes me sound *so* old!"

I hung up and noticed Shonnee staring at me. Some kind of blazin' light danced in her green eyes. "Celia says there's more orientation tomorrow. Can you handle that?"

Shonnee nodded, grinning. "I think I'm up for it."

"So…are you staying at your uncle's house, or are you driving back and forth to Gallagher Springs every day or what?"

"Um…well, my folks made arrangements for me to stay at Gallagher Springs when I work late, otherwise I'll just swing home. It's not so far—only nine miles."

"But it's so late tonight."

"Wesley, it's only eight-thirty!"

"It's eight-thirty *now*, but I wondered if you wouldn't like to get oriented about the island tonight—you know, so we're not so overloaded tomorrow."

Shonnee nodded, a smile turning her pretty mouth. "Oh that's a great idea!"

I grabbed a package of marshmallows and some more sodas, marking them on my tab. "Did you bring a jacket?"

"No, I just didn't even think about it—it was so hot this morning."

"I've got a spare in my pool locker. I'll grab it."

As I breezed past Mark he sang out, "Don't do anything I wouldn't do."

"Those are guidelines I think I can live with," I remarked snidely.

Shonnee and I motored out to the island with the marshmallows, a blanket, and big plans for island orientation. I felt somewhat giddy.

Once we pulled the boat ashore I began goofing in a very professional manner. "Welcome to the heart of Utopia! This is called Grady's island, and it's to be respected. You can only come here with the expectation of having fun." I tromped along the grass and Shonnee scrambled after. "This is Grady's grass and these are Grady's trees."

"Yes, I'm listening," Shonnee said, like a good and proper student.

We lit a fire in the same place we'd burned our last one. Shonnee spread the blanket down and I whittled a couple of roasting sticks from some willows. We roasted marshmallows to golden confection and I popped one in my mouth, saying, "A little Shoog does me good." Shonnee asked all kinds of questions about Howahkan and how I had come to meet him. It felt good talking about him.

"This reminds me of Chapter Six in *Glory Nation*."

Shonnee seriously was as fanatical over Phantom Flynn's writings as I was! "What does?"

"You know—being here with you. Remember how McMillan and Annabelle talked near the crackling magic of the fire?"

"Oh, there's one difference—"

"What?"

"I'm not as tough as McMillan and Annabelle wasn't as cute as you!" Like a raindrop on water, Shonnee's expression rippled with pleasure.

The sun sank low and frogs and crickets serenaded us loudly to the lapping rhythms of the water. The sky was lit with constellations and Shonnee lay back on the blanket saying, "Welcome to Grady's Planetarium." I lay back too, and we studied star formations.

"There's Orion's belt."

"I'm never good at seeing that one."

"Oh Wesley, look—you can't miss it."

"I see the Big Dipper."

"Yes, everyone knows the Big Dipper, but see Orion?" Her hand pointed, trying to get my eyes to follow.

I looked over at her. "Yeah, I see it."

"See, one, two, three; those stars lined up right there, that's his belt, but can you see the rest of him, Orion the Hunter? He's the largest and most recognizable constellation in the sky. He's located on the Celestial Equator, right in our very own Milky Way."

She looked over at me to see if I was seeing it or not. Of course I wasn't trying, as I was gazing at her, just listening to her prattle on and on. "I'm listening."

"I forgot what I was going to say—"

I smoothed a wisp of hair away from her face, caressing the silky tress momentarily. "I like star gazing, and you should teach science, Shonnee. You're more interesting than crabby old Mr. Henry."

Shonnee gulped audibly. "I like space."

"I'm partial to it myself."

Shonnee giggled and I joined in. We were perfect idiots, star gazing and feeling giddy and lit up. We didn't really need a bonfire, for all by themselves, embers were beginning to smolder. I reached for Shonnee's hand and she smiled, giving me a little squeeze.

"You're right, this really is Utopia."

That was a blazin' thing to say and I leaned close to her and whispered a kiss against her full, pretty lips. In all reality I *did* detect a hint of strawberry. It was just a small peck, but enough to light the Celestial Equator into explosions of color! The best summer of my life had officially begun.

Chapter Thirty-Three

Rouree and I were invited to ride in The Days of '47 Rodeo in Salt Lake. Mayor Spinnaker had connections, I guess. Apparently one of the planners of the big event had attended the powwow two years ago. Kenny and Dover would be joining us. Gloria offered Stan, claiming he could now ride as well as the rest of us, but Rouree said, "No thanks, I know he doesn't like to come back here, and it will take some practice." Rouree Greathawk was my best friend and I was grateful to his loyalty!

That's how I found the motivation to start doing chin-ups and push-ups again, most religiously. When Kenny and Dover arrived in Gallagher Springs they would be surprised to see what I could do! I was definitely coming out of my post-appendix slump.

Rouree and I found time to ride together every day, even if it was just for fifteen minutes. He cheered the day I mastered the art of riding straddle backed! His cheering drew others to gather near the corral. Wind whipped through my hair as I loped around and around the corral with one foot on Misty, the other on Old Whip.

Wyatt's eyes were bright. "Is that fun, Wesley?"

"Real fun," I called, making the most of showing off.

"'Cuz it looks fun," Wyatt persisted as I blazed past him again.

"For Heaven's sakes, be careful!" Mother wrung her hands, endlessly worrying about me. "Don't fall and rip your stitches open!"

"They're all healed up, Mother!"

"My boy's okay," Yarrow defended. "My boy is the Little Shoshone!"

Shonnee and I also practiced rowing around Inish Lake every evening after work. We timed ourselves every day, always trying to whittle a few seconds off. It was amazing how we improved. We often challenged Rouree and Celia to races and the competition was healthy. I never mentioned boys against girls, for that sounded so unsatisfactory to me now.

Dover and Kenny showed up on the Fifteenth of July. Dad quickly put them to work in the hayfields, as they had nothing better to do, and Dad always needed help. Uncle Aiden and Wyatt were busy constructing Grady's drive-in and the other cabins. Wyatt was growing stronger every day, and headaches seldom troubled him. Amos Greathawk enlisted to help them and ended up being a very decent carpenter. After lunch every day, Uncle Rob and Dad sat on the corral fence and watched us ride. Occasionally Grandpa Gallagher would wander over and make suggestions or offer critique.

"I'm going to have to get you a couple more horses to train," Grandpa said.

"Why? I'm getting along with Misty just fine."

"Yes, but you need to have a back up mount because Misty won't last forever." I didn't like the sound of that. Misty was trained so perfectly for me, and the thoughts of working another horse seemed daunting, but I agreed, ready for anything.

One night after supper Kenny said, "Let's go cause some trouble somewhere." Dover was game and squashed a cigarette beneath his boot, eager and ready to go.

"Sorry, I'm busy tonight."

Kenny glowered in my direction. "Why, what have you got that's so pressing?"

"I've got a service project. Do you guys wanna come?"

"Work? No, you're Dad's worn me out already. Count me out." Dover spat in the dirt. "Kenny, let's us call some of Celia's friends. Surely there's a few girls left in this town."

I left them talking it over and ran home to shower up. Mom and the girls were gone to Logan on a shopping trip and the house was quiet. I took my time shaving, wanting to do a decent job of it. My bedroom radio was cranked and I sang along with John Denver, "*Thank God I'm a Country Boy.*"

I vacuumed my truck and wiped the dash and the interior until it looked brand new. I then drove to Wyatt's house. He and Avery came out, looking eager to go somewhere. That was my service project. I was taking them somewhere.

"My folks went to Logan today, too," Avery said, looking prim and a little smug to be all dressed up and heading out of town.

"My mom went to town with Wesley's mom," Wyatt explained, and Dad's helping Uncle Bill and Uncle Rob haul hay."

"And I'm away from home on a service project," I chimed innocently.

We headed north toward Eisner. I waved at Pistol Stewart and he lifted a hand, shaking his head, no doubt wondering why I was such a bull-headed cuss. I hit my blinker at the War Bonnet Road, and soon Shonnee O'Shea skipped down her front steps looking blazin' as ever.

I climbed out of the truck and she slid in, sandwiching herself between me and Avery because it wasn't cool to ride in the backseat. Teenagers in Three Lakes preferred stuffing themselves into the front like sardines in a can. Perhaps we all acted this way just to sit closer to each other. If I'd have been mashed into the front seat with Allyson and Yarrow, I'd have gladly volunteered for the back, but this was different, somehow. I wondered if the whole world acted like we did or if it was just a local thing.

We talked and acted crazy and bigger than we were. I pulled my truck into Whitecaps. It was the hottest rage in Three Lakes' cuisine. The interior was decorated like a marina and the tables resembled little boats. The lighting was dim and lanterns glimmered, resembling a harbor at night. The sounds of waves lapping against a shore played over the loudspeakers, interspersed with an occasional calling seagull.

"Cool atmosphere, but we could have just packed a lunch and eaten on the dock at Grady's," Shonnee offered.

I peered at the menu, thinking Shonnee's idea would have been a lot cheaper, but this was a fun change, too. The waitress brought icy mugs of lemonade to the table and a beach pail full of biscuits. She took our orders. Wyatt had a hard time making a suitable choice and had to ask a dozen questions.

"What are the fish and chips made out of?"

Wendy the waitress looked annoyed and one eye shut. "Fish."

Wyatt stole her annoyance and asked, "Yes, but what kind. There is more than one fish in the sea."

"I'll go find out." She turned, seeming aggravated, and we chuckled quietly at her displeasure.

She returned promptly. "They are made out of cod."

"Real cod or processed?"

"I'll go find out."

Avery's nose wrinkled in Wyatt's direction. "Maybe you should just order a burger."

Wendy reappeared. "Real cod."

"Oh, that's good to know. Well…what about the chicken patty? Is it real chicken or processed?"

"I'll go find out."

Now I was getting embarrassed. "Wyatt, don't tick her off! Just get a hotdog or something."

"I don't like processed stuff, and Gloria says it's not good for me."

Wendy stomped back to our table. "It's processed if you order the chicken patty sandwich, but *real* if you get the fried chicken dinner."

"Oh…okay, well—I've actually decided on the halibut fillet."

Wendy's eyes rolled at the sudden selection of something completely new. "What kind of potato would you like with that?"

"Do you have baked?"

"Yes."

"Are they cooked tender? I hate baked potatoes that aren't quite done."

Wendy puffed an angry breath and her bangs flipped up. "I'll go poke a fork in one," she snarled. "I'll be right back."

"Wyatt," Avery groaned. "You're being a pain."

Shonnee giggled softly, trying not to call any attention to our table. "This is the funniest thing, ever."

Stomp, stomp, stomp. Wendy returned with a fork full of white potato. "Is this cooked to your specification?" She shoved the fork in

Wyatt's mouth and he nodded approval. "Fantastic," she said flatly. "Now, I shudder to ask, but would you like soup or salad?"

"What's the soup?"

The waitress's right eye closed again. "Why am I not surprised you asked that?" She huffed away, going to check.

Avery's head tilted at Wyatt. "What?" Wyatt cried, "She really should know the answer to that! These are not difficult questions!"

In a few seconds the waitress returned. "It's chicken noodle. There are carrots, celery, and little tiny dices of onion in it. The chicken looks genuine, w*hite meat.* I don't think it's processed. The broth is medium consistency, and the temperature is hot enough you'll have to blow on it. It is nicely seasoned, and should not require too much salt or pepper. It comes in a blue bowl, this size." She motioned with her hands to illustrate.

"Are the noodles homemade?"

Wendy stared dead panned for several moments. "I'll go ask." She pounded away again, and by this time Shonnee was gasping for air. I was getting a kick out of her getting a kick out of things. Her face was flushed and her eyes were bright. She chewed against the inside of one cheek, trying hard to reign in her amusement. Wendy returned, dragging the chef. "This is Chef Weller. He can answer any other questions you could *possibly* have, and I will *try* and take the orders of your friends."

Chef Weller looked at Wyatt. "Yes?"

"Are the noodles in the soup homemade?"

"Yes."

"Thank you—that's all I wanted to know."

Chef Weller glared at Wendy. "You drug me out of my kitchen for that?"

Wendy puffed another breath and tossed her pen over her shoulder in an exasperated way. "Oh for Heaven's sakes," she muttered. Belligerently she turned on Avery. "What can I get for you?"

Avery tried to make up for Wyatt's questions and answered timidly "What would you like to bring me?"

Wendy's eyes narrowed suspiciously. "Your ticket!"

"But we haven't got our food yet," Wyatt mentioned.

"Exactly."

"I'll just have a cheeseburger with fries," Avery rushed, wanting to show sincere repentance.

"Grilled ham and cheese with tots," Shonnee said, trying hard not to burst into a belly roll.

"I'd also like the halibut, baked potato, and the soup. Thank you." I hoped that was concise enough.

Wendy stomped away and Wyatt watched her go. "She's got a bad attitude and she's not getting a tip out of me."

We chuckled quietly. I looked around the restaurant. It seemed like we were having way more fun than anybody else. I slid my arm around Shonnee's shoulders. If life was a game I was winning! What could be better than summertime, all the right people, and a truck?

"Excuse me, aren't you that Gallagher boy that rides trick ponies?" An older lady stood at the end of our table, grinning down at me.

"Yes Mam."

"I thought that was you! It's a pity you don't cut your hair."

"I'm just growing it out so it's long enough to fasten the feathers in. I'll soon be riding in the Days of '47 Rodeo."

"Oh how marvelous! I'm Rita McCracken. My mother-in-law lives in Gallagher Springs."

Oh, so this was *Ticky Tacky Wicky Wacky Mickey Mackey McCrackey's* kin. I glanced at Wyatt and his head was down, hiding an amused smile. "It's nice to meet you," I said.

"She just thinks the world of you!"

The statement startled me. What had I ever done for her? Nothing—other than shoving that one nice trout in her mailbox when I was eleven. The words pained me, almost. "She might have mistaken me for someone else," I hedged.

"No, no, it's you alright. She invited us all down to Gallagher Springs for the powwow two years ago because she said her wonderful neighbor boy had planned the whole thing."

Geez. Who knew she ever looked up? "Well…thank you."

"She said you *personally* invited her to come."

My mind swam back. I had taken invitations all over town—she wasn't exclusive. I even took one to Agatha Duffy's house, although I made Miles O'Reilly walk to the front door with me just in case she accidentally mistook me for a rooster.

Rita stared at me, expecting a response, so I nodded. "And then you helped her clean her spare apartment so that nice young couple could move in. Ma McCracken claimed you worked like a soldier."

Good grief, I did that for Mark and Michelle, and not for the crazy old land-lady! I fidgeted in my seat since I was quite undeserving of any recognition.

Wendy came tripping back to our table, loaded up with soup and another pail full of biscuits. Rita nodded at us and scurried away, leaving us to our dinner.

Wyatt looked warily at me. "That was weird. I didn't know you were secretly dating old Wicky Wacky."

"I'm not, you blockhead."

Another group of teenagers bustled into the restaurant. Wendy's eyes rolled as they stepped inside. "Welcome to Whitecaps," she snarled. "I'll be with you in a minute!"

Wyatt looked at the group. "Hey Wesley, check it out." I leaned over, just quick enough to see Paul Siskin and Margo Walsh. Margo looked pained and her eyes darted wistfully around the room. Apparently she didn't like Paul any better now than she had in the seventh grade! They were doubling with Ross Moore and one of the nine Cindy's. Paul saw us and wandered over.

"Hi guys, fancy meeting you here."

I nodded, never having too much to say to the poor reader. I'd been angry with him since the fifth grade when he blundered through Grady's book and I got sent to Mr. Mulligan's office. "This is Shonnee O'Shea," I said to the others, introducing the foxy redhead at my side. Margo heaved a martyred sigh, but I refused to let her bring me down.

"So what are you having?" Paul asked Wyatt.

"I ordered the halibut, but I'll give you a little pointer. Ask the waitress lots of questions, because she likes it and the service is better that way."

"Oh yeah? Questions like what?"

"Like what's in the meatloaf and stuff like that," I added.

"Are there real lemons in the lemonade or is it a mix?" Shonnee offered. Avery's eyes grew large at Shonnee's participation in leading Paul Siskin into Waitress Wendy's hot water.

"Oh yeah?" Paul asked. "That's good to know."

Wendy bustled back with a stack of menus in her arms, leading our school mates to another boat. "Don't feel sorry for them Avery," I said. "Ross and Paul sort of baited Stan Tomkins into beating Wyatt on that fateful day so long ago."

"Hmph!" Avery said. "I don't then! I won't have a thing to do with either one of them *forever*."

Wendy reappeared, wheeling a cart full of entrées. She arranged our plates on the table. "Can I get you anything else?"

We shook our heads, eager for her to wait on our friends. She pulled the pen from behind her ear and dodged over to their table, delivering a pail of biscuits and four glasses of icy cold lemonade.

"What's in this lemonade?" Paul asked bluntly.

"Lemons."

Paul's brows furrowed. "Is is freshly squeezed or powdered stuff?"

"I'll go see."

We chuckled amongst ourselves. Soon Wendy tripped past our table again. "It's freshly squeezed."

"Oh," Paul murmured.

"What's the meatloaf made out of?" Ross Moore inquired.

Geez, these guys weren't bright enough to come up with their own kinds of questions. Wyatt was thinking what I was thinking and shook his head at me.

"Meat, you big moron," Wendy grouched.

Ross seemed unimpressed. "Lose the attitude for ten seconds and tell me what's in it."

"I'll go ask."

As soon as she pushed her way through the swinging doors of the kitchen Paul whispered, "Hey Wyatt, I don't think she likes us asking questions."

"Naw, you're just not asking the right ones yet."

"Oh, okay."

Wendy stomped past our table again. "Ground beef—*lean,* of course, eggs, minced onion, bread crumbs, special seasonings, tomato sauce and a mystery ingredient that's Whitecaps own secret."

"Oh."

"Would you like the meatloaf, then?"

"Nope. I can't stand the stuff."

Wendy's foot stomped. "Then why in the name of Pete did you ask me what was in it?"

"Just to improve our service!"

"You impudent little jerk! Get out! Get out of Whitecaps right now!"

"Wait! I haven't asked you what your ham steak is made out of yet!"

"Git! Git out right now or I'll call the cops!"

"But lady, we're hungry and we have some questions about the turkey."

"Turkey? Stuff it!" Wendy grabbed Paul by the ear and tugged him from his boat. Soon Chef Weller came from the kitchen to help clear the riff-raff out of his establishment. Margo was so embarrassed she jerked her shirt collar up over her face so no one could identify her.

The four of us watched, completely stunned, albeit entertained by the unfolding spectacle. Wendy pushed them into the great outdoors and locked the doors behind them. Paul knocked along the windows, trying to get her attention, demanding to know if the chicken fried steak was steak or chicken, but Wendy began pulling the blinds. "Wesley! What did I do wrong?" he hollered, but I shrugged innocently before his face vanished behind a window blind.

Shonnee giggled quietly until she nearly choked to death. I slapped her back, just to help her out a bit. She was so cute, red faced and gasping for air. I was glad to see she could so thoroughly let her hair down and have a little fun. It was prerequisite for spending time with me.

Avery kept shaking her head. "Really Wyatt, you should feel *so* guilty! Poor Margo and poor Cindy Sue, too! I don't care a snit about Paul or Ross—but those poor girls!"

"They can get a burger at Midderkrausse's."

"Oh, but it's just not the same," Avery lamented. "And my burger is so delicious here! Look at this," she said, pointing to a little beach umbrella sticking out of the top of her bun. We finished eating and I flipped two dollars on the table for the flustered waitress. I felt like the last of the big-time spenders!

We skedaddled out of Whitecaps, feeling swanky and superior to the other kids our age. We drove down to the North Beach of Eisner Lake to catch the sunset. We tossed a Frisbee around for a little while, and then Wyatt and I kicked off our shoes and sox, and rolled our pant legs up a bit. Shonnee and Avery were both wearing skirts, and their sandals easily slipped into the sand with little effort. We waded along the shore. Avery and Wyatt went one direction while Shonnee and I splashed in the other.

We discussed one of Grady's books, *Irish Dreams and Idaho Skies*. The wind whipped Shonnee's hair and she kept combing through it with her fingers, trying to keep it under control.

"Just let it go," I whispered.

She peeked up at me, ready to say something, but I kissed her. I kissed her the way Rouree kissed Celia; hard and tender, soft and crazy. My toes curled in the sand and Shonnee's green eyes resembled passionate, fiery emeralds. "I'm falling in love with you, Wesley."

"Oh Shon—that's convenient," I answered huskily, "Since I'm already there." I cupped her chin in my hands, content to study the beauty in her face.

The drive home was great! I walked Shonnee to her door. "I'll see you at work tomorrow." I kissed her again, not caring that Avery and Wyatt were watching from the truck.

"Well, well, well," the lamb said as I climbed back in. "The Little Shoshone must want Grady to build him a house."

"Shut up, Wyatt."

Avery snickered and Wyatt grinned, and I for one, was happy that I could drive them wherever the hello mighty they wanted to go. Service brings such blessings!

The next morning I mowed lawns for Mother and Grandma Gallagher. That was my job on Thursday mornings. When I finished I loaded the mower in the truck and went to Mrs. McCracken's. I needed to earn the praise I'd already been given. I felt like a fink for not really being a swell neighbor kid. I mowed and raked her small yard—which was nothing to crow over. She peered at me from a crack in her heavy living room drapes and I waved nonchalantly.

When I was finished there I loaded the mower and went to Agatha Duffy's ramshackle yard. I decided I owed her after all the mischief I'd taken part in over the years. To my dismay she came trotting out of the house wearing a long red gown trimmed with crimson feathers. Her cheeks were rouged and her lips painted brilliant, flaming red. She tottered on spindly high heels. An ill-fitting wig of golden curls was perched atop her head, but long strands of grey wisps fell in disarray, here and there, tattling on her age and fake cosmetic shell.

"Oh my darling! My darling! I didn't know they made men like you anymore!" Her voice quivered in high soprano notes.

I pushed the mower faster, setting my mind on my work to avoid having to talk to her. She trailed after me, her high voice trilling in appreciative notes which resonated above the noisy mower's engine. I got used to her trailing me after awhile, chalking her presence up to a lonesome, noisy shadow.

"You must come in and have some iced-tea," she sang as I loaded the mower in the truck.

"No thank you, Ms. Duffy. I've got to get to work."

"Come again you handsome, handsome boy, and don't forget your lawnmower!"

I jumped in my truck and headed for home, feeling triumphant for meeting my Boy Scout quota of good deeds done daily. I don't know what on earth possessed me, but I stopped at the Mulligan's yard as I chugged past. I could see Mr. Mulligan from the front room window, holding two bawling babies over his shoulders. Aunt Lace was giving the third one a bottle from the rocking chair, and she looked done-in and tired and it was only ten o'clock in the morning. I stopped my truck and mowed their grass.

Mr. Mulligan nodded every time I rounded the yard, but I pretended not to see. I raked the clippings quickly, loading them into a big garbage bag. As I was backing out of their driveway, Delma Jean hailed me frantically from her front porch. I groaned, but rolled my window down to visit.

"Good morning Delma Jean."

"Wesley Gallagher, Ernie's got the gout! Would you mind mowing our yard? I'll pay you boy, and Godfrey, you know I'm good for it!"

I hesitated, not wanting to do it, but the good angel on my right shoulder outshouted the devil on my left one. I unloaded the mower once again and serviced the Connor's yard although I wouldn't take her money. Had I been worth an ounce of salt, I'd have thought to do it before she could ask.

"Take it Wesley, I'm good for my word," Delma Jean implored, eyes working my entire face at once.

It was hard to look her square in the eye, for I didn't know which one to focus on, exactly. "No Delma Jean, but I'll try to swing by next Thursday morning and mow it again. Tell Ernie to get his sore foot better though, and enjoy the sunshine."

Delma Jean's crazy eyes turned to liquid at my offer and she thanked me all the way to my truck, threatening to bake me brownies.

"Go ahead, for a little shoog does me good!" I called before rumbling away. I should have been doing this for these people all along, but I was fifteen and a half and teenagers aren't always as sensitive as they should be.

When I got home Mother was beaming at me. "I've just received phone calls from four different households in this town. It seems that my Wesley is a good worker." She smiled and I was glad that she could be proud of me occasionally. I doubted she would be too thrilled with me when she found out I drove clear to Eisner for dinner while she was gone to Logan. I hoped the good things I did in life could cancel out the bad, for I was riddled with temptations and bound to attract more mischief than the law allowed. I wasn't supposed to date or drive until I was sixteen, and it seemed like I was doing both with very little pain to my conscience. All things considered, I needed to mow a lot of grass to help sure up my salvation.

Mother hugged me. "You're a good kid! Remember when I said you were the author of your life's story?"

"Yeah."

"Well…I think it's a pretty terrific book so far."

"Yip," Yarrow piped. "My boy is a good boy! My boy is so strong and strong, and triple strong!"

Allyson motioned me into the front room. "Look what I got in the mail this morning Wesley." She handed me an envelope and I slipped a letter out and read.

> *Dear Allyson,*
>
> *I should have cleared this up years ago, and I was remiss in not doing so. I once scolded you, claiming that you would never amount to anything. Allyson, I hope you don't remember those cutting, spiteful words, but I'm afraid you probably do. It was so petty of me! I hope that you will be able to forgive me, for the selfish person who uttered those contemptible things doesn't exist today and never truly felt that way then. I have always loved you—but I have been terribly jealous of your mother for years. It's embarrassing to admit that. Allyson, I look at my new little babies, and it pains me to think that, at some point, some careless, thoughtless, spiteful person may say something cruel and cutting to them. I realize now, more than I ever have before, how I have slighted you and hurt you. I owe an apology to you, and also one to Wesley. I owe an apology to your mother and dad, but very first of all, I needed to square things with you. I am so sincerely sorry! I am asking for your forgiveness. I think you are a beautiful young lady, and full of promise and potential. My little Ainslie reminds me of you, darling Allyson.*
>
> *I love you,*
>
> *Aunt Lace*

"Wonders never cease," I croaked.

"Do you think she means it, Wesley? Or…is she just kissing up so I'll babysit?"

"No, Allyson—you know she means it. It's not like her to do anything she doesn't want to. It's sincere; at least it sounds genuine to me."

Allyson nodded, her strawberry blond curls bobbed. Geez, I hadn't noticed lately, but she really was getting kind of cute. She was sort of Celia-esque. I'd soon have to whip some boy, and I told Allyson as much. Her cheeks flushed, pleased that I noticed.

Shonnee and I took a canoe out that night after work. Summer magic cast its spell on the water and we were part of it. Fish jumped and water rippled beneath the moon's glow. We never ran out of things to say, and the more I learned about Shonnee O'Shea, the more I wanted to know. She was intelligent, fun loving, genuine, and *really* beautiful to me!

"Good luck in Salt Lake."

"Thanks. Hopefully it all goes okay. Basically we'll be doing the same routine we did for the powwow, but we're all doing our super show-off dismounting stunts before we leave the arena. We'll be carrying the colors at the beginning of the rodeo. I just hope I grab the flag as I race by. That's what worries me the most."

"Just rub your bear claw necklace for luck. Howahkan will hand you the flag." The words really made me think, and I couldn't help smiling at the suggestion. I was certain Howahkan wouldn't miss it. "Paint that lucky clover on Misty's flank and you can't fail."

"Thanks Shonnee. I wish you could come with me."

"Someone's got to work around here!"

Grady stood next to the dock, waving to us.

"There is the heart of Utopia," Shonnee whispered, waving back at the old man. Her words formed a lump in my throat! We paddled over and he climbed in.

"Watching the two of you is like looking back in time at my Addie and me. It does my ticker good!" He asked me what time we were leaving for Salt Lake City the next morning. "By Jingo Jones, I'm all packed up and ready to go! I'm researching for a new book, you know."

"Oh? You're going to write another one?" He was ninety-five and going strong.

"Yes-sir-ee, I'm writing about an overly confidant trick rider and his spirited red-headed girlfriend. I figure I've got at least one more book in me, but Wesley, I'm leaving the sequel to you."

The Days of '47 celebration was a big deal in Utah, for it honored the courageous pioneers who blazed a trail across the nation to settle the unwelcoming wilderness of the west. Kenny, Rouree, Dover and I were invited to ride in the parade as well, just to build interest for our performance in the rodeo, I suppose. The celebration committee booked us a string of rooms in the Hotel Utah. We were all nervous as we painted our ponies and faces that morning, but hyper excited as well.

The parade route stretched for miles through Salt Lake City, and I was grateful to be hiding behind a strip of red war paint. I had never seen so many people before, and neither had my Shoshone friends. Camera crews were positioned on every corner. The parade was televised state-wide, not that I thought anyone could possibly still be at home watching. The streets were stuffed with expectant faces, including my folks. I noticed Amos and his new bride as we rode by, as well as the Tanaka's and Good's, Uncle Rob and Aunt Aura Leigh, Monty , Shaylin, and Celia.

I spied Grandpa Grady sitting on the curb with Yarrow, Allyson, Dori Jo, and Wyatt. He stood up, clapping his hands enthusiastically as we passed, and I found it impossible not to smile at him. I could not look fierce while feeling the enthusiasm of my snowy-topped great grandfather! He was in his second springtime...and he planned on racing me to summer.

About the Author

Into the Second Springtime is June Marie Saxton's third novel. "I wrote this book with a happy heart, and my enthusiasm spilled onto the pages of the story," Saxton says. "It's a conquest of *feelings*; those tender emotions we experience as we grow, form relationships and learn about life, death, and the power of becoming who we are meant to be. It's a dedication to the profound influence others have in our lives.

June Marie was raised on a cattle ranch at Sage, Wyoming, and learned to love the freedom associated with such a lifestyle. She loved caring for animals, climbing trees, riding bikes and horses, fishing, and spending time with her parents, brothers, grandparents, and cousins. She learned to respect the history of the land and was always fascinated by the Native American artifacts found on their property. "Our ranch was a training ground for an active imagination!"

June Marie married Mike Saxton and together they have four children, Shannyn, Casey, Justyn, and Tahnee. The Saxton's own and operate Saxton Ranch in Raymond, Idaho. June Marie is grateful to know her children have had the same opportunities to romp and roam, work and play, learning about life in the same zealous and free way.

June Marie owns Bear Necessities of Montpelier, a nutritional counseling center, beauty salon, and day spa. June Marie is a certified nutritional consultant and strives to help others find creative concepts to healthy living. She enjoys the unique personality traits of her clientele, and forges friendships easily.

"Creating identifiable characters is one of my strong suits as a writer. I like taking a one dimensional name on paper, infusing it with cleverly crafted personality traits until it comes to life on the written page."

June Marie is a champion of children and youth, willingly teaching and lecturing at schools and organizations about her adventures in writing. She enjoys being involved with programs that help strengthen and reinforce core values and standards.

To stay abreast of Saxton's current writing projects, log onto www.junemariesaxton.com, or visit www.bearnecessities.us to find out more about her work, business, or to order personally autographed copies of her books.

CPSIA information can be obtained at www.ICGtesting.com
Printed in the USA
270039BV00001B/8/P

9 781452 082714